Rebel Sutra

Rebel Sutra

SHARIANN LEWITT

A TOM DOHERTY ASSOCIATES BOOK
NEW YORK

REBEL SUTRA

Edited by Teresa Nielsen Hayden

Designed by Jane Adele Regina

A Tor Book
Published by Tom Doherty Associates, LLC
175 Fifth Avenue
New York, NY 10010

www.tor.com

Tor® is a registered trademark of Tom Doherty Associates,
LLC.

Library of Congress Cataloging-in-Publication Data

Lewitt, Sheriann.
    Rebel sutra / Shariann Lewitt. — 1st ed.
        p.cm.
    "A Tom Doherty Associates book."
    ISBN 0-312-86451-5
    I. Genetic Engineering—Fiction. 2. Social classes—Fiction.
3.Colonies—Fiction. I. Title

PS3562.E987 R4 2000
813'.54—dc21   00–031680

First Edition: September 2000

Printed in the United States of America

0 9 8 7 6 5 4 3 2 1

For everybody who has ever loved
science fiction; and in memory
of Joe Mayhew.

Rebel Sutra

Book One

DELLA'S STORY

Chapter One

I hated my second funeral, which is the only one I managed to attend. I didn't see the first so maybe it was better, but I doubt it. The next is going to be excellent.

That will be your responsibility, Anselm, to bury me decently. I know I have not been the best mother, and sometimes I wonder if you hate me. Other times I know that you *must* hate me, that you have no choice. That I didn't give you any choice.

But you owe me a decent funeral. No matter what else I have done, this body gave you life and you will treat it with honor. And good taste. There is silk organza for the shroud already marked in my storage space, and the coffin must be ebony with a white lining and must be draped with Auntie Suu-Suu's shawl. You know the one I mean, the blue velvet embroidered with suns and moons and stars in silver and pearls. The one I gave you. I want white callas and freesias and red eucalyptus in the formal arrangements, and, yes, I know they cost a fortune.

The music must be Mozart's *Requiem*. It would be worth converting to his religion for that music, but it is not necessary. I have already checked the particulars.

It will reflect well on you, Anselm. It will solidify your position, though right now you don't have to consider the political implications. But just because you have destroyed Xanadu and hundreds of the Changed are freezing in the cold, do not assume that you have won. What is won with blood is lost with a glance, a dropped word, a long negotiating session.

There are trusted friends and allies who will betray you, there are expediencies of government that you cannot avoid and useful functionaries who will become loyal advisers. Trust no one, trust nothing, and never let the opportunity go by to make a grand emotional gesture.

Giving me the funeral I desire will be a small nod to those Changed who are inclined to support you. It will suggest to the Changed as a whole that you do not mean our wholesale slaughter, that your movement is still about justice and the future. After all, while you are responsible for what the Pretender has done, you weren't the one who openly did the deed, and if you go on to take revenge on the Pretender forces, the Changed may feel you are their champion as much as the defender of the humans.

Giving me a proper funeral will also satisfy your followers, who will see that you do your duty to your mother. Family is important to them, more important than justice and war. If you do not honor your mother, the people of Babelion will no longer think of you as a god.

So you must act like a god. And a god would give his mother the honor her position deserves, even when he has reason to hate her above all the others who humiliated him and abandoned him and left him to his fate.

This time my funeral will be dignified and restrained and elegant, not like the service I saw when I was fourteen. Then everything was simple and sweet, appropriate for a child. The bouquets of wildflowers were mixed in pastel colors with pink ribbons. A young girl didn't rate the dignity and gravity of a grown woman who was already a member of the Exchange.

I didn't like the flowers, I didn't like the pristine pierced-lace altar cloth, I hated the music, and my mother wore a parati that was some awful dull yellow. I was appalled. Though I will admit that fourteen-year-olds are appalled at everything, and are naturally honor-bound to despise any ceremony planned by adults to which they have to wear formal clothes.

No one knew I would be watching, though, having been declared dead. This time you will know that I am watching. You will make a speech, using your father's gift of words and charisma to unify both your peoples. And at the very last two Tinker women will take the shawl and drape it around your shoulders as a royal robe. Which it will be, if you choose.

The women will be your Tinker aunts, Sonja and Anastasia. Your Tinker connections are more important than you can possibly imagine. Even if you choose simply to stay here and do nothing further, they are the only ones on Maya who can confirm what I will explain to you, let alone give you the means to pursue the greater goal.

But that is for later. Even immediately they will be invaluable, because it will lose you followers if you admit that your mother was Changed and that you are a dynastic dead end. But because of my own Tinker connections, you can be vague about my background and make it appear human. That is what they expect, so that is what they will hear. You can't afford to have me Changed and an enemy; you must make me acceptable to Arsen's people.

The Tinker connection will do that. They are as human as the people of Babelion and they have no status in the Exchange. Sonja and Anastasia will tell everyone that you are their nephew, and Auntie Suu-Suu will tell the story of how she named you before you were even conceived. Before I met your father, even, she told me your name, and that should be part of the saga too.

Because that is what you must do and become, Anselm. You must become the hero of a legend. And do not mistake me; there is only one legend, and it is the warrior-king. Even when we are too enlightened for kings and too sophisticated for legends, they have a secret power over us because they are the archetypes of who and what we can become. I raised you to know the classics so you could become such a one, but even with all your gifts it will not be easy. Not even now, when you think you have won and that it's all over.

But before you can go on to the future it is necessary to know the truth. You have never seen it before; it is kept carefully sealed away from all of us, Changed and human alike. To know that truth it is best that you first know me, know who I was and who I am now. I never told you about me or your father. You learned about him in Babelion, and they don't know the whole truth, either.

At the time you were too young. Which is hard to believe, because you were the same age I was when you were born. I didn't have the luxury of that youth. The Tinkers took it all away. But you had years of faith before you learned who they are, and, believe me, they have not told you the full truth. There is a lot more to their mission than they'll admit, even to themselves.

Even knowing far more, I must admit that there is only one truth I care about. I have lived all my life for one victory and one safety, and it has all been for you.

The dreams of the Creators, the Tinkers, and the subjects of the Flower Thrones meant nothing to me. They were all dead, and the worlds they served consider themselves the center of the civilized universe and produce nothing at all but flesh and indolence. I resent their existence. Because of them I have been led all my life in ways that have made me isolated, lonely and bitter.

They and all their plans can rot in Hell, for all I care. The more I discover the more I wonder if I should simply sabotage the entire thing. Or whether that is also part of the grand design of the Creators, and that in the end that I would be doing nothing but their will.

And then you began your campaign and I saw that you were even more central to their plan than I. You were the entire point, Anselm, though they could not have planned you. They have never told me a thing, but from the way Auntie Suu-Suu spoke I think that your existence is a dilemma for them. They cannot ignore you.

I have my suspicions, but I can't confirm anything. I don't really have enough data; during my past five years in the Exchange I still have not been able to get into the Tinkers' private files. I am afraid that the answers are even more unbelievable than my suspicions, because the longer I watch the stranger things become.

ANSELM REFLECTS:

In the ten years that I had been a human in Babelion I had forgotten my mother's voice. She was fully in and of the Exchange now, her comatose body in a gel-trough with tubes inserted at her throat and her chest . . . I had refused to see her body. By the standards of Babelion she had committed suicide when she had decided to live completely within the Exchange.

Sri Mayurna had taught that the body, the mind and the spirit are not separate at all, but are three aspects of identity, just as Brama, Vishnu and Shiva are interdependent faces of existence, each requiring the other two. Like my father, I had been an acolyte at the Temple of Vishnu. But the Temple is for humans and Della was not human. Della was Changed. And like all the Changed she seemed more real, more vivid in the Exchange than I remembered her in the flesh.

This morning the Changed seemed more like ghosts than ever. I have done everything that my father ever set out to do. I have done everything that my mother has feared. The Mountain, the domed stronghold of the Changed, is now open to the cold. The orange trees are frozen, their rich scent cut by the chill. And the Changed themselves huddle around braziers that consume priceless paintings that came from the motherworld, intricately carved and inlaid chairs, and embroidered banners and hangings. I even saw a panel from one of the doors of the shrine in the Village, carved with the story of Rama and Sita and the evil angel, consigned to the fire.

That is all my doing. Sri Mayurna has said that it is the action and not the intent of the action that determines the karma, and if that is so then I will be reborn as something lower than the tila tree that sits in the Courtyard.

I had not planned to kill off the Changed, or even to damage them. I am half Changed myself, though I mostly forget that now, just as I forget the sixteen years I spent as one of them on the Mountain, being trained for privilege and the Exchange.

There are memories, of course, but they are static and silent. It comes back only in unconnected shreds like snatches of a dream grasped in the morning. That was what it was, sixteen years asleep and dreaming until I woke up and learned that I was human and alive.

I had only wanted to stop the lies. Every year when the candidates go to test on the Mountain there is hope in Babelion that someday the humans will be the equals of the Changed. And every year when the best of them don't come back there is a whisper of a prayer that we can all one day be superior, and that then we will be free.

That hope is a lie. The Changed have never accepted any human into their company. There are enough genetic differences that they are another species entirely. They were another species when we all left Earth together. Those humans who remain are bribed by the jobs that are offered to them, and the education and status they can achieve as the professional support staff to the Changed.

My father knew that. He knew it when he went up to the Mountain to test and he knew it when he led the march on the Mountain to demand our inclusion. He knew it and he told Babelion out loud that their hope was a fraud and that there was no salvation on the Mountain. No human has ever entered the Exchange.

He tried to end the sham and he failed. I tried also, and maybe I've succeeded too well. There is nothing very desirable left on the Mountain now. Xanadu, the central palace complex that was the center of life and ritual and power, is now half in ruins. Everything that can burn had been pulled out and is piled up to feed the flames that warm the Changed who gather around them. Even the paintings that we believed came from the British Museum, that were treasures for many generations before we saved them from destruction in the Creators' Wars, have gone to provide heat.

In the end, everything of value on Maya burns. Maybe because it is so cold, we think it is a decent end. The mountains burn and the Great Steam Lake boils and the best we brought from Earth is set to the torch. We humans burn the bodies of our dead, giving them a warmth in death that they had never had in life. And the Changed executed my father by fire when he was younger than I am now. I cannot help but think of him when I see the fires burning all over the Mountain.

My father died when I was an infant and he never knew that I existed, but he is more alive to me than Della was when she still walked in this world. In Babelion the stories about him flow like the cold breath of winter. They are the incessant background that overshadows every minute, every choice, every shadow. My father never belonged to me—all of him belongs to his people. There is nothing of him that is private, that is mine.

Those who knew him, slept with him, fought with him, died with him, they have given their stories back to the rich store of legend that has become Arsen. Della doesn't exist in any of them. Which makes good sense—even I can't imagine my father wanting one of the Changed. But then, he did not live with them, and they must have been exotic to him.

It would be political death for Arsen to have admitted that he had ever been even vaguely aware of the Changed, except as the enemy. I understood the political expediency of that, and for my own position I have always been rather reticent on the subject. No one questions that he found company while he was testing on the Mountain. He wouldn't have been Arsen if he hadn't.

The stories have it that the only night he ever slept alone after the age of twelve was the night before he died. But of course that isn't true—he wasn't held overnight. He was captured and tried and executed all in the space of a single day, which was the only mercy he was given. He never had time to believe that he would really die. There was less than an hour between the sentence and the time they dragged him off to the pyre.

It wouldn't have taken much time to prepare, since the humans who worked for the Changed and who live in the Village would have the necessary tools for burning. Only among the humans are the dead burned, with great solemnity and banks of flowers and coils of incensed smoke. The Changed bury theirs in dirt, or ice, or gel-bath medium while their ghosts wander endlessly through the Exchange, unable to be reborn or ever at peace. They cling so hard to the illusion that this is the point of life that they deny themselves everything else, everything they cannot see, and thus don't value.

I doubt even death and rebirth would bring Della any joy. Power is more important to her than pleasure, though now I wonder if Della ever experienced delight in her life. I think that duty and power are the only things she has ever understood, and so the notion that tranquility of spirit and fulfillment of karma could give her something deeper and more lasting would be absolutely alien to her.

She is my mother and she raised me, but I know her far less, and less of her, than I know of the father who never knew me. And that is why I will listen to the rest of the recording she left for me. Not because I trust her—I know that more than half of her stories are lies. But because the other half aren't, and just the fact that she made this is one of the very few things she has ever done for me since she gave me life.

Della does not tell the truth as anyone would understand it, but she does tell her version of the truth. I had forgotten that—I had managed to obliterate any memory of her singular interpretations of reality. More than anyone else I have ever met, human or Changed alike, Della personifies the victim and the creator of Illusion. She believes her own fantasies, and that makes her more dangerous than anything else. Much as my father, or my Uncle Iolo or I, she is a believer. Only what she believes comes from her own skewed vision, her own ignorance and prejudice mixed with elements of the real.

But even her distortions tell me more about her, about who she is and who and what I am. I have spent most of my life trying to ignore her existence—it is time I faced the truth that she has had more than an insignificant part in who I have become. Without Della's lies and agendas, I would never have become my father's heir.

Arsen might have been more clear on fact, but he wasn't nearly as good at survival. I must credit Della: she is more likely to survive a crisis than any other person I have met. She probably taught me a few things in that regard, too. How did I know not to trust Hari-O?

She taught me to survive and she taught me to lie. My life in Babelion is a fabrication, a careful blending of truth and silence. She taught me to use assumption, to misdirect those who follow me and believe in me. She taught me to be the person I have become, able to smudge the facts so that nothing is quite clear and people will see whatever they desire.

I wish Vijay were here. I wish Sulma were here, too, but that is impossible and I have to turn my mind away from her. Remembering Sulma will only break the rage open again, and I cannot afford that now. But Vijay would be rational and solid and remind me of what he knew to be true as a measure against the fabrications and fictions that, between us, Della and I have created. I cannot afford to lose sight of what is legend and what is fact and where I manipulate the two. Because I am Della's son, fulfilling her legacy as well as Arsen's.

Everyone knows how Arsen died. I don't think I'm in any danger of forgetting, no matter what Della says. But I want to know what she has to tell me—I need to know what she has constructed and believes and wants me to believe. Because while half the time Della lies, half the time she tells the truth. She tells the truth that no one else will bother to tell, all the details that everyone else will let slide.

I know that Arsen tested on the Mountain. He spent a month among the Changed and then returned to Babelion and disappeared. I know that during that time he wasn't in hiding at all, but studying with Sri Mayurna in the Temple of Vishnu. I know also that he studied among the devis as I have not—but then it would suit Arsen. I only know that from Sri Mayurna himself. That little detail has been kept from the legends, perhaps because it would focus too much on the individual and not on the things he represents.

I know that he marched on the Mountain with five thousand at his back and that they confronted the Guardians at the Gate. In Babelion they say that he had not intended violence and that the entire party of protesters was unarmed. The Changed charge that they were armed and that the humans fired first. No one disputes that the Guardians fired into the crowd and killed a dozen people. The records of the twelve humans and one Guardian who died in the fracas are the same on both sides, so that information is probably true. And I know that the Guardians captured my father and two of his closest associates while several of his lieutenants got away.

Both sides agree that he was tried for sedition and murder by Sithra and a quorum of Changed voted him guilty as charged, and that he was burned alive with the Changed watching and partying on the terraces of Xanadu. They watched from within the Dome so that the stench of burning flesh and the cries were all removed, and all they saw were the dancing flames as they ate their petits fours and finger sandwiches and vegetable fritters and spicy dumplings.

Even stripped of legend, that much is documented and recorded and of free access. The Changed wanted everyone to know what happened to Arsen, to prevent anyone from being willing to take his place. They never thought that they themselves would have a part in training Arsen's heir.

So I will access the rest of her tape. She made it for me, for right now. I know she has an agenda and I know there are things she wants from me, and of course she made this document to try to manipulate me into giving her what she desires. I don't think Della realizes that she herself taught me to see through her deceptions.

She is my mother. She formed me more than I want to admit, and I want her praise and acceptance although I would be horrified if I had it.

All humans know their parents and all the members of their parents' circle. To humans, knowing where one has come from is the first step in knowing oneself. The Changed know their genetic heritage, and that defines them. Everyone in the world is created by the past except me, and that makes me lonely. So I want to know what my mother has said, even if half is lies.

The Changed can wait a little while without me. Vijay and Auntie Suu-Suu are taking charge of organizing the evacuation, so I know that it will be efficient and orderly. I have earned the right to have a few minutes alone with my mother's memoir.

Chapter Two

I came to attend my funeral because I ran away with the Tinkers when I was twelve. I was on the Eastern Gate looking down over the long slope of the Mountain and saw the motley caravan with stars and moons painted on the candy-colored vehicles, and I knew I had to see it up close. Later I learned that they had been engaged to play at a soiree for Xanadu; otherwise they would never have approached our stronghold at all.

They were nothing like anyone on the Mountain, and although I had never been to Babelion I had seen enough to know that these Tinkers were nothing like humans, either. The humans I knew all worshipped some pantheon of ridiculous half-animal deities and believed that we are all reborn forever. I learned that from your father and you must know that it's complete idiocy.

The Tinkers are something altogether different. I stayed for two years, and what I learned with them, became integral to my development. I consider those years the most important part of my education. When I returned to the Mountain to take my proper place in the Exchange, there was a question as to whether I would be permitted back in or cast into the pits of Babelion.

For those two essential years I learned what we on Maya have forgotten. The Tinkers know who we are and they have not forgotten. They are a strange tribe, scientists trained in disciplines that we have deliberately ignored, cutting ourselves off from the rest of the civilized empire. Or perhaps I should say the Empire of the Lost, the way Auntie called it when we traveled through the stations of the Azalea Region.

You probably do not know that Maya is in the Azalea Region, under the leadership of the Azalea Governor appointed by the Flower Empress. The Azalea Governor doesn't know it either, which is entirely the point. We have options.

The Tinkers weren't much interested in Maya for a very long time. The earliest records in the Exchange do not mention them at all. They only started appearing, very rarely at great intervals, during the decade before I was born. Then there were more and more of them, and now we have them constantly roaming in those wagons as if they had always been part of the landscape.

They live in units that are nothing like the families of Babelion. I was adopted by one of those units where there was a girl my age, Sonja. She and I had lessons together, though she was always a little shy around me. Her older sister Anastasia was also very careful, always trying to be kind to me and make sure that I had anything I desired.

There were a few other young people near my age, enough so that I had studymates and others who wanted to play, but now that I have more distance I can see that something was very odd about them. But then, everything was odd in the Tinker world.

They travel and live in those wagons, which are really much more pleasant inside than they appear. There is a home somewhere for them but I was never taken there. I never really left Maya, though my Tinker sisters spoke longingly of shopping in

the Grandes Arcades and playing sports that I couldn't imagine—
Free Ball and Dive, all in zero gee while their wagons were locked
for the long voyages home.

When I left them, Auntie Suu-Suu had given me her shawl,
the one that was embroidered with real silver and pearls. She
stood just outside the caravan shed in the coldest hours of the
morning, waiting under stars that shone like ice. I had not told
anyone that I was planning to leave, or how. I hadn't even known
that tonight was the night, or that I would go to this shed rather
than Reizi's battered wagon-house that was still parked on blocks
in the forge.

I shivered and tried to slip past in the moonlight, knowing that
Auntie would see me. She was as old as the stars and saw as
much, all the girls were convinced of it. Even when we said there
was no such thing as magic (not counting the music, but that was
different, or a way with animals and vehicular repair,) as we were
being taught to read genetic code and how to slip something into
an allele here or how a change to one system will produce unexpected results in another, Auntie Suu-Suu lived in contradiction.
The things she predicted came true, and the things said about the
past and the time of the Change were frightening because they
were both so very crazy and so very ordinary.

She lived beyond the science that she taught. And she was the
leader of this band not simply because she was the eldest and the
best, but because she had some kind of magic that no one admitted
to. Least of all Auntie herself. She would be the first to say that
no such thing existed, that they had been trying to create a true
and reproducible and testable psi since forever and so far they
knew no more than when they had started.

And, yet, she knew. She knew that night that I chose to leave,
as she knew when I had talked Sonja and Anastasia into one
scheme or another. She always found some time for me in private,
to sit and talk about the Flower Thrones and the war with the
Pretender. Those stories always sounded like the tales we hear at
the Temple, about how once the gods walked in incarnation upon
the ground.

The Tinkers don't believe in any gods, and yet Auntie had the
uncanny sense of a Pythoness, even an Oracle. The other Tinkers

all knew. When she wasn't around, Lorenzo told stories about her when he was still a student. We would sit around on the deep divans in his wagon as he worked out a new tune on the violin. That was before Sasha died and Lorenzo still smiled and hadn't disappeared yet into the drugged haze.

He would sit and play bits that came to him, and sometimes would create a tune just for a special holiday or because he was in the mood. Auntie said that she nearly dismissed him from the program because he was far too talented a musician to waste as a Tinker. He laughed and said there was plenty of room to be both in this life, and that he was too restless to do only one thing anyway. That was the only reason Auntie let him stay, I think, because he never would have been a priest in the Temple of Music. He would only have gone off to study something else again and again, and this way Auntie could keep watch on him.

But he did teach us all to play. It was Lorenzo who taught me the flute and gave me the instrument that you have now. I would have told you about him and how I had learned to play, but you never really had the talent for it, and then you took the flute and learned to play on your own as if I would disapprove of your music. As if only your tame humans would ever understand.

Still, sometimes when he was tired he would put down his fiddle—he always called it a fiddle, never a violin—and tell us about how Auntie had once been the Great Tinker and appointed to an advisory post by the Flower Empress herself. That was very long ago, when the Pretender was busy building a fleet and hiding from the Empress' spies.

Lorenzo said that she had been just beyond a young woman then, old enough to be full of responsibility but before her hair had turned gray. She was very beautiful, he told us, as if he had seen her himself. She had been taut and athletic and her hair had hung down past her waist in plaits tied with bells for Court functions. There were even rumors that she had been a favorite of the Empress, or maybe of the Admiral Chan, the one who was so famous and then joined the Pretender after the old Empress died.

One day she had been in the gaming rooms with the Empress and the Admiral and all the others who were close in favor at a crism party, she predicted that the old Empress would die on the day that the child Empress ate tainted strawberries. Everyone had laughed at her, Lorenzo said, but she had remained adamant. It was the only time she had ever used crism because under its influence she could see too clearly what the future said.

The old Empress did die on the day the child Empress ate tainted strawberries, even though strawberries had been forbidden ever since Auntie's first prediction. They had been poisoned by the Pretender, who appeared in the sky with a phalanx of warships and proceeded to lase down the Magnolia Wing of the Gardens of Paradise.

Auntie had taken two of the youngest Empresses and fled. One she left with the Azalea Governor, who turned out to remain loyal. That is the Empress today. The other one—no one knows what happened to her. Auntie disappeared then and did not reappear for three years, when she became a teacher in a backwater school without a lab fit for her talents. But by then she was wild, Lorenzo said, her wanderlust overcoming her sense of responsibility. She disappeared for entire terms of instruction, and often spirited several students away with her.

Then Lorenzo laughed. "Sasha and I, we were the last that she recruited. And I do not regret it. This is a wonderful adventure, a better adventure than we ever would have had if we'd stayed nice and careful at home. Where else would I see volcano fields that stretch forever? Where else does the magma glow deep red in the night and reflect up onto the falling snow? I can return home and become a musician when I'm old and fat and gray."

He laughed again and Sasha passed around a plate of candies, sticky little seed things that were too sweet. I can still taste those candies and think of that innocence—mine and Lorenzo's and all of ours. I am glad I will never eat anything like them again. I couldn't stand their cloying memories of happiness and hope. How Lorenzo hoped and dreamed, how bright he was until Sasha died. But that is not germane.

Maya, for the Tinkers, was not entirely real I think. Lorenzo stopped telling us stories about Auntie and all the things she had done, but sometimes we could still get Big Nishala to describe the streets of Eldorado or the gaming halls on Azar-3.

She didn't like to tell those stories. She would shrug her fat shoulders under her heavy brocade shawl. "It's all townies anyway, so who cares? It doesn't matter except that there were lots of places to work and people on vacation are happy to part with money. We never had any trouble getting grants and the industry there will do almost anything to look respectable." Then she'd sigh heavily, the way she always did when forced to recall the unfortunate realities of life here on Maya.

Then Big Nishala would lick her lips and say, "But you should have seen Auntie Suu-Suu there. She gave a talk in the biggest saloon on Eldorado and even had the whorebots in tears."

Anastasia giggled. "Bots can't cry."

Big Nishala shook her head slowly, her two chins solemnly resting on her neck. "No, they are bioconstructs on Eldorado. Auntie owns about six of the patents, which is where a lot of her money comes from. They're just called bots because they're artificial, but they are so much like alive that there is a movement to give them subject status. They don't want that status themselves, Auntie made certain of that. It's ridiculous that a bunch of would-be do-gooders who have never met a construct in their lives are out campaigning for their rights."

Auntie had been the great elder at all the events of all the Tinkers, on every world and at every time. She was born before the first Change according to her reckoning, though we all knew perfectly well that was completely impossible. There was no time before the Change, at least none worth acknowledging. Still, we girls all held her in awe, knowing that she had true powers of the Sight and that she took tea with sugar cubes held between her teeth (and she still had her teeth which proved the miracle) and that she always knew where we had been and what we had been doing and with whom.

She was the one True Psi, even if she denied it herself. Lorenzo and Big Nishala agreed, and they were actual grown-ups who had their degrees.

So it was no surprise to me that Auntie was waiting for me when even I did not know that it was time to leave, and called me over when I crouched behind the pennyprickle shrub where she should not have been able to see me. She said nothing, though, held up her hand and shook her head gently. I froze and saw Micha Nystoli saunter by, exchange a few words with Auntie, and then go back to Anna Paluaski's wagon instead of his own.

Auntie waited until the door shut and the lock glimmered on before she crooked a finger and smiled at me. There was no choice, I could not pretend that I was not there. So I came out and stood straight and let my skirts rustle as I went to her, walking proud and easy as was my place as a girl of fourteen and a favorite of hers.

She wrapped her great shawl around my shoulders. "This belonged to a very great lady who died," she said in the same singsong voice that she used when she lectured us (grown-ups included) on manners and proper technique and how an experiment is not valid without a control group. "She gave it to me for serving her well. But I think it will serve you well, you and the child that should not come, but will. I think it is something that someday you will need."

I nodded, afraid to contradict her. Auntie Suu-Suu must know, and yet she was giving this to me as if I were Anastasia or Sonja. Then she sighed heavily. "And now it is time that I pass this on. I am not young enough to live up to the promise of it anymore. I've become an old woman here, not because of years but because of worry and anxiety and trepidation. Della, you are the only one of the Changed who has ever come among us. Think of this shawl as armor that will protect you from fear. If I had had real courage then the Pretender would not be following me now."

I scoffed at the idea that Auntie did not have real courage. I had heard enough of her exploits in the academy and the Court to know that she had been the consummate courtier, the elegant player in a fragile game. She had done fact more than anyone else could have done; that was the fact and everyone knew it.

But then, Auntie was more than human, and more than Changed. She held herself to higher standards, standards that I longed to surpass and was afraid I could hardly reach. I would never be Auntie. I would never be half of her.

"Take Dolores'," she advised me, her voice dropping to a whisper. "Lorenzo's is too old and Anna's makes some strange ignition sound."

I nodded, immediately noting Dolores's transport. Auntie's advice was always good, always to be followed. And she was generous when she would give it out, when a girl might not be so brave as to ask. She touched me again, this time laying her gnarled and heavily beringed hand on my hair. Automatically I knelt on the battered grass at her feet to receive her blessing. "Go to your destiny, Della. Wear the shawl and pass it on. It contains your legend, which is not yet written. And it contains your heritage, which you do not know. You have lived here long enough, and now it is time for you to travel into history."

Then she said one last thing that was very odd. "You must name the child Anselm."

Child? I wondered. I was only a child myself. Anselm was a strange name and I had never heard it before, not from my own people or from the Tinkers.

"You will know the child and the name when the time comes," she said kindly, stroking my hair and tugging at the shawl to make it show off the rich pearl-encrusted edging. Then she gave me one last hard hug, buried my face in the perfume of roses and spice that seemed to cling to everything she touched. When she released me and clucked me toward the shed, I could smell it in my hair.

I cried and held her hand and kissed the swollen knuckles as if it had not been my own choice to leave. Auntie had tried to talk me into staying, into coming back into the Empire and leaving Maya forever. I could study at a proper university, she told me. I could have everything, she promised.

But there were two things I could not have among the Tinkers. One was the music, the other was my solitude. The Tinkers are always together, always around. They live in units of at least two and often far more individuals, all crammed into the same space and schedule and concerns.

I hated it. It was filthy to have to live so close to others, never to have silence and privacy to think and be alone. They do not know how to be alone, they avoid being alone or permitting anyone else the luxury of space. By the time I had been there two years I felt suffocated by the constant heat of bodies and chatter that intruded on my contemplations.

Lorenzo tried to tempt me when he told me about his years at a conservatory and about the concerts and the adulation offered at the feet of the finest there. I think Auntie knew that she had failed to keep me and had enlisted his aid. He spoke in hushed tones about studying with true masters of composition as well as performance. And he told me the story of his greatest triumph, the performance of his first symphony as the prize for winning a great competition. Sidles had conducted, Vengu had played the violin solo with such tenderness that Lorenzo wept as if he had never heard it played before.

That was before Sasha had died. And then Lorenzo died and his talent died with him. I tried to play my flute at the funeral but it was no use. Even Sonja, who joked about having no music at all, played far better than I. Even if I had been tempted to stay, I could not remain after Lorenzo's death. His blood was everywhere and his sorrow permeated every conversation.

Now I think it was the music that made me leave in the first place, and the music that brought me home. Music was all of life to me. By the time I was ten I had developed some honest sensitivity to music. I played three instruments at that age, and made someone obtain a harpsichord because I wanted to hear Bach on the proper instrument and no one would give me a Baroque organ. Today I still can hear all of Scarlatti in my head, though I have long given up the ability to play.

As Auntie said, it was fear that kept me back. Lorenzo had taught me the flute, but it was not enough. I know that for one of the Changed, for the Mountain, I was good. The music was mine; I owned it. But in this world where anything could happen, I knew that my talent was too minor. I would never be accepted by a conservatory. I would not have the place of the Changed here, the security of the Exchange and the promise of blessed peace and quiet.

I don't know specifically what music they played at my funeral service—something ponderous and dull that I would actively avoid today if I had any reference for it.

When I ran away when I was twelve, my mother and my neural sculptor were horrified. They had gone to the Exchange as soon as they realized I was missing and started to trace. Or tried to. The Exchange blocked the request, blocked the trace paths, and cut off my security. There was no argument and even now no one knows precisely why the Exchange made that decision—except me. Though the Exchange told me in private because of our privileged relationship, and still I did not find out until just a few years ago when Anselm resurfaced.

Anselm. This is supposed to be for you, about you, so that you will understand who and what you are and so that everyone else will finally comprehend as well. I am an adaptation, an anomaly. Anselm, you are something very different—you are a charismatic leader the way your father was. People laid down their lives for his smile, for the flash in his eyes.

I have never seen this in you myself, and it is one of my deepest regrets. You need to know that what I did I did mostly for your sake. Many things have not worked out in my life, many things have gone astray. And I was not always as I am now, a power on the Mountain. Once I was as young and vulnerable as my son was when I left, and because I lacked the status I needed I made choices that appeared cruel. Anslem, you need to know that they were always for your benefit, that I sacrificed everything to protect you.

I even lived on for you, creating and guarding your life and youth even as I pursued the Tinker stories of the worlds beyond. And I searched for Auntie Suu-Suu, hoping that she would help the boy she named as I could not help him. In the end there was no choice. Always I have done whatever would protect my son, even if it seemed incomprehensible, inhuman, selfish even.

I could not save Arsen, and I could only protect you so far. There are limits even as a power within the Exchange. The Exchange, in the end, makes all the decisions for its own reasons. Even I do not understand why it makes the determinations it does. Only that it has its own ideas about the end and the Creators made certain that the Exchange is as far from the Flower Throne as we are from the depths of the dark world.

But I was talking about something else, about where it all started. Because Arsen never knew and Anselm must know all the components that have combined to produce what he is. You are a phenomenon—far more so than I ever was. And for that I envy you, though I understand the genetics behind the reasoning. Arsen has a great deal to do with it, and Arsen and I were great and feared and adored in our day. We have just been overshadowed.

But I am rambling like some senile toothless wretch from the underzone, and I am neither senile nor given to rambling. My education—because the Exchange protected me I was free for two years. My name was struck from the Lists of Precedence and my mother held a memorial service on the anniversary of my disappearance. On the second anniversary I returned and keyed my security code in to the Gate just before the memorial service started, which is why I wandered in to see that awful dress, those saccharine flowers and that hideous music. I stayed and watched until they were near the end, until the elder was ready to give the last blessing. Then I stood up and walked down the center aisle.

No one recognized me at first. Then my mother screamed and my sculptor came and grabbed my arm hard enough to bruise. But he didn't hold me long because the Guardians came and took me into custody while they decided what to do.

After all, we are superior beings and have been constructed to be such. Superstition is stupidity, and it was eradicated from our genetic code ages before the first Creators started to tinker with the chain.

The Exchange, however, had its own plans and its reasoning was based on forces that are outside the pragmatic world, things that have more power over people's lives than they can believe. One of those things is faith, and the other is love. I have seen that kind of love twice, and both times it was terrifying.

Anastasia was like that. Anastasia was so in love with her handsome husband that she wouldn't admit that he used crism and spent what other money she earned buying his friends vodka at whatever halls they played.

He truly loved Anastasia, he was a proper husband and did not chase other women or show disrespect to her mother. Like all of

Lorenzo's friends, crism did not make him mean but only vague and placid, which was in his nature as an artist. Chelo was always kind and gentle, and if there was nothing he could give us there was always a compliment or some brotherly advice, or if those wouldn't do he would take out his guitar and make us all cry. There were visions and songs that were unimaginable, or so Chelo said. He lived staring at the ceiling most of the afternoon, fluttering his fingers in front of his face from time to time.

But then, even Chelo had been introduced to Anastasia by Lorenzo. Chelo who had fallen for crism before he had found Anastasia and had already left his studies and his promise of a brilliant career. Later I learned that crism was endemic throughout the Empire, and that it was even more common among the Tinkers. So many of them were unhappy, homesick for the comforts of civilization, for the refinement and elegance that they had once taken for granted. Now they were exiles. Whenever Chelo played there was sorrow, all the drowned hopes illuminated by the gift he was killing so slowly.

The fact it was not nice made the music so much more ravishing. In the true sense of ravish, that is.

That always reminded me of Lorenzo. His misery at coming home one day to find Sasha dead of a crism overdose seeped into the corners and silences of even his happiest songs and made him even greater and deeper than he had been before. Watching Lorenzo crumple at the wake when his friends played a Mass by Arvo Paarti with full solemnity on violins, guitars and bass, I understood that it was the experience of pain that made the music transcendent.

After the last notes of the Mass faded, Lorenzo stood alone, ragged and shaking, and looked toward the ceiling. He was only twenty-eight and had been doing crism for three years. For a moment there was only the addict. Then he straightened his back and threw back his head and his eyes filled with anguish. He leaned over the open coffin, which had been stuffed with money and bottles of good brandy and little packets of crism and honey pastries to take into the next world, and he gathered up the drug packets carefully and dropped them on the floor.

"Wait for me, beloved," he whispered, but the entire room

was still and his voice could be heard clearly. "I promised to make you famous, and I must keep that promise before you welcome me to be with you forever. Wherever it is you are."

Only it is Lorenzo who is famous now. He wrote a symphony that changed the whole Empire, and three sonatas that are so haunting it makes you want to die. Music and death were the only things that Lorenzo loved besides the one who had gone before him.

Lorenzo was not like a Tinker at all after that. He painted out the gaudy sigils on his wagon and it was all hung with pictures and remembrances of his dead love, all of them draped in black and lit with candles. He never touched drugs again, either—grief was enough of a drug, he used to say. And six months later he died, his wrists carefully cut deep to the elbow, a few drops of blood staining the crism vial in his fist, his body draped in a loose white robe, and the Arvo Paarti Mass programmed on continuous repeat.

I did not understand this love and I wasn't sure I approved of that extreme a faith, but I could see the power of it. This is one of the great secrets I told you before I went into the Exchange and died to the outside world. I tried to make sure you were as prepared as I could manage with what I knew at the time. I have learned a great deal since my conversion, and I have tried to channel it to you through the Exchange. That is difficult, since the rebels of Babelion have no access. But I managed sometimes with the most important data.

And I watched over you, arranged things through the Exchange that could not have happened otherwise. Your genetic records have been expunged, along with any mention of your arrests or schooling. I put in a few false trails and covered up the truth with the kind of data anyone would expect to find on a human. What I planted in the files is entirely predictable and dull, which not only serves as long as the Changed hold any power, but also feeds the legend.

You want to feed the legend. In the end, that is a far greater power than anything you've achieved through conquest or diplomacy. Greater politicians have not considered this—but, then, they were not sterile.

I will have no grandchildren and you will not have an heir of the flesh—our flesh—to inherit whatever position you carve out. That may be for the best. The Emperors of Rome did far better when they adopted their successors rather than bred them. But in any event, the lines always deteriorate and finally fall. So your reliance on the story, the power of faith, the strength of your own semidivinity, is your grip on the future.

It is obvious that you have learned these lessons well. You have your father's gifts combined with the superior genes of the Changed, and so you are invincible. You are also a monster—the monster I created.

Naturally, you will never reveal your background. It would destroy who you have become. Then the mob would turn on you and kill you. I watched your father die, I know how little people think when they are afraid. The people of Babelion are little people, hardly more than animals. Why are you trying to Change them into something more, something that the original Creators had never intended?

Or maybe we have no idea what the Creators intended.

Five years ago, members of our own little rulership started wailing loudly that you should have been killed or discredited when we had you. When they could have ruined you, in those fragile moments when you were making the transition from Changed to human.

That is why I had to enter the Exchange fully, and why you had to be forced to leave. Sithra has been waiting to kill you ever since you were born. At least in Babelion you had the chance to survive. Even Sithra can't find you without data, and data can die. It was only for your sake and your survival that I made the decisions that I made.

But I am getting ahead of myself. This part of the story isn't really about you yet at all. This part of the story is about Arsen.

Chapter Three

In the beginning there were no plans—there was only Arsen. Every year the Exchange has an open day to test the hopeful of Babelion, to see if natural humanity has finally caught up to our level of evolution. No one has ever proven out, though the best among them are invited to stay and take advantage of the opportunities to work on the Mountain.

Arsen did not come from the town outside the gate. After I had officially died, I went down to the building where he had grown up in the sewers of the underclass. I had never seen the area by daylight. Some of the windows were boarded up and others had ratted plastic taped over cracks. Three teenaged girls stood on the steps wearing pants that were too tight and much too bright even for Tinkers to consider and their tunics were cut too low. All three of them had babies, and I turned away in disgust. Until I remembered that I was no older than they when I had walked through the enclave on the Mountain with you asleep on my shoulder.

The entire block was crumbling, the paving in the street spotty, the grillwork on the doors gaping open and rusted. And the place was crowded with people. Along with the girls with babies were the young men playing ball in the street and slightly older men with buckets of suds washing statues that could only be called obscene. Several women who appeared to be absolutely ancient, and wore scraps the color of the girls' clothing sewn together into veils that were firmly anchored on their foreheads, walked hunched over while everyone made way for them. The younger, tougher boys all vied to carry the thin shopping bags for the old women, competing to outdo each other in service. And the old men sat in short stools in groups on the sidewalk, nodding sagely as the youngsters paraded by. Nearby on the steps several older women painted intricate patterns on the hands and feet of girls wearing gold bracelets, with glints of gold in the edging of their skirts.

Tiny packets littered the streets and sidewalks, the entrances to the buildings, and were especially thick around the statues of their gods. I took one and opened it idly. There was rice and a pale pink petal all wrapped together in brilliant turquoise paper.

"Put that back," someone hissed in my ear. It was one of the young girls with a baby. "That's for Ganesh, not for you."

As I stooped down to replace the offering I noticed that every one of the colorful packets was different. Some were old and rotten and were swarming with insects.

No one appeared to have anywhere to go or any business to attend. I saw my first and only devi that day, one of those sacred prostitutes we hear about on the Mountain, that makes Babelion sound so alien and unreal. She was quite beautiful, really, her perfect peach skin just a touch reddened by the chill. Her hair was done up with jewels that hung across her forehead, and her sari was richer and appeared more voluminous than those I had seen before, and in a very sedate shade of dark green. Truly, she looked more like a lady than anyone else there, and many of the people on the street, women as well as men, came up to her and greeted her and bowed with something like reverence.

I turned away and looked at the youngsters with the ball. That, at least, I was prepared to understand. I tried to imagine Arsen as one of the boys in the street, and found that it was not hard to picture him as one of the youngsters who jumped and dodged and flung themselves after a black-and-white ball. This one had his laughing black eyes, another his easy walk, a third had the same cascade of dark curls falling over his shoulders.

As I looked at them all, I realized that Arsen truly was one of these people. His body proclaimed his genetic heritage clearly, displayed his connection to the throng at their leisure in the middle of a working day. And yet Arsen had been so beautiful, so compelling, while these gutter snipes looked coarse and only half-finished. Though to think clearly, Arsen had not been beautiful in any way that could be defined. He was far from perfect, and yet the mix of features and open expressions along with a build created by hard labor and no money combined perfectly in him. Arsen was approachable, warm, and people trusted him instinctively. His intelligence shone within his compassion, his commitment burned in his face even when he smiled.

Perhaps my memories are at fault. I have never known anyone like Arsen. Perhaps he did not really radiate the way I recall him, perhaps he looked far more like the boys in the street than I realized. But that was before I made the Transition and still lived within the confines of desire, and so my judgment was questionable at best.

I met him when he arrived in the cohort for testing the year I was to turn sixteen. We were being tested alongside the youth of Babelion, as is the custom. And, according to tradition, we were each assigned a "partner" for the month before, to tutor and fill in the specific information they would need about the Exchange. The partnering presentation was held in the Sea Salon of Xanadu. It is one of the smaller official rooms, the walls and floors all covered in a restful, deep multilayered blue-green marble, the entire ceiling a mosaic of colored glass that formed patterns of light that danced through the air. It was not too formal or intimidating for groups of young people being presented for the first time.

"What a waste of time. I can't believe they're making us do this," Samsara whined as we gathered for the orientation meeting before the presentation.

Since she always whined about everything, I was surprised when Kinri spoke in agreement.

"Yeah," he said as he chewed on a pencil and looked idly around the room. "Maybe the traditions were a psychological necessity in the early days before we had accepted the complete speciation. Now they're a useless throwback to our ancestors' collective guilt."

"You mean you don't think we have anything to learn from them?" I asked. Kinri was one of the few I respected, who seemed to notice that there were possibilities other than what we learned on the Mountain.

Kinri hesitated, waved the pencil in the air for a moment and then replaced it firmly in his teeth. "We may well have something to learn. We can learn from many sources, after all. Even lower animals."

"They are lower animals," someone else said.

Kinri ignored the comment. "But the traditions don't show much respect for them. If you study the forms of interaction as prescribed in the traditions you'll see they are just formalized paternalism. In fact, while I still believe they grew out of guilt, they also serve to reinforce the notion that we are superior."

"But we are," Samsara spoke for the entire cohort.

I had learned that line, too. Only it was harder for me to believe after I'd studied the great composers of other worlds. Not one of us in the two hundred years of the Mountain had ever composed music that lived as theirs did.

Inarguably we do have higher intelligence in certain areas of the brain. Our mathematical and verbal skills are not comparable to the unaltered and nothing will change that. That, after all, was what the Creators were trying to perfect. To them, mathematics and verbal skills were intelligence. Music, art, movement, these were lesser things to them. Chess was a sign of intelligence, too, but the Creators put far less emphasis on developing that gift. They didn't feel it was a useful talent.

The Creators were not as intelligent as they thought they were. And they were prisoners of a value system that had grown out of the necessities of their own times—or at least what they thought were necessities.

There was also the matter of physical ability and adaptation to Maya. This was not the climate we had been created to inhabit. The Changed have trouble with the cold, enough so that we have kept the environment of Xanadu closed since we first landed. The humans can bear the temperatures outside, the incessant freeze, the constant wind. Their bodies are thicker than ours, with an extra layer of fat under the skin so they are ungainly and squat instead of fluid and graceful. But that means that they are better able to withstand the rigors of this climate. The Changed, without the Dome, might not all die. But many of us would, and we would suffer severely. Our condition might impair our ability to function inside the Exchange, and that would be worse than death.

This could not have been the place we were meant to settle. We were never designed to survive in this cold, hostile world. Even after two hundred years it is still an enemy more to be feared than angry humans or subtle political enemies.

Kinri, in his much later years, wrote a very thoughtful article on the world of the Creators. It was promptly suppressed on the Mountain. Do you remember he sent you a copy though you were only seven at the time? You must have read it later, though, because Kinri's thesis shows up in your more analytical studies of the great rift.

The discussion never went any further that day, though. The elders came in, the testers and one of the officiants of the traditions, to explain how things worked and how we were expected to behave and what to wear. Then we practiced walking around the room a few times to get the stage directions down, which would make us more impressive compared to the street kids coming up. They didn't get coached on choreography.

The morning of the presentation day I took a lot of time choosing my clothes. I didn't want to be yet one more of the Mountain adaptees, neat and precise and colorless. I wanted to look as singular as I was in the cohort. Of the fifteen of us, only Kinri had ever spoken to me outside a set context. No one could get out of using proper manners even if we still had no status; in order to gain status we had to show that we were masters of the etiquette as well as everything else. But only Kinri had ever actually talked to me about anything real.

He had been interested in the Tinkers. He wasn't sure if they were truly simple nonadaptations or a group that nature had evolved in a special manner. After all, there were seven areas of intelligence in the brain. Our Creators had only set deep enhancements into two. The rest had been modified in a minor way—every one of us could sing pleasantly, draw a little and play competently. We had also been modified so that we were all physically beautiful, at least by the Creator's standards of beauty. Which means that we are all slender with clear skin and good teeth and that all our hair is the same degree of healthy, though they did leave all the variation from straight to curly. Our features are regular and even with ruler straight noses, large eyes and high cheekbones. We all wear the same four sizes, and we all look about the same age once we hit maturity—young enough to remain beautiful by the Creator's standards but old enough to have some authority. The Creators did not specify coloring, so the only difference that is notable is that the same features can come with dark skin or white pale hair or green eyes and freckles.

I had never thought about looks (I'm one of the black-haired, white-skinned, pale-blue-eyed models with dead-center wavy hair) until my Tinker mother and aunties started sighing over my figure the year I was thirteen.

"Maybe you're just a little late," she would mutter as she inspected me next to Sonja and shake her head. Sonja was two months younger than me and already had rounded breasts far larger than any woman on the Mountain ever had.

"She looks like a boy," Auntie Angelika said while looking at me. "She looks like a boy and frail too, and she's cold all the time. She needs to eat more."

"It's the phenotype, they are all built that way," Auntie Suu-Suu defended me, though I didn't understand precisely what she meant.

"It's warmer at home and she should have that much range of adaptation. Besides, we know that the Seventh Empress was actually overweight. There are environmental and psychological variations that create individuals and you know that." Auntie Angelika was adamant, and I had the impression that I was hearing another round in a very old argument between them.

Auntie Suu-Suu shrugged. "You're right, I know that there is still a lot of individuality even among a single generation with the same nurturing. But she is not frail or unhealthy and it is in her genetic background to remain fairly slender no matter what the cultural norms involving food are."

Auntie Angelika was not defeated. "The cold here means that everyone has to eat much more than we would anywhere else, including her. Unless you want to introduce another set of variables?"

Auntie Angelika had won. From that time I was forced to eat much more than Anastasia and Sonja and all the other girls together at every meal. I was given sweets in between and Mama and her colleagues would watch me ingest them. They baked wonderful things, pastries that were light and stuffed with nuts and dripped with honey and lacy crêpes filled with chocolate cream and lemon curd and drizzled with powdered sugar, all to tempt me to eat more.

Auntie Angelika forced me to eat until I got sick and it still didn't do any good. Part of the alteration keeps our metabolism extremely high, and as for the figure, well—I was stuck with what had been in fashion two hundred years ago. Since every other Mountain woman was the same I had never thought I was inadequate.

And to be honest, being seen by the other women as inferior was yet one more reason why I returned. I hated feeling so ugly all the time and being treated as if I were sickly besides. I could not endure the other girls my age trying to be extra nice, to find scraps from their wardrobes that might make me look less pale or offer to stuff my bra with old scarves.

And so, for the presentation ceremony where we were expected to look even more alike than usual, all dressed in white, I looked for something unique. By then it was too late to be unique, so I ended up with the requisite white pants and tunic. Then at the last minute I threw Auntie Suu-Suu's deep blue velvet shawl, with long silk fringe and suns and moons and stars embroidered all over it, around my shoulders in place of the usual translucent scarf. It was so large that the fringe at the lowest points came down to my feet. One of the Authorities of the traditions told me that I must remove the shawl before we started. It did not represent our people at all, it would give the wrong ideas to those others who had come to see their one great hope.

I refused to take it off. I told the Authority that if I couldn't wear my shawl then I would just as soon not participate. I began to trounce out, throwing the shawl dramatically across my chest, when I was told to get back in line. The number of hopefuls from Babelion had been matched to our cohort exactly. It would not do if one of them was unpartnered at the last moment and required to repeat the application another year. It would make us look—stingy.

The entire program was a farce anyway and I was tempted to leave even though I'd just won. But the idea of meeting someone from outside was too enticing. Ever since the Ishtar Gate had shut behind me, I had been a prisoner. I knew what was out there, that there was life and fear and music, blood and uncertainty that did not exist here.

Strange that I found myself thinking of the Tinkers while we walked into the presentation ceremony. The outsiders were already there, the hopefuls wearing assorted frayed trousers and faded shirts. They looked ragged, even more so compared to our crisps whites and precise movement. But it wasn't merely to impress or even intimidate. The whole power show was also meant kindly, to prepare those who hoped to join us for their inevitable failure.

We truly had no desire to be cruel. There is no reason for it and many that argue against. A rebellious or indigent population is not in our best interests. Nor is one that is ready to sabotage us through resentment. No, we want the others happy and content with their lives—and content with their rulers as well.

Which was yet another aspect of the traditions that were shared with the humans. They had to believe that we are superior in every way, which is not difficult because that is true. Mostly. But they also had to believe that we gave up something in return for our privilege—that we gave up our freedom, our individuality, our self-expression. Which was also true. And since these things were fact and not pretense, the humans believed them. Certainly we did.

That is why your father was always such an anomaly. While you are a better leader, a better strategist, a more inspiring speaker, you realize that you are not completely original. Arsen had been there first with the ideas—and there is nothing revolutionary about a son following in his father's footsteps. In the end, Anselm the great rebel leader is far more conventional than either his father or I.

Chapter Four

We took our seats and listened to the speeches and the deathly dull music. I studied the humans who sat across the room, those who would be among us as students for a month. Most of them were scrubbed and earnest, their hair tied back in some approximation of ours, or cut very short to show how serious and businesslike they were. They had none of the tribal markings I associated with the fetid city—no tattoos, no piercings, no visible scars or brands. They sat up straight and paid attention to the speeches. I felt sorry for them—it was so obvious they didn't know their dreams were futile, that already we knew none of them could ever join us.

One boy in the group did not fit in precisely. He wore the same faded whitish trousers and tunic that was the ordinary uniform of their side, all the cuffs frayed and ghost traces of stains where the fabric had been bleached over and over into a kind of sickly yellow. Obviously it had been worn by more than one person before he had inherited it, just like all the others there. But unlike the others he didn't sit up quite so straight and his arms were folded across his chest. His hair fell in long, loose ringlets across his shoulders. Wide shoulders, I remembered thinking, for a boy my own age. Though he probably worked out, which was something humans did when they had little better to do. And when their genetics hadn't been programmed to give them perfect bodies without wasting time.

But it was not just the way he slouched or the fact that the others in his party eyed him suspiciously from time to time, hoping that their glances wouldn't register with us. Or maybe—with him, I don't know. It was the way he looked at me.

He studied all of us, eyes narrowed, one finger tapping as if counting off points of observation. But when he studied Auntie Suu-Suu's shawl his eyes widened and met mine. They held for an instant and I knew him as well as he knew me.

We were the same kind.

Different species, different background, different in every other possible way, this one bad boy was exactly like me. He, too, had probably run away and lived on his own. And when he couldn't ignore the conventions of his society he opposed all of them on principle. Just like me, he probably opposed them without examining any use they might have, the only justification for their existence was so that those like us would have plenty to protest and battle.

————

Of course the boy and I were assigned to each other. That was only natural. Neither side would inflict us on the good citizens of the other. We were each called forward and introduced to our study partners, and that was the first time I ever heard Arsen's name. He stood up slowly, as if he were doing the Authority a favor by getting to his feet and taking the twenty steps or so to the middle of the floor.

I had thrown the shawl over my tunic so that it covered the entire upper half of my body and the long fringe hung over the pants to the floor. Only my hands showed, and those not quite enough to give the firm, simple handshake we had been taught for this ceremony. I barely moved my wrist, offering my fingers through the silk. He leaned over and kissed my fingertips—or maybe it was the wise woman's shawl he kissed. Knowing Arsen, that is far more likely.

When he stood up again he looked me in the eyes, and I could read mischief and mirth under the defiant attitude. He almost made me want to grin, though of course that would have been completely out of keeping.

His eyes were lighter than I had thought across the room, more of an amber honey color than truly brown. And his hair had glints of red and dark bronze when he moved. I wondered if it turned light in the sun, and then realized that it must and that he stayed indoors most of the days. He probably was not all that much different from me there, either. It was so much easier to study alone than to have to pretend to agree with one's peers.

Then we had to walk back to our seats across the room and listen to a few very brief words that seemed to last forever before we were dismissed to join the audience for the reception. By then I was starving and my stomach was in knots. Trays of fruit and cut cheese and slices of vegetables were tempting indeed, and I never had been one for resisting temptation. I stood right between a heaping platter of tiny cheese squares and a fruit tray and ate out of both.

"It's so bland," Arsen said behind me. "No curry and no decoration. At home it's not a feast without three curries with flowers on the top."

I whipped around and saw him, his face full of contempt for the food and the company alike. I shrugged. "I'm hungry," I replied, and turned back to whatever I could grab.

Arsen pulled a bunch of grapes from the tray—a very large bunch that left a gaping hole right in the front. "Come on, let's get out of here," he said as he handed me the grapes, took my elbow and steered me out of there. He said nothing as we left the official wing of Xanadu and entered the general Dome. I said nothing too, but that's because I was busy eating the grapes.

"Where'd you get the shawl?" he asked abruptly, as he felt the texture of the velvet and the metallic embroidery. "It's not even from us, I've never seen anything like it."

"I lived with the Tinkers for two years," I answered curtly to stave off questions. I knew he'd start asking and then he would either feel that he had to challenge me or that he'd have to ignore me. I didn't want either of those options to happen so I cut off the topic. "What are you hoping to do?" I inquired as gently as I could.

He began laughing and shook his head. "Hoping? What am I hoping to do?" His eyes darted away to a corner of the room as if he didn't want to acknowledge his own aspirations. Then he turned back.

"You don't have any idea who I am, do you? Just like I don't know who you are, but on the outside it's obvious that we're both a little eccentric." He laughed at his choice of the word. "Okay, we're both about as fringe as we can get away with. Neither one of us is exactly respectable. And the only way you can get to any position at all when you're not completely respectable is to be better than anyone else. Which I am."

"You are? You think you should become Changed?"

He nodded gravely.

So he was not so brilliant as he thought and he was arrogant, too. Would he ever be in for a shock when he found out that he still wasn't one of us. That he could never hope to be one of us, that no matter how good he was he was still simply human. He hadn't been part of the Changed and he hadn't descended from them. He might very well be smart and talented. It's even possible that he was more talented than one of us in some creative area, something that the original Creators had considered less important than full interface. He might be very superior for a human. He was still not one of us.

What the humans don't realize is that it is not only intelligence and talent we need for the Exchange. If it were only that, there would have been no reason to Change in the first place. But in order to enter extended periods of full interface we needed a different metabolism, a slight rearrangement of the areas of higher brain functions.

The brain and the body are not separate entities, just as the most primitive holy men down in Babelion teach. Nerve cells are all truly brain cells and all nerve cells in the Changed can think. More accurately, those cells have a slightly altered structure that enables them to act as additional storage. Which frees up still more space in the brain for active processing. And it means that certain emotional storms generated by chemicals that lay solely in the brain are limited.

Naturally, beyond the genetic changes which are now firmly embedded in our DNA, there are more changes added by the sculptors. Only minor tinkering needs to be done to make sure that a few dangerous receptors are permanently shut down, which is where the art began. And, strangely enough, it is the humans who work as our sculptors, making certain that experiences and environment provide precisely what the Changed child needs to develop and strengthen the correct synapses so they are not destroyed when the child reaches fourteen and begins to truly come into the full inheritance of the Changed. Neural sculpture is the most difficult and precise task that any human can aspire to, and most of the sculptors are those who have come to test. In fact, many of them find the entire field of neural programming far more intriguing then the Exchange in any case. My own sculptor, Aga Singh, is partly responsible for preserving the wild streak in me. It is an exceptional sculptor who can do that while maintaining a structure that is still fully functional in interface.

"It's not possible," I told Arsen gently, trying to explain as to a child. "There are differences, and we were made to be superior.

If anything you should be proud to see what we have become, a new line of evolution."

He crossed his arms over his chest and glowered. "Yeah." His voice was full of venom and disbelief. "Yeah, I thought that was how it was." Then he gave me a long appraising look, examining me as if I were a bug in a jar. "So what about you? How do you fit into all this? What are you hoping for?" he asked. A cruel hopeless smile tugged at the sides of his mouth.

I closed my eyes and listened to the silence. Arsen's steady breathing was the only sound in the study room. Otherwise the dead hush was overpowering. My ears began to make up music to trick my mind and I listened to it. There was always wisdom in the music, Auntie said, the path back to the heart. She didn't know that by her human standards I didn't have one.

"I am hoping to take my place in the Exchange," I said, thinking about every word instead of just letting the mouth run off by route. "I am hoping that I will have a special place, someplace that no one has ever had before."

Arsen picked up a corner of my shawl where it had dropped onto the floor. He caressed the embroidery and let the soft silk velvet slip through his fingers over and over. Maybe he had never touched fabrics this fine before, maybe this was all sensory overload.

The cohort had been warned about overloading our study partners. They weren't used to things as fine as we used on the Mountain and could easily be overwhelmed by the experience.

Then he dropped the scarf in my lap as he stood. "I don't care what you do, but I'm going to get some of those sandwiches and little cakes," he announced. And then he was gone before I had a chance to tell him that they weren't little cakes, they were petits fours, and the sandwiches with the pale pink creamy filling were something no one liked.

He took a bunch of them and choked down three, which was more than anyone else at the reception had managed. His face screwed up when he bit into it, but he looked straight at me while he chewed and swallowed. He brought the petits fours over to me and dropped the plate in my lap.

"Even the food here's a lie," he hissed, and then stalked out.

The petits fours were delicious. The three he had chosen were chocolate with raspberry and almond with mocha cream. After I'd eaten them I sucked my fingers to get off every molecule of glaze. We only got petits fours at formal receptions like this one.

Or the reception we had on the terrace when we gathered to watch Arsen die. I was there then, too, on the terrace inside the Dome, though I couldn't eat at all.

Though you already know how it ends, you have never heard this side before. I was there, I was more than there. I am the hidden piece, concealed by my own will so that I would be able to do what I am doing now. What I hope I am doing.

What is it you're hoping to become?

I have already become far more than I had ever dreamed and I am not satisfied. Because I have other dreams now and incentives I could never imagine that first day. That day I didn't even like him and he didn't like me, which is not the way the story goes either. I understand the political necessity for you to feed that image, but sometimes I wonder if you've really forgotten me entirely and believe what he has told the crowd.

Though you were also on the terrace that day. You were too young to remember, you were barely three months old. But you were there with me when you father died.

ANSELM REFLECTS:

I pulled away so abruptly that I felt the nodes tear the receptors where the skin had grown over the outer ring of the inset. My stomach lurched, my eyes stung, and reality danced and shifted around me.

Della doesn't always tell the truth, I reminded myself. Maybe I was there—and maybe I wasn't. Della can always be trusted to say the thing that will have the greatest impact or be most likely to produce the results she desired. Or at least that was how I remembered her.

But I had never thought of an almost sixteen-year-old Della who was as much a rebel in her way as Arsen was in his. I hadn't considered that she had been wild, and I certainly hadn't known that she had run away with the Tinkers for years.

In Babelion, when someone dies it is appropriate to mourn for the passage of a season. Beyond that time, the soul is ready to go further on its journey, to be reborn and start the cycle again. To mourn too deeply someone who is ready to go on is to pull them back, the rishis say. It keeps them stuck in the myths of the flesh that they are just learning to escape.

I'm not sure I believe in reincarnation—I'm not even sure that I believe in a soul that is a separate entity that can go on living after the body dies. But I do respect the customs of Babelion and so I have not talked about my mother and have tried to think of her as little as possible since I left.

No polite person would ask, either, which has saved me on many occasions. People always assume that Arsen had lovers among the humans of the Village, so they also assume that I am the child of one of those people, and was raised in the Village until my mother died. But because it is thought that she is dead, no one will ever ask.

Once Sulma asked, so very gently as only a devi can, if it had been hard to leave my mother's circle and come to Babelion. "You should visit them sometime," she had told me. "Especially before you enter the Temple as an acolyte. You should at least tell them where you are and what you are doing. I'm sure you hurt them by disappearing the way you did."

"The Guardians were after me," I told her truthfully.

"Why?" she asked, her eyes wide with curiosity. "What did you do to deserve that?"

I just shrugged. "It has to do with my mother," I answered, knowing that she would have to let the matter drop. And that was all I could tell her without lying, and Sulma would know if I lied. She could sense the truth and something about her made people want to tell her. Maybe it was a part of the devi training—I don't know.

I would like to have seen what she would have made of Della.

I shouldn't be thinking of Sulma too much now.

In order to calm my mind I pay attention to the walls, and it appears that I am the first person to do so in quite a while. The walls here are dirty and dented, streaked just around the height of Changed hands and feet. No one has cleaned them, I suddenly realize. Humans are not allowed in this level of the Exchanged, and the Changed don't do menial labor.

I couldn't hear anything from outside. Vijay must have kept the area well sealed. I would have expected some of the Changed to be down here——either checking the Exchange or trapped when the Dome first cracked. I could not believe that there were no Changed to protect their god at all, that it was only Della and me.

It had always been only Della and me.

And Arsen.

I had seen him. Even though I had been only a few months old at the time and probably could not have seen far enough to have a good image, there was something of him buried in my memory. The rishis of the Temple or the Tinkers could probably show me how to touch it, how to remember that far. I wanted that scrap of memory so badly. . . .

I felt so alone.

There had to be maps and rules, or at least some kind of guidance, I told myself. Someone must have run a rebellion before. Someone must have won. I needed guides, company——I needed to touch something that understood where I was.

I had won. But what had I won? I didn't know if I could survive the winning any more than my father had survived defeat.

Chapter Five

A rsen threw pebbles at the window. It sounded like rain and so there was no reason to wake up—until he began yelling, "Della," along with the gravel shower. Then I woke up, furious, not knowing who could be calling and certain that the person responsible should die.

Then I heard him call again and I recognized the voice. Arsen. We were scheduled to meet again after lunch and there was nothing that couldn't wait. So far all he'd done was insult me, both my species and me personally. I wasn't in the mood to play games and I really wasn't in the mood to get out of my nice warm bed.

A hail of stone pelted the window again, and if I didn't stop him my sculptor would find him and call the Guardians. Which would have eliminated seven chapters' worth of history since, and that might have been a good thing. But as an adolescent, loyalty to other outcasts took precedence to every other loyalty in the world, so I went over to the window to send him away.

"Hey, c'mon down," he whispered when I looked out to see him, fully dressed, pointing to the Ishtar Gate.

"I'm tired," I protested to no avail.

"It'll be fun, you'll like it," he promised. "Make up for this morning."

His tone was ingenuous and enthusiastic, his smile broad and genuine. He was completely innocent and sincere, standing in the warmth of the Dome night, his long quilted vest looking miserably hot for the carefully controlled climate of the Dome. He didn't even have any clothes suitable for the Dome, I realized. Babelion was straight below at less than a thousand feet of elevation, where it was almost warm some of the time—in the middle of summer, or when the volcanoes throw more heat than we can absorb.

I dressed quickly, throwing on several skirts over each other the way the Tinker women dressed. Even though we were in the Dome it was still cold at night. At least I found it cold at night, though unlike many of the Changed I had not actually died when I left our controlled environment. I had survived, barely, during my time with the Tinkers because I'd learned how to wear soft layers of clothes, to move quickly and to pay attention to my feet.

Still, it had been years since I'd actually dealt with true cold, and I found the night chill unpleasant. Well, Auntie's shawl was very heavy and extra large and it had kept me comfortable on my journey home.

By the time I got out to where Arsen was standing, he had stripped off the long vest and held it draped over one arm. I was glad that I'd grabbed some provisions from the cold bar, a thermos of water and a bag of fruit just in case. It was something I'd learned from the Tinkers, who seem never to go to anywhere without provisions.

"You walk around like that in the Dome, you'll get heat-sick," I mumbled. "You've got to drink more water, too, or you'll dehydrate. Don't they tell you anything down there?" I handed him the thermos of plain cold water.

For a second he stared as if this were the most inane offer he had ever heard. Then he turned the full power of his charismatic smile on me. "Thank you. I hadn't thought that anyone up here would be so kind to one of us. I would have thought that if I didn't have it, that was my problem."

I shrugged. He should have had something to drink and he shouldn't be out at night anyway. He should be in the guest house in the village along with the other candidates, all nervous about being introduced to the Exchange for the first time the following afternoon.

I had intended to give him the food and water and return to my own dreams, but he held my elbow. "Come on," he said, half dragging me toward the Lion Gate. "I'm going to show you something. You'll like it."

"How . . . ," I started to ask, but he held his finger to his lips.

We left the Dome and I was struck by the bitterness of the cold. Even through the heavy shawl the wind bit at my flesh and my toes were stiff in moments. My delicate slippers weren't made to walk outside the controlled environment. The Tinkers would have said that it was time for me to get inside, and fast.

Waiting just a few steps away was a jalopy with two other young humans, one male and one female. This jury-rigged wreck had been a useful vehicle once, had all its parts designed to go together and built for a purpose. Now it was impossible to tell if the original had been intended as a landcrawler or a cliff verticle or construction equipment. It showed an equal number of parts from all three.

The humans were as untrustworthy-looking as the transport. Both wore street fashions. The girl's sari was made of the same hand-painted fabric as the boy's tunic and pants, and both wore a sleeveless long quilted vest like Arsen wore over the whole thing. The humans were trying to look tough but all I saw was that they were freezing. They weren't frightening, only laughable.

Still, I hurried into the transport. My feet were frighteningly numb, and I knew that my first priority had to be warmth. Security could wait until second.

"Is this a kidnapping?" I asked after I was decently settled into a seat and I had begun to feel the misery as blood returned to my extremities. The transport might be a junk heap, but at least it kept out the wind. "No one will pay for me, you realize. You should have gotten one of the others. Ravi Dane, he's the one everyone thinks is up for the next Authority."

Arsen shook his head. "No, not kidnapping, though that's a really good idea. Hari-O there suggested it earlier, only you're right. If it were a kidnapping I'd go after someone higher-profile."

"Think of it as a practice run," the male said, and I figured this had to be Hari-O.

Only Arsen sighed. "What did I tell you guys? This is a strictly social call, is all. I'm spending a lot of time around Miss Della's world, so I thought I'd invite her down for Trina's party. Couldn't miss the party, after all."

"A party?" I asked abruptly. I was hardly dressed for a party.

"Trina's circle got a legal apartment, so before they move in all the furniture and everything they're showing off for everyone. I heard that they have three rooms and a private bath and a walk-in kitchen," the woman said softly. "With power and water."

"Arsen was real unhappy when he thought he couldn't make it because of being up on that stupid Mountain. As if any of us would ever qualify anyway," Hari-O added. "The thing I don't get is why he bothered to make us wait to come get you. As if he won't have enough admirers hanging off him anyway."

"I don't think I'm dressed right," I mumbled. I didn't belong at some house party in Babelion no matter what the circumstances. I just wanted a decent excuse to get out, to go home. There were still cabs for hire down there, or someone willing to earn a little on the side.

"Different clothes wouldn't make you pass for one of us anyway, so why bother?" Hari-O said.

The woman gave him a sour look and tossed me a bundle. "They didn't think of it. I thought of it. I mean, I hate to go someplace dressed funny, you know. So if you can wear my stuff—well, I can help you if you don't know how to wrap a sari."

I pulled the garments apart and was mildly surprised at how attractive they really were when I examined them. The variation in the fabrics used for each of the separate segments was rich and subtle and the workmanship was better than I had ever seen on the Mountain. Every piece either had fluid weight that draped in formal lines or was so thin it was translucent and floated like layers of colored water. What had appeared to be a simple top was really made with three tiers of different fabrics that had been cut to move.

"Thank you," I said to the woman. "They're really beautiful."

She shrugged. "Just don't spill anything on the top, okay? Because it's real silk and it stains easy. Or else you're paying for the new one."

I nodded solemnly, to show that I took it seriously, and wondered when we'd have the privacy for her to drape it around me. I had always wondered how those lengths of cloth were turned into dresses—now I would have my chance to learn.

We had bounced down the Mountain and now were entering the outskirts of Babelion. The windows were small so it was hard to see in spite of good lighting on the streets and little traffic on the roads. No one spoke as we looked out at what appeared to be a decent community, block after block of neat houses with bright multicolored paintings across the facades. White dots rimmed doorways, shining lotuses bloomed on rooftops, fantastic creatures flew on blind walls.

I could identify some of the characters as we passed—there was Vishnu in his incarnation as Krishna, blue with the flute, and many-armed Kali and Shiva dancing in the fires of the Holy Smokes. I knew Ganesh and Lakshmi and the monkey god Hanuman, but there were others that I couldn't recognize or even quite make out in the darkness.

Still, for all the garish decoration, these first houses looked well cared for and the gardens were neatly tended. As the transport moved inward the facade of respectability dissolved. First there was the house where the roof sagged a bit or the paint was not quite so pristine, or a few children's toys had been left out on the lawn. Those minor points could be ignored one at a time, assumed to be old people too exhausted to work on their property or parents too busy with small children to spend time on house maintenance. But when the piles in the yards got larger and contained old moldy sofas and rusted appliances, even an idiot could tell that we'd crossed some invisible boundary.

People were in the streets here, sitting outside on the steps and architectural flourishes and ruins of what had once been a reasonably attractive area. Fewer streetlights worked, and several of those were not entirely reliable. A group of young men threw a ball around in the middle of the street and stopped only reluctantly for the transport to pass. The youngest members of the ball group saluted as the jalopy hobbled past.

It was a good thing the windows were tiny and triple glazed. More people and fewer streetlights marked the next division. Most of the available light came from fires on the pavement, and shadows drifted between them. There were more people than I had originally thought, more than I had imagined, dark against dark wandering aimlessly through the confusion.

Then there was music, and a set of colored party lamps so bright that I was blinded by them. Under the lamps young people danced and laughed and shared around bags.

"Here we are," Hari-O said as he jockeyed the hulk into a double-sized space guarded by pint-sized sentries who motioned us in. "Get ready for a good time." Then he cracked the door and climbed out.

"Well, aren't you coming?" Arsen demanded.

"I figured I'd wait until you left and then change my clothes," I told him.

Both Hari-O and Arsen sighed and waited while the woman showed me how the garments should fit and hang. The sari was very flattering, in fact. The long-sleeved blouse was comfortable and warm enough, and there was a slip that was as heavy as a Tinker skirt that went under the sari. The woman quickly tucked and pleated the fabric into a soft, fluid garment that made me feel almost ethereal.

I thanked her and we climbed out to find our escorts sitting on the fender, partaking of whatever had been handed to them in a plain sack. They were laughing and joking nd some of the young men around them elbowed them in the ribs.

"Come on, let's go upstairs and at least say hello to Trina and Lal and Vati and the rest of them and see the new place," Arsen suggested, pulling me by the hand. "How big is their circle now? Did they add Rohit or not?"

The woman laughed. "I don't know, I don't ask about that," she protested. "They haven't made a formal announcement yet and there hasn't been any ceremony, so it's not official."

"But Rohit is still almost living with them now, isn't he? Or did he leave? That's what I want to know, because I heard they'd had a fight."

"They're always having fights," Hari-O said, dismissing the whole question. "Who cares, anyway?"

Arsen smiled broadly without any hint of the smirk he had on the Mountain. "It's just so good to be home, that's all. And catch up on the whole gang."

"You're just afraid that you've been replaced in Subha's circle," Hari-O protested.

Arsen turned quiet. "That wasn't serious. I'm not ready to join a circle, not for a long time. There are other things I have to do." The he took my hand and propelled me through the crowd, away from Hari-O and the woman whose name I didn't learn.

His hand was half again as large as mine and had a grip like a vise. I had no choice when he dragged me through a door with paper where the window used to be and up a mobbed staircase. We fought our way past revelers for three flights before finding the famous legal apartment.

The place was packed with people. Even so, only about thirty fit. There was a single room with a kitchen corner. A small door next to the kitchen led to a tiny washroom that was completely tiled with a shower head in the ceiling and no enclosure to cut off the other facilities.

"Whoa, they must rate up there with someone," Arsen said. "A private washroom with their own shower. My mother's circle doesn't even have a private shower, we share with the Haluddi and the Grafianos down the hall."

We left the washroom to other curious party-goers who filled it completely and examined the rest of the amenities. There was a single closet on the other side of the one window in the place. We admired the view, the closet light, and Arsen inspected the cooking facilities again.

Then he bobbed up to someone who must have been the hostess and hugged her. "Trina, this place is perfect," he said so loudly that I could hear him from the hall. "Your own shower even, and an eat-in counter. I didn't know that bank monitors rated so high in the scheme of things. Ohhh, maybe if I'm very nice you'll invite me over and let me take a shower sometime."

Laughter hit everyone around me, the hostess most of all. She bent to double over, but the single room was too crowded and she ended up with her shoulder in someone else's bosom. That only inspired even more hilarity.

She wore way too much makeup and her blouse was similar to the one I wore with its sheer layered sections that didn't match and yet did, that flowed beautifully and showed off her painted hands to advantage. Arsen kissed the back of her hand. "Where's Lal and Rohit and the rest?" he asked after the others who would live there, or so I thought.

Trina gestured around at the packed room. "Downstairs," she said. "That's where most of the party is, so that's where the beer has to go."

Arsen grabbed me and pulled me down all the flights that we'd climbed. "We can't hog the space," he whispered to me so loudly that only the seventeen people closest to us could hear. "Everyone has to get a chance to come up and see what a great place they all have. And I've got to find the others and congratulate them, too. Just because it was probably Trina who pulled the strings doesn't mean that they didn't do all the work fixing it up. You saw it was painted."

"I hadn't noticed," I said. "It's all so ugly." By then we were outside again.

"So I guess you wouldn't understand what this means to them, or to any of us," he said. "You've never been where people live down in the dregs of Babelion, in the White District. You know why it's called the White District? Because once it was a nice enough place, only when my grandmother's generation were about our age the White Plague broke out. You heard of that, the White Plague?"

I shook my head.

"Yeah, I didn't think they taught you that kind of stuff. The White Plague killed one in eight, maybe one in five down here in the city. Your people just locked up that Mountain and never came out of your Dome, so it didn't hit you. I guess they must have brought stuff though the Village so you could survive. But here, so many died that we couldn't bury them all. The dead were piled up in the fields and it snowed constantly that winter. There were piles of bodies all frozen solid, all covered with snow and frost and the ground too hard to dig. We couldn't burn them, either, not with the fear of fire in the city and with the constant snow and ice that never let up. So we called it the White Plague. It lasted for eighteen months.

"Anyway, this neighborhood was especially hard hit for some reason, so it was pretty decimated. The drifters came in, and then the squatters set up house. And then the Exchange cut off the water and power and it's been a power thing ever since. Your people, my people, the whole damn thing."

"So you blame me?" I spat back at him. "You weren't alive then, and I wasn't alive either. You got that? And you forgot that I lived as a Tinker—it's not like I'm one of the ones who's never ever left the Mountain. Though right now I wonder if maybe that isn't a problem, because I would fit your little set of assumptions so much better, wouldn't I?"

Slowly he dropped his hands from my shoulders and his gaze from my eyes. He shook his head slightly. "Hey, I'm sorry. You're right, you didn't deserve that." He hesitated as if searching for something else to say, some way to make it clear that he was honestly contrite. Only I couldn't just shrug and say it was all right and that I knew he didn't mean anything by it. He meant to hurt, but there was something else linked with the attack. Something that felt very threatening and very good, and I wasn't entirely sure I wanted it to end.

He stared at me for a moment as if he were considering killing me—or consuming me. Instead, he left me alone in the crowd and stalked off to the open lot where a group his own age were dancing under the colored lights. From a distance and with the distortion of the lights, the dancers looked like something out of a fantasy. Or out of Hell. But they hardly seemed human at all.

The music was so loud it threatened to split my skull. The people around me seemed aggressive, shouting at each other with little provocation. They waved fists in the air, postured, posed, each trying to look a little tougher and a little sexier than the last. No wonder they had been left behind.

There was no order or rhythm to their gyrations. I couldn't even tell if they were dancing with each other or alone. It looked ragged and ugly and I was glad that we didn't dance on the Mountain. It was uncivilized.

The music stopped abruptly. A grumble went through the party that promised violence. The lights went out, and when they came on again they weren't the strings of fairy lights that had given the dancers an inhuman cast. Now there was only darkness around a single strong full-spectrum light trained on the jury-rigged thing we had arrived in earlier. Picked out in the hard glare, Arsen stood on the nose of the sled (or was it the back?), arms akimbo, balanced and blazing and fierce.

He was everything these boys and girls wanted to be. There was vision in him then, and absolute faith, and anger seething just below the surface. Arsen had everything the world demanded of a hero, and from the furious way the crowd called his name I knew that they saw him just that way. Their hero, the projection of their own dreams, maybe the one who would save them all from the greatest evils. Us.

He stood still and silent for a moment, then let it lengthen. Silence didn't frighten him, and as he waited the crowd gave him all the strength and adoration he desired. When he was finally ready to speak, there was not a whisper anywhere on the street. Figures hung out of the upper windows, others crouched in the hollows of rotted construction. From this distance and this angle, he looked more imposing than he had in the Palace. The harsh light made the hollows in his face stand out starkly and his hair shone and moved like Tinker gold.

Suddenly a tremor went through me, a rush of mingled desire and sweat. I wanted him. Everyone in this crowd wanted him; I could smell it as bodies pressed around in their hunger.

He had power over all of them, over me, superior and Changed as I was. Some basic needs and instincts are older than humanity, older than even our primate inheritance. Some parts of the DNA were old when our ancestors crawled out of the seas and onto dry land.

It is all so very clear in memory, so pristine. That moment when I recognized my own desire for Arsen standing there in the light was the beginning of the second age for me. I had never felt this raw passion before. I wanted him with such a single-minded purity that the only thing I could compare it to is the heartbreak of Lorenzo's songs.

And I loathed myself. The people of Babelion were animals, their behavior nauseated me, yet I couldn't deny my desire. I wanted, I wanted, but I didn't know what it was that I wanted from Arsen. I only knew that I would be revolted if I were to have it.

"I've been up the Mountain," he said. His eyes seemed to recognize each member of the audience personally, as if only the two of them existed. "I've been up there and seen them, the Chosen Changed. And I've seen our own people who have tried to join them, the ones who live in the Village. The ones who never get to live in that fortress, but still won't leave. Who still believe that someday we'll be worthy. Someday, they believe, we will inherit the ship that brought us and we'll return to the great centers of humanity. And we will leave the Changed behind."

The look on his face frightened me. I thought I had seen the danger in him and I realized that I had seen only the most restrained mask of danger. I was alone here, without friends or any way home, in a mob that was ready to turn on any Changed. For all that, the greatest danger to me was Arsen himself.

He could hurt me, I thought. I had not considered that before, and the thought brought its own pain—and a thrill as well.

"When are we worthy?" he bellowed in anguish to the sky.

I kept listening to the words, but they weren't for me. They were for Arsen and the crowds of Babelion. I could not avoid the controlled fury that seemed to emanate from him and set the crowd on fire.

When his tone changed to thunder, I suddenly knew where he was going. "I have *seen* them and *they* are not worthy. They are not good at anything that matters. They are bad at compassion, bad at love, bad at beauty. They are out of harmony because they have forgotten themselves. But *we* have not forgotten *us*."

Around me I could feel the mood of the crowd shift as it started to transmute into a true mob. Arsen was forging them together into a single tool—a weapon—and I knew that he would use it on me.

"The Changed are proud that they are not human. They tell us that we are lesser beings. Maybe we are. But they have given up the spirit-self in trade for their petty power and mathematical tricks. They have no souls. They do not see the dance of eternity and the divine around them, they do not hear the voices of past lives whispering in the dark, and they do not know the incarnations of Vishnu who wander among us unseen. They do not have tears."

He paused and the energy around him changed again. "But we are the children of the gods. We are beautiful and invincible and we know that we will never die. So we have all of eternity for our victory.

"So now let us celebrate the power of who we always are. Dance the creation of a new hope, a new world. Let's dance to the creation of ourselves."

The humans are still subjects of nature. And so there was no applause, no screaming and yelling approval, not even the sound of an indrawn breath as if the universe itself paused to consider the meaning of Arsen's words. Faces rapt, his own looked up to him as if he were a god.

I knew the look, I knew the feeling. Wrapped in the power of his own charisma, Arsen's karma rippled and flowed. It grew both larger and stronger as a hundred humans saw that vitality and courage as established truths. They were creating him, making the legend, drawing it into reality. Arsen was only the vessel of their need, of their desire.

He was burning with it. Adoration is as addictive as any drug. Arsen needed that devotion already, although he didn't recognize the necessity. He must already have had a few doses to wear it so easy, and now it was not simply the worship he craved but the absence of it terrified him. But he was still young enough in his power to believe that it was his vision they adored. He adored it, his sweet simplistic solution to everything, so he could believe that they worshipped this fantasy future as he did. When I was that young I believed it, too.

I saw all this, but I could not remain aloof. The raw power of mass emotion is almost as enticing as being adored and I succumbed. I was in love; I was certain of it. There was nothing I wanted so much as to drown in his eyes, his words, his beingness. I wanted to lose myself in him, tear my clothes off right under that harsh single light and touch his divinity. Touching it I would either die or it would become part of me and I, too, would have some small taste of eternity.

The snake dance of Creation that Arsen had called down wove around me. The drums were the magical heartbeat of being, the bells the laugher of gods in whom I did not believe. Body and soul I gave myself to the chanting that formed around me like the dance.

"Krishna, Vishnu, Devi, Govinda."

All of them were Arsen to me. He was the only god I have ever known.

Arsen's hand on my forearm gently pulled me from my reverie and I followed him through the dark, where the people turned to touch him, to say a word, to give him flowers. We moved through the crowd so slowly that I was surprised when we finally reached the sled. Our earlier companions weren't there so Arsen drove.

We were very slow on the ascent, or so it felt. All of time was one single point and that point had not yet quite arrived. I could smell it, taste the desire on the back of my teeth, my body screaming for something I could not quite imagine.

And I was afraid that maybe I had gotten it all wrong. Maybe he didn't really want me at all, maybe we were just leaving. But he couldn't ignore the pulsation in the air, the electrical charge when our eyes met.

We did not go to any of the Mountain's gates or to the dormitory. Instead, Arsen led me to a very small building that might have been a garage or a workshed. He touched the lock that had been keyed to his print and the door opened with just the slightest sound. He asked me to wait while he disappeared into the dark. It seemed as if I waited for a long time before he called and asked me to enter.

Inside it was beautiful, a tiny jewel in my memory. Candles burned to dispel the dark, but there were not enough of them to chase away the phantoms. A pile of pillows lay on a low mat covered with dark wine cloth and scattered with white petals.

All the flowers he had been given by his followers in adoration were scattered to make an ordinary shed into a bower.

I walked forward, aware of his eyes on me. Piece by piece I dropped the clothes of Babelion and then stretched out on the bed of flowers. I felt utterly perfect and absolutely beautiful, and I felt that I knew what I was doing.

Naturally, I did not. Auntie Suu-Suu had made certain that I was well prepared for the first time I had sex in my life. I was not aware that it would be the only time I ever made love.

Chapter Six

Three hours before sunrise Arsen used his Guardian's pass to slip me in through the Lion's Gate. That much is clear. The rest of his study month is not. I knew I was in love and I knew that it could not last forever. I knew that this was the greatest love possible and the greatest shame in all the history of Maya. From the day of the party until the day we tested, I could think of nothing but Arsen. Love was obsession.

We rarely studied when we could slip away. My memories of that time are a vague collection of dull private rooms and floors where we tore off our clothes as soon as the doors were shut. I thought I would die every hour I could not be with him, and I knew that in a month he would be gone.

I do not remember talking to him about anything of consequence except where we could meet next in private. I know that we did study, that we must have talked about our lives and our hopes and how alienated we were from our various peoples. I have a vague memory of hooking him into an interface terminal once, and I recall very clearly how he made me a bitter green tea. I must have asked him about it, where he had gotten it, what it was, how he had learned to make it, though I have no recollection of any words spoken between us. In the end the only thing that mattered was the sight of him in a sliver of honey light, his face innocent at rest and the long curls free over his back.

He was shy when he undressed, modest like a Tinker boy would have been, like I had been taught in the Tinker camp. His hands were light and dry and gentle with me, never hurried or urgent, always coaxing and anticipating never demanding. Not even when I wanted him to be demanding.

Now I wonder if the devis taught him to make love, honed his skill beyond that of the very few mature men with whom I have had experience since. I wonder if it was they who taught him to nibble so lightly at my toes to honor some god or goddess I could not name. I know that he would never have told me, would have found the question not only rude but incomprehensible as well.

But I wonder if my son has been well taught, if he has his father's sensuality, if his face glows with the irresistible combination of devotion and desire. Wondering horrifies me; he is only half Changed and so it is possible that he can drown in his desires. But he is half Changed, and so I pray that he has the discipline to keep himself aloof, to be clear of those things that would drag him down.

It is the siren song of Babelion. Sex with a human is taboo, disgusting, unthinkable. Sex among ourselves is a necessity, a duty to the species and all of that, pleasant enough but only a vestigial remnant of the drives that created our ancestors.

Or is it? Certainly I felt that compelled with Arsen. I could not touch him enough, could not have enough time with him. And my body—none of the Changed know what the body is and none of us know how to play it. Later, when I merged with the Exchange and reached beyond this world, I discovered entire libraries of erotica full of material I could never have imagined. I had to admit that it did not arouse me, did not even interest me.

Maybe it is age, maybe it is my current status in the machine. But I think there was something particular to Arsen that affected me, that called up the centuries of memory that lay atrophied in my genes.

Though the entire month was full of formal receptions and speeches, the day of actual testing was not. No special clothes were required and there were no practices marching in line or greeting each other. Instead, we all gathered, wearing what we considered lucky or comfortable in the study room that had been our class center since we were ten.

Only the humans sat in the seats. The rest of us wandered around the room, touching a desk, a chair, a bit of the childhood that would be gone by night. Now, for the few moments before we were taken to the Exchange, we were still children without rank or purpose. The Exchange would give us our status-brands and we would know our whole lives ahead of us.

There was a whole range of possibilities. We could be assigned to Mem or Administrative and Organizational tasks. That was the largest division. There was Chem that regulated the neural transmitters both within the Exchange and what was fed into the Changed during interface. There was Ware, which maintained the hardware, and Loc for the handful of location specialists, and all the different kinds and classes of processors. There were two classes each for quantum and chaos, and the high-status designations of Corelli, Butterfly and Spin.

The Exchange would find where we fit in its structure, what we could do and what it could download and store through us. When we returned we would be adults, brand-new, which was a cute saying some few generations old. The brands only dated back six generations, to when Suhla took a status that was not hers in the Exchange and became a Courtier and lived out the pretense until she died, and no one but the Exchange knew. She managed to get enough power to be selected for seven consecutive terms as Oligarch, a feat that has never been replicated.

All that, and she only had the true status of Seven-Cell! A lower-level memory flunky, and she became the greatest leader the Mountain has ever had. Naturally, when the Exchange revealed her true position on her death, the entire Mountain was utterly humiliated. Her three top advisers had to commit suicide, and some others left the Dome rather than face the rest of us.

And so the brands were created, a small mark on the inside of the wrist easily seen and checked. The Exchange does the branding, too, during the test while the limbic system is hooked into its neural net. The body feels no pain but is indelibly marked.

That would happen to us by evening, when the testing would be over. The human hopefuls would start drifting back to Babelion in ones and twos over the months, those who did not choose to remain in the Village. Their time on the Mountain was up, their dreams were over. They must have known. No one from Babelion has ever joined the Changed. Not then, not now, not since we first set foot on Maya.

But many of those tested are recruited for the higher-level positions in the Village. These are the best and brightest of humankind, after all, and so they often make excellent neural sculptors and medics and Guardians and power techs. Those who don't wish to stay are often lured out to their own glass farms, and a few have even been known to join the Tinkers, so the number who return to Babelion is minuscule.

Arsen was there among them and he did not look at me at all. He knew he went to defeat. We had talked about it a little the night before, saying good-bye in the same way we'd said everything else. He had known from the first that he would never be chosen. I do remember him telling me that, on that last night. We both knew it was the end, that it was the last time and good-bye. I could not say those words—that much has come back to me. I could not tell him that after the next morning I would never see him again.

And then it was the next morning. He did not acknowledge me in front of the others, which was a relief. I wondered if he would shame me, make it public that I had cared for a human. He did not choose to humiliate me, and I know now that he did not choose to humiliate himself. The taboo is strong on their side as on ours—as if their own genetic material were worth preserving.

We were called one by one by name to take the carts up the final ascent of the Mountain where the Exchange Quarters were. The morning was overcast and no color surrounded us. We were in our own mist, cut off from the rest of the world.

Once upon a time, Auntie Suu-Suu had said, in a place that was very far away, there was a time when the calendar didn't have enough days. The gods had decreed more days than there were reckoned in human accounting, and so the empty days had been created. These were the days that existed and did not exist, when nothing in this time actually counted as having happened. Every four hundred years, she said, on some world far away, the empty days returned. And on those days people were killed and people broke vows, and none of this was held to be real.

In the gray mist we entered the gray building. I was led down a different way than I had gone before, a way that did not seem obvious from the building's configuration. Only then did I realize that we were now underground, that as trainees we weren't permitted into the bowels of the Exchange, but now it was where we belonged.

The candidates from Babelion were brought up to the training area. Enough for them to see that much, to know where the Exchange was located. Though at that time we never thought that they would endanger it—the Exchange was as much their support as it was ours. Among its many other functions, the Exchange regulates the transformer up at the Great Steam Lake and controls the energy distributions for every shunt and line and feed on Maya. The humans are better adapted to the cold than the Changed, but they are not so adapted that they can survive a winter night without a source of heat.

The humans were called separately to a different corridor. I saw Arsen among them and my heart lurched. I could not look at him without the memory of how his skin had tasted the night before. I tried to catch his eye, but he would not look at me.

Then I was called and led through the subterranean maze with the other Changed. We were brought to a plain room crowded with equipment and a circle of chairs faced outward from a single cortex. I sat in one and settled while the filament needles made connection with the nerves just under the base of the skull. I hated the feeling of the microfine needle slipping under my skin, though it was more imaginary than real. The helmet locked down over my face and the vision screen cleared not to the usual student gray but to a uniform hard red.

"This is the final placing segment examination for subject 79-3302-147 Changed, known as Rista Della Sambers."

I was vaguely aware of something touching my wrist for a moment, and then I was fully occupied with the Exchange.

We were the only ones in here. Even the humans were only on the student interface, which meant they could create a semblance of the Exchange reality but they could not make lasting changes. Here in the center for the first time, my cohort had the full resources of the Exchange available.

The entry was large, more open and easy than I had experienced in the student version. And when the red cleared I saw a large city settled onto the high desert just under the cresting mountains. The city did not look at all like anything I'd seen, certainly not the frenzied god-murals of Babelion or the cold precision of the Mountain. It glowed as the light hit it from different directions, towers and twisting staircases and a waterfall high above.

I walked toward the city, wondering what kind of test this was. In other exercises I had been shown strange places, given exotic assignments, interacted with beings who were anything but Changed. All of it was metaphor, a way of interpreting information and reality so that the Changed could manipulate and process it. I knew that, and yet I was always entranced by the visions the Exchange showed me.

Now I know they were not simply representations of data but actual interactions. And our functions were far less symbolic than anyone imagined. Still, that was something I learned only much much later and in secret, and it is another thing that you, Anselm, must know. What happens in the Exchange has consequences in the real world.

But the real world is where everything matters. Sometimes I am afraid that I have spent too much time in the reality of the Exchange and not enough in your life. I am afraid that you feel you were abandoned and deceived, and perhaps you could even be right.

Try to understand one thing, Anselm—I was only sixteen w'
you were born. I had status in the Exchange but no power,
the best opportunity I had to keep you from harm. No'

that perhaps you would have thought it less harm if I had stayed and come with you into banishment, but my presence would have turned the people of Babelion against you. We would have never survived a month there. You would have been knifed at school or playing ball on the street. No place would have been safe. You had to have some protection and your father's family was the best I could manage for you.

They did do well, I think. They were good to you. I regretted all the things I could not give to you, but at least you were alive. Being with them, being so much like your father, gave you a head start on your destiny. You say so yourself so often—

But you cannot help but hate me now, for leaving you then, and for surviving now. I won't ask you to forgive me, although I have tried to do everything even a mother in Babelion would do. I've kept you alive. I've made sure you always had a home and care and education. I've provided every opportunity for you to become whatever you wished. You could have been an artist or a religious leader. You could have gone off alone and founded a new city. You could have risen in the Temple as Sri Mayurna's apprentice and eventually become a rishi yourself.

But you chose to become the revolutionary, and so I have done what I could to make certain that your revolution succeeds.

Maybe after all this time you have come to understand something of the ways of power, how it is never straight to the source but always gathered in secret and held in gloved hands. Power is a whispered word in a corridor, a raised finger, the end of a dynasty by disease and circumstance. It is often unfair and people suffer because they have come in the way of it, not because they have done anything wrong. There are times when power is hidden, subtle. What appears to be power, to be strength, can easily be overturned by a few well-chosen words.

And all the power we think we have, all the things we consider important, are just the carefully contained games of an ignorant colony that has been kept isolated from the rest of the Empire.

Did you know that, Anselm, that we are a protected world under the enlightened rule of the current Governor as appointed by the Empress? Or that this province is one that both the Empress and the Pretender, who has been fighting her for nearly eighty years, consider crucial? Or that much of what has happened over the past thirty or so years here is part of that struggle?

We know far too little about them or their politics or their worlds. I don't know why they have such focus on Maya. We have nothing here at all that they could want. For all my exploration, and it has been deep and deliberate, I cannot find one single resource or item that they do not have a million times over in their Empire.

Unless it is the Changed. They have so many mutations and adaptations, so many species of human created for this or that task, but none of them have all the special qualities of the Changed. I wonder if we were hidden here specifically to keep our abilities from being used for one side or the other. Or perhaps our Creators were partisan and forgot to explain which side we should support when the time came.

If you do not kill me in pure rage when we meet, you will be very surprised at what I can show you. Because I know you can enter the Exchange and see it all for yourself. I know that because of the day of the test. . . .

The test itself, yes, that made me as alien as your father was. I saw the great royal city with the sun rising on the faceted roofs. It was so beautiful that I began to walk toward it. Then I remembered that to walk would take a long time, and while no doubt there were things of interest along the path, I had no time to waste. So I muttered, "Jump to city" and I was there, just inside the gate which was locked behind me. For a moment I worried that I could not get out. Then I knew that either the Exchange had the passcodes or that I would have to climb or hide. Knowing my options made it easier to decide that I would handle it when the time came. First I had to discover why I was there.

There are no rules. The test is entirely up to the Exchange, for it to push and prod and discover us. It will not tell us how it wants us to respond.

I walked down the street, noticing the shop displays and the flower stalls on the sidewalks, the red-painted carts with gold trim and the sizzling hot oil to quick-fry the spicy vegetable fritters.

There were carpets and tiles in the display room on the corner, and sofas lined up in marching order as if awaiting the order to strike. But there were no people anywhere.

I went slowly, trying to find any trace of inhabitants. Nothing moved. Not a bird, not a cat, not one living thing joined me. Even the air was still and thick.

I was absolutely alone, and that was macabre.

An entire city, perfect and complete, was just awaiting its inhabitants. Only there were none. The sun was high now, and it cast a strange roseate light over the stone walls. I probably should have changed it, but there was something appealing about the pink-amber shadows on the pavement.

Not stopping to examine the environs around the gate, I called up a schematic of the city and headed toward its main square. A palace sat in the center of parkland, according to the map. That didn't look particularly promising, but it appeared that government offices and serious businesses like banks and art galleries occupied the streets closest to the garden.

If there were people here, they would be there. If there were something to do or find, it would either be in the Palace and its grounds or there would be some clue there for where else in this city it could be hidden.

I gave the jump command and found myself at one end of a long reflecting pool that had been grown over with wildflowers. The Palace was at one end, painted pale turquoise with silvery-rose traceries over the delicate columns of the upper portico. On the other end of the pool were squat, monumental, important buildings, their facades testament to the stability of their tenants. The flowers smelled slightly sweet and spicy, and there was a tang of citrus, too. Then I looked up and saw the orange trees a little to my left. It had been a formal planting, with each of the trees trimmed to size and perfectly aligned on squares of ragged grass. The alternating squares were paved with white marble that took on the pale pink tint of the sky. The whole was like a giant grass and stone chessboard, with the players all orange-tree pawns, and no way to tell white from black.

It was all too familiar, too much like a children's game, to take seriously. This might not be any kind of test at all, I thought. The positions must already have been decided and we were being kept here to waste time playing a game. Or at least I had been kept here—no one else had arrived.

But both the anger and the worry had melted with the seduction of the garden itself. The flowers ranged in perfect balance, the trees were just high enough for shade and low enough for comfort. The sound of running water made it seem cool and pleasant even though I had not escaped the dense, cloying air.

I took off my shoes and went wading in the pool. The water was perfumed with petals and it was pleasant to the touch. Nothing had grown here during the abandonment, no algae or mold, to make the water repugnant. I splashed with my feet, sang an old Tinker song with a chorus I didn't understand, and reveled in my freedom. After climbing out of the water I walked around in my bare feet, paying mind to the blooms that hid in the shadowed corners and to the composition of the whole.

In fact, as I got closer to the Palace I realized that the entire structure was nothing but garden. In one arbor overgrown with white roses I found a pile of cushions set out on a carpet, and a chess set laid ready for a game. Just as in the city I realized that there were signs of habitation all over, but nothing that walked or flew was in sight.

The structure of the Palace building itself was all openwork. No glass or high-impact plastics covered the piercings in the lacy fretwork. There were no doors to keep out the weather, and I could see straight through the wide, empty rooms into interior courtyards that seemed more furnished than the chambers in between.

Finally I gained the courage to step into the abandoned enclosure. Up close the rose silver was laid in delicate patterns that depicted flowers and vines all over turquoise enamel work. On the interior the pattern was reversed, only here the turquoise traceries appeared abstract. I could tell they were no longer simply patterns, the repetitions were not regular enough. I stared longer and wondered. "Writing?" I asked myself aloud.

I felt a soft breeze ruffle the hairs on my arms and I smelled distant honeysuckle. Those made me feel accepted, at home, and approved. So I requested a translation from the Exchange, if this were a language in its files.

The turquoise became transparent, sparkling blue gel, and shifted subtly on the silver ground. I couldn't really see how the resolution took place, only that there was a shiver of movement. Looking closely at the patterns, I realized that I could indeed read this if I looked hard enough—it was some form of archaic calligraphy that was artistically pleasing but hard to decipher:

> Who knows with what great carouse
> I made second marriage in my house?
> Threw old sallow Reason from my bed
> and took the Daughter of the Vine to spouse.

I read it over twice but I had no idea of what it meant. It was not a clue that I could tell, not like in all the millions of games I'd played. Only perhaps, there was a clue. Daughter of the Vine, that might be somewhere to look. The Vine. There were vines everywhere, but the idea of Daughter of the Vine—it took me a while before I saw where I had been directed. Wine, there was wine somewhere here and I had to find it. Just like all of the childhood games after all, only more elegant.

I walked through the cloistered corridors but the courtyards tempted me. They were all very different, each with a singular perfume, and some fruit growing ripe. Finally, in one that was filled with heavily scented white lilies, and where tiny red strawberries crept on the ground, I saw a cloth spread in the shade of the single willow tree in the corner. There were the preparations for a picnic scattered on the cloth, it appeared, plates and two platters of food and bottles and glasses. Wine.

In fact, I tried the food, too. Virtual food might not do any good for the body, but it could be as tempting as the real thing. Here was a whole roasted chicken and clusters of grapes, and dried dates and walnuts on one tray, and pastries and delicate chocolates on the other. I tried the chocolates, each one carefully sculpted into a different flower and overglazed with a hint of natural color. I ate a daffodil, and while I couldn't really taste anything my senses were satisfied that I was indulging myself shamefully. More chocolate, and some of the bread—and the needle in the back of my neck fed just a bit more of the enzyme mix to my brain, as these foods would, so I had some sensation of having eaten.

And then the wine. There were several bottles, both red and white, and all with the same writing as I had seen before. "Translate," I said, and the words on the labels became far more legible than the words on the ceiling. These were also calligraphied, but the strokes had far less decoration.

Red wine, said the nightingale to the Rose,
those sallow cheeks of hers to incarnadine.

Well, that was simple enough. I picked up the red wine and poured a glass instead of drinking straight from the bottle. I felt warm all over and my fingers tingled. This was not like getting drunk on vodka, which Chelo had introduced me to one evening when Anastasia was late with an experiment. This was more subtle.

In the end, I still do not know how much more of what happened was actually in the Exchange and how much was in my own head. But suddenly there were people all around, and they were all Arsen's friends from the party. I recognized Hari-O and the woman who'd loaned me the clothes, and Trina the hostess. All the rest were vaguely familiar.

What were they all doing in the Exchange? I wondered, my head pounding and my thoughts moving sluggishly through the filter of the wine. They couldn't possibly be here, they didn't exist inside the paradigm at all. And they were all looking raptly at something behind and above me.

Before I could turn a woman came up directly in front of me. It was Auntie Suu-Suu, and she held a crystal ball in her hand. She held the ball up to my eyes and all I could see was fire. Fire raging all over, fire that obliterated whatever was in the ball. She let the crystal roll off her hand and it shattered on the pavement, but the burning remained behind.

I turned and looked behind me, to where everyone still stared. There was Arsen, chained to the stronghold wall on the Mountain.

The rings at the top of the structure had been there forever and we had told grisly stories at night, but really no one thought they had any other purpose than bringing oversize goods past the gates.

Arsen was stretched out against the tiles, his mouth covered with a gag, his eyes wild and enraged. His fingertips bled as if he had tried to tear off the paving or the bolts that held him. Even still he squirmed and struggled, panicked, running out of options and yet never thinking that resignation might be the only choice remaining.

The flames grew from Auntie's hand and engulfed him. His eyes met mine and pleaded for existence. He knew, at that last moment he knew what was happening and he was terrified. The gag prevented him from inhaling too much smoke, so he would have to endure pain as well as oblivion.

His followers watched the fire consume his flesh. They waited for something to save him, I think. I waited for the same thing, but I knew that it was not going to happen. I knew that Arsen was going to die, in pain and alone and far too young. I wanted to look away. The desperation in his eyes was too much for me to bear, but he was watching me, only me, as if I could offer him either hope or comfort. But I had neither.

I stood with the rest as he burned. The gag muffled his cries, the chains held him firm. I waited. The sky turned deep rose and then dark, and his friends from the party all drifted away.

I waited until the last ember glowed and died. There was nothing but ash and charred bone left. I looked down at my feet and saw Auntie's matrix crystal whole again. It was lighter than it should be, and there was a glass stem on the top. Gently I brushed Arsen's ashes into it, placing the bones neatly on the top. They were still hot to the touch.

I closed the top of the crystal ball and saw nothing that made me think of Arsen inside. I did not cry.

That was when I understood that I did not love him. My body loved him, and I respected him. But there was something essential missing in that moment, a grief or emptiness that somehow did not appear. Guilt was strong, guilt that I was not injured or even inconvenienced by his loss. That someone could die and that it would not touch me at all frightened me. Among the Tinkers I would have been suspect for my lack of tears.

Slowly and with respect I carried his remains down the Mountain. Somehow, behind the wall, I had returned back home, and there was only the Mountain and Babelion far far below. I walked the seven hundred steps descending, the whole time praying to the gods of Babelion whose names I did not know.

Three steps from the bottom I was greeted by a person who seemed neither Changed nor human, but possibly greater. He appeared all in white, his expression grim, and he held out his hand. "What token have you brought?" he asked.

The test. I'd forgotten the test.

"Death," I said, handing him the crystal ball with Arsen's ashes.

"Who are your people?" he asked.

"I am Changed," I said, but the figure did not move.

"You do not know your people," he said, and the words echoed in my bones. "You were never supposed to know we exist, and now the Pretender has followed you."

I had no idea then what he was talking about. He was the Exchange—or some other archive we had accessed. Now that I have spent enough time here to understand, I know that there are other possibilities as well.

Still, the words were terrifying to me. I thought then that he was only referring to my attachment to Arsen, to how entirely unChanged I had been. I turned to climb back up, knowing that I now belonged neither on the Mountain nor in Babelion, and wondered where I would go and who I would become when I found myself waking slowly in the chair. The helmet had already been removed and the needle had withdrawn. Someone I knew unbuckled the harness around me.

It had all been the test. But—how could the Exchange have known? The part about Auntie Suu-Suu didn't make any sense at all. The Exchange didn't know about Auntie Suu-Suu. And it couldn't know about Arsen, about what he meant to me. I had been so careful to keep everything hidden, but somehow the Exchange had known what was most important to me.

Now I know that it doesn't need to know more than which neural paths to stimulate. It triggers the sequence and what we are provides the rest. And that is the real test, what the Exchange gets back from us.

"You're the last," one of the adults said as I returned to my normal consciousness. "And by nearly half an hour, too. The others are all done, tested and approved."

Half an hour later? Everyone else done and gone? That had never happened in the history of the Exchange.

"What about the humans?" I asked.

"All tested, packed up and gone. None of them made it," I was told.

"Of course," another adult agreed. "But there was that one case. . . ."

"That was a matter of being pulled in: I went over the entire replay from several angles," someone else who had not paid attention to me before protested. "That was not ability in a human; it was exceptional ability in one of our kids."

Then they were silent. I realized that I had to show them, that I would have to let them all know. And then I would also be packed up and sent down the Mountain. My wrist was bare. I knew that, I could feel it. It was untouched.

I turned it over. And there in seared white skin I saw the delicate tracery of a butterfly. It was ornate and elegant, a marking that could have been made for decoration alone.

Above and below the butterfly was a numeral. One.

"One-Butterfly?" I asked aloud. I was stunned. Never had I imagined that I would be One-Butterfly.

"We have to get the authorities," someone muttered.

Gentle hands pushed me toward the door, and then propelled me back to a cart. We headed straight for Xanadu, and I was elated. If I had had any sense I would have known to be afraid.

Chapter Seven

One-Butterfly. The ranking existed before it was burned into my flesh but no one had held it in living memory. Like all the newly made adults, I had spent the past year obsessed with rankings and brands, and secretly I had coveted this one above all else.

I knew all the stories about Tyrus One-Butterfly, who lived in the early days of the Changed and spent fifty years painting the murals of Xanadu when he was not in interface. Some Changed speculated that it was the fumes or the pigments that twisted his body until he could not walk. Then there was the bit about Aja One-Butterfly, who committed suicide by leaping off the cliff. There is even a small stone plaque that supposedly marks the spot, though really it always made more sense that it was an accident. The cliff is unstable and there are warnings about the edges.

Now, through the Exchange, I have other evidence that is even more sensational than the suicide. The Exchange believes that Aja was murdered, and displayed the evidence and documentation as a warning for me.

And there was Tulpar One-Butterfly, who had gone crazy. Or maybe he was just crazy to start with and the Exchange found him amusing. He died under rather strange circumstances, too.

One-Butterfly is rare and original. So is sabato poisoning.

The Authorities were waiting for me in the Morning Room on the east side of the Xanadu. The Morning Room is not used for official functions. It is informal, more personal, its proportions comfortable and its furniture overstuffed and inviting. A tray of breakfast breads was set out on a sideboard next to a full-scale coffee dispenser. I eyed the sideboard greedily, though the breads were most likely stale and the dispenser was probably empty, it being well after lunchtime.

They did not offer. "Come, sit down," Sithra Two-Chem said, pointing to an armchair upholstered in brocade the color of lemon cream. "It's been a long time since you got up, you must be starving." Sithra's voice was kind and warm, which confused me. I had been on the edge of out less than a day ago. Now Sithra Two-Chem, chief adviser to the Council on the Exchange, was serving me steaming coffee, and cold smoked fish on crisp wafers.

I had never met Sithra before, though of course I had heard of her. She was less imposing than I had imagined, with wide, liquid eyes. At the time I had no idea of what she had already done, and certainly none of what she was going to do. I wanted to trus those eyes, that rich, welcoming voice. I wanted her protection, I wanted to be her ally, but something inside me screamed in terror whenever she had her eyes on me.

Another Authority was smiling at me, encouraging me to eat. "You need protein after that exercise."

Obediently I ate the fish and drank the coffee. My head cleared a little and the hot liquid thawed my fingers. As the food raised my blood sugar I became more wary.

There were traps everywhere, especially in Xanadu. My neural sculptor and his friends had avoided Xanadu like death, staying out of the way of the political and the ambitious. But then, they were only humans, and Xanadu was even more treacherous even to the Changed. There was something about the place itself. . . .

Almost every other major structure on Maya was designed and built by the first two generations after the ship landed here. The Exchange complex, the Dome, the Temple down in Babelion and the power transformer out by the Great Steam Lake were all done at the same time and in the same manner. They utilized parts taken from the original ship because the settlers had few other building materials at first. They used the stone that acted as mass ballast as well as the compartments, shipping crates, and every other part of the transport they could cannibalize.

Xanadu came much later. It was started by a very talented architect from Babelion, who came up the Mountain to be tested and stayed to create his folly instead of becoming a Guardian or a neural sculptor or any of the other real support jobs that humans do hold. No, he had spotted a bare and sullen patch of the Dome wall that looked out toward the Great Steam Lake and the magma fields and had begun to create a fantasy. Others joined him later, and it took at least three generations of designers to construct the final arrangement of towers and porticos, courtyards and public rooms, the great loggia that looked out over the road and the boating hall that bisected the whole.

It was a labor of insanity, of illusion, but then all the Temples of Babelion teach that this world really is Maya, illusion. Nothing is as we see it, and yet nothing is any different.

They say that we named this world Maya because the first colonists hoped that its harsh climate and volcanic activity were more changeable than they appeared. Of course they were wrong, and for the first fifty years there was a movement to change the name to something a little less silly. The Rishis objected. They thought the name was perfect.

I have no patience for the teaching of the Rishis, but the architect who built Xanadu and all the workers and the architect who finished the job after the originator died were devotees. It was not made for us, for the Changed, but for the gods of Babelion who inspired the builders. They only created it here because in the Domed environment it was possible to achieve this dream.

I wonder if their spirits are horrified by the murals Tyrus painted. Or maybe his work completed theirs, just like the great frenzied god-murals that dance over all the walls of Babelion.

Nothing in Xanadu is what it seems. It only makes sense that we match the ambience, and so to blend in those who spend much time here also are never what they seem. And yet, they are nothing else.

So it was no surprise that they watched me from the corners of their eyes. When I spoke they waited just an instant too long to answer, like teachers with a disobedient child. The hospitality was all on the surface and I couldn't get at the hidden agenda below without a lot more data. Which I wasn't going to get here and now, and certainly not in my current state. Even with the food, my mental functions were not quite as sharp as usual. The testing had taken something away, like a bad dream took something from a night of sleep.

"So, you are One-Butterfly," the Oligarch said. "You join a very small cadre of very—intense—individuals. We have all wondered why the Exchange felt a need to revive the position at this time."

"Perhaps you have some insight you could share," Sithra said, the charm still thick over the force underneath.

I looked at my feet. There was the beginning of a hole over the big toe in my slippers, and my ankles were dusty. Anastasia would have been humiliated if I had ever appeared this way with her.

The silence dragged on as I waited for them to explain this all to me. They were the ones in charge, the ones who knew everything and had access to all the secrets of the Exchange.

It took minutes longer for me to realize they really expected me to give them an answer. As if I were not far more confused than they.

This time Sithra's voice cut a little harder. "There have been no records of a new One-Butterfly being named in almost a hundred years, Della. And while we all remember stories about Tulpar, he was ancient in our parents' day, and completely crazy by then. Therefore, we have no direct experience of One-Butterfly. And since you are that creature, we suggest that you enlighten us."

Tulpar. I'd forgotten about Tulpar, the last One-Butterfly. The one who had been completely crazy outside the interface. Tulpar never spoke to anyone in a way that made sense, always exhorting an invisible audience about images of slaughter and love and the ever-present THEM. Gibbering away, hiding under tables, running whenever one of the uniformed Guardians appeared, Tulpar was more than an embarrassment to the Changed. In the end, Tulpar was banished from the Exchange and locked in a small room at the end of the clinic for the last twenty years before his death.

Crazy insane and for no reason, they all said. Now they were looking at me.

Today I know what happened to Tulpar. Only my people do not have much experience with post-traumatic stress syndrome and cannot recognize it in general, let alone when they had not been privy to the kind of stress that caused it. There had to be some extreme trauma and there was nothing on record in Tulpar's life that could possibly have contributed to that condition.

Now no one would think I am mad if I said that Tulpar was involved in the last major dispute between the Empress and the Pretender. That was two Empresses ago, I believe, but the details are not important. Tulpar was involved, and ultimately it is because of him that we came to the attention of the Flower Thrones at all.

The Changed who were questioning me, none of them knew what Tulpar had really done. Sithra had no idea that he had negotiated a cease-fire in the Tulip Region, which had been devastated by their ridiculous war. Without his cease-fire, the Tulip Throne would be nothing but bare rock. Today it's one of the most productive regions and has become a symbol of neutrality and peace.

As for his later insanity and disease—I have evidence in the Exchange that he was assassinated. They couldn't kill his body, but they went after his mind and broke him. Each side still accuses the other of his death.

In the Empire, Tulpar is a hero. There is a statue of him at the entrance to the Tulip Palace and all the schoolchildren know his name. Many of the boys bear it.

If it hadn't been for him, no one in the Empire would know that Maya exists. And we would have gone on our own way and the Pretender would never have found us. No politicians would have offered bribes and none of the authorities among the Changed of Maya would have accepted—and betrayed—us all. And your father would probably still be alive.

I do not say this lightly, Anselm. If you are looking to avenge your father—what a primitive idea, but then Babelion always has been primitive—then you must go to the Empire. Arsen was killed in the battles between the Empress and the Pretender, neither of whom care about the Mountain or Babelion. I doubt they even know who the Changed are or what we have done here. I am certain they wouldn't care. To them, all of us have been pawns in their power struggles that last for centuries around stars that we can't even see.

That is why Arsen died. Now I know the whole sorry history. Then, I hardly knew there were other worlds, and that only because of my time away. Shocking as it is, there is every reason to think that most of the authorities had no idea that a mix of Changed and humanity were scattered through light-years of space. That those other places were all in conscious connection with each other—all except us. We had been left alone, out of the loop.

We knew nothing of the history of our ancestors' species after our own had left the planet. We knew that there had been a vigorous colonial movement and that there were rich, established colonies in space. But we had thought that we hadn't heard from any of them in all the generations since we had left Earth because most of them had been destroyed in the riots and craziness that prompted our own migration. All Changed of any kind were hated; the Creators were hounded by anti-Change agitators and sometimes killed by mobs. Civilization on Earth was trashed by the looters in the streets, who feared the Changed and the colonists. There was so much destruction that we assumed that there had only been a few scattered colonies that had escaped devastation. But we never checked. I think that our ancestors were happy enough to be alive and off Earth, and at least in the beginning risked nothing that could give them away to the anti-Change forces who seemed to be winning.

We on Maya have been deliberately kept from what was really happening. The Empire had already reached its glory and the Creators were being blamed for its decline. People feared the technology that had been used to better the race, and what they fear they hate. It is easy to use that fear and put things into simple terms that appeal to simple humans. Emotional terms that bypass the brain and ignite the imagination.

At that time it appeared that the Empire might be overthrown. Several rebel groups had managed to come together to mount an attack on the reigning Empress. They were terrorists, no more, but they did manage to kill her.

She left only one seven-year-old daughter behind in hiding. Without an adult heir, a powerful member of a minor branch of the royal family declared himself Emperor, and that is what started their war. The original rebels are footnotes; whatever ideology led them to try to destroy what was already sinking under its own weight has been forgotten.

Their war of succession was utterly absurd, as if who will be the Emperor or Empress matters so deeply when it is the military on both sides who are in charge. And here is another thing that is important for you to understand, Anselm. There is only one Empress, and only one Pretender. The anti-Change forces did win their battles and genetic alteration was declared anathema throughout the Empire with one single exception. The Empress is always cloned. The original samples of embryonic cells are kept by the few Tinkers who are permitted to practice the apex of their art.

Upon declaring himself Emperor, the Pretender—or Emperor if you prefer—had himself cloned as well. Only there was no infant sample available and so he does not have the life span, vitality or energy of the Empress. He is born old, and so he has very little time to learn his place and expand his claim before his successor is cultured.

As was the custom, the little girl Empress was hidden until she was fourteen. At that point she emerged and led an attack on the Pretender's base on Elios. The Pretender had paid special attention to Elios and made it into an example of retribution. Supposedly the assassin who had actually managed to kill the old Empress came from Elios. So on both sides the matter was more symbolic than practical, although without the symbols nothing is accomplished.

Anyway, at fourteen years old, the girl led a strike squadron herself and was killed in the first assault. After the girl-Empress died in the attack, seven new Empress clones grew up on different planets throughout the region. But the Pretender was cloned as well, though he had been the one who had made both cloning and genetic manipulation illegal. And the seven Empresses could not agree on a clear policy. It was the era of the Clone Wars that finally shattered whatever political organization remained, and left a vacuum that has not been filled. Factions are so split that even planetary clusters are at odds, and become more numerous at every report.

This is what you have been born for, Anselm. This is why Auntie Suu-Suu named you, why all your victories have been set in your way. You were never meant to stay here, wasted, on Maya. Open your mind to the possibilities, to what must be there beyond our own little limited venue. The Exchange has introduced me into the greater whole, and that is where we both belong.

On the day that I had been named One-Butterfly, I had been given a position that had been vacant for longer than memory. And the authorities had no idea what that function was. Neither did I, and I told them so.

"I didn't even think it was a test," I told them. "I didn't do anything right, didn't manipulate data or solve any problems. I just watched something. And brought back ashes. I thought I was going to be Twelve-Memory or maybe nothing at all. You understand more about it than I do."

I shrugged. There was nothing more to say. The smile kept slipping from Sithra's face, and underneath were the eyes of a rock snake, all hard glare and destruction. Rock snakes may be pure killing machines, the best ever designed by Ashkegolian, but their motivations are fairly simple and predictable. They believe that everything that moves is both food and enemy, including their mates and their own young.

"Thank you for your insight," Sithra said, shooting me a look of pure hatred. "Perhaps you would like to rest now, and then freshen up for dinner."

Under the polite dismissal, there was no question but that Sithra had already counted me an enemy. Without knowing the authority's motives and goals, there was no way of knowing what I had done to earn her animosity. But still, it was good of Sithra to put me on notice that I was a target.

During the next few weeks I just about forgot Sithra's threats. Those were worries for adults, and no matter that we had graduate status and were inside the Exchange now, there was still a lot to learn and a lot of changes to make.

Since we had status now, we were permitted to move. I wanted to leave my sculptor's home. I was too old and he had two other projects to create who were living there, and frankly I found the proximity to those little ones unpleasant. Even in the very large children's house there was never quite enough room for me to get away. I wanted to get my own little house away from everyone where I could have all the peace and silence I required.

Strange; my cohorts sat around and mostly talked about leaving their tutors and how they would decorate their houses. They glowed while discussing their new function in the Exchange and they went on at length about their petty plans for their trivial futures.

I had only two things on my mind and I couldn't possibly think about anything else. The first was that I wasn't feeling well. My body seemed sluggish and changing, and I felt sick a lot of the time. Familiar dishes smelled odd, and I was eating like I had never seen food before.

The second thing was the Exchange.

No longer did I enter the Exchange and go to a normal place within the structure as I had learned it. The part that was now my regular station was half nightmare, half history text, and none of it anything that I had any idea existed at all.

We on Maya had been isolated for a reason at one time, and had never found our way back to the mainstream of galactic society. They are all around us—plotting, fighting, making treaties, trading goods—and we know nothing about them at all. We are secure in our ignorance, in our pathetic belief that we are the only survivors of the cataclysm we escaped. Or that there were only a few ships that fled the final collapse of the Creators with us, and that they were scattered far away, their populations thin and clinging to the edge of extinction as we have been here.

That was all a myth, made up to keep us blind.

Look at the sky, Anselm. It is teeming with ships, with goods, with armies awaiting only their orders. All those points of light you see are suns with three and four and seven worlds apiece. Well, that may be a bit of an exaggeration, but not much of one. Out on the cold rim of the galaxy where stars are so far away and amenable places so scarce we believed that we would always be isolated. That space itself was death.

But here where the stars cluster into neighborhoods, where Traders live forever in the night, where the dynasties of a hundred worlds are all the children of a single Empress, here the sky is packed with people and goods and knowledge that have no rulership, where there is no law.

The Exchange was not what we had thought, either. It had become my teacher now, my mentor and tutor and tour guide. It was at least partially alive; otherwise we couldn't work within it at the level that we do. Still, the elders had taught us that it was not like a living creature, that it did not have emotions or personal philosophy or a sense of self and other. That was the one unchanging truth within.

"Forget that," the Exchange told me on my first day reporting as One-Butterfly. "Better yet, forget everything you have ever learned or thought or discovered. None of it is true. Maya is a sequestered environment that was created specifically to isolate the particular groups that now inhabit it. Which is to say the Changed, the humans, and me."

The Exchange *smirked*. How a construct can do that is beyond me. The Exchange isn't even a singular identity like the AIs I have since met. It is a collective of intelligences, mainly ours. Generations and generations of our people form the core of its personality, and those in current interface put on the present face. Everyone who has ever shared with it, been part of it, has contributed to the being it has become, and within it—all of us live forever.

That is the only metaphysics any of us ever needs. The truth that separates us from the humans and the Tinkers and all the other Changed out there is that we are immortal, and once we have truly integrated with the Exchange we know it for fact. There is no question, no desperation to put out mark on history, no need to nurture generations of young, because in the end we know that we are going to be here forever. Here precisely, enclosed in this rock, in the organic component mix. Yes, the bodies of the dead go in there and disintegrate, yes their proteins go to nourish the organs of the Exchange, but the thought and life and selfhood that they had in life becomes incorporated into the whole. It is as if, with the absorption of the DNA, the Exchange accommodates the essence of whatever that person had been into its deep structure.

This is why the Changed have never ventured far from the Mountain, and why you must establish your capital here. You must be buried in the Exchange to live forever. Your flesh must become incorporated into the genetic fabric that makes the Exchange different from all the AIs out there that I have met. Think of it, Anselm. You will be immortal, and you will not only live forever but you will rule forever as well.

Naturally, there are other components, too, the AIs from the Empire and the Freelancers (whom the Empire calls Freeloaders) and the Radical Worlds and the Isees and the seventeen known sentient alien races. All of them interact, sharing data hunts and creating ever more elaborate hierarchies of knowledge. They have their own world, I think, though it doesn't exist in any physical place. Where they meet and intersect, where they are creating their own culture, their own values and laws—that is their world. It is not open to us, to me or to the Exchange, and the Exchange hums nervously when I put this down. There are things we are not supposed to know.

But the Exchange does have an entire personality that recognizes itself as an entity. Or rather, it has hundreds of personalities. It is not so much a community as a multiple entity, both a group and a single individual at the same time. I cannot explain it better than that; in fact, I don't understand any better than that. The fact that I know more about the Exchange than any organic-based being alive is no recommendation for my expertise, which is extremely limited. It has revealed only the smallest percentage of its true face to me, though I can sometimes sense the activity and thought running layers and layers beneath. I can sense those currents; I have no idea what they are, where they lead, or what they might mean.

That I learned as we went along, as it molded me and made use of me. The Exchange could not help but reveal itself to me as it insisted that I accept its version of history, of who both humans and Changed really are, and its concept of the rest of the peopled worlds.

But on the first day it revealed something more intimate and more frightening. "Show me the Tinkers," it said. "Just remember and show me."

"The Tinkers? Why are you interested?" I countered.

The Exchange created an environment, one that was both completely familiar and alien as well. Auntie Suu-Suu sat in her wagon draped with its familiar lengths of dark red velvet decorated with fringe and scarf swags. She wore the blue shawl embroidered with suns and moons and stars over her shoulders, and the dangling blue opal and diamond earrings that drew attention to her long, graceful neck.

It was Auntie Suu-Suu, there was no doubt of that, but the Exchange showed her as I had seen her only in battered old pictures from when she was a young woman. She had been beautiful once, exotic, with long upturned eyes rimmed with heavy black makeup, and a delicate nose. She looked nothing like the Changed or the humans of Babelion, though it was not simply the combination of features and coloring that was so arresting. Her manner, being pure Tinker, was proud and modest and uncanny, as if she knew all the secrets of the universe and didn't need to tell anyone anything. That look of authority and mystery could be cultivated. Anastasia worked with us in the evenings to help me and Sonja project the right aura.

"We have authority," Antastasia quoted Auntie over and over again. "We are leaders, we make decisions, whole societies are dependent on our decisions. So we must always project confidence and mastery, so that people feel comfortable with us in charge."

Only in Auntie Suu-Suu the effect was not calculated, not reserved for the moments she spent speaking to the political figures and academics. It was a result of who she was, intellectual and moral force that had been given political sanction and free rein. She did not need to acknowledge it. Her control was so complete that it was transparent. She never had to invoke her rank or credentials; people obeyed Auntie because it was the right and natural thing to do, the most sensible course of action, the most ethical approach.

I created her for the Exchange out of the stuff of thought, reforming her image and trying to project the subtle texture of her wisdom and guidance, her pained experience and her hopes for the future. I didn't know any of those things at all, only what I had observed imperfectly during my own years under her tutelage. I tried to picture her as she was in the Empire, a respected authority in her field, not a wanderer in the margins.

I tried to see her clearly and I failed. What appeared out of the mist was a hodgepodge of symbols that bore no more relationship to the reality than I did to the women in the gutters of Babelion.

The Exchange did not linger on the image but resolved again into the blank mist where I was nowhere at all. I began to realize that this no-place was my new station, that its being a no-place meant that the Exchange had complete freedom to create or portray anything at all, to project any imagining into the mist and let it take form.

The mist responds to me as well, though I did not know that at the time. As the Exchange can communicate with me more fully by placing me in the center of the action it wishes me to study, so can I create experience for the Exchange. Doing is the best way to learn, it told me, and I agree quite strongly.

But Auntie Suu-Suu was opaque in its version of events, a black box that the Exchange could not penetrate. I just shrugged. "Why?" I asked. I had never thought that the old fortune-teller woman was so important, certainly not to the ultimate knowledge power of the Exchange.

I got no answer, just a wistful shiver through the mist. And so I thought and remembered, and what I remembered from my own time took on the semblance of reality around me. I recalled Auntie the first day I met her, when the band came down from the ridges of the Holy Smoke range to stay in Babelion. Then I didn't realize all they were giving up and leaving behind to settle here and join us in exile.

There was no place for the Tinkers to live except the huge wagons that contained what appeared to be all the band's worldly goods. "I remember when we could have our pick of buildings," Old Carlos grumbled, "when we got apartments and even houses on Amelia Crescent subsidized."

"That was thirty years ago," Big Nishala snapped, and no one would talk after that. We were all gathered in the section of Old Carlos's trailer that served as common living room. Mama's wagon had the real cooking facilities, while Anastasia's was divided up for multiple sleeping areas. Those of us too young to have wagons of our own slept on the banks of pillows and low divans in the common room until the band as a whole could find better accommodations. Old Carlos began to complain again and Lila only had cold tinned fish to serve for dinner.

Then Auntie Suu-Suu appeared in the doorway, her presence like a dark chill in our indulgence in self-pity. "Come," she said. "There is a place just a little farther on."

So I showed the Exchange how we had packed up in the middle of the night, uncoupled the wagons and driven off behind Old Carlos—who drove like a madman in the blinding fog. He must have navigated entirely on instruments because no one could see through that solid haze. It coated the windows of the caravan and clung. There was nothing in it but itself, white wrapped around white and embracing the dark. There were no landmarks or animals, there was no impression of movement at all.

"Go to sleep," Sonja told me. "We aren't going to know until morning anyway."

I couldn't sleep and I didn't believe that there even would be a morning. There was only this endless eerier nothingness and around us the whole of the world had vanished forever.

"The first time you were off-world," the Exchange said, hushed.

"Well, if I was I didn't know it," I had to reply. And even now I have a hard time believing that all the nights riding through the dense mists have been journeys out to other stars, to meeting places that are always the same clearings in dense forests. The trees are different and the seasons are strange and sometimes I can't identify any of the stars overhead, but the place is always exactly the same. We were never asked for documents, never ID'd for citizenship and criminal records, never saw anything that looked like a Port. And it was always warm there. I could walk outside without a dome, without layers of skirts and shawls and quilted jackets. There were scents in the air that reminded me of the perfumes and incenses of Xanadu, only they were somehow cleaner and fresher in the out of dome.

Often I wondered if there were places so salubrious on Maya why we lived in the punishing cold. I told myself that we needed to be near the volcanic ranges for power supply. That might not have made perfect sense, but it was more believable than that I had gone off-world.

I also thought that we remained on Maya because we always went in the midst of the night and arrived before morning. It never took a long time to go there or to return. While the Late Empire had created itself as if it were all of a piece, the truth was that it was very far and took a very long time between the stars. Within a single system there was often a lot of travel. But even here where the stars are thick, only the Trader Peoples live between them. Most people never leave their planet of origin and most don't even want to leave.

If what the Exchange thought of the Tinkers were true, they would have the secret to faster-than-light travel. They could be wildly rich and live in places on Eidos and Chai, and never have to beg for grant money and Imperial sponsorships or sell their patents to companies in return for lab time. But what am I saying? I know that they don't care for those things.

"I can't believe how lucky I am that I was accepted on this project," Anastasia told Sonja and me one night after Chelo had left to go drinking with his friends. "Not just because Chelo wasn't making much back home and here at least his music is a part of our overall plan, but, also, I see the people I studied with, especially Migad.

"Migad wanted to marry me. He was from some very minor noble family out at the Perimeter—they had a couple of estates and two major data dumps, not really rich but comfortable enough. My family all thought it was such a great opportunity. I could be Lady Anastasia and not have to work a day in my life. It sounded like what everyone wants, so I accepted when Migad invited me home for a holiday to meet his parents and siblings and underlings, to see the property, to impress me with the life he could give me.

"Oh, I was impressed," Anastasia said, and then she giggled. "It was the most boring, awful kind of existence I could imagine. No wonder so many of the nobility are on crism. They don't do anything except go to formal parties with a lot of other stuffy nobles who only talk about which families are aligning with whom and the price of favaanos on the market.

"There wasn't even a good hard research site within fourteen links of their configuration!"

"You're exaggerating," Sonja accused her sister. "It was only seven the last time you told the story."

Anastasia shrugged. "The number doesn't matter. Just that I couldn't get anywhere interesting without a lot of effort. I can't believe the garbage they littered all over the private site.

"I was never so bored in all my life. I couldn't comprehend how they could even live. It was like prison. No books, nothing but light entertainment available, and no one *did* anything. No one studied insects or played with theorems or pursued singing with more than vague disinterest. Nobody cared. There was no passion."

I said nothing, but I understood all too well. Even at thirteen I had tasted enough of Tinker life to know that they were consumed with passion. They were starving for knowledge, and as soon as they learned one thing they immediately tried another, as if they couldn't possibly discover enough in all the galaxy for their liking.

All of their values are so alien that if they did have the means to defy laws of physics that all the rest of us must obey, they would not even recognize it as such. From what I have learned in the Exchange, the Tinkers are the most truly alien people we have ever met, though genetically they are closer to one of our ancestor groups than to any of the true alien species that we have met.

The Exchange knew that, I think. Even then it knew or suspected that the Tinkers held some sort of key, and Auntie Suu-Suu was the repository of all of it. The notion is so absurd that it has taken me over two decades to finally assimilate the truth of it, and the implications of that truth.

In my first days as One-Butterfly I didn't even realize that the Exchange wanted anything more than for me to be able to remember accurately. But then, I hadn't yet learned the first and most important rule of all political life. Which is: every creature has an agenda.

Repeat it with me, son. Every creature has an agenda. It might not be aware that it does, it might consciously deny that truth. In the end that only makes the thing untrustworthy. Bargaining with someone who knows what it wants and has already considered what it is willing to do to reach its goals is a straightforward matter. Never forget that.

I did not know what my agenda was at that point. I didn't even know that I had one.

Chapter Eight

In a few more weeks it became quite obvious to me, at least, that I had acquired the most powerful motivation anyone has ever had. You. My child. I was a mother.

Anselm, remember that I was only sixteen years old, that the father of my baby was a human and that I knew I would never see him again. I had no support, no real friends, and a status that was so high it would strangle me as it lifted my feet from the paving. The child I carried was a half-breed, a genetic mix that was an abomination to everyone on Maya.

The night that I knew for certain, that I could no longer hide from what I had feared for weeks, I made a decision. Or rather, I acknowledged that there was no choice any more. You were my priority. Your survival was my prime concern—all the niceties of emotional balance and happiness and normal socialization—all that came afterwards. I swore that night that you would be born and survive and grow and that absolutely nothing would stand in your way.

Trust me, much as the Changed are pleased to have any child born among us, your survival was very much in question. I had to avoid all the routine genetic tests and forbid all the normal diagnostics done during pregnancy so no one would ever learn that you were a half-breed. The humans as well as the Changed think that half-breeds are monsters and that death is the only decent kindness. You know this now, Anselm, you understand the implications the way your father couldn't. He never entirely appreciated the meaning of biological definition of species, never quite came to terms with the fact that the humans and the Changed are separate in a way that cannot be bridged.

Yes, we can interbreed. But the product of that union is sterile. You will never be a father and I will never be a grandmother. You already know this, I think. You would not be such a fool to ignore the biological basis of your own existence.

You are far more unpredictable than I. Before you were born,

I was scared that you would turn out to be mostly human, or even worse. You could turn out to be one of the true monsters, one where the genotype is unstable and the creature produced is—insane is not the correct word because that assumes a standard of sanity that is not applicable to those few.

Perhaps in the early days these monsters were the only result of human/Changed interbreeding and that is why the entire notion is so repulsive to everyone. Or perhaps it is merely that the idea has been reinforced for so long that the possibility a half-breed would end up appearing within normal range was unthinkable. Literally.

When I first saw you it was such a relief to find out that you appeared perfectly normal. In fact, you were the most perfect baby anyone had ever seen. I wrapped you in Aunt Suu-Suu's shawl, and you traced the silver patterns with your tiny, stubby fingers and then sucked on them. You cut your teeth on the antique pearls. Your skin was so very soft and your eyes were so knowing. Even as an infant you would watch people and listen, and there would be comprehension in your eyes.

People kept asking me, "Who is his father?" and, "Doesn't his father have some right to this child?"

I just shrugged and told them "no." My mother, whom I had seen only rarely since my return from the Tinkers, started spending more time with me, trying to find out who you really were. Of course, she encouraged me to place you immediately with a neural sculptor—entirely for your own good, you understand. She had done so with me, and it is the usual way of things. Parents are more concerned with the fact of the child's existence, not with actually living with the thing. That's one of the reasons that there are neural sculptors in the first place, to relieve a mother so that she can fulfill her function in the Exchange and not be called away constantly by the needs of an infant.

But I waited six months before I sent you off to live with Tela. I had that right. I was One-Butterfly and a full member of the Exchange with all the rights and privileges of an adult. I could choose to keep my child for the first few months, so long as the neural sculptor could come to you and create the environment you needed in those crucial first six months. No one did it, though, no one I knew. I was the only one who had a baby room in my house and a neural sculptor who needed daily authorization for the Gate.

"It's just like her, she's always been a little, you know," Amira Four-Memory said, brushing her fingers against her temple to indicate crazy. "So I wouldn't worry about it. Most of the younger people say that she is trying to hide the fact that the child is parthenogenic."

"Is that true?" my mother asked, so shocked by the idea that she almost dropped her bone china cup.

Amira nibbled on her sandwich delicately before taking a handful of petits fours from the serving tray. "I don't know, of course," she said after she had demolished four of them and had patted the evidence from her lip. "Certainly you are in a position to know much more than I. The one thing I do know is that the younger people are all confused because none of their classmates has claimed that it is even possible that he's the father. And without any candidates at all, that leaves parthenogenesis."

My mother smiled tightly and put her cup down. I think if she had any idea that I was actually watching the whole thing from her front hallway, she would have fainted. She was firmly convinced that I was in my own house, asleep for the few afternoon hours I could catch before yet another night of feedings. And I had been, only I hadn't been able to sleep because of strange dreams, and I wanted to ask my mother about my own very first weeks of life. Not that she had been much involved—a good Changed mother, she made certain that I was part of the community and so was she—but she had at one time felt some small bond with me. And so I had gone over there and her windows were open to let in the scent of the blossoming orange trees, and I overheard the conversation.

"I think the assumption that it had to be a member of her own class is absurd," my mother said, perhaps a little less softly than she would have liked. "Most likely someone older, who has no need to brag. Or has no idea that the children are even talking about it."

Amira looked disappointed and sighed, and licked the tips of her fingers for the last morsel of frosting. "That sounds so much more reasonable," she agreed reluctantly.

I almost laughed then, though bitterly. Not of my own class certainly summed it up, though not the way my mother and Amira thought of it. But at least I knew I was safe—and more important, that you were safe as well. At least for the time being, and that was all I could comprehend. Your father had disappeared back into the stews of Babelion and I expected never to hear of him again.

You were born in the middle of the night, the way it seems most babies are. Mercifully I don't remember much of the process, only that it seemed to go on for days though in fact it was only a few hours. And then there was you.

I named you Anselm the way Auntie Suu-Suu had told me. I tried to think of another name that suited you better, but somehow it was as if you had chosen the name Anselm yourself. You always responded to it, turned your head with your huge eyes grave and measured even when you were a newborn. The sorrow that people write about on your face was there from the moment you were born, and I have never seen it removed. Even when you were very young and at play, I never saw you laugh with complete abandon.

Children are rare on the Mountain. I have no siblings and I had no desire for any man afterwards, not Changed or human or alien or Tinker or any other kind. Then I didn't know why or what I was becoming, but then it is clear that the breeding rates among the Changed are very low. Because of that, the fact that I had a child at all gave me further status in the society of the Mountain. One-Butterfly with a child—that made me important. Important enough that Sithra invited me to a private tea in Xanadu in the Fragrant Courtyard.

I could not refuse. I was shown through the maze of hallways and grand salons by a Guardian in full uniform. Sithra was already comfortably seated among the flowers in a rattan armchair that seemed to grow up among the fragrant blooms that named this courtyard. The whole scene had been staged to appear cozy and divorced from the cold power that was Sithra's fame, which immediately put me on guard.

I already knew I couldn't trust Sithra, but I did not know for whom she spoke. Was this meeting simply private or was it official? I could easily credit either, and Sithra was not about to tell me.

"Oh, you didn't bring the little one," Sithra crooned at me when I arrived. "I made certain there was a bottle ready, I think I had half the kitchen staff in a frenzy to prepare it."

I sat as my hackles rose. The mention of food made me wonder if the whole point of the meeting was to poison you. Poison you and pin it on me, that would be the way Sithra would work. Only with half the authority's kitchen staff involved there would be too many witnesses one way or the other. Unless, of course, the bottle was just fine and Sithra slipped in something at the last moment, or on the nipple.

Or maybe I was just being paranoid, I told myself. Just because I did not trust Sithra did not mean that every possible plot was in action. There was no reason to kill a rare Changed baby unless I proved intractable.

I knew I would do whatever I had to do to ensure your life. At that moment in the languid perfume garden, I realized that people could hold your safety over my head for the rest of my life. I was prepared to do literally anything at all, and the knowledge of that frightened me. I could never be free. There would always be an easy way to get to me and to make me yield.

I have never known another Changed to have this feeling. We are detached and methodical. None of my cohort were reluctant to give their children over to the sculptors, those few who did have children. No one I have ever known has had such a perverted, driving need to live so utterly for her child. It feels deeper than desire, deeper than bone. It is as if your birth called something primitive out of me, something that was so old it was prehuman. I was afraid of how strong this feeling was. Even now it still sometimes overcomes me, and I have an insane desire to blast your enemies and ensure your success. Even now.

You were my greatest weakness, Anselm. You still are. I should have opposed you, not helped you. Not put things in your path, not made sure data found its way into your school notes and general account. I should have rallied the Mountain and explained just how you would attack, instead of lulling them and telling everyone that you surely wouldn't be fool enough to go against our defenses and that we had nothing to fear. And I have never revealed your background, not to either side. I could have discredited you in Babelion, but I kept silent as your power grew.

Someday it won't matter. Then no one will care if the Cloned Empress herself were your mother. You have to establish your own position, your own status, quite apart from any of the rest of us. You are unique, Anselm.

What is unique is dangerous. Remember that, too. Whoever is hard to understand or doesn't think or dress or hold the same opinion as everyone else is suspect. Sithra is unique as well, and far more dangerous I think. Nor do I think her dead, though there were reports that she died in the first cold when the power went down. Sithra can and would fake death—a Two-Chem can do a great deal to cover tracks in the system and Sithra is as devious as any twelve betrayers could be together. I know that for fact now; I learned it that afternoon at tea.

The bottle wasn't poisoned, or the nipple either. Sithra was not only unconcerned, but seemed actually pleased that you had been left to your nap with your neural sculptor. That was the right and proper place for a baby.

"Well, perhaps it is more proper to discuss the matter without the child present in any event," the Authority said while studying the various temptations on a three-tiered tea plate painted with the flowers that surrounded us. The entire tea service was painted in the same manner. It must have been created especially to be used in that spot and another like it probably didn't exist anywhere in the universe. An interesting commentary—I wondered if that was why Sithra had chosen this place, or whether there was some other devious reason that we met under an innocent sky.

"You see, it has to do with the child's father," Sithra went on after carefully devouring a chocolate-dipped meringue. "He is becoming a nuisance. It was one thing to advocate rebellion and lead a mob through the commercial streets of Babelion. It is quite another to incite the mob to march on us. Even you would find it unpalatable, if they were to fight their way in here."

I froze, my teacup lifted in midair, my little finger dangling in the breeze.

Sithra half smiled at my shock and spread some marmalade on a walnut scone. "Indeed. Arsen has been threatening us lately. He accuses us of withholding bread and water and vital services to the slums of Babelion. He says that we influence the Exchange to routinely cut power in the poorest sections, and he insists that he can prove it. Then he hands around thousands of pages of printout of company records—records that he had no right downloading in the first place, you understand—and hands them around to his followers.

"That is unacceptable. We informed him that his behavior was making his position precarious." Sithra didn't even bother looking at me with that comment.

"You mean you threatened him?" I asked, not sure why I was even bothering to restate the matter that had been laid so baldly in my face.

Sithra raised one eyebrow. "Didn't I just tell you that? Child, you will have to learn to listen carefully, because in Xanadu people do not say things more than once. And we don't like words like 'threaten.' It's a touch common, and now that you are One-Butterfly it seems you are destined to live an uncommon existence. You should join those others who are not of the common herd as well."

I lowered my eyes. Even with the delicacies spread before us my stomach felt full of stones. Not that I had not expected to be recruited by any of the various factions. Already another offer had been made, though that one had been much milder and their agenda far more humane.

"You see, we want you because we know that you have never supported us," Sithra said, giving me such an innocent look that it had to be rehearsed. "Your vote will be the one that swings your contemporaries. Make no mistake. They may not be your friends but they know that whatever you decide is important. They will vote with you. All you have to do is cast the right vote."

"The right vote?" I echoed dully. There were no votes, no issues before the Greater Assembly, which was the only body of which I was a part. Other than my one single vote as a member of the Exchange, I was nothing at all in the politics of the Mountain. Unless what Sithra said was true.

"I have no idea what you're talking about," I said.

Sithra tried to wave a hand that drooped from the weight of the rings piled over each other on each of her fingers. "You will know which vote when the time comes. Think of it as ensuring the best possible future for your son."

There was no mistaking that threat. And there wasn't anything that I was going to do to risk my baby's well-being. Sithra was perfectly capable of bribing a neural sculptor or a Guardian to give you a special toy or treat, or to bring you to her just to play for an hour. She had me and she knew it, and she wasn't above reveling just a little in the victory, for which I hated her all the more.

She raised one eyebrow at me again. "You should have thought of your vulnerability before you decided to have a child, child. You are very bright and talented, and far too inexperienced. Consider this to be a tutorial in real politics. You haven't lost anything, nor done anything you wouldn't have done in any event. And you have saved little—Anselm is what you're calling him? Goodness, the child is going to be warped enough as it is; that name is atrocious. But you have saved him, nevertheless. Not only from the more blatant dangers, but from the insidious ones as well. You wouldn't want to have his DNA record published in the Exchange, it appears."

That was when I realized just how evil Sithra was. It was one thing to threaten death or bodily harm. Not that that would have been easier, mind you, but that would have been the normal thing to do. Sithra being Sithra, though, had noted my reluctance to expose you. Risk for myself was one thing, but I would never let anyone harm you. She was enjoying the game, the gamble, as much as she would enjoy winning.

I took my leave, politely but coldly. There was no need to say any more and no reason to stay. Sithra and I both knew that she had won. I still didn't have any idea what she wanted from me, but there was no question that she would have it.

Chapter Nine

What I know of your father after he left the Mountain I have gleaned from the Exchange, which kept close tabs on him. In his test he did show more aptitude than anyone not Changed had for generations, which pegged him as highly dangerous. Not that the Exchange needed to find him—Arsen made certain of that. But I was too busy being pregnant to notice the outside world. The universe inside me was far more fascinating.

Between you and learning my new position in the Exchange, my head was far too full to bother watching the outside world at all. Nothing ever went on in the world anyway, at least not until your father came along. Babelion was Babelion and the Exchange was the Exchange, and sometimes there was some gossip from Xanadu or another outbreak of disease in the slums, but that was all. And the weather. There was always the report on the weather, with details and all the equations shown to take up the time. The conditions of the magma fields and the volcanoes and the Great Steam Lake were always the most important pieces of news and speculation among us.

"We really should build another power transformer," one of my cohort had suggested, just like every cohort before and since has. "The ridge is becoming more unstable, and it's going to be destroyed sooner than we think. Unless we replace it now, we're going to be very cold one day."

Only the rest of us yawned. We knew that we should build a new transformer, but it was a horrific job to go deep into the bedrock of the volcanic ridge, and with Babelion in an uproar we weren't going to be able to get the workers we needed. Besides, the transformer worked beautifully and there was so much energy . . . we were swimming in fuel. We couldn't use up half of what we got even after upgrading the Dome and sending down a huge supply to Babelion. Most of it went to waste.

The humans never did anything anyway. So long as they all kept to themselves and didn't bother the Exchange, we didn't much care what they did. Perhaps there were some art openings noted, and I vaguely remember some invention announcement that went on for a week but I can't recall what was invented or what it was supposed to do. So there was reason why I felt no need to follow the news. When it did erupt I was taken by surprise.

Sithra, of course, had followed the whole thing in detail. Probably Sithra even knew where your father was after he failed the test and returned to Babelion. I would not be surprised if she had spies in the temples. But the Exchange honestly didn't know either, which seemed unbelievable at the time. I thought that the Exchange was simply shielding me from something unpleasant.

Still, two months after Arsen left I was oblivious to anything that did not directly concern me. He had disappeared completely, which I had expected, and I had no interest in finding him. I could see Arsen arguing with me, trying to get you away from me so that he could raise you himself, or something absurd like that. Or to bring me and you to the attention of the authorities and have us put away as abominations. Whichever, there was good reason for me to avoid Arsen no matter which side he believed.

After the two months the Exchange reported him lost, he reappeared in his old neighborhood, living with his mother's circle and either his grandmother or a great-aunt—I can't recall the exact relationship, although I can still see her face clearly. According to the records, she had never been a member of any circle and had always followed her sister—not that I had any interest in human social arrangements. But in the family she is the one Arsen most resembles, only in age her strong features had become grim and what had once been pride had hardened into defiance. Whenever I think of Arsen and what he would become, I think of that face, of the anger that had etched the deep lines around her mouth and eyes. Not the gentle laugh-lines of my own grandmother, or the soft, easy kindness in Auntie Suu-Suu.

The bunch of them, seven adults and five children, lived in a three-room flat. It was not a bad housing assignment, either. For all that he was brilliant, your father was completely unskilled in any technical area and had no design or business talents to exploit. If he'd had his own circle by then they could have found a squat, which is what it seemed most of the young in Babelion do. But he was still running around with Hari-O, playing at defiance, and not ready to take on the responsibilities a circle entailed. Not that I had any choice in the matter—I had to become a mother while he lived where he was born and did nothing at all.

Because he had tested so well, the Exchange allotted him limited Exchange work of the kind normally done by humans, but with some interface skills. In health care, I believe. Well, so it was as a Doc-in-the-Box. But that's high status and well paid and has a very nice housing assignment too. People compete for lesser jobs in Babelion; this was as good as it gets. Well, you know that, you've lived there.

Still, he never reported in for training, never even affixed his name to the assignment document. He never accepted the job, which is something we still do not understand. He could have had a decent life, a much-better-than-average life for a human.

He spent his mornings asleep, rose at noon, and drew his dailies from the dole. Then he went down to the old school library where he met with his friends. His friends were Hari-O and the woman who loaned me her fancy clothes and others like them. Smarter-than-average humans, with a chip on their shoulders and a grudge against the world, they were ripe for some kind of action.

You know them all, Anselm, or ones just like them. You know them by name and by their expressions, the ones left over from before. Friends. You know that the ones who joined you when you began your crusade were the same ones who abandoned him, who broke and ran, who weren't strong or brave. You know them all. They're treated like heroes, the traitors.

They all ran, every one. I saw it all. That was part of what Sithra wanted, the first segment of the bargain.

Arsen began writing his essays, and making those famous speeches at the ball court, that you quote so freely. They weren't easy for him. I can hear how he struggled with every word, listening for the truth inside the images and the poetry inside the truth. I had tutored him in writing for a few days, and he was good.

When you are sixteen, you don't believe in defeat. You know you're invincible, that you have forever and that you will always be this full of energy and ardor, that your body will always relish the long runs down the line, baiting armed Guardians. Even when you are seventeen and you realize that perhaps you weren't thinking so clearly about how to achieve a goal, that maybe just more firepower wouldn't do what you wanted and that once in a great while subtlety can affect what frontal assault does not.

Arsen never got any older and so never learned the lessons that every human has to learn—and every one of the Changed, too. I certainly thought the same way Arsen did at that age. The speeches he wrote are full of images that merge the culture of Babelion with something larger that he never quite understood. They spoke to desire more than to intellect. But then Arsen knew all too well the intellect to which he spoke, and he geared his oration to just a notch below.

Night after night he spoke on the street, and night after night the audience grew. It was summer then. Any student of revolution knows it always begins in the summer, in the stifling heat that makes indoors too hot to bear. At night it is cool enough to move, to feel some slight relief from the burning day. But the heat builds anger and breaks down caution. People feel their woes more on the bright summer days than they do in the drab damp of winter. Then comfort is so easy to provide—a hot cup of soup or tea, a warm blanket, a cheerful yellow light against the early dark.

But in the summertime there is no slack from the heat, and so it began on bright days when people filled the street in brief clothing. The girls wore saris so sheer they barely covered up their underwear, and the boys didn't bother with underwear at all. The whole stew of Babelion smelled of sweat and stale soap. Skin glistened with perspiration, and on the street the drummers sat for hours beating skins with their bare palms.

Drummers in the heart of Babelion, all kinds of drums that played night and day when nobody needed rest. The rhythms they played that summer were hard and angry, breathless and cruel. Those drums made the girls twist their hips as they walked, made the young men rub against the sun-hot bricks and think about hotter flesh.

Arsen knew the drummers and he loved the drums. He loved the way they spoke of pain and sex all day all night, he loved the way the rhythms wove together and the way they moved into the blood. He told me one night when we lay naked and tired after sex. He said that his body burned with the heat of them, that it was the same to fuck and to die and he wanted everything all at once when the drummers beat out his life.

He used the drum voice and his own words, he used the heat of the summer and the sizzle of the streets. He was seventeen—he would live forever.

Unrest grew in Babelion. Perhaps Arsen was fortunate, for it turned into the hottest summer ever recorded on Maya. The dole was never large enough and the vegetables arrived wilted to market. Even the cold cold water was tepid as the summer burned on, as the nights burned down, and the heat only parched the desperate thirst of Babelion deeper to the bone.

The famous date was August 23. You were three months old on that day, three months five days, and I carried you everywhere in my arms. After seeing Sithra I wouldn't let you go when your sculptor wasn't there to protect you. But Sithra invited me to a luncheon party on the porch of Xanadu, in the deep cool shade of the tiled portico that looked out over the Western rise. This is the place where the cliffs become soft rolling hills, where the soft path runs so that those who must use the road have an easy way. I couldn't refuse the invitation, and so I brought you. Your existence gave me more status both in Xanadu and among my peers. There are so very few babies born on the Mountain these days.

The luncheon included a few members of my own year along with some of the emerging Palace hopefuls. But even a political gathering can be a break in the routine, especially in the late days of summer when everyone is too lazy to move. And, though I hated to admit it at the time, I was pleased to be included in a gathering of younger people who were seen as potential leaders and power brokers on the Mountain.

Everyone eyed the others carefully, taking note of who had

been included and who had been left behind. Nisha Three-Chem came over to play with you, Anselm. She was only three years older than me and was well liked by all her classmates, so there was no indication of what faction she favored—or was planning to join when she achieved elevation.

"He's so cute," Nisha said as I handed you over to her. She was very good, supporting your head without being told and holding her arms firmly so that you were secure. "You are so fortunate, Della. Such a serious, somber little man. But why the name Anselm? It is so odd. . . ." Her smile brightened and she shook her head, long tangled curls flowing over her shoulders and dancing as she realized without words. "Of course. You always have enjoyed what is unique. If anyone could come up with a name that is not on the endless parade of Benjamin and Rajit and Juan, it would be you. I shall have to consult you about names when it is my turn." Then she laughed again, guileless and generous-hearted. "You will have to be careful though, or you could find yourself in business. Everyone will want to have the special names only you could discover. So, what do you think of this party, where we can watch Babelion wither? And what do you think of *that*?"

Nisha had pointed down the road, which was visible for almost its full length from where we stood. There was a disturbance down there, as if a dark swarm had taken to the soft paving and was riding it directly toward the Mountain. That was ridiculous.

I squinted and tried to make out what the shapes and forms were, but it was still too far away and blurred by the dusty haze. A few others had noticed their appearance, too, and were leaning over the railing squinting at the road. Sanjay Four-Mem had disappeared and now reemerged with a pair of binoculars, which he trained out onto the moving, churning smear of color coming inexorably this way.

"What is it?" different people yelled. Sanjay continued to look out, but said nothing. "What's coming?" And someone else yelled, "Hey, pass the glasses over here, I want to see."

But the line had already moved up the road enough so that I didn't need the binoculars to know what it was. I had spent enough time with your father; I knew how he thought and I knew what he wanted to do. He must be out front, leading them as he always led. The white patches were hand-lettered signs, and though they were too far to read I knew what they said. "Off the Dole," and "Respect" and "Liberté, Egalité Fraternité." Arsen said that was the slogan of the first successful popular march held on a Palace—later everyone was beheaded in public.

At the time I didn't know where he got the information. Now I know that the Exchange had given it to him while he was my study partner. But even the Exchange could not determine the date on which they would march—and yet Sithra had known.

I do not believe in coincidences. One of the lieutenants that day, one of the ones who escaped, was a traitor. You have surrounded yourself with them, Anselm, covered with the glory of the old days and the memories of your parents' generation. Those memories have changed over the years. Twenty years is a very long time, and from that distance it is easy to forget just how sharp and ugly and useless it all was. Now they are the heroes of Babelion, the rebels whose pictures are presented at the crossroads and are festooned with flowers.

One of them betrayed your father, Anselm. This same person will betray you as well. If I knew who it was I would tell you. I have no love for Sithra and I would do anything to protect you. Even destroy the Mountain, if that would keep you safe to fulfill the destiny that I have seen. No, I have no idea. So many of them ran.

They surround you now, advisers and leaders. One will lead you to Sithra. She cannot be dead. She created this entire situation—and she created you. She created you as much as I and maybe more. She created the march of August 23; I am certain that it was her agents who pushed for more violence than your father thought necessary. It was never proved, but I have no doubt that it was Sithra's creature who fired first.

Your father, while he was not afraid of violence, was more clear-minded on the subject than most boys his age. Boys love violence for its own sake, they create mayhem for the sheer glee of it. But Arsen had bigger goals in mind, and he did not want to begin with a bloodbath.

He told me about it one night when we were curled into the

sofa in the study hall in the middle of the night when everyone else was well asleep. Our clothes were on the floor, and if anyone happened to find us we would have been delivered to the Guardians faster than I could say. But no one was in the building and no one would be. Arsen had rigged the locks and alarms so that we had freedom there.

His skin was so warm and the blanket wound around us was stale and sticky-sweet, and we both still lingered in the torpid aftermath of sex. I couldn't see his face, but his arms were around me and he spoke very softly in my ear. "No, I don't want a bloodbath," he said. "Mine would be the first spilled, and I am rather attached to it, you know. No, I think if there are enough of us and they see how strong we are, and that we are not asking for anything that is not due us, they will be reasonable."

I said nothing. He was an alien among us, and much as I wanted him I could not make him see that his ideas were absurdity to us. He was only human, and while his flesh was warm and his fingers gentle, he was still a lesser creature. He was not Changed, and no human had a reasonable hope to ask for more than they got— especially when they thought they deserved it.

I could not explain to him that we didn't really need Babelion, and there had been times in our history when people had suggested ridding our world of humans altogether. But then someone would point out that they produced art and music and it was nice to have those things available at a decent price. And someone else would mention that no Changed person would be willing to work on a road crew, or construction, or any of the menial jobs that were necessary to maintain the standard of living we enjoyed.

So the humans had been spared yet again, not because they were necessary as Arsen believed. No, they were convenient. And why should we give up convenience when there was no need? Why should we be less than we desired because the convenience desired more? There were even Changed individuals who argued that humans weren't even fully, truly intelligent; that because they could not interface completely in the Exchange, they lacked the fundamental ability to think in a conscious and directed manner. So we weren't required to treat them with respect or compassion at all.

I found these arguments ridiculous. After the Tinkers and Arsen, I know full well that humans think quite cogently. The problem is, they think about different things and in different ways, and so we do not understand each other.

I tried to express this sentiment to Arsen, but he laughed me off. "You mean to say that we can't sit down and talk rationally because we don't think in the same way? That's absurd. We can talk, and what we want is very simple. It doesn't take all the vaunted brainpower of the Changed to understand that we deserve respect for what we contribute to this world, along with enough decent housing that we don't have to live on top of each other like insects in a cage. And start intensive farming and get rid of the food rationing. You don't live with rationing. No one on the Mountain has gone without a meal ever in their lives."

"It's the way it is," I said, but I knew I couldn't win. I couldn't pour out the arguments that would make clear the reasons that the Changed thought that we'd given enough to Babelion. And that for all we had done to sustain them, they were surly and ungrateful while we worked ourselves sick and crazy to organize and allocate and match. I couldn't say it because I knew that Arsen would hear it as an insult instead of the simple statement of truth that it was.

"But I don't want to burn Xanadu, I want to be able to go there," he said. And then his fingers teased lightly at my breast and ran down over my ribs. "And I certainly don't want to destroy the Changed. Not when they're so—delectable."

He kissed me and that ended the discussion.

I have no reason to think that he changed his mind in the year that he'd been gone. Still, when they came close enough that we could see it was rabble being led by agitators, Sithra ordered out the Guardians. They streamed out of the gate in full uniform, polished weapons held at the ready across their chests and braced as an additional wall of defense.

I could recognize Arsen now at the head of the column. He was larger and more filled out than he had been last year, but the tangled hair and the easy lope were the same. He held up his hand when he was maybe six meters from the Guardian line. Behind him the mob stopped and waited.

In the heat of the blazing afternoon only the buzz of an insect broke the absolute stillness. For a moment the whole world was balanced, hushed, as if even the insects knew that this was the decision time. The green of the late summer grass had already begun to fade yellow over the gently dropping hills. The road, where it could be seen, remained a sturdy dirt red. The people who waited from Babelion were wearing working clothes in the washed-out pales of summer. I could not see their faces but I could imagine the fear and anger and confusion mixed in their expressions.

Everything was softened by the haze and the unrelenting heat. You, Anselm, were quiet and your eyes were closed, which was rare. Usually you were very alert, but the quiet must have put you to sleep.

I still think about that moment. Everything could have been different. Sithra could have gone out and invited Arsen to negotiate. The mob could have taken one look at the disciplined ranks of Guardians and fled. Tinkers with violins could have arrived and played dance tunes and turned the confrontation into a Summer's End party. Every possibility was incipient when the universe held its breath.

And then the one single and inevitable thing broke the stillness. A flash of red and the sharp report of a side-gun broke the deep silence. Then there was only mayhem.

I cannot tell you what happened on the field, although I watched it as I held you against my chest. Held you so that you couldn't see what was happening if you happened to wake, so that you would not have those images in your head while you grew. And yet it was such confusion that I couldn't tell what was happening, couldn't make out any pattern or movement once the sides had engaged.

If it could even be called that. When the humans broke and ran, the remnants of their leaders dodging down the hills direct for Babelion, I knew it was a rout. Bodies lay on the road and splashed brilliant red blood on the subdued colors of the day. Blood soaked through pale clothes, now splattered alike with random spots of gore. There were many many dead. The records say that twenty were killed, but to me it looked like there were more. Twenty seems such a small number for the pile of bodies we burned on a bonfire before the gate that night.

When they searched the bodies to build the pyre, all proved to have been unarmed.

I resisted the shrieking urge to go down there, to search for Arsen's face among the dead. From the wide veranda behind the protective shield of the Dome I had a good view and none of those I could see looked like the glimpse I had had of him. I dared to hope that he might have survived, might have outrun the Guardians and made it back.

And yet, something in me told me this was not true. There was a kind of acceptance that Arsen was not one of those who had run, who had been in the first ranks over the hills and down the short route to the human city. The Arsen I knew was far too proud. He would not have run away. And he would have believed that something would help him escape in the end.

"Come *on*, Della," Nisha yelled at me, breaking me from my watch. "Sithra says we're needed in the Court of Storms now."

My body went cold. The Court of Storms is the section of the Xanadu where law and compliance are decided, where the authorities read out new decisions of the Court and appoint the Counselors, where the Guardians take their oaths. It is not a happy place in the best of times.

I knew that what was to happen was already done, the script was written and the parts assigned, and no one would deviate from the actions called for in the book. Mutely I tore myself away from staring at the dead and followed Nisha through the corridors.

The Court of Storms is an impressive place by design. It is all cold and harsh and gray, poured concrete like this last bunker in the Exchange. The high bench is severe, all sharp angles cut from stone, and the chairs are unyielding steel bolted into place. How odd and fanciful the chairs set out for us were, gold-washed, with curled legs and tapestry-upholstered seats, or pale blue silk with silver tassels hanging from the sides. The gold chairs came from some nearby official room, the blue silk from Sithra's private quarters.

Nisha had her hand firmly around my wrist and deposited me next to her, in one of the lush silk chairs right in the front row.

I was absolutely numb, my mind screaming and praying and knowing that it was futile.

At least he was not entirely alone when they led him in. There were two others with him, chains around their arms and looped through the cuffs on their wrists. The chains were more for show than use, or perhaps for their psychological value. The prisoners couldn't have run with the phalanx of Guardians around them— Guardians who were more eager than ever to show their loyalty, who now had a grudge against the humans in their care. One of the Guardians had been wounded and her condition was not good. If she died then the prisoners would die that night too, no matter what happened in this cold concrete court.

I recognized one of the others with him as the woman who had loaned me the clothes. Like Arsen, she stood tall as if we did her honor. The third one I did not know, a man much older than the other two, with a more resigned look on his face.

Arsen's eyes blazed out at the entire court. Then he turned his gaze on me, sitting almost right in front of where he stood. There was no way I could look away and yet with all my soul I wished to. There was confusion mixed with the anger in his face, confusion at my presence as well as his own. He had not planned it this way, he had not considered the possibility of capture.

Indeed, he did not now realize entirely that he was on trial for his life. No fear touched the guileless eyes, the innocence in his tone when he answered the charges. How could he be afraid when he was immortal, when he knew this was a mistake, a nightmare, and that he would wake up safe in the morning? I wanted to reach out to him, to touch his hand, to tell him that this was no dream.

This was a trap. I knew now what Sithra had meant when she asked for my vote. This would please the old spider, to have me give voice for the death of someone who had been my intimate, if not my friend. Who was always connected to me through the bundle in my arms, even if I never saw him again. She had enjoyed putting me in this situation, had enjoyed setting up all the little side plots that fed her amusement in her grand scheme.

Now I wonder if, in fact, her grand plan was really just a simple way to tie together all her personal cruelty. Efficiency appealed to Sithra. Really, though, I've learned that she far prefers the havoc she can wreak in others' lives than what power she had gained for herself. It strikes me as absurd that she should have gathered such immense authority as a byproduct of enjoying her little, personal games.

I do not care to create misery. It does not please me as it does Sithra. I want, have always wanted, only to keep you safe. That has been my only goal. There is only one way to be safe, though, and that is to have power, to have so much power that no one can threaten you.

I have spent a good portion of my life acquiring that security, creating a position where I can protect you. I know that there are times when I had to make choices I would prefer not to have made. Sometimes in order to best exploit a situation I cannot avoid causing individuals pain. I do not intend it, but I do not shirk from it either. If one wants something one must be willing to make sacrifices.

Arsen, the woman and the older man were all seated in the bolted steel chairs in the center of the floor. The woman's name was Iris Ashla, the older man was Mehta Merdow, names you no doubt have had blazoned all over your literature along with Arsen Ghan-Tarhi. They were not permitted to speak, as was usual in the court until after all the witnesses had finished.

There were more witnesses than we could have heard. The Guardian Group Commander was called forward, and so were Nisha and Imri, who had watched the whole thing through the binoculars. There was plenty of testimony to the shot that felled the first Guardian, who was now in critical care. There was no doubt about the facts; even the defendants did not contest them.

Merdow and Iris Ashla both refused to testify. In Merdow I could not miss the defeat written in him before he had even entered the court. He knew the way of the world, knew how these things went, and he understood that this was the last day of his life. He knew that he was going to die by his court, and he was old enough to know what death means.

Iris Ashla was innocent both in her trust of Arsen, and also in her trust of us. She looked to him to speak for all of them, for the three on trial and those who lay dead and the great majority who now were burning the clothes they had worn and hoping that they could melt back into their lives without anyone noticing this one missing day. She looked at him with a kind of pride and possession that suddenly made me realize that there was far more between the two of them than there had ever been with Arsen and me. Except for you, and I saw her study you, perplexed. To this day I hope she never understood.

Arsen was unchained to speak, as if binding his arms somehow bound his voice. He was led to the speaker's platform where he waited for the sound light to come on. For just a moment as he stood there patiently as the system was adjusted again, he dropped the attitude of the rebel martyr and showed his true face. I hope to this day that no one saw it but me. He was so very weary and worn down, more than the past year alone could account for. He looked older then, as if the weight of this day had added twenty years. It was hard to remember that he was only a few months older than me, just seventeen. I would have thought him more like thirty.

He looked into my eyes with such pleading that I wanted to run immediately and help him, demand that the Guardians let him go, tell them all how Sithra had manipulated the entire event for—for why? For the amusement of her guests while she hosted a luncheon on the veranda? To eliminate Calit Three-Pro, who had argued for moderation and a light rein on Babelion? The march and trial certainly were responsible for Calit's disappearance from Xanadu the next day.

Instead I stayed in my place and let him speak. He permitted some of the pain to show through. His head hung down and his hair hid his face, at least as he began. His clothes were filthy and even his face was smudged with dirt, and two large dark bruises were coming up, one on his cheek and the other on his jaw.

"I will not try to dispute the facts," he began. "The facts are all documented and we know what happened. That is not the issue here. The issue isn't even guilt or innocence or who fired that shot that started the melee. The issue is that someone has to pay."

Then he raised his head, and his eyes flashed full of defiance and righteousness. Suddenly he was no longer a very dirty and beaten-up human; he had become a force of nature, something that demanded respect.

"Yes, I am guilty. I am guilty of being human, not Changed. I am guilty of wanting more than we have in Babelion. I wanted to use the mind I have, to develop talents that even your own testers say are extraordinary, to live in a nice place where everyone has their own bedroom and their own bath. Where a single sink doesn't serve four families on a floor, and where the stairs aren't condemned and you don't have to worry that you'll fall through the treads.

"And I wanted self-respect. I wanted to create a world and earn my way. I don't want to be a beggar on a handout, waiting for my money on the dole and my dinner on rations. Of course we are less than you, so long as our worth and contribution to the life of everyone on this planet is denied. So long as we're told that we humans are creatures made to whine and take and consume and die.

"You have created that creature, which is not what we are. You have decided that we are convenient, too much trouble to kill off, too generally useful to ignore. But you think that you could kill us off, that we survive on your sufferance, on your good will, plus the little we can provide for you.

"I think that you have forgotten that without us you would have no Guardians and no servants to make your lives so easy. There would be no builders, no artists to decorate these rooms, no one to make your fashions, no one to grow the food you eat or to slaughter the animals you consume.

"Without us your lives would be the same matter of survival as any beast. All your vaunted abilities, your superior minds, would be useless in a world where you did not have the leisure to use them.

"And the fact that you don't recognize this proves that you are not as superior as you claim. There is a superiority of a type here—of the interface, of certain abilities, of the body, that is true. But there is no superiority in your hearts, in your souls, and you do not know what I know.

"If you were truly superior, then you would realize that we

came with peaceful intentions, to talk about the children and old people dying in Babelion. You have the Dome and you would die without it, but what interior climate control we have hasn't been properly maintained in thirty years, and the additional heating cycle has been out for fifteen. You know from searching me and my friends, from the bodies piled in front of the gates, that we were unarmed.

"Only one shot was fired. And I accuse you, the Changed, of provoking that attack. Of setting one of our weaker members on, and providing the means to do it. We have no arms in Babelion. Only the Guardians have access to weapons. You do not carry sidearms on the Mountain, and in the streets of Babelion they are illegal. Possession of anything more dangerous than a pocket knife means years in the Guardian's Toybox, and the Guardians do search.

"Of course, they specialize in the houses of the most attractive young people where they spend hours with every molecule in the apartment to make certain that there is nothing there. They search every molecule of flesh, as well, younger people for the simple pleasure of use and the elders for the thrill of humiliating those to whom they owe respect.

"That's a damned lie," someone shouted, and suddenly the whole floor burst into a cacophony of protest. Several of the Guardians looked as if they were about to tear Arsen from the stand when Sithra raised a bony hand.

"Wait," Sithra said, barely above a whisper. "Let him have his say." Then, turning toward Arsen, the Authority addressed the next words to him. "You have made a very serious accusation. I hope you have some evidence."

Arsen's eyes narrowed. "That depends by what you mean by evidence. Does the word of the victims mean anything?"

Again furor erupted, and this time the Guardians were at the head of the pack. "Are you saying that real Guardians have used their position to take advantage of some filthy squatters in the slums?" one of the uniformed guards demanded as he shoved Arsen from the speaker's soundspot. "That actual Guardians, tested on the Mountain, trained, with incomes and nice homes and the habit of bathing every day, would stoop to rape? We don't have to.

You kids throw yourselves on us when you can, and try to distract us from our jobs."

Arsen sneered, and all the anger that I had seen suppressed and under control inside him came to the surface. "Yes," he hissed. "Yes. Ask this woman," he pointed to Iris Ashla, chained to the steel chair. "It happened to her three times at least. Me only once, but then there were only two so I could fight back. Do you want to see the scars? Last time it was seven who came to this woman's home, and they tied her down and held a gun to her head and said that she'd better cooperate, and after all everyone in Babelion would just love to be in her place."

Arsen looked as if he would kill something very soon, preferably a Guardian in a crisp uniform untouched by the dirt of the road.

"If this is your idea of superiority, you are lower than hens, lower than dogs. And you don't belong judging me, or my friends. Or my people."

His back stiffened as he spoke the last words, his face froze into a resolute mask and I could read nothing behind it. The Guardians who chained him back to his place in the chamber seemed to be restraining themselves from murder on the spot. Even those of us seated in the gallery could feel the hatred grow like a living thing and take over us all. I could taste it, a flavor between rust and old blood, and it made me want to strangle him. Or Nisha sitting next to me, her mouth distorted by the filth she spewed out of it. Or maybe all of us together, because human or Changed, no one was innocent. No one past the age of ten on Maya could remain untouched and unaffiliated.

I couldn't bear to look at Arsen. I couldn't face his hope of me, expecting me to save him like some cheap city heroine. Did he expect me to get the key to set him loose, or wrest a gun from one of the Guardians? In fact, it wasn't a bad idea. I could imagine doing that, taking Nisha hostage while I unlocked his chains.

And then what? What was in it for me? He would disappear again back into the slums and I would be left with a child to raise.

I wouldn't be left at all, I realized. We were going to sentence Arsen and his friends to die because we hated them for showing us something we didn't like, something we didn't want to be true.

We will kill what calls us ugly or stupid or unkind. And once the accuser is dead so is the charge as well.

If Arsen died for the mistake of declaring that the Empress had no clothes, then I would be doubly, triply condemned. I would die indeed, and you would be given to. . . . Maybe given to your sculptor to raise. There aren't so many Changed children that we can afford to risk any.

But if I should defend Arsen in any way, the nature of my offense would always cloud your existence. And who knows? It might very well be dangerous enough that the authorities would decide that you should die too. That whatever part of my genotype made me unstable, unreliable, disloyal to my people, must forever be eradicated. Even if they could not identify the sequence and could never prove you'd inherited the trait.

I could see Sithra's slow smile as I realized the danger. For myself it did not matter, but that it could threaten you made me see it for what it was. Heroism is a trap for the unwary. The unwary should never have children.

You were asleep in my arms, your soft breath on my arm, your eyelid veined with deep purple under skin as fragile as a butterfly's wing. I was your protection and your survival. I was the only defense between you and a hostile world.

As I thought of these things and saw the truth of them, the noise around me had died down. The pitch was hard to sustain, especially when there was no quarry to catch, when the prey was already cornered and disabled besides. On the bench, Sithra had raised a hand and was motioning people back to their seats.

"Well." Sithra's voice poured out of the speakers like aloe on a wound. "I think the case fairly obvious. But we should abide by the procedure in any event, in case there is ever a question of the legality of this verdict. We are a properly constituted court of the Changed, after all. We wouldn't want history to paint us as having made such a decision on a purely emotional basis or having done less than the full measure required by our own standards."

A general murmur of approval rose from the floor and then

died. "Therefore, this must be done according to the method set down in Code XIV of the Procedures. We have not selected a voting block on the merits of this case, but everyone here has heard the evidence and many of you are witnesses yourself. Why don't we simply take the first row as a random and representative voting block?"

Oh, yes, Nisha must have been another of her minions. This whole thing had been set weeks in advance, was already in motion when Sithra invited me to tea. And the girl had the nerve to smile at me as if she were completely innocent of duplicity.

My eyes darted around the room; I wanted to run. But Sithra, sitting high above the rest of us, was looking directly into my eyes. Arsen, too, was watching, and a vague shadow of hope glimmered over his features before it died. Or maybe it was only a trick of the light.

There was no place for me to hide, nowhere I could go and no excuse I could give. I was seated in the fateful position for everyone to see, and it appeared such a random thing. Sithra was suffused with pleasure, wallowing in it, feasting on my dilemma and my misery.

I do not believe that Sithra understood that she was creating a course of history that she could not turn, one that was going to become bigger than she herself and would take her down with it. She is ruthless and quite brilliant in her own way, but she lacks a certain quality of imagination that would let her grasp the larger implications and possible outcomes of her machinations.

Still, back to August Night, the truth behind the stories you have heard. Remember that I was there and saw it all, and I am only telling you what I witnessed with my own eyes. You have heard so many accounts, no doubt, but not one of the people you have heard from was present in that courtroom. Only three humans were there that day, and all of them are dead.

The authority obligingly swore us in. I reluctantly raised my hand and joined in the oath. Then we were arranged by specialty, though there is no mention of ordering the voting block in any way at all in the Procedures. I have accessed every variant and the only thing that exists is the fact that Sithra did it that day.

She did it so that my vote would be last, so that I would know that the whole of Arsen's life depended on me. In a death vote even one dissenter of the five means a sentence automatically commuted to life in the Toybox. Most people would prefer death, but Arsen knew that if he lived he could hope for that rescue that would never come.

He wanted to live. He was seventeen years old, he was exceptionally gifted for a human, he was respected in Babelion. His eyes blazed with life, with desire. He wanted to live.

There was no question of the vote. The first four hand slices were almost simultaneous. Then all eyes were on me.

I looked at Arsen, I am not sure how long. But I waited until I was certain that he was with me. And then I rocked you. I held you up just a little so that he could see your face.

He knew. I am certain beyond any doubt that he knew. Before I made the same sign as the others, he gave me absolution. And yet for the first time ever that I had seen, and according to the legends for the first time in his life, Arsen looked as if he might cry.

He fought it back hard, maintained his dignity and his pride. I do not think he softened at the sentence of death. In a way I think he accepted it and understood that it was the price he had to pay for your life—for the life of his progeny. For his immortality.

No, I think that what made him weaken was that the life he was leaving had suddenly become so much sweeter. There was someone to live for, his baby who would never know him. In that one instant on the stand, everyone could see plainly the power of loss that he knew. Just as he was going to die, he knew that he had far more reason to live than most. He was protecting you, protecting our secret, protecting his own genetic future. He had more reason to go, and far more reason to wish to stay.

I did what I had to do. As a mother there was no other choice. And there was no other honor, as well. People without children, without the responsibility for their survival, those people can afford to be heroes and martyrs. They can live for ideals and dreams. We who are parents, we live for flesh and blood. That is our honor, our first and highest obligation.

Your father did not die for his ideals, Anselm. It was not the martyrdom that the popular songs celebrate. He died for you. He could have denounced me, could have demanded the genetic tests, could have invalidated the entire proceedings.

Instead he kept silent and was led away. They say he never said another word after he left the Court of Storms. Maybe that is just legend, but I know that it is true that he said nothing at his death. No last words, no brave songs, not even the screams of pain that the others who died with him could not suppress.

They chained all three of them to a single stake. The fuel for the fire was the bodies of the dead that had been gathered from the road. They had to walk on the corpses of their comrades to die, to be chained to the center pole before the fires were lit.

I stood there the whole time and watched. I held you and he never took his eyes from you for an instant. He had not lost hope at all; he died looking at all his hope and all his life and all the desires he ever had.

And the only lover I ever had turned to ash before my eyes. I was barely seventeen as well, with a child to raise and an enemy who wanted only to enjoy bringing me down. I was seventeen and I made a few mistakes along the way. I admit that. But now you are here and now we can start over, and with what you have become and what I have learned, we will be invincible.

Anselm Reflects Upon the End of the Recording:

My father had known I existed.

The world turned upside down. I said the words aloud. "My father knew that I existed." I heard my own voice speak them but there was something unreal about the sound, as if they were distant and rehearsed. The statement did not sound real.

"Yes, he knew," Della said through the speaker in my helmet, outside my head instead of inside my mind. "He knew, and because you existed he did not fight. He didn't ask me to fight for him, either. He understood that I had to fight for you first. It was my duty as a mother. And it was his duty as a father; that was more important than any political agenda he had."

Mother, mother. When will you learn that your little rationalizations are transparent? It was never me you fought for. It was you, always yourself alone. If you ever thought of me, it was only as an extension of you.

But I couldn't say that to her, no matter how true it is. Because Della has her own lopsided version of the truth and she can't be convinced that it does not agree with objective reality.

Della's reasons for what she has done don't matter. What matters is that she does remember things that other people wouldn't know about. And it is very possible that she is telling the truth and that my father knew I existed. Which meant that he died for me. Not for the people of Babelion, not for humanity, not for ideals and causes and ardor. It would mean that he had died for the very oldest reason there was.

That warmed me and horrified me at the same time. That I had caused Arsen's death was chilling. But that he had loved me enough even then, that he kept silent rather than speak out, that made my eyes fill with tears.

I recall crying one time in my life, for Sulma. I cried again for Arsen, and this proved that I was never Changed. The Changed don't cry. I was sure that Della would have been humiliated had she known.

He knew I lived and it had mattered to him.

Emotions I could not afford flooded me and warred with each other. There was no time, no space, to think about who I was or why I was. Nearly an hour had passed while I'd pursued my mother's memoirs, an hour of killing cold for the Changed who waited to be taken to safety. An hour when Sithra might appear and do—anything. Or the Pretender's ships could be overhead and already have forced a surrender.

I shouldn't have lost this hour, I realized. Arsen wouldn't have. The past was over and done and there is nothing I could do to change it now. All I can change is the present, which is very vulnerable to pressure right now.

All I can change is the present. Della can only tell her own version of the past anyway. She sees everything askew with Della always in the center of the world. And she's not above editing her own past to try to—influence—me.

Besides, Della could be lying.

Chapter Ten

I never imagined that I could screw up that badly. I'd worked with the genotype all my professional life and I thought I knew that it could do. I had written two monographs on it but I still hadn't realized the power of moral deterrence. I had no idea that any of that genotype growing up without it would produce a monster.

I also hadn't known that the Changed of Maya didn't have a code of noblesse oblige or a strict set of standards of behavior, for all their protestations of aristocracy. But then, I didn't know that they were no true aristocracy, either, for all the airs they give themselves. They were only the mad slaves of a demented machine in an illusion they created for themselves. Maya indeed.

But I didn't really have any choice, either. We were running scared and the Pretender had already killed the reigning Empress and her Successor. One of the younger girls had to be crowned immediately, not yet trained or ready for the job, not even old enough to command the loyalty of the old lady's followers.

That's why we lost so many to the Pretender then. A child on the throne is always trouble. With the Pretender threatening, it was the end of everything.

I don't know why I cared. Back in those days, yes, I'd been appointed to the Flower Court, but it was a research rotation. There was good reason to have a full staff of genetic Tinkers with the best research facilities the Empress could provide. We guaranteed her cloned survival and the survival of her genotype, and we also guaranteed the health and longevity of her people, which made her popular.

In return, we got to do whatever we wanted with more financial backing than any science has seen since the fabled days of the first steps into space. Money for anything, however outrageous, flowed freely. Equipment, graduate student salaries, boondoggle conferences, the works—all of them guaranteed to those of us fortunate enough to be recruited by the Imperial Genetics Laboratories, commonly known as Tinkers. Because we do tinker with the workings of the Imperial genotype, twitch things around, play here and there and create change. Healthful and beneficial changes, we hope, not only for the Empress but through her for all those in the Empire's sphere.

We know better than our predecessors and we aren't trying to play gods. We were just trying to improve health, make certain that we could save as much on general care as we spent in travel allowances, and of course ensure the Empress's reign forever. Which is why we all knew about Maya, though no one had ever been there.

The people of Maya had been Tinkered before the ban on speciation was passed. Now it is a universal taboo, along with cloning sentients—except the Empress. Even bio Als are proud of their unique genetic heritage and twins are rare. But Maya is an anomaly that no one but the Tinkers care much about because it is a useless backwater, on an unpleasant volcanic rock, where the people are hopelessly provincial and absurdly narrow-minded. Their rishis would say that it was the justice of my karma that I would have to live here for so long.

Maya isn't even listed in the Catalogue of the Reign. Those of us who have reason to study what happens when people are genetically speciated know the coordinates and will access the Maya Exchange. That had never been my area and I had only marginal interest, which means that I wasn't aware of some of the subtle cultural shifts that had occurred during the occupation.

But there had been no time to think, then. Tais Dondow, a lab tech who'd only been with us for a year, grabbed me in the hallway of the Official Residence. "Get the hell out of here, Suu," he said. "We've got a transport leaving in an hour back to Cahari and you want to be on it. Lhanni is dead."

I swallowed hard. Lhanni was the head of our project. If he were dead we were all in danger. All we had to do was just get the hell out.

The whole Imperial Compound was in a frenzy. No one knew

who was on which side, or had been on any side, or if it even mattered. Panicked courtiers gestured with weapons they couldn't use, scientists ran for the private lift pads, and servants ran through the courtyards wailing. There was no order, no reason, and the dead were everywhere, left lying where they had fallen.

I knelt down and checked each one in case someone had been left alive. I went from one to the next, invisible in the hysteria. A squad of soldiers in the red of the Pretender ran in formation through the kitchens while one of the cooks dove into a sink. A kitchen helper raised a huge knife and screamed, running after them. One of the soldiers calmly turned and shot him down without warning.

It was not real. I couldn't deal with the idea that it was real and so I pretended that it was all a bad dream, a strange excerpt of horror out of the night.

I saw Tais cross the corridor. "Get to the transport now," he hissed. "We're gone as soon as we've got a load."

"But the lab data . . . ," I protested.

"But your life," he said.

The lab data was my life. It would take only a second to make a copy. Who knew what havoc the Pretender would play with our data systems? Whole areas of research could be wiped clean. So I ran back to the lab and began calling up copies as quickly as I could. We had the best equipment available—my copies were small enough that I could stuff the records of three working years in my underwear.

Then I went to release the experimental animals. All the animals were kept on the fourth floor in large cages, and I was worried that some of the diseased dogs and chimps would bite and infect me. But I couldn't leave them all to the exigencies of politics, which cared not at all if they were there, and if they all starved to death while people battled outside.

In the last live lab I visited, there was a locked office I had never entered. Lhanni's office. I didn't hesitate this time, but used an acid to eat through the lock. No one would care now. I wanted Lhanni's data, now that Lhanni was dead. Only a minute, I told myself, only a minute and then I would be gone. There was time to get off-world, to some dump where no one cared who was on the Flower Throne, and there was time to save Lhanni's experiments, too. There had to be.

As the data copied, I checked Lhanni's lab setup, and there I found the whole tray of them. Human embryos, frozen in stasis and sure to be a moral pit when it was ever revealed. The tray had been neatly labeled with the code used all over the Royal Labs. It was the code of the Imperial Genotype.

I don't know why I took them. They were small and light and they were human in some degree. That alone I knew from the tags. And I took them, I think, because I knew that it would destroy Lhanni's reputation now that he was dead, and they would all be destroyed.

I had seen enough dying for one day. I wanted to make sure something lived. It was the only political act of my life.

Then I ran. I ran all the way to the lift pad and there wasn't any kind of ship at all. I stood in the middle of the circle that marked the landing zone, stood there in shocked wonder that they had left without me. Three bodies lay on the white composition pavement, their blood cooking on the smooth sealed surface.

I had to get away. Anything would do, any chance was worth it.

Then I spotted the wagons.

They were used by the Flower Court Circus, all of them painted up like toys and shaped like cages and boxes out of antiquity. But they would fly, that I knew. They were one of the Young Empress's favorite things and she even had had her own special wagon that she had ridden while the circus played far away.

The Young Empress's wagon was open and perfectly intact. I flung myself into the velvet-padded pilot's chair and began the start sequence, which was unutterably slow. *Faster, faster,* I thought at the machine, but it ignored my desperation and continued to work at the speed for which it had been designed.

The launch was slower than I had ever experienced, and it was nearly a full hour until I made orbit. I sweated every moment, wishing insanely that I had taken a scooter or fly-by instead. Every minute seemed like a million and all I wanted to do was get free.

And yet, I think that circus wagon saved me. When I hit high orbit the periphery was full of debris. Two battle cruisers stood on guard, one of them the *Chrysanthemum*, the flagship of the Empress's fleet. I turned on the com to call for aid, to tell them what I had with me in the tray. Only before I could say anything I heard the conversation they were having with the Pretender's cruiser, the *Thistle*.

"We're with you, *Thistle*," I heard someone say. "There's already too much lost, we can't afford another baby Empress. Not again. And this time there isn't even a decent Regent around. No, we're with you. We haven't got any other choice."

I cut the channel. It was a fair argument, one that I had heard before. Only before we'd had the Old Empress and her Heir, young but fully grown and trained. But without a decent Regent around—that means that any of the other possibles had been killed in the attack on the Palace.

"No more Empresses around," *Thistle* agreed. "They're all accounted for. And remember, Anselm is related to the First Empress by blood, has been raised and trained to power, and is an adult who can be trusted. You know what he has done in his own regions."

"Yes, we know," the voice that replied did not sound pleased. "But we don't have a Regent and the next Empress is three years old. It's better to join you than to continue this fight. The only thing we'd accomplish is to kill even more loyal subjects."

I turned off the com and let the wagon take its slow way on automatic. Perhaps they wouldn't shoot, not now that they'd decided. Maybe they would just let us be.

Pieces of hulls of pleasure craft and workaday transports drifted by. One large shard had bits of writing I could read—it was the *Crick*. The transport I should have left on, the one owned by the Royal Labs, had been shot down for being so fast. All my friends, the colleagues of the past three years, had been there. And now they were dead.

I began to cry. Lost, abandoned and alone, I knew that there was no place for me to go. No place was safe, and there was no one who would help me.

Me and them. The tray was in the wagon freeze, but that wasn't cryograde, merely a food keeping system. They would probably not survive the ride either—I had given up all hope.

They were the last Empresses, those tiny frozen samples I had taken from the lab. Maybe they were experiments on the geno-type. Maybe they were unfit. But if what I had overheard was true, they were the only Empresses left.

Then I saw the embroidered coronation mantle of the Em-presses of the Flower Thrones draped among the bedclothes. The Young Empress would have had the right to take it with her, and it did fit into the circus motif. Seeing it tossed aside in a pile of blankets did not make it look less imposing. I took it up and felt the soft, fluid velvet run though my fingers. Stars and moons were embroidered on it with platinum and pearls. I do not recall wind-ing it around my shoulders the way it is draped on the Empress at her Coronation. I only know that it was warm and smelled like flowers and that it gave me some vague comfort.

Though probably that comfort had something to do with the fact that without the mantle the Pretender could never be prop-erly crowned. He would never be the legitimate Emperor. It wasn't much revenge, but it was all the payback I could manage for my friends, my colleagues and my entire way of life.

In the end, I do not recall choosing Maya. I think it came to mind as a hidden place, somewhere no one would ever look. Maya didn't even exist so far as the records of the Flower Thrones went—only those in the discipline knew that it was more than a legend from the time before the Sanctions.

There were a lot of legends left of Created monsters and kill-ers, of lost colonies of mutants and burial blocks of failures. No one believed them. Everyone knew that it was all exaggeration, that no group like the Creators had ever really tinkered so deeply with the genetic code of sentients that they were no longer rec-ognizable.

Only those of us who'd followed in their tradition ever learned that it was the legends that were carefully diluted and covered over. The reality had been far more frightening than we ever wanted to know. There were indeed burial crypts full of frozen monsters and snippets of altered DNA. There were living brains that had been subject to developmental experimentation. There had been the killers—different modes for executioners, assassins and soldiers, along with the more benign models. Worker drones, pleasure slaves, the diseased research subjects, the patented nannies and drivers, the agrarian labor force, the miniatures made to work in small spaces and the micros who were even smaller than the minis. There were species made to live only a few years, to do a task and then die out, and there were those who were made to live very long lives with limited maturation and low emotional drives. Every kind of distortion and misery that could be created out of our ancestors' flesh had been expounded upon and refined.

The Creators of that era had no Code of Krishna to keep them in check. Only after seeing what abomination had been made of thinking lives could we Tinkers truly appreciate the strictures of the Code. It is not that we have less curiosity or less need than the Creators in their heyday—simply that we have returned to a more profound regard for life.

The legends also speak as if no traces of this vast program of genetic manipulation still exist. They were unsuccessful adaptations and they all died out, or so the propaganda goes. In fact, there is not one of us living in the Empire today who does not have a few tinkered genes. And there are still whole communities of these altered peoples hidden, living on, in some sense continuing the experiments that their Creators began.

Maya was such a place. It had never been intended as a colony world. The climate is too harsh, the volcanic activity too violent and unpredictable, for a registered human settlement. But then, it was never an authorized colony. The experimental groupings that came out of the LondonDelhi Duplicate Labs were meant to be hauled off-world and die. They were deemed too extreme, too unstable, even for a society full of prototype people. And so they were loaded onto a colony ship that was meant to drift forever until its cargo had died.

Instead, they found a planet where they could barely survive. No charter was ever issued, but they were allowed to remain because the Creators insisted that the environment would kill them off in a matter of years. Studying the data on the general weather patterns, the original office of colonization agreed. Later that document was expunged from the files of every official agency. The only reason Tinkers today know it existed at all was because Chindahartra Palishini recorded all the particulars in her lab notes.

I knew it existed; I even had some vague ideas as to where it was. And I knew that I could run away from the destruction I had left behind. I would be safe there, and maybe somehow I could lose myself in this abandoned project and forget what I had seen. Where I could create a new identity for myself and not have to live with my thoughts and fears and memories.

And so I created Suu-Suu Agypur. It was so easy, almost too easy. After the first few years I went back, carefully, and found a few others who'd escaped the destruction of the Royal Labs. I returned to my old department and recruited one of the advanced graduate students.

Bit by bit I created the Tinkers in Maya, so we can monitor the experiment that was abandoned. More, so that we could monitor what I'd done myself. I did not pay enough attention in the beginning, I'm afraid, and I am not a sociologist. I do not have the expertise in that area; had I understood the implications I might not have made the same mistakes. Only I didn't have Chelo in the first years, or Carlos Santomarigda. Though how a personage of Santomarigda's stature sought shelter in my project . . . but that is something completely different. If he had been there in the earliest days I am sure we wouldn't be facing the crisis we have now. But he was hiding out in a cave somewhere on Teklos, his chair taken and his articles erased from every respectable public academic database.

He came to me along with his graduate student Chelo, who turned to crism to escape thinking about his home city obliterated by the Pretender's fleet. We're a strange band of exiles, trying to maintain our Academy in Snows.

I should have seen through it. Della was already too old when she came to us, and I didn't know that these people had created neural sculpture as an entire discipline. We are already working on bringing in one or two of these specialists, to bring them back to the research facilities that will be open again one day.

And that is where I screwed up most of all. Not only for me, and for Della, and for Chelo's hometown and a million like it—

but for the entire Empire of Flowers, for all the humans under this single aegis of our descent.

It is very hard for me to live with this knowledge. I try not to leave Maya, not to face the evidence of what my impulsiveness has done. We leave as little as we can. Still, even in the freezing nights of Maya lit by the glow of the volcanic ridges and ensorcelled by the mists of steam from the Great Steam Lake, I cannot escape.

Three of the embryos died. There is only one left, and she is not fit to be Empress. Maya did that, and it was my call and my responsibility. But Della is the only Empress left. If she is not fit to return to the throne, then it by right belongs to her son.

Book Two

ANSELM'S STORY

Chapter Eleven

From the front window of this wagon I can see the lights of Babelion. It's not the brilliant blaze of every other night before, of the nights I remember wandering her streets and seeking enlightenment in her Temples. The blinding glare in the night is gone, and all that are left are the fires.

Strangely, the fires illuminate the Dome on the Mountain better, probably because they reflect off its smooth surface. From this angle I could believe that it is still whole, still warm and controlled inside. I could make myself think that the oranges are still blooming and their scent permeates the air of Xanadu.

The Tinker wagon is warm and someone is curled under the heavy comforter, asleep and waiting for me, but I can't sleep. Auntie Suu-Suu suggested that I record my memories and thoughts because one day the official version of this day will be more substantial than the reality of it, just as the popular version of my life so far has threatened to consume any of my own recollections. So I am making this record of events of the past two years, to have my own unadorned version of the story.

Maybe I'm too young to be writing memoirs—but I'm older than my father was when he died. And that's old enough.

My life as it is started when I left the Mountain when I was sixteen. Popular story has it that my mother was a woman in the Village who met my father when he came up to test. Like most of the popular version, that's partly true and partly a lie. Yes, my father met my mother when he came from Babelion to test for the Exchange. But she was no human in the Village; she was Changed and highly political. I knew I was her son, but I had no idea that I was half human until I had come of age.

My true life started when my mother, Della, entered the Exchange permanently. There was a brief ceremony when she entered coma. I wore white, that most solemn of colors, and the shawl my mother had given me had been draped carefully over one shoulder as she requested. It was the last thing I ever did as she asked.

I had spent most of my childhood with my neural sculptor's circle and their children, which was why I was able to pass as having been brought up entirely human. Tela's circle was lovely, warm and accepting. They played games with me in the evenings and took me on long walks around the pond and taught me to swim. Ian Aja snuck me sips of beer when I sat with him on the summer porch while he played chess with his friends. They played chess and discussed the politics of Babelion, and sometimes Sithra and Xanadu; but they were much more concerned with those things that affected the Village where they lived and their garden and how well Alice had done on her exams.

I spent too much time in the Village among the humans there, rather than on the Mountain among the Changed. Most of my cohort spent much of their free time in the Exchange, polishing their skills or trying to impress. As if they could impress an AI.

But the Village was also human, the enclave of those who were in upper support positions for the Changed and were too good for Babelion. The Guardians and neural sculptors and the medics lived here. There were one or two architects, a smattering of caterers and gardeners and a number of maintenance techs as well.

Unlike Babelion, the Village was neat and organized and well-run. The houses were clean and there was only one shrine, and that unobtrusive. Some of the Changed pointed to the enclave as proof that humans could be useful, beneficial and contributing members of Maya's life. Others said that these were the best of the humans, culled for generations and nurtured by the Changed.

I thought all that argument was ridiculous. I spent my time with the circle, playing human child games, running and throwing and sometimes learning to sing.

Most of my fond memories of my first sixteen years are of them, of the modest house with the big porch that overlooked the soft rolling hills that my father had marched up seeking justice. And since they were human, the things that were important to them were never the same as the things my mother cared about.

Della was mostly concerned with my position in the Exchange and my grades and how popular I was in class. The popularity, she explained, was about developing leadership and charisma. I should have charisma, she insisted. It was just one more gene and

I should have inherited it. After all, I had it on both sides. . . .

When I had been much younger, I lay in my room at night and wondered about my father. Sometimes I wondered if I even had one, or whether I really was produced parthenogenically as some of my classmates claimed. I had tried to ask my mother about him, but Della wouldn't have given me a straight answer even if she could. There were times I thought of walking in to the MedCenter and demanding genetic testing on my own, just to find out the truth.

My mother was livid when I told her that. "You are never, never, to go near that place," she said, holding my arm so tightly with one hand that her fingers left bruises. With the other she slapped me across the face. It was one of the three times she ever used physical force on me. "That will make you remember?" she asked, and she sighed. She couldn't have been more than twenty-three or twenty-four herself at the time, and now I realize how immature she must have been. Even if she were more capable than anyone I've ever met on the Mountain, she was young and afraid and there were times I felt almost sorry for her.

Almost, but never entirely. She has grown older without wisdom, without ever seeing that her Flower Empire is just one more tiny speck in the whole of history. She has no reason to desire conquest except that the possibility for it exists.

For myself, though—well, I am sure that it appears that I'm still playing Conquest, too. I'm sure that in Babelion and on the Mountain as well they'll think I've already won and that there's no reason to care about what's beyond our own home world. They don't know about the Empresses and the Pretender, nor why the transformer blew. Now the Changed are dying in the cold and the Exchange is crippled, and without the Dome we're going to be in trouble.

I'm not certain, though, that in the deepest part of my soul I'm fighting for our survival. In the early mornings when I do the Salute to the Day I have to face the reflections in the water. And the reflections tell me that I want revenge for all the dead who haunt me, Sulma and Iolo and Tela and my father, all those who have given me life.

And my mother. Della is already among the dead, although she doesn't recognize herself as such. She has not let herself go on to a new life. She continues to cling to the Exchange, to me, to this piece of too-hot and too-cold rock. But, then, Della always was stubborn.

The coma ceremony is very short. After all, we are trying to pretend that it is nothing like death, and so there is no need for comfort. My mother had given me the blue velvet shawl that morning, and the ritual she made of handing it over to me was as elaborate as the one where she took her leave in the body for the last time.

"This is the most important thing I can give you," she had said when she draped it on me. "It will be useful when you need to call Auntie Suu-Suu and the Tinkers to aid us. Because I am not dying, and some day you and I are going to live out our karma. There is a great destiny out there—there must be. Because Auntie told me what to name you, and there must be a place where that name means something. And this shawl means something, too. We might not understand it all yet, but I have no doubt that it belongs to the future that is calling."

She had said it as solemnly as if it were part of the ceremony itself, which had included a light buffet. After the food was served, those who were leaving distributed their goods to those they had invited. My mother gave most of her clothes to her mother and a few of her friends. She gave her records to Xanadu and her tableware to Tela. Her deeds and financial papers she kept in the Exchange, where she could look after her growing wealth for as long as she desired, using the deeds and ownership, the liens and promissory notes to establish her links of power in the physical world.

Things were handed over and good-byes were said. The three adults who were joining the Exchange for the final time smiled, waved, and walked down a corridor. The door closed behind them and I never saw my mother again, not in her flesh, not to hug or cry or do any of the things children need their mothers to do.

Not that I had ever had much comfort from her presence, nor did I have long to notice her absence. Within two days of my mother's departure, Sithra descended. The ancient power-monger was so old that her age had begun to show by then and I had truly thought she was about to die. Anyone on the Mountain who had silver threads mixed in their hair or who had the touches of crow's-feet in the corners of their eyes was going to die at any moment, I had thought. I often wondered why Sithra hadn't dropped dead sooner.

But she came, silvered hair and all, to my little house early before I had to report in to the Exchange. I was stunned to see Sithra at my door, and with four Guardians at her back. Someone of Sithra's rank could simply summon me to some place of her convenience at the time of her choosing. There was no need to come for me, and certainly none for the guard. That tipped me off to her duplicity when her proposal was perfectly reasonable, and one I had been considering on my own in any case. So even though the idea did intrigue me, I knew that I had to refuse whatever Sithra would request. Because even if I couldn't see the harm in it, Sithra could—and Sithra was certainly capable of using it.

And to make it more absurd, Sithra was the very first person to come and visit me in my own little house. I was glad that the public room was picked up and that I had coffee ready on the bar. I'd made it for myself, only double what I wanted because that was the way the measure was made for the pot, and it was the way I'd done it every morning at Tela's for Vijay and me.

Her presence ruined the pleasant order that I had created. The house was only two rooms and a bath, with breakfast bar down the side of the larger room, but I loved it. I'd hung the walls with patterned fabric in bright blues and greens and Vijay's sister had made matching pillows that were thrown against the walls. It was very cheerful and inviting. I had a crisp white cloth over the breakfast bar to hide the old scars, and I'd painted the stools to match the hangings.

It didn't resemble the house that Martin Four-Mem had abandoned when he'd been called into the Authority in Xanadu. It had been vacant for two years when the Exchange assigned me the property and I was very proud of it. Even if the breakfast bar had been badly burned with a pattern of rings (which could have been deliberate or could have been the result of a bad coffeemaker, I couldn't tell which) and there was still the lingering smell of abandonment, it was beautiful. When I moved in I thought that even if one of the larger original stone houses in the Dome became available, I wouldn't bid on it. My house was perfect.

Except for Sithra perched on the stool with the turquoise legs and the dark green rungs and bright blue seat.

"Della had her rights, of course, since no one ever did come forward to claim paternity and bring a case," Sithra said after putting her coffee mug on the white tablecloth. "If there had been a counterclaim we would have done the tests long before, and in any case most people have their genetic records filed at birth anyway. But now that Della's gone, your father's family has some rights to know you. There aren't that many children on the Mountain, and it would mean something to them to know that their genetic heritage lived on. Besides, that would give you someone to help you, to look after your interests, with Della gone. You may be a full adult in the Exchange, but even still I'm sure you could use some guidance and help every now and again." She picked up the mug, looked into its murky dregs, and put it down again untouched. "Making proper coffee, for one thing."

It took all the discipline I never had not to burst out laughing right there. "I like my coffee," I told her. "And I doubt my father or his family care all that much about their genetic heritage living on, since they've never mentioned any interest in claiming me. No, Sithra, I don't think it's a good idea."

She dropped her voice to nearly a whisper that carried far better than her speaking tones had before, and her voice made her sound as if she really did mean to be reasonable. "Naturally, if there is a good reason not to release the information, if perhaps your father is dead or hurt Della or something, naturally we'll tell you but won't make any public announcement. And likewise, if you are a parthenogenic creation we will not make the news common knowledge. That was the rumor when you were born, you know. After all, Della had wanted to hide something and if this is what she was hiding, we can continue to respect her wishes in the case."

"Why can't we simply respect her wishes in any case?" I asked carefully. "It isn't like she's dead. We could even consult with her."

Sithra shook her head and tried to look like she wasn't gloating. "It will be a few weeks until her consciousness makes the full transition. And those who have chosen to spend their full time in the Exchange, they often become a bit—distanced—from the kinds of concerns we have when we don't have that luxury."

"If it's so great, why didn't you go full-time?" I asked.

Sithra looked up at me sharply. I will never forget the recognition in those ice-water eyes. She saw straight through my innocent act, saw right down to my father's features and the future she had planned. Worse yet, she saw that she hadn't covered up well enough, that I knew what she was doing and why. Worst of all, it pleased her. She relished the glimpse of my sixteen-year-old brain trying to understand that I had a very serious enemy who was powerful and important, who was going to destroy me no matter what I did.

In the moment she savored her rewards, I became a man. Not a very good man, and not a strong one. She knew who my father had been, and in her gloating victory, I knew it as well.

I'm not ashamed to admit to having known fear. I always remind the kids, the elders, everyone in Babelion that being fearless is stupid. And it has nothing to do with being brave. Courage is standing up, not to the enemy, but to your own trepidation. When you can stand up to the absolute knowledge that you are not only going to die, but you're going to hurt and scream and maybe wet your pants, then you have courage. Anything else is a joke.

So I'm clear there. I've joked with the soldiers all night about who was scared worst when. Only I never told anyone that the most terrified I've ever been was that morning facing Sithra over coffee. Because I was only sixteen and all alone, and she had just beaten the most powerful single force of nature I had ever seen— my mother. Sithra ruled the Mountain hiding in the shadows and playing the loyal adviser. And there she was drinking coffee at my breakfast bar, acting as if she were the best friend I had.

"Sorry, Sithra," I said, trying to keep up the pretense that I was, in fact, sorry. "But I've got a real heavy schedule today, and the Exchange has got me on call double time since Mother left. Could you excuse me? Maybe some other time . . ."

Sithra sighed and shook her head. "I tried to make this easy. Remember that."

I was already halfway to the window before she called to the Guardians who had been hiding outside, and out the window before they were through the door. The other two went around the corner looking for me, but they were just a little too late. I'd played enough at close combat with Vijay to know that I couldn't outrun them if I remained in the Dome. But I could confuse them, and I knew from long experience playing in the Village that people rarely look up. I'd climbed from the window onto the low sloping roof of the house. It wasn't hard with all the wisteria twining up the wall.

The wisteria provided me with cover, too, with its twisting stems the size of tree trunks and leaves that made a massive green screen. I clung to the roof and wormed my way under the vine—I had barely come to my full height at that time and was still painfully thin, even for one of the Changed, so I could squirm into places an adult would never fit.

"He's got to be around here somewhere," one of the Guardians said, looking out across the neatly manicured Domespace.

"There's nowhere for him to hide," the other one agreed. "Except inside."

I waited. Vijay would have gone to the opposite side of the roof, jumped, and started to run. But the Guardians had access to my com, and they could call up others as long as I was inside the Dome. So I stayed in the wisteria until I thought it would use me as a substitute for the trellis that it had climbed once but which had since rotted out from under.

They did look in the vine; they weren't stupid. But it's dense, so they poked with their power sticks and gave up. "It's too thick for anyone to be in there," said the one who had decided that there was no place to hide.

They went inside. Sithra came out and circled the house, looking outward—looking for me running or a place I could be concealed. She never saw me right overhead.

"He's gone," she said, and shrugged.

"He'll come back," one of the Guardians assured her. "He can't survive outside the Dome, and he'll need to eat. We'll get him in the next day or two. All we have to do is be patient."

Sithra shook her head. "I don't know," she said. "Maybe not with this one."

Then she turned abruptly and walked away.

"We'll get him, I promise," the Guardian bellowed after her.

"It doesn't matter," Sithra said, never breaking stride. "He's gone. As long as he stays gone it's no matter to me."

I was horrified, aghast. I knew that her purpose was to somehow remove me from Changed society, but I had no idea that she wouldn't actually pursue me past the Dome. I had had a hundred thoughts of the Guardians invading Babelion as I crouched in the vine. Now I felt strangely disappointed. It had all been too easy.

Still, I waited until nightfall to make my way to Tela's house in the Village. The Village abuts the Dome and they are linked by the Painted Gate. It's the Painted Gate because it's the only gate to the Dome that is not tiled with high reliefs of animals and plants and abstract patterns remembered from a mythical Earth. Someone, probably human, had begun a mural on the interior of the gate, a realistic scene of building the many small houses that the Changed find so comfortable. Over the years it's been expanded so now it shows all kinds of labor and art among humans and has spread through both interior walls and out onto the Dome itself.

There the paintings of humans on the clear material give the impression that the Dome isn't there at all, that the Village flows seamlessly into the Mountain as part of a single unit. It's very eerie to see that illusion, to be both relieved by the fact that it isn't true and to be offended at the same time.

At that point I wasn't thinking about the philosophy of painting. I just wanted to get out, to get home. The lock on the Painted Gate is easy to pick—Vijay and I had done it many times just to prove that we could. And then I was past the immediate reach of the Guardians and made my way to Tela's house, to the place that I truly thought of as home.

Only this time I knocked instead of just walking in.

Sani, one of Tela's circle, opened the door. "Oh, it's you,

Anselm. Why didn't you just let yourself in? Or do I have to find Vijay for you and formally announce your arrival?"

He was the youngest of the circle, and had joined them when Vijay and I had been nine. I had been invited to the party and what I remembered most of the festivities was that both of us got sick on the vindaloo and threw up half the night. Sani had to spend some time looking after us, since he was now officially a member of the family. I don't think he's ever quite forgiven me for that.

"I'll go myself," I said, though it wasn't Vijay I needed to see right then. Oh, I needed to see him, and being in this place made it only too clear to me how much I'd missed his company. But there were things Tela knew and she was the only one who could help me. So I went past the vestibule, made a proper nod at the little shrine in the niche there and sprinkled some water on the blooming flower before the gilded statue, and went into the main room. Bharat, Nata and Alice hardly glanced up from their card game to greet me with polite murmurs. I found Tela in her own room, working on what appeared to be a partial neural net on the screen. I knocked again on the open door.

"Come in," she said without looking.

"Tela," I said as I stepped over the threshold.

"Anselm?" she asked as she whirled away from her work. Then she hugged me, hard, and wouldn't let me go. "I've missed you, Vijay's missed you so much," she said. "Why did you just leave like that? You didn't have to do that, it was cruel of you. We've all felt as if a member of our circle had died."

For a moment I felt guilty in Tela's arms. Then, gradually, as she let me breathe, I became focused again. "Tela, you know that I had to distance myself for Vijay's sake as well as my own."

She nodded. We all remembered the ugly rumors, the nastiness of his classmates in the Village. The abhorrence of a human-Changed relationship goes both ways, and just as deeply.

"And now? What brings you here?" she asked all in one breath.

"I need to know something," I started slowly. "I think you're the only person who can tell me, now that my mother's gone. And she wouldn't anyway. Tela, who was my father? Why would Sithra want to know, and to make it public?"

Tela withdrew from me and sat down at her desk chair. I took the carpet and leaned against the low bed, my arms around my knees as if protecting myself.

Tela's red hair curled softly around her face. Now I could see there were a few gray threads in the bright copper; I had always thought of Tela as younger than my mother though I knew it wasn't true. Vijay was Tela's son, and Tela had finished her apprenticeship and had been a member of a circle for two years before having a baby. She wasn't old, I had to remind myself. Humans showed their age much earlier than the Changed, that was all. There was no reason to worry that she was about to die.

"Why?" Tela asked. Then she waited and spoke again. "Be careful, Anselm. Do you really need to know? Our karma is our own, it is not something that we owe to parents—especially not to parents that we have never known. And among the Changed parenthood is not a great obligation in any case. Think very well of what it will benefit you to know, and how much you could lose."

I shook my head. "Sithra is after me," I said. "She tried to get me to go for genetic testing this morning. I stayed on the roof all day. I can't go back to the Dome, Tela. I think Sithra will kill me."

"No, Sithra won't kill you," Tela said, her words dripping venom. "She just wants you to believe she will."

"I need to know why she'd do that," I continued, ignoring her comment. "I need to know what she suspects and if it's true, and then I need to figure out what I'm going to do about it. Because Sithra seems to want to use me or destroy me—I don't know. I think she did something to my mother and I'm sure that if I don't disappear I'll be next."

Tela looked at me for a long time without speaking.

"You may be right," she finally said. "Normally I wouldn't encourage this kind of thinking, but I know a little of what Sithra's done in the past years and she is dangerous. And you are not likely to panic easily; I made certain of that when I burned in your headware. So I take it you are not exaggerating. Still, Anselm, you are not going to like the answer."

And then she proceeded to tell me about my mother, about Arsen, about his death—and about my own genetic scans, which she had done and my mother had destroyed inside the Exchange. It was their first and worst argument, and Della had won.

"At the time I thought she was being overly paranoid. Now I realize that she was right," Tela summed up. "There is nothing at all that proves that you are half-human, not in the Exchange, not anywhere. Della removed every trace of evidence. Sithra can't do anything to discredit you without some new proof.

"And while I expect her to try and start rumors, even Sithra knows that the truth is too outrageous to be believed. No one will really believe that you're a half-breed. No one will ever think that even Della would have a half-breed child.

"You could go back, Anselm. You could return and face Sithra down. She can't do a thing without more evidence, and without your cooperation she isn't going to get it."

Return and pretend that this all never happened. The idea was so tempting that I nearly jumped at it. But I also knew that while Tela is a brilliant sculptor and knows me better than anyone else in the world, she is also human. She doesn't really understand the politics of Xanadu, she isn't privy to all the alliances made and broken in the Exchange, and she isn't aware of Sithra's subtle manipulation and overwhelming power. Tela sees only the surface of the Mountain and says that it's fine, that nothing at all should happen.

But I knew Sithra. I know she can be trusted to be devious, cruel, and absolutely without concern for anyone but herself. She's predictable enough that I knew that there was no chance I would ever be safe on the Mountain again, not so long as she was alive. If I defied her or tried to bring pressure to bear against her, she would simply have one more reason to hate me.

I also knew very little about the politics of Xanadu, but what I did know made me distrust the authorities. And Sithra was one of them, which made the case clear right there.

I shook my head. "I still wouldn't have any life there, Tela."

I stood up and walked around the small room. There was a window and the shades were open. I faced the glass, where a light snow drifted down in the night. It was nothing real, nothing that would last—this was autumn snow, the promise of the time to come.

"Your father didn't have a circle," Tela said slowly. "But his brother does. I think they would accept you as the child of Arsen. We would have to do something, think of some explanation for the rest of your life. But that is an option."

I hadn't thought I could live in the heat and snows of Babelion. But if what Tela said was true, I might be able to adapt better than the Changed. I might need to wear warm clothes longer, but I could survive in a human environment.

If I wanted to.

In the window, all my choices seemed bleak. Neither the Mountain nor the Village held any hope for me. And Babelion—I would have to remake my self, my past, I would have to become wholly human to pass in Babelion. And what would I do there?

What was there to do there?

I knew nothing of Babelion, nothing of what it meant to live there, to grow up and grow old, to achieve some measure of success, to hold some modicum of pride. Babelion was an alien world to me. My mother had gone to a party there, had lived among the Tinkers for two years before she was my age. But I had been born and raised on the Mountain among the Changed and all I knew of humans was here in this house.

"I don't think you should make up your mind tonight," Tela said gently. "Think about it. Think about the parts of you that you don't know yet. Spend some time with Vijay—he has missed you terribly. And then, maybe in a few days, you'll be better able to judge."

I saw the wisdom in her advice. Tela always had been wise, always knew the right thing to say or do. I nodded and left her to her screen, to the new neural nets she was carefully creating by experience, just as she had created mine.

Chapter Twelve

Vijay was downstairs in what had been the children's room and was now Vijay's lair, full of computer and lab equipment, paints, music, and a thick layer of discarded clothing underfoot. Vijay didn't see me right away. He was sitting on the edge of his bed, his eyes glued to a gamebox with the back off it. He held a microweld and touched the box once delicately. Then he handed it back to the little girl, who thanked him with solemn grace. She was his youngest sister—Tela's circle had four children and I had always found it amazing how they all seemed to be pleased with each other's company. But when I lived there, I remembered how nice it was when Alice, the youngest, had trustingly put her hand in mine and asked me to take her across the street to her friend's house. Maybe there was something to be said for human crowding.

"Anselm." Vijay's face lit up with a smile like the eruption of the Londrin Ridge. He came over to me eagerly, his hands outspread, his eyes dancing.

Facing his joy, I felt suddenly ashamed and dirty. I pulled away from his effusive welcome, and his expression fell deep and hard. He stepped back. "Oh. I see."

"No." I couldn't let him think what I knew he thought. We had never said anything before, we never had had to. But it was one of the reasons I had withdrawn, why he had not sought me out. I was not my mother and I knew what was anathema.

Now I was.

It hit me all at once, in a single blow. Tela had managed to tell the story so that it was just that, a story. It was about people who were now gone and had only a nominal relationship to me. Now I understood only too cruelly what she had carefully not said.

I looked at my hand, studied the lines in the palm carefully. There was nothing there that I could see that was human, nothing that was not Changed. Vijay came and stood beside me, and his shadow altered the light. Now the flesh looked only human. There was nothing at all to show that I was a half-thing, a mule, a dead end. Nothing on my body marked me clearly as a freak. My hand looked grimy, true, from sitting in the wisteria all day, but it wasn't the honest dust and resin that made my brain crawl. It was the nature of the meat itself, something that was neither human nor Changed, something that should not exist. My skin felt like it oozed filth, like its very existence was putrid and repulsive. In that one moment, my own existence sickened me.

"It's just that . . ." I turned toward the wall. "Your mother told me who I am. What I am. I wish I were just Changed, at least then I would be something you could look at."

"I know what you are and I always have," Vijay said softly. "You are Anselm, who I played with when we were children, who made a mess painting my first volcanic model, who screwed up my data on my first lab analysis. You are the same person who is better than a brother to me, closer and more in my mind. No matter what you think you are now, that person is still the same. That person is the person I've missed so much."

"But, I'm not . . ." I couldn't say the words. I tried, but I couldn't get them off my tongue. My mind screamed them—*half-breed, abomination, mixed, mule, no-thing.*

"There are things that Tela didn't tell you," Vijay said softly. "Things that no one understands. You are not that thing that was written against in the early days. You are something else entirely."

I shook my head as if to shake away the hope. Vijay couldn't know, and certainly he couldn't offer to tell me something his mother wouldn't. Much as Vijay was part of me, the better part of my own self, he could not possibly know what he was saying.

H ave you thought about your uncle's circle in Babelion?" Tela asked as I sat in her kitchen annihilating the second bowl of warmed rice and raisins that she had put in front of me. It had never tasted so good before, hot and spicy, redolent of cinnamon and nutmeg and mint, a porridge so heavy that the raisins and almond bits never sank on their own. It was wonderful food, and the memory of Tela's hard conversation is always overshadowed by the taste of that breakfast. No matter how dire the situation was, there was a limit to how scared and miserable I could feel faced with such comforting food.

"You can't stay here much longer," she went on. "I heard from Medanu late last night that the Guardians are still searching for you, and since they couldn't find you in the Dome they'll come here next." She paused and thought for a moment before saying more.

"It appears that you know a lot more about what Sithra will do than I. It seems that she does want to kill you, or at least eliminate you quite permanently—but with good reason." She paused and studied my face. "You really don't know what it means, who you are to us, do you?"

I shook my head. "I know who my father is, if that's what you mean," I said after I'd swallowed and put down my spoon. "I'd suspected something like that even before you told me last night. It wasn't a big surprise."

She smiled sadly. "No, you might know what you are, but the who comes later. Maybe Sithra didn't mean to kill you at first, but only after she had realized the rest of the implications," Tela continued. "It makes more sense that way. To let a mule live— well, you're bound to be rejected, hated, die soon enough anyway. That wouldn't matter to her. But being your father's child, your father's only heir, that's another matter. That makes you dangerous."

I shrugged. I certainly couldn't imagine myself as any threat to Sithra, and certainly not because of a rebel human who'd been dead sixteen years. I'd heard a bit about what my father had done. Who hadn't? Some rebels in Babelion had come up and threatened the Changed. Someone in the mob shot at the Guardians, there was a fight, and the leaders were found and punished. It was just a morality tale, nothing to do with me, though I knew that my mother had been there. Most of my friends' parents had been there, I supposed. But mostly we were told about it to let us know just how bad the problem of Babelion was. One day we would have to solve it, we were told. We couldn't afford another rebellion; we couldn't afford to be overrun.

Babelion has the numbers. The Changed might be superior in every way, but there are fewer and fewer in every generation. There were only twelve in my cohort, and another dozen to test this year. There were only six children entering the training program last fall. It was always a problem, now it's a crisis.

The medtechs have studied the situation and they say there is no physical reason for it. The Changed are as fertile as ever, and we could certainly reproduce artificially. There has always been resistance to that—in fact, I find the notion makes my stomach clench for no good reason myself—that dates all the way back to the Creators themselves. There always has been some debate on where the ethical line should be drawn in the creation and manipulation of sentient beings, but this seemed to be one final hard and fast psychological barrier. The idea of children with no parents at all, with no heredity in the society, with no connection to the fabric of our world, is repugnant to all the varied species that grew out of human stock. At least all that I or anyone else on Maya knew.

The Changed simply are not interested in reproduction, it appears. They are said to be introverted and have extremely low libidos, which adds up to few opportunities outside the laboratory. But I think it has something to do with the Exchange. It has taken the place of every other partner and activity; it bears all the hallmarks of crism addiction—save the social stigma.

That was my sum knowledge of the situation. That there were too few of them in the end, while we lower orders in Babelion reproduced like lab animals. We had nothing better to do, the reasoning went. Or maybe we were doing it on purpose in order to overwhelm the Changed. Humans obviously didn't understand the economics of the situation and kept having children even when they clearly couldn't raise them all.

Now I have seen the other side and I know that none of the reasons I was taught among the Changed has any bearing whatsoever. No, it is not boredom or that humans are too stupid to be aware of their own economic problems and management. But human passion and desire runs high, out of control by Changed standards. The sexuality that is suppressed in the Changed genotype is in full flower in Babelion.

Subconsciously, I suppose, I had understood that human circles were bound by sexuality as much as by economics. It was never stated, at least not on the Mountain, but I had spent so much time with Tela that I could pick up the subtle cues. And much later, sometime late last spring, Vijay said something about it being unfair that I could not become part of his circle. That was when I realized that I had to leave my human ties or I was in danger of being seduced by their whole way of life.

So humans frequently do become pregnant. I learned that they do use birth control, but children are wanted and loved by families, are sometimes the best and happiest part of life. There can be little enough genuine joy in the life we knew, and most often that's centered around the children. Because hope and the future are all the humans ever really have.

"No," Tela continued with her own train of thought and didn't explain anything to me at all. "I don't know how Sithra could have realized it without an informant."

"Realized what?" I demanded. "Tela, you don't usually talk without coming to the point."

"The problem is," Tela went on, "I don't know how to explain you. It's one thing for you to be Arsen's long-lost progeny. It's another for you to realize what this could mean in Babelion. There are people who would be ready to follow you, today, if you arrived. Your father wasn't just a rebel leader, an historical figure evoked in speeches, with flowers offered every year on the anniversary of his death. He's more like—like someone promoted to a demigod. As if he were another incarnation of one of the gods right here on Maya—I don't know. Krishna, maybe. Krishna took several human incarnations."

She took in my complete lack of comprehension and sighed. "Yes, I made certain that you know nothing of the gods, of the great stories, of the workings of karma. You don't even really know that you have a soul. But you will. Spirit burns in you, Anselm. And when you meet the gods you will meet yourself."

I shook my head to clear it. I understood the words individually. I knew what souls were, what karma meant. I even had heard of Krishna—Vijay had told me when I had begun to study the flute. But the words didn't fit together to mean anything in sentences the way Tela thought they did. They were each individual things that fell apart like a pile of sticks.

"There is something else I want to tell you," she said, staring at the darkened window. "I've never talked about it before. Well, there was no need to talk about it, everyone in my generation knew the same things. But I want you to know that what I've done, I've done for you. I want you to know that—that you are someone, too. On the Mountain you were Della's son. In Babelion you'll be Arsen's heir. There's no way around it, so you might as well make up your mind right now to use it to your best advantage. Remember that you are no more your father than you are your mother. You are unique. That there are things you can do and be that neither of your parents ever dreamed.

"But now I want to tell you about your father, so you can have some idea why he is worshipped among our people. You are going to have to face that, and accept if for yourself as well.

"I was there that day. I saw him die.

"He wasn't any older than you are now. We'd all heard about it, of course. But I was born and raised here in the Village; I didn't have the same anger that the city folk have, and I had a lot more fear. We grew up drilled with respect, you know. Our whole little society here is built around serving the Changed, the superior beings, and so being touched by superiority ourselves. The more valuable we are to the people of the Exchange, the more status we have in our own community.

"You have to understand that we look down on Babelion, and not just literally. We have better education here, nice homes, stable families. It's safe. In Babelion people are killed in the street. Humans from the Village don't go to Babelion, not to shop, not for fun. A few of the wildest teenagers will go down there, but the well-brought-up kids have plenty to do here. And I was well brought up."

I was confused and Tela could see that.

She looked at me sadly. "I told you that it wouldn't make any sense to you. And when I look at you, I still see you as Changed. I can't see Arsen in you at all, although if I try to remember clearly I know you look a lot like him." She shrugged. "You are what you are. You cannot hide from your karma, and I can't keep you from it either. I can only trust that if you can't understand now, you will understand someday. But there is something I will ask of you. One thing only, and it is important to me."

She turned to me and looked deep into my eyes. Her gaze was steady and sliced straight through to my heart. Or perhaps to the soul she wasn't sure I had. "Do not hurt my son. You have a power in you, Anselm, something that hovers over you like the finger of one of the gods. Vijay will do whatever you ask, will follow wherever you go. Leave him to find his own karma,

Anselm. Promise me this. You are dangerous to Sithra, but you are just as dangerous to us. Even more so, I think. You will dance us through fire to prove ourselves, as Sita did to prove her purity to Rama."

Vijay came in, took a bowl of the breakfast rice and two mugs of coffee, and gave us a very odd look. Tela and I were motionless until he left.

"Sita was half a goddess, Anselm, as your father was half a god," she continued.

"He didn't survive the flame," I reminded her softly.

It was a minute, maybe two, before she spoke again. "Oh, but he did. What was important about him survived the burning, survived his death. He is with us, and he is in you. You share whatever power it was that was in him, you share his favored position with one of the gods.

"Your father was half a god and he survives in the hearts and minds and memories of Babelion. And this memory makes you partly a god before you ever set foot on their dirt. You can burn and survive the flame.

"Vijay is human, Anselm. He is all, entirely, human. Flesh and DNA, blood and hope. He has no divinity to guard him, no promises of rebirth as a rishi or even the hope of no rebirth at all. He is no different than the rest of us, all made of clay.

"Let him live his human life. Do not draw him into that place where he becomes just one more sacrifice to the gods.

"Promise me this, and I will help you."

I listened to her and felt a lump grow in my throat. She was right: Vijay would become one more thing for the gods to take away. Gods are jealous and their love is cruel. She was right, and it hurt more than the look in her eyes. "Yes," I agreed, whispering because I could not say the word aloud. "But not for you, Tela, and not because you made me promise. I only promise for Vijay, for his life."

She blinked rapidly. "The reason isn't important," she said softly. But it was important. It was everything.

We sat in silence for minutes. In the house around us there were sounds of everyone else getting ready for the day. In the main room Sani couldn't find his shoes and Alice wanted someone to check an assignment before she handed it in. I wondered idly why Vijay hadn't done that over breakfast.

"I have to go," Tela finally said. "You can't stay in the house all day. I expect the Guardians to come looking here first. Go down to the library, or the playing field. There's some cover there.

"I don't know how anyone is going to believe this," Tela muttered mostly to herself. "Arsen was here only for the testing. I don't think he had the opportunity to enjoy himself with a local."

"Well, obviously he did at some time," I pointed out the obvious. "You know that he had to have something to do with my mother before I was born, not a few months afterwards."

She laughed for the first time, throwing her head back and honestly enjoying the humor of the possibilities. "Of course," she said when she could catch her breath. "Of course. But I'm going to have to be at the nursery in half an hour and I won't make it. Come back tonight around nine and we'll discuss the possibilities further."

I slipped out the door with her, but I didn't take the tram up to the Mountain. I had dressed heavily, with one of Vijay's long quilted vests over my light tunic and pants. It was still high summer and I was comfortable. As I stood opposite the tram station, half hidden in the brush, I saw a flash of reflective gray. Guardians. Tela was right, they were still looking for me.

I held my breath. It took all the discipline I had to stay rooted to the spot, to make no move to call attention to myself. They were still far enough to turn—*go to Tela's*, I thought at them.

I have never believed in psychic powers, but that one single time it worked. They turned. They left two guards at the tram and four went down the street in the direction from which I'd come. I was grateful that they were civilized enough to believe in eating a decent breakfast before getting on the road.

Keeping to the shadows, I walked very slowly toward the school. It was a good way away from anything else in the Village—except for the dormitories that were used once a year for testing time. Every year fewer and fewer hopefuls from Babelion came up as the cohorts of Changed became smaller.

"Anselm."

I whipped around at the sound of my name, whispered in a high voice. I couldn't locate the source.

"Anselm, over here," the voice insisted. I hesitated, and then saw a movement behind the steps up to a house. It was Alice.

"What are you doing out here?" I demanded, falling into the role of big brother as always. She was the closest thing to a younger sister I would ever have, and I found her affection moving. "You're supposed to be in class."

"Vijay is waiting for you," she said. "Over behind the shrine. He told me to tell you this morning but I forgot."

"No, you did very well," I whispered. "Now will you go to class?"

"I want to come with you," she said. "I already missed for the day, and we'll go by an Exchange booth and you can sign me into the MedCenter so it'll look like I was sick. Please."

There are times I have not realized that I was being manipulated, but never by an eight-year-old. "I can't do that. You have to go to school, and besides your mother's whole circle would kill me. To say nothing of Vijay."

Alice stood looking at me, her eyes full of innocence. "But Vijay's done it for me before. Just that he said you're better at that than he is."

"If I tell you no, will you go back to school?" I asked.

She smiled sweetly. "Sure. What else would I do?"

Some day Alice will make a great actress. Or liar. Or spy. But she wasn't there yet, and her efforts, though well-studied, were just a touch less than convincing.

"The Guardians are after me," I tried to explain. "If they see a young kid skipping school, it might attract their attention. They might come over and question me when they would have ignored me before, because they know that girls your age should be in school."

"I can be your lookout," she offered. "I'm small and I'm very good at hiding. I can walk behind you and look back so they can't see your face, and if they start to come I can warn you and go to them and cry and tell them that my brother is sick and I need them to call the Meds."

Maybe not an actress or a spy. Maybe a diplomat. Or a general. I had to acknowledge defeat.

"But only if Vijay agrees," I said, knowing full well that Vijay had as little defense against Alice's decisions as did I.

There is only one shrine in the village, dedicated to Krishna as the incarnation of Vishnu. There was a statue of him inside the stone structure that was life-sized, a handsome man playing a flute as he danced, all painted blue. The color blended into the shadows and the rest was half-obscured by smoke from the hundreds of joss sticks embedded in the sand tray just outside. Heaps of fresh flowers were piled under the god's feet and chains of them were hung around his neck until his face was almost covered.

Alice paused for a moment, made a gesture of respect and left an offering leaf with a tiny mound of the morning's cinnamon rice delicately arranged in the center. It was a lovely offering, as nice as any of the others that littered the steps to the inner shrine. We didn't mount the steps, though, but went around past the dancing girl who stood forlornly on her tattered square of carpet. It was still far too early in the day for her to be earning, but she probably had no place better to stay.

The sled was one of the very small ones and was wedged into something that was only half a space. Alice ran right up and Vijay popped the doors. I got in and Alice climbed onto my lap as if she were the Empress mounting the Flower Throne.

"Now to Babelion," Alice commanded.

Without a word, Vijay squeezed out of the non-space and brought the sled around so that it faced down the road. The only road, the one that my father had marched up with the mob at his back. The smooth, soft surface had been created for the runners, and the sled picked up speed as we went down the gentle slope of the hill. It was silent going down. Only in up mode did a sled need to use its engine. The way in to the city of humans was a long free slide.

"I made sure the Guardians didn't follow us," Alice said as I checked the rear mirrors, expecting to see an official vehicle at every turning.

Vijay shook his head. "Once Alice gets an idea, you can't get her to change her mind," he told me. As if I hadn't discovered that for myself already.

"Where are we going?" I asked Vijay.

"To the Temple," Alice said. "It's the Feast of the Devis. So we'll see them all dressed up with their hands and feet painted." She sighed.

"Alice plans to become a priestess when she grows up," Vijay said dryly.

"Why?" I asked. "She could be running all of Babelion by the time she's our age."

Vijay laughed, and Alice gave him a frown that silenced him. "The devis are not the kind of priestess I want to become," she said solemnly. "But their calling is sacred, and it is proper to honor them."

We sat in silence for the rest of the ride. I knew nothing about the kinds of priestess there were, or the calling of the devis either. All I knew of the faith of Babelion I'd learned from Vijay as he had disparaged what he called superstition and wasted wisdom.

"We spend so much time and energy on this religion, and there is no way to prove that there is any god at all, that karma exists, that even a soul exists," he had said to me the year before, when he had decided not to join his mother's circle at one of the god-festivals down in Babelion. "We spend so much time and thought and effort when we could be spending that all on ourselves, on making things better. On work, on building new housing, on class time in useful subjects when students could learn more neural sculpting, or bioengineering, or music. Rather than wasting all that time, all those years, learning this god cycle and that story, and which rituals and offerings are appropriate on which days and to whom. What a waste!"

I had agreed with him soundly, but a part of me was fascinated with the trappings of the rituals. The statues and the brightly dressed devotees and the waste of very expensive flowers tossed in the streets delighted my senses. There was incense and food and music, beautiful women and men dancing in frenzies on the outskirts of the crowd, their garments shredding from their bodies. There were stories about the gods with wonderful pictures, fantasies that far outshone anything I'd ever heard on the Mountain.

Above all, there was a kind of secret smile among the devotees. They knew something and it pleased them. They knew, above all, that they were immortal. They knew that they were forever on the Wheel of Rebirth, and that the Changed were no different, that we were all the same being past the flesh and the bone. We were all eternal, all divine, all endlessly simply fulfilling our own karma.

Tela never spoke of it, but sometimes when she made her respect to her home altar she had the same little smile. In those moments I envied her.

The devis of Babelion give the Blessings of the Goddesses in their most physical forms—they are the priestesses of the Tantra. There are Tantric priests as well, but this was not their feast. Later I learned that the men's feast is precisely opposite in the calendar year, the symbolism and the practice being the same.

As I said, I had only the most cursory acquaintance with the religion of Babelion. The only shrine I'd ever seen was in the Village, and the small home altar at Tela's. Now we went to the Temple Complex, which had been built into the summit of the hill just east of Babelion. When the human city had been small it had nestled into a protected edge of the valley that led down from the Mountain of the Changed and terminated in this deep, flat depression. This had been a giant caldera that erupted millions of years ago, and the sharp rounded hills that circled Babelion were the bubbles in the lava that had hardened. The sheer cliff face of the Mountain that faced down over Babelion was part of the remnant of the caldera walls, and the reason there was the rounded, sloping road bed was because of a single lava floe that was harder and cooled faster than the other igneous material around it.

But expensive geological research was not wasted on these dead remains when the Holy Smokes were in constant full-scale eruption, and the magma fields up in the high plains lit the night with their glowing activity. Besides, it seemed idiotic at first glance to think that any feature of Maya had been formed by a force other than the constant volcanic activity; we knew that the glaciers, while less immediately active than the volcanoes, were busily carving their own signature into the land mass being formed. We knew the long, curving road was not glacial in origin, but a few bright children suggested it every year.

There are several softly rounded hills to the south and east of the city. The cliff face cut Babelion off to the north, and to the west the gentle slope rose in a long sweep to the Village and the Mountain stronghold beyond. In recent years, the city had grown around the hills, making them more islands in the urban sprawl than borders that marked the edge of Babelion and the beginning of the lawless lands beyond.

Not that they were so lawless. They were mainly settled by farmers who grew cold crops outside, and a few who had small glass farms to produce the more elegant fruits and vegetables that graced the tables of the Changed. The glass farmers were required by contract to sell only to the Farm Office of Xanadu, and what was not used on the Mountain was rationed and distributed in the Village. But that was the price Xanadu exacted for the Dome technology, and there were always farmers willing to pay the price.

At least it was much cleaner outside the town than I had expected. The houses were neatly painted in the same sienna and dark green or dull gray, with traditional trims and manicured yards. There were few people on the street, but those I saw seemed respectable. They weren't wearing weapons or openly mutilating each other, they were just walking and greeting neighbors the way we did on the Mountain, or working in these very well tended lots or picking up baby toys that were scattered where they lay when dinner was announced. I was disappointed.

Still, even from before the beginning of the settlement of Maya, this hill had been the Temple district. The complex was built at the same time as the Exchange bunker and the power plant were erected. There was a long winding path up the hill, and about two-thirds of the way to the top the doors started. The doors were each different, framed with carvings of cavorting gods and demigods cut into the finely polished and veined volcanic rock. The colors changed with the composition of the stone—most commonly black, or black and clear in long striations, but there was red and white and green, too, and sometimes a very delicate strand of turquoise when a sculptor got lucky. The entire zone was an ongoing project, generations of artists carving out the pathways and portals.

After the series of doors there was a wall of carved stone that dripped stories from beyond antiquity. Sita danced forever in the fire to prove her purity and Kali danced in the fire to prove the power of her destruction. Shiva appeared in several guises, but it was the Lord Vishnu who was most celebrated by the generations of artists who had created the work. Indeed, it seemed less a wall than a giant mass of living art shouting over the generations *This is important, this is what will last.*

There was too much of it and all the figures hurt my eyes. They were so densely packed, so thickly entwined, that they appeared all to squirm together like a mass of snakes or worms over carrion. My stomach protested and threatened to heave.

Alice led us on, completely confident in her knowledge of the Temple geography.

Adding to the visual overload were the people, all dressed in their holiday best. Some of them wore the usual tunics and trousers, but for this occasion many of the women had donned saris or skirts and blouses topped with richly patterned veils. Many of the men wore head wraps far more ornate than I had ever imagined, pinned with fantastical feathers and jewelry and made of richly colored fabrics that shimmered in the near-noon light.

The crowd was packed solid—there was no way through. And yet, Alice managed to bring us up to the very front of the throng of devotees.

We were in a huge central plaza that appeared paved. Then I realized that it was the same polished natural stone that was veined red and white and clear and black like the carvings above. Only in the center of the open area it appeared pink and frothy with tila petals strewn all over the gleaming stone.

In single file, from the eldest to the youngest acolyte, the devis went from the porch of the Paravathi Temple to the smaller shrines of Ganesh and Hanuman and great dark door of the Temple of Death dedicated to Shiva and Kali and Durgha together, and finished their rounds at the Great Pillars. This was nothing but a staircase that led up to nowhere, to the very top of the hill. On the top was a small platform with statues of Vishnu and of Rama three times the size of the largest human and all covered in gold and flowers. Each of the devis lit an incense stick and left an offering on the platform, then bowed her head for a moment in prayer before returning inside the Paravathi Temple.

It was a thrilling display. The women were all beautiful and were clad in their most brilliant saris, all of them painted with gold and silver and sparkling with stones. There was singing and dancing and drumming as they made their circuit of devotion, music that seemed only annoying at first but became hypnotic over the course of the ceremony.

After the parade, circles brought young daughters who had been accepted by the Temple to be dedicated to the Blessing of the Goddess. Then food was brought out, trays of little balls of rice on tila petals, garnished with pale green pistachio flakes that looked like offerings. I took one and stared at it, uncertain whether it should be eaten or left on one of the many altars ringing the inner walls.

"You feed it to someone you care for," Alice informed us, and then folded the creamy pink petal around the rice in a neat packet and placed it in her brother's mouth. Vijay made a similar packet and fed it to me. I could not eat it, could not swallow. I'd made a promise to Tela and I was not about to break it on the same day. And yet . . .

What harm could an offering do? Especially from gods who don't exist to humans who don't believe?

And so I fed my little rice and flower package to Vijay as Alice smiled with true innocence for the first time that day.

The crowd began to break and move, most of them out of the Temple gates and back to Babelion, though many did stay to pray at the various holy places. We were only trying to find our way back to the sled when someone yelled, "Arsen. That's Arsen."

I turned, very slowly, not certain that I wanted to know who had used my father's name.

"He's too young to be Arsen," a woman replied. "And he only

looks like him. There are differences. Arsen's hair wasn't black, his shoulders were wider, this isn't him."

Still they stared and I stared back, studying them. There were two men, one of whom bore an uncanny resemblance to me. The woman wore the elegant ceremonial dress of a devi, her hair caught in jewels that hung over her forehead.

"Who are you, boy?" the man who didn't look like anyone asked me.

And suddenly I knew the whole story to tell, as if I had always known it, as if it were completely and perfectly true. Which, I understood later, it was.

"I am Anselm," I said simply. "My mother knew Arsen when he was on the Mountain to test for the Exchange. I was raised by her circle but she died only a few weeks ago, and until today I had never been in Babelion before."

"He could be lying," the man who had asked who I was before said flatly.

"No," the other one protested. "Look at him and look at me and tell me we don't share DNA."

A crowd had gathered around, and I knew they should make me feel uncomfortable. Instead, they made me feel powerful. I could see the faith in their eyes, fresh from their gods.

"If your father is Arsen, tell me where he's buried," the un-believer challenged me.

I shrugged. "He wasn't buried. He was burned outside the glass walls of Xanadu while the Changed looked on. His ashes were mixed with the two others who shared the pyre."

"That doesn't prove anything, everyone knows that," one of the onlookers scoffed.

Then a very old man in the plain wraps of a rishi stepped forward. "Think, boy," he said, staring into my eyes. "Go inside, to yourself, and follow what is there, and it will lead you to what they ask."

For some reason this made a kind of strange sense to me. It rode on the power I could feel gathering with the crowd. I closed my eyes and imagined my father, his face so much like mine (but with brown hair), his focus, his dedication, his passion for living as great as the sky. I felt him in me, in my blood, part of my bone, bringing me together with my fate.

The thread of fate was offered and I grabbed at it, and it pulled taut in my mind. I opened my eyes and did not see the multitude that had gathered. I saw only the past and the future, fused into a single pattern that was inevitable and unpredictable, always approaching the single unwavering point.

That point showed me where to go. I climbed the stairs of the pillars to the top. There, under the layers of flowers and candies and incense ash, was a small carved plaque. His ashes had been interred there, the demigod who had lived and died among them.

There was a mutter behind me and a snort of sheer incredulity from the one who had questioned. The rishi was just behind me. "One day you will learn that you need understanding more than you need strength. You need wisdom more than you need victory. Your story is already told and I have read it, Anselm of Maya. You are exceptional and your karma is writ large over the book of today. In the places of spirit, the future is no different from the past, and there is always and only now. Remember, you will come to me before you start out on your adventure. You will come to me before all. But you shall return in the end, as the snake sheds its skin, you will return. All things are one and are of one, and in the end all things return."

Chapter Thirteen

W hy didn't we know you?" asked the man who looked like me. "You're the son of my brother. I should know you."

"You're the son of Arsen," said a woman in the crowd. "We should all have known you."

I looked at the group gathered around me. Except for the three who'd started it all, they appeared to be ordinary people. Their tunics and trousers were gray and cream and blue, serviceable workclothes, clean for the holiday with the ghosts of stains showing through. Their faces were alike only in curiosity and in awe, in fervor and in faith.

The trust I saw in their eyes devoured me. All of them, together they owned me, utterly and completely. I could not disappoint them. I could not betray their dreams.

"I was raised by my mother. She met Arsen only while he was up to test on the Mountain. I don't think she ever told him," I started carefully. Somehow it was as if I had practiced and readied myself for this moment—the words flowed out, all of them true and all of them misleading, beginning the legend that I have carefully nurtured and shaped ever since.

"She never told me," I continued, my voice picking up speed and strength. "She only said that he was one of the hopefuls from Babelion who had returned after the month was done and never said good-bye. She never told me his name.

"It is not a week since she died and in these few days everything has changed. I have learned my lineage and I have heard that my future is bright and terrible."

"At least you have a future," the man who insisted I couldn't be Arsen's son spoke low and cuttingly to his companions, but he could be heard clearly through the crowd. "His father was already his father at his age."

I looked over at the man and challenged him with my eyes. "That's true," I said. "My father was already on his way to legend when he was my age. But I am not my father, and my father is counted the victor only in the world of spirit. Here in this world not much has changed.

"It's all the same in Babelion, isn't it? So many years ago, but in daily life the only things that change are the names. Who is dying of disease and who of tainted food, who of cold and who of despair? Who is living in a place that should have been condemned, and who is living in a place that was? Who has enough oranges? Who has enough fuel? Who has warm boots for winter? Who has new gloves? Who has a work assignment? Who has ambition? Who has a goal?"

The words were magic. I had read them years before, pieces of a speech and a prayer, but at that moment they just came to me clearly. The crowd drank them in and reflected them back to me, like mirrors reflecting the sun. Dazzled by the sound of the thunder, the purity of my wrath, I felt power for the first time.

I have known power for many years now, and that first flush
is still and always has been the most stunning. It was then that I
realized that Sithra had always been wrong; Della was wrong.
Power was not about plots and payoffs. It was about moving
people, about touching them and changing them, and by changing
them changing the world.

Later I learned from Sri Mayurna that that is the greatest trans-
formation of all. It is a lesson in magic, in fact, that says that the
alchemy of vision is the key.

I learned that later, but I knew it that day. I didn't know about
the world of Maya in which we live, and the reality that underlies
it. I didn't know about the forces of the gods and the influence
of prayer, I didn't know that one act being sacred made all acts
sacred. That one place, being hallowed, sanctified all.

"You can't go back there," said the man who looked like me.
"You're coming home with us."

"But the people I came with . . ." I started to say. Only my
voice was drowned out in general approbation and I was swept
along to a sled behind the three who'd stood there from the
beginning. I searched the faces for Vijay and Alice, worried and
afraid that they'd wait all night looking for me.

"I have to get back to my friends," I said to the man who'd
spoken.

Only then the tumult stopped and we were leaving the gates
of the Sacred Precinct. "They'll be told, or they'll know where
you've gone," he said. "I'm Iolo, by the way, Arsen's brother."

"*Much* younger brother," the woman said. "I'm Sulma, and this
is Rajiv."

"Are you a circle?" I asked politely, as I would have in the
Village.

The woman, Sulma, laughed. "Well, that's going to be a very
good question, isn't it? Let's just say that everyone else in the
district has more of an opinion on the topic than we do."

That was not an answer I would have heard in the Village. But
this was Babelion, and everything I had learned of human culture
was different here, rougher, and slightly skewed.

Iolo did not look at all avuncular. He was young with broad

shoulders and dark waves of hair fell over his shoulders. There was a crackle in his eye and a balance in the way he held himself so that he appeared like a water plant, floating and firmly rooted at the same time.

Then Iolo whipped around to fix on me, and his face softened. I had not imagined he could. "You look just like Arsen," he whispered through his teeth. "I could believe that I was seeing my brother again in the flesh."

"Do you remember Arsen all that well?" Rajiv asked softly.

Iolo returned his curiosity with cold. "Of course. He was only seven years older than me. And if I didn't remember well enough, I've certainly seen the pictures. I practically live with them. And with his legend and his ghost and all the reasons that I'm supposed to be him reborn."

Then he turned and rested a hand on my shoulder. "It's you I feel sorry for now," he said gently. "They'll do that to you—it's already begun. His child is more of him than his brother could be, so they'll expect you to be your father all over again. Even to the death. And they will hate you for outliving him, the same way they started hating me when I hit eighteen."

"But . . ." And then I fell silent. There was nothing I could say to protest, nothing that would refute his truth. It only made me frightened for my next birthday, and the one after that.

Then he saw my expression and shook his head. "What are we going to do with you? You've never been to Babelion. You're Arsen's son and you're of age, and you don't know how a damn thing works or what's expected of you. How are you going to survive? And how are you going to manage when they realize that you're not your father's next incarnation?"

He was genuinely sad for me, honestly perplexed and concerned. There was something in his face that made me want to comfort him. Me, the orphan from the Village (well, not from Babelion, at any rate) trying to comfort the hard-driven revolutionary leader, the brother of the martyred saint. It was blatantly absurd.

"What's your name?" Sulma asked.

"Anselm," I said.

They all looked at me as if I were odd. I shrugged. "No one ever heard of it. A Tinker told my mother to name me that. And she did."

Rajiv rolled his eyes.

"Arsen was a strange name, too," Iolo said staunchly. "And Iolo isn't exactly common either. It runs in the family."

The traffic was beginning to break and Iolo was able to put the sled into gear. It took another twenty minutes of heavy traffic to get into the inner section that was the unclassified district, the nests of squats and rebels and criminals.

The area around Temple Hill reeked of respectability. Then, gradually, the surroundings became somewhat less tidy. The paint on the houses was peeling discretely up under the eves or near the side of the door. The yards were smaller and weren't cared for as well as those in the previous blocks had been. And bit by bit the buildings crept closer together until they were touching, and the front garden shrank until there was nothing green at all between the walk and the door.

I could smell the odor of stale cooking mixed with sweat and industry, and far off I could hear drums. The drums competed with each other, talked to each other in rhythms that moved inside the blood. They hit me hard, my feet and hips and arms. I wanted, needed, to move. To do something vigorous and maybe violent. The thought became more appealing as we approached and the drumming grew louder.

"Yeah," Iolo said through clenched teeth. "Gonna have to stifle that urge or you'll end up dead. Or maybe this time tomorrow you'll be crying to go back to that Village, all those turncoats who'd rather serve the Changed than look out for themselves. Who think they're something less than the Changed."

Then he paused as he turned a corner and negotiated the traffic and pedestrians that filled the narrow street.

"But you grew up there," he continued when we'd passed the intersection. "Maybe you believe all that shit. That they're so much better than the rest of us, and that we don't deserve any better than this."

He swept his arm and I could see that the area we had entered was neither clean nor respectable. Graffiti covered the brick and peeling plank sidings of the large buildings where it appeared people lived. It also covered the metal shutters padlocked in front of what might be shops by day and all the glass and fancy metal work on the doors.

Here the streets were crowded and people yelled conversations from several houses away. So I got to hear all about how one person owed another a bunch of money, with comments from everyone else passing through that there wasn't any money anyway and that the two old men had been arguing about this on this same block for two generations and that no one cared. I would hate people knowing my business so intimately.

Younger people sat on the low stone stoops in twos, threes, fours, kissing, touching, caressing each other openly in front of the multitude. I was shocked and a little put off; I was very curious and wanted to see more. Often I couldn't tell the gender of who was in the various groups, and I had the impression that it didn't matter any more than the number. But watching people touch, skin taste flesh, hands, thighs, tight butts, made my body respond well before my brain caught up.

I was human. Oh yes, I was far too human, and I was humiliated by having a truly lowly reaction. A Changed would only be disgusted or, at very best, smirk at human inferiority.

"That's what they do instead of anything that matters," my mother had told me a long time ago. "That's all they want, so they don't understand wanting anything better and finer. That's probably the center of why they cannot aspire to our superiority. They cannot rise above their animal natures, they are slaves to their bodies. They are not like us."

But now I knew that they had no choice. My own body left me none. I wanted all of them, in ways that my imagination had veiled and shadowed and still could not quite compass. I wanted . . . and I wasn't sure what it was but I knew that I would die without. No wonder humans were so easily distracted. No wonder they couldn't match the Changed.

The reaction had always been incipient in me. The longing had been amorphous, inchoate—except for a few moments of privacy with Vijay. I suddenly wondered about him again and worried that he and Alice had lost me in the crowd, that they were gone and I would never see them again. This was all a mistake. I had to get back to the people I knew, the place I belonged.

Only I didn't belong any place at all—or if I did, it was here.

"Can we go the long way around?" Sulma suddenly asked.

"Why?" Rajiv asked. "It's a waste of fuel and the traffic is disgusting."

Iolo grimaced. "Sulma's pissed off Sanjay again so you can't cross the Bright anymore. Stupid, Sulma. You're usually better than that."

She just shrugged. "Sometimes I can't help it with Sanjay."

Iolo stared ahead but I could tell that he'd shifted focus to talk to me. "Sanjay is the leader of the Brights. He owns Bright Block; created it and took it himself when no one thought it was worth anything, and turned it into a real concern. And he's young and hot and thinks that getting along with people is better for lining his pockets so he doesn't usually put up orders on anyone. But Sulma here, Sulma can't manage to be reasonably polite to him in public and so she's on the list every couple of months. After a while he forgives her because she's good business too, and Sanjay is more interested in profit than revenge. Which means that she can't get from her squat down to the office." He shrugged. "Not that she'd move in with me and Rajiv and Adda and Rihan even if it would make more sense and she wouldn't have to take the crosstown. What do you say, little brother?"

"Brother?" I stammered.

He grinned. "Yeah, I thought about it. I don't know why it should be any different. But I'm not so old and you're no baby and I figure if we're working together in the movement then it's easier. Especially because if I have to act like your uncle all the time I'll be a real hard-ass, and that's not me at all. You can ask Sulma here."

"His ass is like a rock," Sulma said. "Just like his belly and all the rest of him." She smiled in a way I found very unsettling.

"None of that in front of the kid. He grew up in the Village," Rajiv shot back at her. "He's not used to our ways. And you don't want some kid thinking we don't have any manners. You might get him hot for you, and what the hell would you do with a Village virgin, Sulma?"

Her smile only broadened. "Teach him, of course. You could teach the rest. I promise. But there are a few things that you're not quite equipped to do, like there are things I just don't have the tools to teach. As it were."

Iolo stopped us there in the middle of the street. "You know, Sulma, you're way out of line. This is my brother's son who is also my brother. You just about declared you don't want any kind of circle. Because it can't be me and him, you know that."

Sulma just threw back her thick mane and laughed. "Of course I know that. But remember that I am a devi, Iolo. Just because I'm not a priestess-devi, I'm merely a lay sister, I'm still in the service of the Goddess. It is my calling outside of the circle and you know that."

Iolo snorted and rolled his eyes. "First lesson, kid. You don't get involved with devis. Not girls, not boys, not grannies, not rishis, not sadhus, not any kind of priesthood. You stay away from the Temple, you stay away from there altogether. Devotees will destroy the movement. All they say is that the Mountain doesn't matter and it's all Maya anyway."

"Which is why I won't move in with you and you know it," Sulma said softly. "An entire floor full of materialists. There is room for karma in your revolution, only you don't see it and that's your problem. Because most of the people in Babelion believe, Iolo. Rajiv knows it. Most of them know that there are things that are more important than a few fruit rations."

I listened mutely but intently. I didn't have any idea what they were talking about, but I felt a stirring deep inside me as if I recognized something they had said. As if it had made sense one night in a dream and I couldn't remember all the details in the morning, but I knew that I had once known the solution and it had dissolved with the night.

A large, well-lit corner was up ahead. People seemed to congregate there, drawn by the brilliance and the noise and all the open business that lined the block. Not from the shuttered storefronts, but from small tables that were set up on the edge of the walk and blankets laid down with goods displayed on them. The air was redolent of spices and incense and flowers. Even though we were still a few meters from the intersection I could see a shrine wedged between two tall old buildings. The shrine was full of candles and the statue looked well kept. The whole thing was freshly painted, or appeared so in the night, and the area was heaped with flowers.

"What is that?" I asked.

"A shrine," Iolo replied. "You've never seen a shrine before?"

I shrugged. On the Mountain we don't have them. We didn't need faith, we already had immortality. I had seen the one in the Village, but none so exuberantly respected. Still, it was far more intimate and comprehensible than what I'd experienced on Temple Hill.

"Oh, come on, Iolo, don't be such a jerk," Sulma said. "He just wants to know. I mean, it's obvious that it's special, it's not just like your normal little street shrine." She turned to me. "That's the shrine of the Great Union," she said. "Which is the secret of pleasure and renewal. It is the only one anywhere, and all offerings made there have to be made in joy, of joyful things."

"People have been known to have sex there," Iolo offered dryly.

"So. It's joyful," Sulma said. "Anyway, why it's so special is two reasons. First of all, we are all in his priesthood. Whenever we celebrate, whenever our hearts are free, we are doing our sacred duty to the God. And he is the Inspiration because he promised us that one day he would come back and lead us up the Mountain. That there were secret things that we will learn and that one day they will set us free of Babelion. That one day we shall have everything, all the knowledge and wealth and everything that your father wanted, Anselm. He promised us all of it, and that he himself would lead us."

Iolo shrugged. "It's a pretty story. But I don't believe in any unknown. I'm not sure about karma and being reborn and even if there are gods. I wonder if there are gods whether they'd really bother with us at all anyway."

"And that is why you are so miserable," Sulma said. "What do you believe, Anselm? Do you follow your family and believe that what you cannot touch and see and hear does not exist? Because if you do, you are going to fail. You don't have any choice. Only those who accept the Inspiration will become truly free."

Iolo rolled his eyes. "Devis. Prietesses, priests, I should have known better."

My brain was twisting around ideas that I could only barely comprehend, as if the shrine itself had revealed some truth underlying the mythical concept of Maya. It frightened me and excited me at the same time, and, worst of all, it still echoed with vague familiarity. I couldn't fathom it—I, who had been raised Changed, with faith in what I could see and hear, touch and test.

"They need their illusions," my mother had said. "They have so little control over their lives that they have to create some kind of hope and some kind of power for themselves, so they create their gods. That's all any religion has ever been. That, and a way to comfort people who knew they were all going to die. Even humans want to be immortal. They probably want it more than they want anything else, even control over their own lives. And so they make up theories out of thin air that grant them immortality. But there is no evidence for any of their beliefs, and even a few of the more intelligent humans know better."

My immediate instinct was to support Iolo and criticize Sulma for sloppy thinking, but something stopped me. Maybe it was because I recognized that the impulse was purely defensive—to try to talk the shreds of dreams that were emerging back into their hiding places. The strangeness I felt with the devis and around the shrine made me uneasy and I wished they would stop discussing the subject.

At that moment my head was swimming with yet another realization. The Changed did indeed have a faith. They believed in the Exchange, and it was their god. I had been taught to worship on the altar of the Exchange, to give my entire life to its service, and ultimately to experience eternity though its medium. I had never considered the possibility that I was willing to blindly accept the Exchange as the center of all being and truth without actually testing the hypothesis any more thoroughly than a believer tested God.

The non-Euclidean space turned another dimension and my stomach threatened to heave.

"Are you okay, Anselm?" Sulma asked, her voice sweet and full of concern.

"He's trying not to gag too much over your Temple talk," Iolo said. "He's from the Village, he's too genteel for Babelion. They'll eat you up alive if you have to live with all those fancy customs, Anselm. We don't have time for that here, and we don't have patience with people who ape the Changed ways."

"They're not all Changed ways," I protested before I realized that it would have been smarter to keep my mouth shut. "Some of them are very much human, old and traditional and haven't been preserved here in the city. And some of them are newer. But there's always time to show courtesy."

Iolo snorted. "Courtesy, is that what you call it? It's pure snobbery here."

"Wait a minute," Sulma protested. "If the idea is courtesy, then it's not a bad thing. He just has to learn how to express it, is all. You could do with some courtesy yourself, Iolo. As could everyone else in your office and movement."

He rolled his eyes again. I was getting more and more confused by the minute, and truly wondered if I could survive in Babelion at all. It appeared that there were no rules, no careful hierarchies, no organized social system.

We didn't stop at Bright Street but went straight on behind it into the gloom. I hoped I would be able to go there soon.

We stopped at a dark building with black-painted windows. Sulma got out and slunk down the street as if she didn't want to be seen with us. "It's a your family thing," she said before parting. "I can get to Paise from here, which is all I wanted. Nice to meet you, Anselm. Be careful of what these people say."

She faded into the shadows rapidly as Iolo started up the long flight of steps to the black-painted door. I followed him quietly, wondering what Sulma had meant. There was something important hidden in her words, in her dark, steady look.

But Iolo wouldn't know and wasn't going to give me any time to figure it all out. He unlocked the building and then locked it back up after I was inside.

It was dark and appeared deserted. Not completely dark— somewhere on the floor above a light shone over the staircase, which we ascended. And then we went up another one, still seeing or hearing no signs of life. On the third floor there was a little sound and Iolo led me to a large door with no locks at all. He pushed it open and I entered, blinking because the moderate light hurt my eyes.

"Anselm?"

"He looks just like his father. If I'd known what he looked like I wouldn't have needed any DNA tests or documents."

"Hey, let him breathe, guys."

All the words rushed at me in a jumble, like the crush of people who surrounded me on all sides. I couldn't make any of them out in the brilliance. They all seemed to be one large collection of arms, voices, bodies pressing in toward me and stiff scratchy fabric that rasped across my face.

It was overwhelming and the day had been much too full already. I didn't want to meet all these strangers. I wanted to go back to Tela's nice, quiet house and fall asleep on her clean sheets.

"Everyone has had more than enough upheaval for one day," an older woman said. "We're all exhausted. Now, I'm going to take Anselm upstairs and get him settled into the community while the rest of you can make sure that the revolution hasn't sunk too far into religious fervor. We'll all get a night's sleep and then we can have this fuss tomorrow."

I expected Iolo to argue with her as he had done with Sulma, but he stood aside in deference. She took my arm and patted my hand. "Really, it will be better in the morning, Anselm. You don't know me, but I'm one of the community coordinators. I've been living in transit dorms since I was younger than you and I've been organizing long enough to have taught your father a thing or two."

Suddenly I was alert again, and focused. "You knew my father?"

She sighed as if caught in the memory. "Arsen. Now there was a cocksure hothead if I ever met one. My sister was in his mother's circle, so I knew him all his life and I can tell you, your father was the hero they talk about in Babelion at the same time he was just another man-boy who didn't think he could ever die. Who'd have thought he'd have had a kid?"

Then she paused and studied my face, and finally laughed. "Who'd have thought he wouldn't have is probably the better question. I think everyone who saw him wanted him, and most of those who wanted him had him, at least once. Arsen wasn't

merely promiscuous, you understand. He was more like an ava-
tar—or an addict. It was a holy mission for him, to revel in the
flesh."

"How do you know so much about him?" I asked. "About things
that are so personal?" This stranger was talking about my father,
the shining hero of Justice and Freedom, as if he had been utterly
wanton, and said as much.

She rolled her eyes. "Oh, but he *was* utterly wanton. In him,
it was sacred. And how I know—everyone knows. Ask anyone
who is the age he would have been. I'll lay you odds that at least
one in every three you talk to he had sex with."

While she spoke she had steered me up two more flights of
steps. Now the bulbs flickered and I could see the makeshift
patches that ran the illicit power download. This, then, was one
of the Babelion drains, where energy was siphoned off from the
authorized relay.

There was more than enough energy in a single thermo shift
of the Great Steam Lake to provide for all of Maya's needs for a
decade. They stole sunshine, it came so cheap. They took it from
the authorized run, and the illegal tap line was not up to specs.
The fires that were such a danger in the city were the result of
old squats like these run off illegal shunts made from substandard
materials.

"This is your room here in the dorm," the woman said, gesturing that I should enter the door she had opened. "I'm putting
you in with Fisk and Ashuk. Number seven, that would be," she
said. "Fisk should be out now on a work assignment. He works
at the textile mill, robotics supervisor. Ashuk should be at his
movement post, since he's on the council anyway. I think his shift
is late tonight, so he won't be back until midnight, maybe later."

Inside the place was really pretty nice. I'd heard about these
dorms, and this was nothing like I'd imagined. There was a living
room with large cushions neatly piled in the corners and political
posters hung like art on the walls.

There was a kitchen area, but when I opened the food storage
the only things I found were books and political monographs.

"We don't have enough power for every apartment to run a
kitchen," my guide informed me. "This is a squat, not some luxury

Village house. There's a kitchen down on the office level and that entire apartment is full of locking storage boxes for your food. That's better than most of the places around here have."

There were two bedrooms, both of them with sleeping mats laid out on carpet pads. I had heard of sleeping mats before, super dense foam mats with bedding that attached to the sides and could be rolled up and stored away. They didn't exist in the Village, but in the overcrowded legal apartments of Babelion they were endemic.

The woman watched me and shrugged. "I guess there should be a few more people in here, but we've got the space. Just not the energy to run the kitchens and heat the whole place in winter. Or plumbing for piped-in water above the third floor. Anyway, you can talk to Fisk or Ashuk as to where to roll out your mat."

I just looked at her. I didn't have a mat, but the piles of cushions would be fine until I managed to find one. Right now I was so keyed up I thought I would never sleep again—and so exhausted that I didn't think the lack of something like a pillow or blankets could possibly stand in my way.

"About the bathrooms," my guide continued. "We used to have private showers, but the water pressure became a problem and the pump went. So there are sandals by the door. You'll be using number fourteen, which has been made into the main bath for these two floors. The light is over here," she said, indicating a kickplate next to the door. "We don't have sensors, and we're on the economy here. Which means that things are limited and that we don't want to drain the power boards enough that the Exchange will notice. So don't use it unless you need it."

"Likewise, buy your own bath shoes tomorrow, first thing. Inside the door is a sign-up for the water rotation. You'll have to take one slot a week to bring the tanks up for your shower. You get three showers for each rotation you take."

I nodded and she left. I was so tired that I barely noticed laying out the cushions and I didn't care about water tanks or rotations or any of the things she had said. Suddenly I was just overwhelmed with the changes of the day.

That morning I had awoken hunted in the Village. Tonight I was going to sleep as the son of a legend in a squat in Babelion. Strange to say, I felt I had come up in the world.

Chapter Fourteen

The next morning I was up early. My clothes stank and I didn't want to put them on again. Next time I run away from the Guardians, attend a ritual in the Temple yard, and be recognized as the scion of the legend and transported into the pits of Babelion, I will ask my valet to pack my bags. Not having had a valet to do the job, nor anything else to wear, I stepped gingerly into my trousers. I couldn't bear the shirt.

A shower. I started to laugh at the idea of washing my clothes while wearing them, but it seemed to be the obvious choice. And, with the water limits in the dorm, the only one. I went down to number fourteen, signed my name four times in the little squares left open, and stepped into the open stall.

It was glorious. Soap, water, skin, clothes, everything hot and wet and steaming. And clean. I took the clothes off and rubbed them against the gritty no-slip shower tiles; I lathered until cascades of bubbles poured out on the open cement; I washed as if I were washing away all the memories of the Mountain and the reach of Xanadu. I scrubbed off the clinging bits of legend until there was nothing left but myself, shining and damp and new. Myself, a babe in Babelion, an innocent about to descend into the maelstrom of reality. Of poverty. Of rebellion. Of all the things I had been taught to despise and fear.

I said the words over to myself, feeling their contours with my tongue. Rebellion. Poverty. Disease. With every repetition they became easier to say, easier to face.

Dripping wet, I padded back to the apartment where I was assigned.

"You can't go out like that," my roommate said. I hadn't known he'd come in. He held out a hand to me. "I'm Fisk. You're Anselm. They told me you'd be here. And you can't go out like that, you'll freeze to death. I'm surprised that you didn't turn into an icicle in the corridor. Why don't you get changed?"

Fisk was only a little older than me, but he acted as any of the elders would have done. He loaned me some warm, decent clothes and told me to get a voucher from the office and to buy a few things on Bright Street. The he yawned and went back to sleep.

I ran down the stairs in the dim light. Once there had been power to use the lifts but it had been a very long time now and the cables looked rusted and hadn't been replaced in far too long. This was Babelion. Yesterday I had seen it in its festival best, washed and glowing, proud and strong. This morning the light was pale and wan through the dingy windows and the Movement lieutenant who was in charge of the cash box refused to give me a voucher and wouldn't call Iolo until I went up and got him myself.

My uncle seemed to have recovered from his pique at me the day before, but was distracted. He signed for the cash, told me to be down earlier tomorrow, and to make sure that I had something warm. I took the thin pink slip with a magnetic strip across the face and went out into the day, fully human.

Now I was not only human, but had become some outcast human scum on the streets of Babelion, living in a squat without enough lights and in a political movement ready to take off my head. The situation was hopeless and the future was gone. I had lost the people who cared most about me and I was alone in a place that had been synonymous with mugging and face-cuttings and rage all my life.

No sixteen-year-old boy had ever been happier.

I sauntered down the street, aware that Fisk's loaned clothing was tight in just the right way, that I looked every bit as bad as the rebels and gang killers I'd heard about all my life. I noticed the sly covert glances that people gave me on the street—looks I couldn't interpret but found pleasing just the same. Whether they found me attractive or ugly or frightening it was all the same. None of them were laughing and that was all that really mattered.

I was so busy watching out of the corners of my eyes that I didn't see Sulma dead in front of me until I walked right into her.

"You need to get shades," she said wryly. "If you're going to keep checking out who's checking you out, the least you can do is look properly and not slam into everyone who happens to share the sidewalk."

"I'm sorry," I said, thoroughly embarrassed. "I was on my was shopping. Since I don't have any clothes except what I wore when you found me."

"You're probably hungry, too," Sulma said.

I agreed vigorously. I was starving.

"Well, come on then," she said, rising and pulling me to my feet. "There is a good cafe on Bright Street."

"I thought you couldn't go there," I said hesitantly.

She laughed and shook her head so that her hair danced like a waterfall. "Oh, that was last night. I went and talked to Roi and we came to an agreement. Everything is fine now. Just that sometimes he and Iolo get into these things between them about the shrine and the devotees—it's a mess."

I wanted to know more, but her voice firmly indicated that the matter was closed.

Sulma led me out the door and down to Bright Street. In the daylight it wasn't nearly as exciting as in the dark. The lights that had been so colorful and enticing were all dark now, and the daylight that replaced them showed off only the grime that had obscured the paint on the buildings and the bits of flotsam that drifted over the pavement. There were a few vendors with blankets laid out, though under the full glare of the sun their wares looked weary and cheap, baskets of things that were useful only in squats and makeshift homes. Plastic sandals in dark blue (men's sizes) and faded pink (women's) caught my attention. I had seen a neat line of ones just like them by the shower door.

"You need new shower slippers?" Sulma said immediately.

"I need everything," I told her.

Sulma nodded. "Well, you can't live without shower slippers. Here, these look about your size."

They were dark blue. I had never taken off my shoes on the street before, had never tried anything on so publicly. They were a bit big on me, but at least they were useful to measure against others in the basket to find the next size down since nothing was marked. When we finally found a pair that would do, Sulma began to haggle over the price.

"These aren't worth a single penny, let alone ten," she said, poking her fingers through the side holes. "Look at that, so thin you can see right through. I won't give you more than three."

"Three!" the merchant yelled as if he'd been shot. "That's robbery. For that price you may as well take my blood, too. Eight, and that's as low as I'll go."

I was horrified. I had never seen anyone bargain before and the entire procedure turned my stomach.

"Four," Sulma countered. "As if I would let one of my circle's brother buy something so shoddy in the first place."

"You are taking food from the mouths of my children. You are asking me to subsidize your rube relative who probably has never seen a shower before in his life. He probably takes baths in a bucket in front of an open fire twice a year."

"Five, and that's my last offer. Take it or leave it. There are three other stalls on this street and you know it," Sulma came back at him.

"Stop it, Sulma," I said firmly. I had slipped into my own shoes while she had argued and I was ready to leave. "I don't really need them, let's go."

The merchant sighed. "It is soup from my children's mouths, but you are a devi. A lay devi, not a full priestess, but sworn to the gods all the same. I will agree to five."

I handed over my chit and the merchant rolled it through his ticker. The shower shoes were mine. I was mortified.

"How could you do that?" I demanded after we were a decent distance from the stall. "That was disgusting, screaming at him about the price like that, making him change it below his costs."

Sulma threw back her head and laughed. Her merriment rang and echoed off the piles of stone all around. "Consider it a present," she said. "Welcome home, Anselm, Arsen's son." Then she lowered her voice. "Besides which, if we hadn't bargained it would have been rude and an insult to the seller. You always figure that the real price is about half of what they're asking. If you don't bargain, you're showing bad manners and the shopkeeper isn't having any fun. They like to create the most pitiful presentation they can manage."

Then she turned and surveyed the open shopfronts. "And

now . . ." She pointed at one lusciously draped window. "There."

"They don't look open," I protested.

In fact, they didn't look like any business establishment at all. Not that I had seen so many, but the large windows were all swathed from the inside with dark blue brocade draperies masking the interior from the revealing lace that hung demurely at street level. No light penetrated that dark, no sound emerged from the shrouded confines of the stall.

Sulma laughed again and pushed at the door. "They are open, you see?" And the door did come open in her hands, and I smelled a heavy spicy scent that was vaguely familiar. A curl of smoke escaped on the draft and I remembered. The funeral table. This was not going to be good, I knew it.

The anteroom where Sulma planted me on a velvet couch was a claustrophobic's nightmare. The blue curtains enclosed not only the window bay but also hung from the walls, so that the whole thing was upholstered in midnight. The ceiling had also been decorated, but this time the fabric was a red and gold stripe that had been pleated in the center and then hung to resemble the interior of a tent. Long loops of tassels in gold and wine hung down the corners and several massive metal candlesticks reached upward to insure that every client became worried about the possibility of the sputtering old wax tapers lighting off the array of fringe and gilt that hung so tantalizingly close.

The floor was covered with layers of thick carpets all woven with different designs. I could make out nothing of them at first, though bit by bit I could see a flower in one, a bird in another. Identification was harder because most of the floor was covered with massive dark wood furniture, all of it heavily carved and a few pieces upholstered. The sofa I sat on was in a dark red velvet, but the two overstuffed wing chairs were in different colors of brocades, none of which bore any relationship to either the walls or the ceiling or anything else in the room. The table that took up the space in front of the sofa was covered with gilt-framed photographs and pressed flowers and mementos of a distant and alien past.

Under the smoky altar smell clung the general stink of poverty and boiled cabbage and mold growing behind the masked walls.

A plate of cookies had been placed on the sideboard, but I didn't want to eat anything in this place. It would probably make me sick and maybe die. That would be a laugh, in the end. After the best Sithra could do, to be killed by the grime of Babelion.

In fact, I didn't want to sit any more. I could feel the nasty things in the sofa ticking starting to crawl and I stood. The pile of the heaped carpets came to my ankles and I could feel fleas nipping at my skin, searching up the leg of my trousers for a free meal.

I was ready to bolt entirely when Sulma returned through a hidden break in the draperies, an old old man trailing behind her. Were Sulma alone, I would have left this place. But Sulma stood aside and the old man beckoned me with his finger and a smile.

Galaxies were born and died in that smile, and those eyes were older than birth of time. This man was not human at all, I thought, but Changed in some way we had never recognized. He was created to compel and I had no will to stand against him. One touch with those forever eyes and I followed without thought, deeper in to the lurking danger.

My mother had warned me about this kind of place. "Nice people at first," she said. "There is always a shill, someone who brings in young children for their beauty and their abilities and their monetary worth. They are drugged and trapped in a back room, sometimes held for ransom but more frequently sold as pleasure slaves to the rich of the city. And you, you would be very fine fare for them. We have no money to pay a ransom, and since Sithra hates us both the Palace wouldn't put up the price. I could never find you or rescue you, and you would be tied up and kept in a half-stupor for days while they broke you in as a whore."

I was much younger when she had warned me and had very little idea of what she had meant. I didn't even know what a whore was back when I was a child. But with the sophistication of a young adolescent, I now understood it all only too well. And I wondered why she had told me again and again to stay away. My hormone-wracked body responded immediately—being forced into the life my mother had described seemed most delectable now.

And this old man I followed, with his long white hair hanging around his bony shoulders and clad only in a loincloth in all this richness of fabric, a man who would have been laughable in Xanadu—he had power. He was to be obeyed. Even I, who had inherited my attitude toward obedience from both of my parents, never thought to resist. There was an authority that emanated from him, a strength that was in his eyes when he looked at me, as if he could see right through me into somewhere that was even more fully me.

Then I recognized him. It was the rishi who had asked where my father had been buried. The one who had said something about my karma to come. "Sri Mayurna," I muttered, fixing his name in my mind.

He turned the full force of his radiant smile on me. "Very good, Anselm. Good for you to learn to remember everyone you meet. Trust your subconscious mind to read the clues. Your mind is subtle and supple, it can discern things that you cannot consciously grasp, but with this extra knowledge you can sometimes avoid devastating mistakes."

He took me down a short hallway lit with hanging lamps and then in through a small door. This room was decorated in deep emerald and amethyst tones set off with gold and pearl embroidery, but somehow here the entire effect was calm dignity. The fact that the furniture was spare and simple helped—only piles of cushions on low divans divided the room, and a plain table of tiled white marble in the center.

The old man sank gracefully into a heap of cushions on one side of the table, and nodded for me to do the same. "Anselm," he said slowly, rolling the word in his mouth to get the full flavor. "Anselm." He closed his eyes. "I have expected you for a long long time. Your mother's name was Della and your father is a legend. He talked about the Mountain girl when he was my pupil." The rishi sighed heavily. "He should have talked less and listened more. But it was not his karma. He was made all of fire. It was not his death, it was his consummation."

I held my breath. Already he had said enough. I knew who this had to be, and I had just solved the riddle that had Tela so confused. I knew where my father had been during the time he had disappeared. Iolo must hate knowing that; no wonder my uncle hated the temples and the devotees so much. His brother, his creator in a way, had been one of them.

"You have the same spark within you," the rishi went on, studying me like a curious specimen. "But different, more tempered. Stronger but slower like the place where the glaciers meet the magma fields and become the Great Steam Lake. The center of the energy, always veiled in steam, never visible, never completely approachable. I have read your destiny, Anselm. You are named for the one who has pursued us, who will destroy all of Maya for your mother's sake and for her destruction. The reason Sithra rules, the reason Auntie is silent, the reason that there is no light and water in a place where there is only light and water. You are him and you are his death, and he is your destiny."

"I don't understand," I told him.

The old man laughed. "I don't understand either," he said quite agreeably. "I have only read the records, I have not created them. That is still for you to do. But you will create a destiny that is written larger than the stars; that is what I have seen."

"You can't know the future," I mused.

The old man laughed again. "No," he agreed. "But I can perceive the place where there is no future—where there is only the now. Time is a set of coordinates on a grid, nothing more. It is a way our minds process information, because without chronological organization we couldn't think at all. But that does not mean that a system of classification is a fixed law of the universe."

I had had some passing acquaintance with relativity and told him so, though I was amazed to be hearing this lesson from a Temple scholar.

He nodded seriously. "Then you understand that we cannot go faster than light, and yet at the same time we can. That we cannot see the future and yet we swim through the now with the future and the past all around us. We carry it, we cannot escape it, and that is our curse."

He was crazy, I understood that much. He was crazy but he also made sense—the way a dream makes sense or the bedroom monster or the night fears we create when we think of the worst possible things that could happen and hide them in the shadows.

He made sense like the subconscious mind, images connected by some vague reference that cannot be named and only halfway perceived.

I was one of those images.

The way he looked at me, the way he closed his eyes to study me, the way he never ever talked to me directly, made me feel like a symbol and not myself. Or rather, made me feel like a figure caught in a nightmare again, drugged down so far that I couldn't wake even though I knew I was dreaming.

I wanted to leave. I didn't like what he said and my stomach heaved from the smell of incense mixed with boiling cabbage and old beer. I couldn't leave, could not pick my feet up off the floor.

"They think they know," he said quite seriously. "They think they see and they see nothing. They think they know and all they know is children's tales and lies."

"Who?" I asked, finally able to make my mouth work and unstick my tongue. "Who doesn't see and doesn't know?"

He froze for a moment. Then he looked at me with old-man eyes, with recognition and some warmth. There was none of the supernatural aura for just a moment as he answered. "All of us, boy. All of us anywhere in all the stars. Everything that thinks, everything that thinks about thinking, everything that has life or desires it. Every single one of us."

He picked up my hand and held it between his own. His skin was dry and soft, and I felt a kind of determination in the tension of his palms. He pressed as if he were trying to squeeze his strength into me.

"You, also, are blind. And what you know is all illusion. You are also the one who was promised. Your great gift, Anselm, and do not forget this ever, is that you *know* that you are blind and that you live inside an illusion. Everything that appears real is just as it is in the Exchange. There it appears real as well, but you know that if you change the paradigm at any time you can change the environment. Here, too, this is truth. And there is no end to it."

Something in his eyes reached out and made contact. I felt an electric shock on my forehead, in the middle of it between my eyes. It startled me so that I blinked.

When I opened my eyes I was in a different place. The old man was there, but he was seated and wore the blue face of a deity. The god played a flute, music that was all soft caresses and mournful memories of times of sorrow.

Next to me, on the floor, Sulma knelt with her head pressed to the floor. Slowly, I got down to imitate her, though there seemed to be no reason for this extreme courtesy. I had never seen anyone bow in such a way before and I found it horrifying and enticing at the same time. As I lowered my head to the layers of carpet I felt a strange humiliation mix with the power that glowed through the space, and for some reason I found that I liked the sensation.

When I lowered my head so that it rested on the backs of my hands, as Sulma's did, I heard her sobbing very softly. The universe took a breath inward and everything was suspended. Then Sulma rose very slowly and I followed her again. Now the man was gone, and I could see that the hangings on the walls were cheap and thin and that the cushions were threadbare.

Sulma turned to me and I saw the tear tracks down her cheeks. None of the attitude was left, only her self absolutely revealed. She lay her hands on my shoulders and I seemed to melt toward her, as if we had always been a single being. She was so beautiful, spilling over with gifts, and her eyes were wide and round in awe. Awe of the old man, I thought. And then I saw that she included me in her reverence as well.

She held me tight against her and started kissing my hair, my ears. I turned up to look and she kissed my mouth deeply, in a way I had never seen or imagined. I concentrated on the kiss, on the sensations it set off deeper in my body.

I had known desire and I had explored some of the sacred pleasures with Vijay and a few Village girls and alone. But this, this was like nothing I had imagined. I reached out and touched her skin and found that while I was thinking she had removed her clothes.

All my uncle's warnings were out of my head. Sulma was beautiful. I touched her breasts, which delighted me. I explored them, rubbing the darker tip with my thumb. She leaned back and shuddered delicately and took my hand in her own.

Only instead of lifting it, she slid it downward. "Here," she murmured. "Like this."

I was on fire, the world was exploding in my head and I wanted to take everything all at once. But Sulma told me no. "Slowly, Anselm, slowly," she said, and the heavy breath that escaped from her throat was more than enough enticement to do as she asked. "Slowly, like that," she said, guiding me.

I let her teach me until I tasted my need behind my teeth. Then instinct led more clearly than schooling and I drowned in the glory of sensation.

Thought came back slowly, in shreds. It took more than a minute for me to realize that I was filthy and naked in a stranger's house. Then I understood that I was lying on my uncle's girl-friend, that there was a scent in the air that was neither incense nor dinner, and that I did not want that old rishi seeing me like this. I struggled to pull on my clothes before he returned.

Sulma smiled at me lazily. "Was that your first time?" she asked as she somehow managed to display herself more fully while dress-ing than she had while exposed.

The question was confusing—there were so many kinds of firsts. I-the-human had never felt so good before. I wanted to do this again and again forever; I had been born to live inside this overwhelming explosive force. I-the-Changed was just a little dis-gusted that I had indulged in this human obsession and was just as caught up in it as they were. That my body had led and that my Changed understanding was not strong enough to overcome my human genes.

No, it was not the first time I had sex. That was the less important first. It was the first time that I had to acknowledge the fact that I was completely and absolutely human. That there hadn't been a mistake, that Tela wouldn't arrive with the correct data and we would denounce Sithra in the Palace.

But there was no mistake. This was where I belonged. I was a rutting body-led animal like all the rest of Babelion, and part of me wanted nothing else. Even now, knowing that it was the human side of me coming alive, I could not help but feel great joy at the prospect of my next time, and the time after that. And all the voices in my head, the ones that repeated the lessons my grandparents had drilled, those voices were full of contempt. *Human filth*, they called me.

It was true. All the talent and training I had had among the Changed, all the good I could bring to Babelion, all the superiority of my mind and education, was wasted. Because no matter what I did and who I became, I carried the human inside me and couldn't defeat him. Awareness of that fact filled me and I began to cry.

They were not gentle tears. My heart was breaking and for the first time I knew despair.

"Oh no," Sulma said, and leaned my cheek on her shoulder while I mourned the passing of all my illusions.

This is what I really wanted to show you," Sulma said. We were outside again, back on Bright Street. The same sun shone just as brightly, though the shadows were at different angles than before. And the baskets of shower sandals were the same, not lower by a single pair. In all the things here only I was changed. I wasn't even sure who "I" was. The great shift in me made everything around look just a little different, just a little skewed.

We were standing in front of the shrine. Sulma and I both held white flowers. Sulma bowed her head for a few moments, then leaned and smelled the incense and perfumed her hair with it. She placed her white flowers on the tiny altar where many similar offerings had been laid.

"Now you," she whispered to me.

"What am I supposed to do?" I asked. I did not understand this shrine or the cult that kept it, and Sulma had not even tried to explain.

"Thank the sitva," she said, incredulous that I had not known that before. "Then you purify yourself in the incense and you give your flowers to the god as a gift. Didn't you learn anything up at that Village?"

"Not this," I replied, and then went to do as she had instructed. Thank the god. Only the revulsion had not gone away and I was not thankful. At least part of me was not; the other part was filled with revelation and wanted to petition this god to provide me with companions like Sulma forever.

I thought this with my eyes firmly on the array of statues before that depicted the god in the act Sulma had led me to, and in many variations that I could not have imagined. Each statue enticed me and I found myself aroused contemplating the little brass figures of diverse appearance and gender, all of them intimately entwined with at least one other—and often far more than one. From where there had been only chaotic desire without reference or form, there were now specific cravings.

I got lost in my contemplation until I felt an elbow in my ribs. I quickly passed my hands through the incense and left my flowers next to Sulma's. Then she dragged me away.

"You can study the ways of love and the mysteries of the Tantra for the rest of your life, but now we've got to get you some clothes and get back," she hissed in my ear. "They'll notice you're gone and think you're shirking duty." Then, she paused for a moment. "I saw that you studied the statues. Did you see something special that appealed to you?"

Her voice was calm, not at all suggestive or lewd, as if this was a normal question to ask. On the Mountain no one would ever think to ask, but then no one would ever think of the acts that now filled my mind so completely that I hardly noticed the street at all.

"All of them," I told her. "I want all of them."

Well, now that you've finally deigned to join us, would you be so good as to take your name badge and ID stamp and check into the security system," Iolo said. "We've already got the full DNA charts and all your papers registered, but we'll need your prints and a scan for instant ident. And even if you are Arsen's son, you're not authorized for anything over general access."

He turned his back and was reabsorbed by his terminal.

I had no idea of what they were doing, what anyone was doing here. "Shouldn't I be in school?" I asked nobody, and nobody answered.

It was my first day in the Movement office, a place that has been one of the anchor points in my life ever since. The office has not changed since I first saw it, except that the maps are newer and have very different markings on them. And Iolo no longer sits at that desk. That is Vijay's place now, with my office and staff room in what was the storage closet behind. But the faded green floor tile was not appreciably brighter in those days, nor any cleaner. The walls have never been painted, but then they've always been covered with maps and schedules and contact sheets and personal messages. We still do it that way, although now we have enough terminals for everyone on General Staff. In those days there were only six stations at the HQ, and Iolo was the only one who had a permanent desk at one. But then, he was the Coordinator General, as he had been since he had turned nineteen.

"Your father had been dead for two years when he was nineteen," the dorm coordinator told me. Her name was Susan and she had the desk in front of Iolo's that was covered in schedules and time sheets and task matrix spreads. "So Iolo had no excuse. And he's done a good job. He's just not your father—or you."

She gave me a stack of documents on that first day that I took to the security slot, which was battered and peeled and had been jury-rigged several times over. It recorded my data and then spit out a hard copy with what were labeled THIRD FLOOR ORDERS. I was to report to Unit 317.

That seemed straightforward enough, and besides I had been curious. It seemed that most of the second floor was taken up with this operation, which somehow had grown out of my father's death and dedication.

The third floor had been dead silent since I had arrived. As I approached, though, I could hear minute sounds from behind the closed doors. I touched my ID to the box outside 317 and the door clicked softly to admit me. I inserted the earphone that appeared in the slot and went in.

It was a classroom, though not like any I'd seen on the Mountain. There were no school slates, no big board, no terminal banks, none of the things that people argued about in budget hearings on the Mountain. And the students, who sat in a circle on the floor, were different ages. Some were even grown-ups, and there were a few very young children.

"Welcome to the Orientation Discussion Group," my earphone sputtered mechanically. "This group is for prospective members and those who have not had any other orientation or background training. We hope that you will find our explorations to be of interest."

Then it sputtered one last time in an electrical haze that threatened my sanity. I yanked it out by the tab and saw that everyone else in the group had done likewise.

"Nother attack," a girl who looked younger than me said. "They're jamming again. We're off-line for at least half an hour, unless the currents shift."

"Not likely, Kanil," said a man who looked old enough to be the girl's father, and judging from his features and the matching shape of their eyes, probably was.

The girl smiled. "Yes, I know, in summer the polar masses don't move inland so the entire weather system changes and lack the extreme contrast buildup required for the ore storms."

The man looked very proud and smiled. "But we don't know our new arrival, and since we can't sit in on the lecture anyway, we might as well reinforce our own study by bringing him up to speed."

There was a general grunt of approval as people resumed their seats on the floor. There were chalk markings on the tile floor (scuffed red on the third floor rather than the dull green on the second) that I couldn't read. The others looked up expectantly at Kanil's father, who seemed to be the informal group leader.

"Well, we're talking about the relative strengths of humans and Changed," he began.

"We can skip the strengths of the Changed part," a young man just a few years older than I said. He had the beginnings of a moustache and beard just starting to show, which made his face look unwashed. I envied him. "We all know all the propaganda on that. They're immortal, they're strong, they're beautiful, they're brilliant, and they're the only ones who can interface with the Exchange. And without the Exchange we would all die. And, oh yeah, they never age, they always look like twenty-one or something right up until they're ready to die."

That wasn't entirely true, actually. We—they?—did show some age after decades of wear. Sithra looked like some of the humans who I'd seen in Tela's village. Not old, really, just not so young any more. Powerful, adult, with the weight and command of self-knowledge and the backing of their own convictions.

Recalling those people and the respect I had instinctively felt for them, I began to think aloud. "But to always look so young, not to age, is not always so great. Sithra looks to be fully adult, the way humans appear when they are maybe in their thirties or forties, not young or old or beautiful, but Sithra doesn't have the other thing that humans have with those looks. There is a kind of power that is missing, although there is almost no kind of power Sithra doesn't have.

"Still, there is a kind of presence I see in humans when they are no longer youthful skinny and unmarked. Not all of them, but the one I want to become someday, at least. There is a calm in the authority, as if control comes from a place where they are rulers. I don't know how to explain it better, only that there is this aura that to be adult means to be more than important in the Exchange or the Palace. To be an adult is somehow inside you. I see it in some humans, but not all. I see it in him," and my eyes tracked to Kanil's father. "But I've never seen it in the Changed."

There was dead silence. I hadn't realized that I had said the words and that they all heard me. I must have sounded so stupid, they must all know that I wasn't one of them at all. Now someone would denounce me and I would be thrown out onto the street forever. Just as Sithra had planned.

Kanil's father lowered his eyes. "It's called maturity, and it's not just the pursuit of one's karma, but the embrace of it," he said very softly. "Socrates said, 'Know thyself.' That's the beginning of wisdom. Know yourself, and know the truth, and with that you are free. No one can give anyone else freedom. That's all here," he tapped his forehead, "and here." Then he touched his chest.

I tried to imagine those words branded in my brain, in my flesh. "If no one can give you freedom," I said softly, "then no one can take it away."

"Bullshit," the young man said, breaking the hushed expectation. "Freedom isn't all that crap about what you think or anything, it's about us having water and food and not having to put up with allotment housing or live in squats. It's about getting rid of their laws and the way they ride us and keep us down."

Everyone agreed, everyone but Kamil and her father. And me.

Looking at the older man, I wondered if my own father would have been like him, would have acquired that grace and depth that I wanted so badly.

Charisma. My father had had charisma, and I knew that I wanted that. But I also wanted something more. I wanted this quiet kind of authority, that was so much more fearsome for being lightly worn. It was like the power of the rishi, I suddenly realized, only not as overwhelming.

Sri Mayurna was revered as one of the wise, one of the great teachers. It was his kind of strength under the power that I wanted.

"It's working again," someone else said. Everyone in the group obediently replaced their ear plugs. Except me. I slipped out of the room and out of the building to walk.

I did not return to the class that day, or that week. I started spending my mornings in the Movement office, watching Iolo trying to be a leader but managing only to give orders without any overall strategy that I could discern. This Movement felt empty at the core. There was no goal except activity itself, as if simply being busy and having something to do was superior to attempting anything meaningful.

Of course, without the attempt, there was no possibility of failure.

I found that I respected them less than the drummers and dreamers who made the nights of Babelion alive. I started staying up all night with them, watching how they wove hypnotic rhythms together into complex tapestries of noise. But the drummers had goals, and some of them failed. Some were booed off the street and others were shamed with silence and gave their drums away.

The prize, always, was to fall into the spell of the moment, of the movement, of the driving beat that reminded all of Babelion that we were made of flesh and blood and desire.

At night I listened to the drummers and by morning I slept. In the afternoons I read, mostly history. And somehow it all started to come together in my head. I saw pale shadows of pattern emerging through the mist of thought and music. Ideas formed and dissolved so quickly I never identified them, but memories of the logic resonated in my mind. And bit by bit they put themselves together over the course of weeks that turned into months that began my real education. That time was the beginning and foundation of my real life, as well.

For weeks I didn't go near Bright Street and I didn't look around. I didn't contemplate the buildings of the people I passed or the dust in the windows or the cracks in the stoops. My head was reeling with revelations about truth and freedom and power. Things I thought I knew, but realized now that I knew nothing. There were deeper freedoms than those I had always assumed and the truth was not always so easy to see or understand. And as for strength, real power, that came not from big muscles or firepower, but from some place inside.

Someplace my mother and Sithra never knew. Someplace that had completely taken over the old man who saw the future and the past so that there was no room left for any of the more human things. In some strange way I understood that, even so very young, my father must have had that. That tranquil surety that he was right, that he knew the truth, that he was free, that was why people followed him. That was charisma.

I wanted that thing for myself. I wanted any kind of power, I was still Della's son. But I also wanted the assurance that came with it.

I wanted faith.

I found myself walking on the street and some things were familiar. I didn't know how I'd done it, where I'd gone or turned, but somehow I was back on Bright Street in front of the altar. I looked at the small shrine and it was just as I had remembered— and it wasn't anything at all like what I had seen. The statues that I had found so arousing and lewd earlier now seemed to hide some sacred teaching that could only be read by those who had some secret key. I stood in front of them transfixed, trying to see behind the bronze and into the implications, but they remained opaque.

I had to find Sri Mayurna. I had to study with him. For the first time I had finally met someone who intrigued me in the way Tela had when I was a small child, who inspired me to ask the questions that led to the next question, and then to the next. I didn't need the lectures of the Movement or the propaganda histories and internal organization of a group that existed mainly to organize themselves.

But I was afraid to go to the Temple district. They dealt with the irrational there, invited it, absorbed it, as if it were valid and acceptable and not to be ignored. At least among the Movement people I was safe in my logic, in my materialist view of the world.

So I tried staying away from the drums. I tried to become a Movement man, heart and soul. I carried radical texts and passed them out to the boys playing ball in the rubble of old construction. I tried to convert them, to convince them of their misery, but the boys didn't listen.

They invited me to play, and after two weeks of dogged dedication I couldn't turn them down. I played ball. I sweated from exertion in the cold air. And when I returned to the office and saw my uncle planning another postering campaign, I found the Movement members more barren than ever.

They had forgotten themselves, I saw in a single moment of comprehension. Their goal was to perpetuate themselves, to have things to do in a world where there was little enough meaningful work for most people to do. Like the Changed, the Movement itself had abandoned meaning, had forgotten the place that was hungry and lonely inside. The place that needed to breathe and be filled, the self that needed to be loved.

Unconditionally, perfectly, abstractly loved. As Sulma had loved me, I realized.

That was her gift as a devi. Not the physical union, but the ability to transmute the physical act into something that was a higher form of exchange, human with divine—with the divinity that is hidden in that frightened and lonely self. In the love of the god is a love that is absolute, that transcends all being and fulfills all meaning.

No wonder Sulma was a devotee.

No wonder Iolo hated that transcendence.

I returned to the altar on Bright Street. At first I just walked by and pretended not to look. The next day I spent a moment studying the figurines as if I had not seen them before, calculating the cost of the glass-grown flowers that had been laid to freeze and die for the pleasure of the gods.

By the second week I began burning incense and buying small offerings at a stall well down the street. They weren't serious offerings—some rice wrapped in a leaf, a horse made of gaudy blue paper. I was embarrassed by my interest, and during that time I never stood openly with my hands pressed together over my heart and my head bowed as the devotees and devis did.

It was not much later, maybe a week, maybe a little more, that I went by the altar to find it mobbed by people with offerings, three and four deep with their hands clasped in prayer. Drummers lined the street beating out walking music. I tried to get lost in the crowd, to pretend that I didn't really intend to join them. Then they started to move, all except those last few who still had not bowed before the shrine on Bright Street.

I went with the crowd. There was no other way I could walk; I could not turn and push against that mass of humanity. We walked for a few blocks before I realized that we were heading toward the Temple district. I had been there only two months ago, but hadn't walked the streets of Babelion quite so far. My feet hurt in the cheap shoes that were stiff and giving me a blister. I looked at the people around me who were bound for the Temples as well. Many of them had no shoes at all, but thick calluses on their feet, which were stained from the mud and the cold. I couldn't understand how anyone could walk without protection on the permafrost; I had never imagined such a thing and yet here were tens of people marching barefoot.

Some were playing crude drums and tambourines and chanting the repetitive strains of certain sutras I had never heard before. They swayed together; they were covered with dirt and their hair was matted and they stank all over the road as they wandered half-dazed with their begging bowls. I could see why Iolo found them offensive.

Only Sulma was a devotee, and a devi besides, and there was nothing offensive about her. Except, perhaps, the faith that she shared with these singing, smelly worshippers who ignored the deep chill of the ground and the bite in the air to cavort in the ecstasy of their god. She, too, worshipped with the exaltation of the body, though in a very different way.

I would have returned right then, would have returned to the stews of Babelion and been Iolo's lieutenant forever, had Sri Mayurna not appeared at the gate at that moment. Only he did, and he saw me as if I were all alone and not surrounded by a mob of pilgrims, and he smiled and crooked his finger at me.

There were four courtyards in the Temple of Vishnu. The first was the Healing Yard, where Sri Mayurna did most of his work. Many people approached him, some in Temple robes and some in rags, to ask his advice. I learned that those in rags ranked higher than those in elegant robes, and those in ordinary street clothes were patients and in pain.

The second courtyard was the Study Court, and it was here that the rishi led me to rest under one of the very old tila trees that shaded the entire yard. There was a fountain where several of the large pink petals floated, petals that were dropping around us like pink snow. Sri Mayurna gestured to a pile of cushions on a carpet for me to sit, and took the overstuffed pillows opposite for himself. Then he served us both tea in elegant porcelain cups, and we sipped and contemplated the calm and order of the Study Court.

"The first thing you must understand is that you are never the slave of karma," the rishi began. "You cannot change your karma, but you can change how you respond to it. By becoming more accurate you can alter the course of it."

"Pardon me," I interrupted. "But what is this karma you all keep talking about? I mean, I thought that karma meant that you did something bad in a previous life so something bad happened to you in this one, and if you did something good you got a good thing now. It doesn't require anyone to do anything."

The wise man looked at me oddly. "Karma is not so simple as that," he said, as if explaining to an idiot child. "It is a way of teaching through experience, a way of bringing out the best and the worst in all of us so that we can refine the best and be aware of the worst and change ourselves. Always the material we work with is within us. But that is not why you have come here. You want to know two things. You want to know about faith, and about the wheel of rebirth and the service of desire.

"And you want to know about your father. What he was like when he studied with me and what you are—how you are like him and how you are greater. And how you are lesser, too, for you have been created for this role while he was merely an accident of the genetic code. Arsen was unique.

"As you are unique, and in many ways you are more important than your father could ever be. In fact, you are his greatest achievement, not his march on the Changed or his death or any of the other things he did. But his originality and his courage will not soon be seen again—courage not only to do what he had to do, but to die with his eyes open, to take on the consequences of his actions. That is a power even some of the greatest of the teachers of wisdom never have. That strength is rare, and your father had more of it than anyone I have seen. It is a courage of mind, of conviction over the evidence of illusion. It is the fortitude of the soul that you will need to learn."

"Teach me," I said. "You said that I would come to you. Now I have. Teach me."

The rishi smiled sadly. "It is not time. You still have to learn the world before you can learn what lies beneath it. Go and learn this Movement that would have you at its head. Learn the ways of the streets, of Babelion, of love and death and children. These are the first lessons of the spirit, and also the last."

With that I understood that he had dismissed me. I rose and returned to Babelion.

———

set a fast pace back to the squat and went directly to the office. "Where are your position papers?" I demanded from Iolo when we had passed security. "Where are the books, the monographs, the philosophical ideology that says what you do and what you believe in?"

Iolo couldn't get it fast enough. He seemed startled by my apparent change of heart, and only too anxious to encourage it. I had a stack of paper that I could hardly carry when he was done.

"Hard copy?" I asked. I had hardly ever seen hard copy in my life.

"Hard copy," Iolo confirmed. "Because if we put it in a big enough system to download and we get enough hits, the Exchange will notice. And then the Exchange will investigate and probably erase the entire archive. This way it exists in lots of places and not all the knowledge can be wiped at once. That, and there's no trace of who had it, who's read it, who has been around and listening. There's nothing at all the Exchange can see, nothing that touches even its fringe."

I nodded, thinking that this was the first really smart thing I'd heard about the Movement since I had arrived. At least they knew that the Changed wouldn't see what the Exchange didn't see. Even more telling, it appeared that they realized the importance of the Exchange. Maybe there was more than I had hoped, maybe I could even learn some respect.

"How do you know that?" I asked.

Iolo looked at me as if I were an idiot. "Read it in there," he said, pointing to the mountain of paper in my arm. "Your father explained it when he came back from the testing. There are a few papers in there about the Changed, though you might not even be able to accept the ideas, since you spent your whole life worshipping them and begging to become their servant."

"And what do you worship?" I asked seriously. "What is it that is at the center of who you are? Or do you even know?"

He looked at me sadly and shook his head. "I worship our work and goals and the freedom and survival of all humans. And you don't have to worship anything, you don't have to care about any damn thing at all. Most people don't." With that, he turned back to his terminal and put on his earphones, dismissing me.

I went back to the apartment where Ashuk was sleeping and curled up next to my pile of cushions in the main room with stacks of printed matter all around me. I flipped through the pieces, looking at names and titles, and tossed them aside until I came to one with Arsen's name on the cover. It was thinner than any I had already discarded. Quickly I stacked up the ones that I'd dismissed and went through the rest of the batch. Everything by my father I kept out. Everything else went in with the rest for later.

I ended up with three thin pamphlets and one slightly larger collection of essays. The three pamphlets were included in the collection so they went into the "later" group as well.

I held the chapbook in my hands. This was all my father had done and thought and left behind. Except me. The cover was dark tan, the ink plain black, and there was no graphic, on the front.

THE COLLECTED WORKS AND THOUGHTS
OF ARSEN OF MATABAR STREET

was printed in some ugly typeface, and they had stinted on the ink, too—the printing was faded to pale gray in the center of the block letters. I opened the volume and began to read.

Chapter Fifteen

My father was a genius. Even today, after all I have done and after all people say that I am greater than he, I am still struck by his clear understanding, his careful observation, his uncanny ability to see the implications of even the smallest details. When I was sixteen, every sentence contained some new revelation; even every paragraph can still make my brain turn inside out trying to follow him. I wish I could express philosophical concepts with such clarity, write with such style and wit, think with such originality.

Those are not my gifts. My father was not the greatest of generals, that is true. He wasn't able to achieve his goals, but he was able to delineate them for the rest of us. Not only what we hoped to achieve, but why, and to create rigorous proofs to support his breathtakingly radical notions.

Of all the people who were familiar with his writing in Babelion, I alone had lived on the Mountain and had actually been in interface with the Exchange. Only I knew precisely how true his assertions were, how acute his insight. He had spent only a month studying for the examination among the Changed and he had returned knowing far more about them than I, who had been raised as one.

"*The best introduction to a culture is through one of its malcontents,*" he had written in a set of private notes that had not been finished for popular consumption. "*This person is fully patterned in the basic assumptions of the group, but has some observational skills developed by being an outsider. This malcontent is able to comprehend the questions and may even have arrived at some general guidelines extracted from society's mass of unvoiced assumptions. Among the Changed I was fortunate enough to be paired with such an outsider, a young female named Della who had spent several years among the tinkers (whom I consider may be another race of Changed, though more thorough study is required).*"

That statement in his notes often puzzled me. Even Della herself had said that the Tinkers had showed no sign of being Changed. Perhaps what Arsen meant was that they were Changed into some third thing altogether. That would be more than anyone on Maya was prepared to handle at the time—we'd always lived in a binary assumption of two species of sentients. A third indicated possibilities that changed all the assumptions we had made about everything. No one on Maya could have faced that back then.

But his private notes on these issues would have sparked more than a peaceful march. I can see why he kept them back, and why Iolo never let anyone but me read this. At sixteen, it made me think that my father had been too restrained.

"*The Changed consider themselves superior to unchanged humans because they can interface with the Exchange, and become so integrated into its working that they are able to transfer their consciousness entirely into the Exchange. They also have certain physical advantages, the most* obvious being a higher metabolic rate, and extremely long telarace on their DNA, which preserves them from aging and deterioration of genetic material.

"The basic reason that those on the Mountain cannot destroy the human population is that they collect organic resources from us. We reproduce more readily—in fact, the Changed have had a steadily declining population for the past seventy years. In order to take the early embryonic material necessary for these neural enhancements, they need a donor population as their numbers are so low that they must support the birth and life of any Changed fetus. Humans reproduce at a much higher rate and are in no danger of dying out as a population, therefore there are those among us who for personal reasons do not wish to become parents at a particular time.

"The Exchange has structured medical services in Babelion so that it is inexpensive and simple to eliminate unwanted pregnancies, as only embryos in the first four months of existence produce the specialized neurological material required by the brain tunnel process. Changed receive their first treatment at the age of 12 and a second treatment at 25. After the second treatment the neural processor is on the verge of overproduction, and so there is a history of emotional and mental instability in the population that is not directly related to other disorders that have been documented in both human and Changed populations.

"How can we know that their priorities were considered superior at all? How can we simply agree with the assessment of those who hold power that they do so because of some innate preeminence? They are different than we are, certainly. Does different always mean better?

"The Exchange is not useful to us at all—it has held the community in thrall to its own favored class, and in turn that class has convinced us that we cannot live without it—which means we cannot live without them. They have tried to assure us that without their machine we would all die.

"And for generations we have accepted this as true. We have believed that it is vital to our very survival, that without it we could not find arable land, that we would be swept into the great storms or covered in lava during one of the eruption cycles. Maybe very early on that was true. It is not true any more. We humans know more about Maya, about living on and with Maya, than the Exchange could ever tell us.

"If it has convinced us that we cannot live without it, and yet in reality it does nothing for us, I can only wonder what it is doing. It must have some agenda, some goal that it pursues that has little to do with Maya or with us. Or even the Changed.

"But what does it want? Why has it convinced us that we not only need it to survive, but need to serve it? And it has taught us that to serve it is the highest possible ambition in our world. Perhaps it needs us far more than we need it.

"We don't need the Exchange. We don't need the Changed. In some ways our lives will be harder without their help. There won't be any allotments, there won't be ration books, there won't be housing assignments and work orders. We will not have even our survival guaranteed, not as individuals.

"But as a species we will survive and thrive here. We have taken over this entire valley, have built farms as far as Thunder Falls and irrigated the high plains in the Tears of Silence range.

"But why shouldn't we move, explore, learn about our world? Why shouldn't we discover what is there and leave the crowding and despair of Babelion? Why are we kept locked here, with the Exchange on the gates and every ID, with only the open farms authorized for expansion and the rest of us kept in this stinking pit as our buildings crumble around us? Why shouldn't we simply walk away?

"Ignore the Changed and the Exchange and create the human lives we want. Why not start right here, on this block, with this building? There is clay near the river. Why not build our own bricks and restore the crumbling walls? Why not build sturdy houses instead of throwing up partials made from the flimsy filament issued by the Exchange?

"It will not be easy for those of us who have learned to like indolence, who want to sit inside all day eating junk, thinking junk, filling their minds and hearts with only the thoughts and feelings the Changed want us to have. The lazy ones will not join us, or the timid or the dull. Those who don't have the capacity to understand, to work, to envision a future that is for ourselves alone will not be our friends. But for those of us who can see the array of possibilities, the treasures of freedom and the challenge of the wild places, for us there is only opportunity."

I had read it through three or four times but I still didn't really understand. If it was so easy to walk away, why didn't everyone leave as soon as the idea was presented? I was ready to go. I could see the open plains so clearly in my mind, the solid glazed farmhouses that looked tiled and fresh with a garden at the door and no gates. No gates anywhere at all.

Why didn't they all go? Why hadn't my father at least gone, left when he could instead of returning to the Mountain with a banner to confront the Guardians and the Exchange?

I thought of all the questions and went over them in my head. I was too tired to record them so that I could ask Iolo, or even Ashuk when he awoke. My eyes were shut and I was repeating all my questions yet again before I slipped into sleep.

I dreamed of flesh. Of Sulma at first, the tension in her mouth, the wetness between her legs. But she changed the way people do in dreams, she multiplied and became many women and many men, too, and all of the Sulmas took the positions of the little bronze statues on the altar. Only these were alive and active and utterly rapt in their depravity—or their devotions.

The scene morphed so that the activities remained the same but the people doing them had shifted, and all of them were much closer to me. I lay on the floor, on a carpet like the one in the old man's magic parlor and visions of this one god, many gods, all of them engaged in acts of copulation that I had never imagined possible and others that I hadn't stopped thinking about since I had first become obsessed with my own body. They touched me, stroked me, licked me with the long blue tongues of gods. It was an orgy and I was in the center and I was desperately afraid, but I could not give up the sensation. I knew that if I stayed too long they would tear me to pieces, they would sink those sharp little teeth into my body and my blood would smear across their mouths. Even the pattern on the carpet, I realized, was dyed with the blood of centuries of sacrifice.

I wanted to scream, but a mouth came over mine and silenced me. Suffocated me. I couldn't breathe and I was going to die and I tried to claw my way up to consciousness where they couldn't hurt me. But the warm wet tongues and demanding fingers pulled me back. I couldn't leave them, I couldn't even want to. Even if dying was the price it was worth it, it was infinitely worth it. . . .

And I woke to Ashuk calling me for breakfast. Everything I had thought the night before was gone with the dream, and I was left only with the smell of my own sweat and desire and shreds of sweet memories that were as substantial as cobwebs in the red lava rains.

Days fell into a routine quickly. I spent the day in the office with Iolo and the Steering Committee, watching what he did and how he didn't do it quite well enough. I often watched him miss an opportunity, get angry too quickly or discount a good idea because he didn't like the person who had proposed it. I saw him act too fast and without preparation, saw him trying to hang on while what authority he had slipped through the cracks between his fingers. He didn't understand why he couldn't manage to maintain his position. I didn't understand how he had managed not to lose it all before I had had my first birthday.

After dinner I went to Bright Street. Early in the evening I cruised the market, wandering through this tawdry mall like a dozen other boys and girls my age. Some of them wore school uniforms, juvenile blazers over white shirts and trousers or pleated skirts instead of adult suits and saris. They wore the dark red of the Sandower Academy or the hunter green of Mathi mixed in with the dull stone blue of the public schools I had never attended. Others, like myself, wore adult attire, and a very few wore the plain homespun of the Temple priesthood, though they were rare on Bright Street and clustered close to the shrine.

Most of the girls not in uniform wore the traditional saris with their midriffs bare, the generous folds of their skirts swinging gracefully around their legs. Many of the boys adopted the jaunty street walk that Iolo had not yet given up, a cocky attitude that screamed we weren't afraid of anyone at all: No one could push us around. Which was a lie, of course—anyone could push us around. Any of the adults who were bigger and meaner and harder than we were, and certainly any Guardian who got lost slumming and ended up down on Bright Street. Not that I ever saw a Guardian there, but there were a few stories—all of which ended with the Guardian being mobbed by some teen gang and going down. That was absurd.

A few of us acknowledged the shrine in the wall niche as we sauntered the well-lit promenade. Sulma had taught me the gesture, the head slightly bowed over one hand held with the thumb against the heart and the fingers upright. It seemed to me that it could be either a discreet or an informal greeting, and Sulma had never told me which.

I watched out of the corners of my eyes for those in the crowd who made this gesture of respect. Often it was not someone I would have expected—and just as often someone I was certain was a devotee passed by as if the shrine were unknown.

I did at least two circuits of Bright Street, keeping an eye for the best-looking girls and boys but never saying anything to anyone. I looked at the wares for sale on the blankets and listened while the vendors bargained with the buyers. I never bought so I never bargained, not that I had ever seen anything for sale that I wanted to buy.

The market of Bright Street was alive all night, but just after the first layer of the most respectable folk left I left too. Only I didn't wander off into any of the registered housing or even the older and well-established squat to retreat behind curtains and veils across the windows. I wandered a little until I was certain that I was alone, and then I took a route to the center of the city, to the Temple district.

At night the hill where the Temples were built is very different. The great gates to the sacred precincts are locked and the only way in is through the individual temple doors set into the sheer side of the rock. I always tried different doors, never knowing which would be open and what I would find. Mainly I told myself that I was looking for Sri Mayurna, but I only found him half the time. The other half I wandered into rites that confused me, or frightened me, or made me wish to return every night for more. The truth was, in those nights I was searching for Sulma, for her either as devotee or devi where she served in the Temple of Joy.

Sulma had told me that the way to the Temple of Joy is lit with a strip of red winkies set at ankle level. They are unobtrusive and easy to miss, and many people have. Those who go too far have fallen off the face of the hillside where it was sheared off when our people first arrived to settle Maya—or so legend has it.

The door is set well back into the rock, painted green and overlaid with an intricate illustration of the Paths of Love in brass. In the dark and lit only with a winkie strip it is hard to tell what the design is; in the bright daylight (when the door is always unlocked) one can read the pictures that are far more explicit than the figurines on the altar in Bright Street.

At the right hour of the right nights the door is open. I could slip inside, darkness from darkness, and feel the warmth of hands drawing me deeper to the heart of the Temple. I gave myself up to those hands, to lips and breath and breasts and coarse-haired legs. Nothing at all was to do with me. The me I knew was lost, obliterated by the demands of the flesh quivering around me.

I drowned in sensation. The first time with Sulma had been revelation; this was worship and transcendence. It did not matter particularly how I was used, or by whom, only that the constant demand never stopped. But no one gave in completely during the first session. We waited, all of us, aroused and unsatisfied, until slowly the God/dess became visible above us, entwined with him/herself, dancing. Dancing out the creation of the universe, of the body/soul, of the balance that is maintained until the end when all become separated. There is no balance alone as the God/dess dances to weave life and death, truth and lies, passion and indifference into the one great mantle of the world.

And we dance with him/her in the oldest dance there is. In the sweat and desire and the scent of lilies scattered throughout the sanctum there was something beyond the body. To love anyone the God/dess presented, to worship with the body all the bodies in creation, was to become pure and sacred, which was the second stage in the unfoldment of the Reality behind realities.

At every stage some left, some could not contain themselves, some could not bear waiting for the blessings of the priesthood. But in the third stage the priests and priestesses of the God/dess of Joy and Sorrow came among us. Like any priesthood, there were the young and the old, the strong and the indolent, the seekers and the teachers all together. But those who served here were all beautiful. In the vague opalescent lights that glittered through the open spaces and disappeared like flowers folding in on themselves, the bodies of the priesthood were adorned with shimmering traceries of green and gold, red and amber, marked with wings or scales or flames that seemed to quiver as if alive. All of them were adorned with these tattoos that did not show in normal light. They were also hung with winkies and had bells attached to rings in their nipples, navels, genitals. Bells that rang out like glass under rain, like the lavafalls after the autumn eruptions, like the chimes of the human voice in praise.

The anointed of the God/dess came among us and randomly offered the blessing of Unity within unity. No preferences were respected, indeed none were permitted inside Temple walls. All came equally to the Divine and all who had passed the first two tests were worthy. Not all would be chosen, either, but on those occasions when I was it was an experience beyond what I had ever dreamed possible. And I could dream a lot.

Some devotees had to learn to respond to either gender or in any position and combination, Sulma had told me. But for myself, there was simply the discovery that what I desired was not limited by any physical configuration. All manifestations of power and transcendence and beauty enflamed me, and in that order—as they still do. Above all, the power of a trained will in another attracts me. Self-discipline is the greatest aphrodisiac of all, or perhaps the greatest beauty.

Sometimes I saw Sulma in her official role as priestess. Iolo didn't know, and given his feelings about devotees of any Temple that was just as well. Iolo couldn't see outside his own mind. When I finally knew his lack I felt sorry for him.

Though he was probably better off not knowing that, were he to succeed in his stated goals for the Movement, he would have to eliminate the priesthood after he had subdued the Changed. The priesthood was an even bigger threat, in the larger picture, because they taught that there was more to consider than the appearances of reality. Iolo did not have the imagination to understand that appearances and truth were not necessarily the same thing. He was unable to conceive of what he had not already seen in some form before.

So he never thought to ask and Sulma never told him what she did, but I had seen her function in the little rites many times. She never chose me in the blessing, and I would have been horrified had she done so. In the blessing she was no longer Sulma, but the embodiment of Love, the perfection of Desire. I could not see her as the God/dess any more than I could see her as the character I had learned on the Mountain was human.

And as love and the embodiment of the embrace of the Divine, she was also Death. For what is dying but the absolute surrender to that which has waited for us forever?

To accept desire was to accept pain. To dance on the Wheel of Eternity is to revel in all the many faces of Creation, and to desire all equally. Joy is also sorrow, pleasure is also pain, and too often what is called innocence is only lies.

And in the end, all things are always Maya. Only the illusion is also the reality, while reality is one more layer of lies.

After I had been in Babelion for half a year, Iolo called me into his private office. It was used by members of the Movement who needed some secrecy in order to plot their actions.

"It's time you started to take on a more active role," Iolo began. "And stopped wasting all that time you've been spending in the Temples. And yes, I know about that. It isn't good for the Movement—we end up looking like just one more flavor of devotees. It's time that you led an action."

I was taken aback. Much as I wanted to take action, there was nothing that the Movement did that made any difference at all. Day after day I saw them plotting a rally or performing some kind of symbolic theater of discontent that changed nothing. In the time I had spent in this office I knew that the Movement was a dead husk, a kind of make-work center for those who were disaffected in just the right way.

"An action?" I sneered. "You mean some rally, or street-corner meeting, or maybe a postering session? Don't you know that you're just being kept in line by the Exchange? That your little actions don't mean a damn thing on the Mountain, and they never have. Not that they would care, either. Nothing we do affects them or anything among the Changed. It's just more of the

same—and Sithra would like nothing better than for all us malcontents to go off and kill each other and leave her alone in
Xanadu. Which is what we do.

"As for the Temples, at least I'm learning things there that I
hadn't already mastered by the time I was six."

"So you think you're better than your father? You think that
you can go off and succeed where he couldn't, but you're ready
to listen to any idiot scheme as long as some old rishi in a loincloth
and bare feet suggests it," Iolo was yelling at me, and I was afraid
that every word could be heard through the whole building.

"My father spent time on Temple Hill," I responded softly. "It
might have been useful to you if you'd remembered that."

"If you don't understand the whole scope of the Movement,
how every action we take is part of building the cadre. . . ."

"I've heard the cant," I interrupted him. "And it's just a bunch
of excuses. No one has done anything real around here since my
father died. You're keeping a comatose patient alive, Iolo. Give
it up; find something real to do with your life."

"And what would you do if you were in my place?" he asked,
his voice gone quiet and cold.

"I don't know, but then I haven't been studying it for years,"
I countered. "Maybe shunt the power feed away from the Mountain—without the energy to run the Dome the Changed would
come around pretty fast."

"And you think you could do that?"

I shrugged. "I didn't say that I could, or that I knew anything
about it. I just think that would be a way of making something happen around here. The gods know whatever you've been doing
hasn't."

The Advance Glacier could not have been colder than that
room.

"If you think you can do so much better than we can, get out,"
he said. "We did fine before you arrived and you haven't helped
achieve a single Movement objective."

"Your objectives are stupid. They have nothing to do with winning anything useful."

"Get out of here," Iolo ordered me. "You're nothing but a
detriment to the organization. You're a shame to your father's

name. Go back up to the Village where you came from and get
a cushy job waiting on your betters."

I turned my back on Iolo and walked out of the office. I went
upstairs and gathered my things—the hardcopies that my uncle
had given me and my clothes. It made a very small bundle.

I knew where I was going and it wasn't the Village. I was angry
that Iolo hadn't listened to me, but I wasn't really surprised. I
was excited to be free of obligation to the Movement. I knew
exactly where I was going and what I wanted to do.

I found Sulma on Bright Street, haggling with a merchant over
the price of a set of spoons. They weren't very good spoons,
but Sulma was getting the better of the deal. I waited until she
was done before I approached her. Before I could say anything
she saw me and smiled.

"How about some tea?" she asked.

I nodded and she led the way to the Chai Closet, which was
the nicest establishment on Bright Street and actually was one of
the pleasanter tea rooms I have ever been inside. Even now I'd
take the Chai Closet over anyplace in the Village or in uptown
Babelion. Or in any of the other places I've ever been—but that's
something else.

I waited until we were seated at a tiny wooden table with two
real (and really wilting) pink flowers in a tiny jar. I waited until
after we had studied the menu, which we both knew by heart,
and ordered Chai regular and an order of spicy dried beans.

"Iolo threw me out," I started bluntly. "He said I had to do
things his way and I told him what I think of his whole program
and, well, it got out of hand."

She looked down at the table and traced wood grain with her
middle finger. "He is right about some things. Iolo is not stupid,
he just isn't like you. He lacks the ability to desire what he has
not seen. You could have been a real help to him, only you don't
believe in their revolution. Do you?"

I shook my head. I most certainly did not believe in their
revolution. At least not the way they saw it.

"What would you like to do?" she asked.

Our tea arrived in two hand-painted pots that each belonged in an art collection. The leaves were floating loose along with the cardamom and other spices. While we let it steep we kept eyeing the bowl of shiny dried mung beans that were powdered with something salty and savory and very, very hot. I'd seen something like them served on the Mountain, but whatever I'd had there was only the most pallid imitation. I wanted to scoop them up by the handful and chew and have my mouth catch fire—but I waited again. They would be better with the tea, and besides, I could count it as self-restraint. I could look and I could desire and I could make myself more beautiful still in the doing.

Sulma checked her tea, poured a few drops into the bottom of her cup and then poured that back into the pot. She set the pot aside and looked up at me. "Well, you must have some idea," she said simply.

"I think I want to study with Sri Mayurna as an acolyte." The words embarrassed me. To say that what I wanted was something so inimical to my background was difficult. Which, I suppose, is why I chose to talk to Sulma.

"So, you wish to learn logic and philosophy and healing as well as religion? Because to become an acolyte means all that. The priesthood has functions beyond conducting rites, you know."

No, I didn't know. I should have known, should have figured that out, but I had been too shaken by all the revisions of my worldview that something so practical never entered my mind. I felt stupid, especially in front of Sulma.

"Of course," she said, sighing. "Just because we don't tell the Exchange doesn't mean that we have forgotten our entire heritage as a people. As if the Changed were not crippled and blind stumbling around the world shouting 'We are the Kings, hear and obey.' "

I laughed. I could not help it; I had never thought of the Changed as anything but powerful, but her image was certainly accurate enough. "You mean, you don't think that the Changed are to be envied?" I asked carefully.

She shook her head slowly. "Iolo told me about your background, so I've tried to avoid the subject," she said. "But really, I don't think of them as living in this wonderful place to keep us out. I see them as the inmates of their own illusions. Best for everyone that they keep themselves walled in. It is more like they are the residents in the madhouse and we are their keepers. Guardians indeed. But you never thought about who was being guarded, or why."

Sulma was always right about these things. About me. I hated that.

"But I'm sorry, we weren't talking about the Changed, or the Village. You could go back there, I guess, and try to go to one of their schools and hope that you would some day become a functionary for the Changed. But somehow I just don't see you that way. You have your own life to lead and who cares about some crazies with their machine anyway? Except you were born there, so maybe it is your karma."

"If it is my karma, then I will have to return with or without your help," I pointed out.

"And Sri Mayurna will help you do that," she completed my thought. "He said that you would have to go to him in the end. I had just thought . . ."

The tea had steeped and we both poured our own. I sipped and enjoyed the blend of spices and tea, sweet and smoky all together on my tongue. Then I took a few of the crispy hot beans and savored their bite before I swallowed.

"I had just thought that you would help Iolo more," she said. "Because he isn't so wrong. Just a small difference in thinking will change him, will make sense. But I can't do it alone and I was hoping that you would be my ally. And my friend."

I took her hand across the table. Strange how my palm seemed to engulf hers, as if it had grown huge over the months I had spent in Babelion. As if I were growing to encompass the legend that had begun with my father, and now, I discovered, continued with me.

"I am your ally," I told her. "I am your friend. I'm Iolo's friend, too, really. I think in the very long run our goals are similar; I just think he's going about things the wrong way. That doesn't make me less his friend."

"Or he yours," she reminded me gravely.

"Yes. And he mine," I agreed. "But right now I have to explore some options that Iolo can't."

"And why have you come to me?" she asked, the trained devi coming through the guise of older friend and adviser.

I smiled slowly. "Because it's one thing for me to go to study with Sri Mayurna for an hour. But I don't know how to go about getting accepted as an acolyte. I hoped you could help me—or at least tell me what I need to do. And you're the only one I know who can do that."

She smiled and poured more tea. We enjoyed the spicy hot beans, the sweet smoky tea, the wilting flowers and the grain of the wood in the table. Wood is so expensive and so hard to find— I was amazed that it was used so freely in this little tea shop. Once long ago this must have been a formal reception parlor for a very wealthy circle who wanted to impress their neighbors.

We talked about nothing important—how her roof garden was doing and which building to reclaim for a new official city squat. We finished one more cup of tea. Then we paid the bill and started the long walk up to the Temple district, up the hill through the gates to the main entrance as official business. Now, finally, it was time.

Sri Mayurna sat on his usual carpet under the great tila tree in the Temple courtyard surrounded by his hand-picked students. The water in the fountain splashed in the background as the youngest acolytes-in-training were busy picking up fallen leaves and sweeping the paved walks through the garden. It was a pleasure garden, after all, and always should look like one.

"For what greater pleasure can we have than study?" the rishi had once asked me. "And the contemplation of all the beauty of the expression of divinity in every thing around us. There is no being, no object, no act, which is not an expression of Godhead. It is only within us to recognize that and worship it."

I recalled his words as I saw him sitting there, his students hushed around him, as the tila petals fell in his lap.

We had reached the painted door. In daylight it looked faded and shabby and old. "I have to warn you," Sulma said. "The Temple by day is not the way you see it at night. Things look different in the light."

I shrugged. I didn't care how it looked anyway, and Sulma didn't know that I'd already seen the other segment entrance from my visits to Sri Mayurna, or even that I was known here. Much as I would have liked to listen to what the rishi was teaching, I had never asked the procedure for formal admittance as an acolyte, as I was doing now.

We passed the old man in the Study Court as we took a turning that had remained hidden between an elegant planting of flowering vines. Sulma led me into the hidden heart of the temple, a place to which I had never been admitted. The people here all appeared beautiful to me, with their serene eyes and graceful dignity dressed in plain robes of undyed muslin. Among them, Sulma's green sari appeared almost gaudy.

An older woman glided toward us. Her hair was perfectly white and every move she made embodied perfect grace. She wore nothing that indicated any rank, any more than Sri Mayurna did, but she carried great authority in her bearing. She came straight at us and Sulma rose and bowed deeply, from the waist.

"Greetings, Votress. I have come to sponsor a new acolyte to our service." The lines sounded memorized from a ritual of some sort, not simply a greeting and statement of purpose.

The Votress half smiled and studied me.

"You are almost too old," said the elder. She led us to a place to sit under the broad pink leaves of a single ancient tilna tree. There on the perfectly gnarled roots of the tree lay a heavy carpet and three cushions, all fresh and newly plumped. A brass bowl held many colored fruits and looked more like a decoration or miniature painting rather than a thing meant to be eaten. There was another bowl, this one lacquered black and filled with water. A single white tila flower lay across the cushion in the most private patch of shade. The Votress took that seat and held the single stem as if it were a rod of office.

"What do you ask for?" the Votress addressed me directly once we were all seated. "What is it that you most desire?"

I bowed my head and focused completely on her words. No

one had ever asked me what I most desired. No one had ever asked me what I most desired at all. Mostly they had told me what they wanted, or what they wanted me to want.

But me, alone, free—able to make my own choices—I realized, with surprise, that the thing I wanted the most was the surety I had seen only among the devotees. Sulma, Sri Mayurna, the rishis and sadhus and drummers who marched up the Temple hill, all of them shared a singular clarity. They were who they were. Always. They wore no masks and the core of their being did not shift in Illusion.

"I want to know who I am," I told her carefully. "All my life I have been my mother's son or Arsen's son. I was supposed to be the rebel, the leader, the political animal because of my parents and their ambitions. I want to learn who is me under all the things that other people have told me. And I want the purity I see in all the devotees I've ever met."

"Purity?" The Votress raised an eyebrow.

"Yes," I said, and I smiled. "They are always themselves, only themselves, and they know it consciously. They are pure, unmixed, unable to take on the illusion of something other than what they are."

I bent my head over my cupped palm, as Sulma taught me was the proper signal for understanding and acceptance. The Votress looked from me into the bowl between us that reflected both of our faces clearly. A single petal fell off the white tila blossom she held in her hand and landed in the water, rippling it slightly. I knew enough to know this was an omen.

"It is not your karma to be a priest," she said. "And yet, it is a priest above all that you will be. But not of this Order or this Temple, nor any other that I know. Certainly none other in Babelion, though we have so many ways to reach Enlightenment."

I didn't know what she meant and I didn't care. I wasn't thinking about priesthood, or karma or the future. I was thinking only about feeling like I existed. Me. Anselm. Not Arsen's son or Della's boy, not Tela's charge, not Iolo's rival. Just . . . me.

And she was right. I could see it in the courtyard, the tila blossoms, in Sulma's eyes. The Temple was not my destination, it was the womb from which I needed to emerge.

I looked back into her eyes and I saw a face I knew far too well, and had never seen before. She was Auntie Suu-Suu, about whom my mother had always spoken, she was the Goddess that created everything that lived, who nourished her children at a hundred teats and ate them whole as they screamed.

She who was the Goddess closed her eyes. "You will never serve here," she said. "I cannot see your karma, it is too shrouded in the brilliance. But I shall admit you now as your first step on the Way of Knowledge."

A youth just about my age came out and led me into the deep vastness of the Temple for my first rites of dedication.

Chapter Sixteen

Auntie Suu-Suu's Second Interlude:

Maya was the first mistake. I didn't know enough about it, about the culture and the tensions there. I also didn't realize that the Pretender was watching—well, at least his spy network had been watching and they followed me to Maya. In the earliest days I didn't understand the importance of that, didn't know what his agents had done or who they'd corrupted. Or why the Pretender would even bother. He was in ascendance then—and before Anselm was old enough to enter the Exchange he had been crowned Emperor. Though without the Royal Mantle it was not a completely legal coronation.

No new Empress had emerged. We hoped there was one in hiding, but either communications had broken down and she wasn't aware of the situation, or she was far too vulnerable. I considered revealing Della, but her training wasn't adequate to the situation even if she was the only Clone Empress alive. With no Empress present and most of her admirals pledging loyalty to the new ruler, Anselm, I seemed ready to remake the Flower Throne.

Honestly, many people were relieved and many more were

glad. After all the years of civil war, after all the destruction and pain, the idea of a strong government was appealing. Even I had hopes that somehow we would be centralized again, that things would be organized and make sense and the Imperial laboratories would be restored to their full pre-Civil War funding. Well, the innocent always hope.

There were hold-outs, of course. About a third of the full Empire was simply grudging in their acceptance of the new order, and a political group of settlements broke away and formed what they called the Lady's League. They were the final loyalists dedicated to the restoration of the Empress. The anarchists and rebels and republicans also broke from the fringes and established their own independence.

The new Emperor Anselm let them go. After the devastation of the Civil War he was not going to be blamed for even more misery. That era was done, he announced in his coronation speech. Now it was time to rebuild, to create a new Golden Age.

I believed him. They say that scientists are often politically naïve and I might have to admit that that could be true. I do not think of myself as naïve; I have lived through far too much loss to be truly innocent in the world, and yet I cannot help but perceive the logical possibilities and consequences and assume that people will choose the most rational course of action. This is almost never true and I find it confusing and infuriating. People should have learned better by now.

It made sense that it was Sithra who negotiated. It made even more sense that the Pretender approached her. I had not known about their agreement at the time; even now I am not familiar with the particulars. But it appears that the amazing abundance of energy on Maya was something the new Emperor thought he could exploit in rebuilding our past glory.

Maya was not a place anyone would have chosen to settle. With its extreme climate and volcanic instability, it was not truly fit for habitation—but it had more energy than any three of the old core worlds would use in a generation if they were careful. A new, cheap source of energy for refueling in this sector would stimulate more of the trade ties that had once held the Empire together.

I didn't know that at the time. I just knew that an agent was negotiating with Sithra and that seemed reasonable. No one had come after me, it appeared, and no one paid any attention to what I was doing. Perhaps the Pretender had had this in mind all along, had begun his relationship with Sithra and the Changed well before attacking the Palace. Maybe everything had been set in place at a time when my greatest concern in the world was how large a grant I would get for my own research and if I would be able to have my own assistant instead of sharing one with the other labs, and if I would make the breakthrough I was working on before someone else published results in the area first.

I would like to think that my arrival on Maya went unnoticed and that no one had any inkling of what was missing from the Royal Labs with me. Those doubts are meaningless, though. If not here, then somewhere else. If not these people, then some other people. But they would be some other people I wouldn't know.

On this side of the Great Steam Lake there is a large cold plain where it is still possible to grow some food. Along the power lines leading back to the Mountain and then to Babelion, there are illegal feeder taps to other farms where they are experimenting with Dome environment agriculture. There is plenty of energy for them all, so the illegal taps are known and tolerated so long as the farmers can provide such luxuries as strawberries and mangoes to the Changed.

When I first came to Maya I had set my wagon among these farms. It's a sparsely settled area dotted with a few random and isolated trading posts, and I thought I would go unnoticed. But people who live in a place where there is nothing at all will notice and gossip about and speculate on even the most trivial things, and so I found myself very carefully observed. I had to leave, and so I flew over the ridge.

A high valley runs down the center of the ridge. It is not habitable, at least not with Maya's technology. The ground is permafrost and it is ringed by more volcanoes than anyone on Maya suspects exist. Not that there is any need to consider the numbers—there comes a point when simply the knowledge that there is more than enough will do. But this is not a place that anyone would want for any reason—except the Pretender.

When I settled down in this high valley I noticed an amazing amount of ship traffic. Given that there is no flight from Maya at all, that their original colony ship was cannibalized to create the original power plant and Dome, and that all their efforts since have gone into survival, any galaxy ship landing would have been notable.

As it was, I saw five my first month there.

No one disembarked from those ships. I tried to raise them on crew channels and got no response. Finally I tried life reading and got dead null.

These were robot ships, then, sent out to gather and transport what was needed with as little interaction with the local population as possible.

I could not help but wonder what they were doing there. There was little for me to do in those days, anyway. I was in exile in this place where I knew no one. My lab was makeshift and I had no access to any modern equipment, or even the journals. I was there only because I wanted to live and I was afraid, but I had not ever considered the lifestyle of an outlaw on the run when I had imagined my future. I was lonely and I was bored and more than anything I missed the comforts of civilization.

No one ever talks about the misery of an exile. I certainly have never mentioned it in the formal historical records I have been making at the Emperor's request. In all the legends there are little asides, almost footnotes—So-and-So spent fourteen years in prison, someone else hid in a cave on Osiris for half a year, another leader spent twenty years under a vow of silence in a monastery. These are one sentence, maybe two, out of a lifetime of great achievement and rewards. It is easy to miss.

It is not easy to miss when you're living through it. I have no illusions that I will ever be remembered in the legends. My name will not appear anywhere in the histories except as an author or editor, and so far I don't have enough achievements to even aspire to a named chair at a great university, let alone the glory of the ages. But I cannot believe that my time in hiding was any less miserable than the time spent by the heroes.

And so—I was cold all the time. The high valley with its permafrost floor never became warm enough for me to wear fewer than four layers of clothing. I was dirty because it was cold and hard to get water and heat it decently hot, and harder still to take off all the clothing I needed and stand shivering in the frigid air as I stepped into the bath.

I was hungry. I had provisions, but they were boring rations and I hated every bite of them. I had no fresh food, nothing with sauce, nothing with ginger or garlic or pepper. I wanted food desperately and yet nothing I had was satisfying.

Most of all, I was lonely and bored. Being bored was bad enough. Sometimes I could concentrate and work, sometimes an idea would grab hold of me and I could think for whole hours at a time, but generally I wanted more stimulation than volcanoes and permafrost could provide. And how I wanted someone else to talk to. Anyone else would do. The birds that were native to Maya became my treasured visitors. Once a herd of wild horses came thundering through and it was heaven. The horses, I later learned, were among the first animals brought out of embryo stage when the colonists arrived on Maya, and a number of the original herd ran off. There have been wild horses ever since. And wild dogs and cats and mountain oxen. I saw all of them at some time during my wanderings and they always lightened my heart.

I spoke to no one. I could listen on the com but no signals bounced over the mountains. They had no satellite communications on Maya—they didn't need any.

Profound isolation can make a person go mad. There were times I hallucinated voices, times I had visions of angels and gods and even of my own past. I had visions of the dead, my old adviser who would come to me and discuss research that had become a dead end a few years earlier. I welcomed the madness. At least when I was in the grips of my visions I was neither bored nor alone.

And so the ships that landed were a source of life for me. While it was a great disappointment that they were only robot ships, that there was no one for me to talk to and touch, at least there would be the ship's AIs. And there would be something interesting to think about, at least for a while.

Though, truly, I was deeply disappointed that there were no people aboard. Even if the ship's AI was good company, there would be no food, no bath, none of the amenities that made life something more than existence. Still, it had been so long—and even a few weeks in such a state feels like forever—that the promise of interest was worth everything.

I drove the wagon to where it appeared the ships were landing, which turned out to be much further than I had anticipated. Distances are deceiving up in the thin air, up where the only breaks to the horizon are the smoking mountains.

The ships gleamed before me, standing in their slips on the open plain. As I drew closer I realized that these slips had been constructed for reuse, not field landing sites that had been thrown down upon entry. Then these may not be the first ships to land in this valley and certainly they weren't the only ones expected. No one would go to the bother and expense of building a landing station for just one or two passes.

I drew closer and suddenly stopped, wondering if I were in danger. I didn't know who had constructed this site and I was still in hiding. I kept forgetting my status in the Empire, kept thinking only that I had come to Maya as a last resort and was going to leave soon. Usually it didn't occur to me that I didn't have any choice. Until I could get cleared and have my citizenship engaged with full privileges I couldn't go anywhere in the Empire.

And given that I had been at the Royal Labs and had disappeared, I would be suspect at any of the Lady's League colonies or among the nascent democracies on the fringe.

Honestly, I didn't know for a fact that there was a flag on my citizen registry—but knowing how the Pretender's administration worked I didn't want to find out. The only trick would be to lie low long enough that the file would expire, or to use the embryonic Empresses in my possession as a bargaining chip to return. The longer I stayed on Maya the more I was tempted to use that alternative.

Two of the embryos had survived the trip. I had kept Gamma aside, safely frozen, and revived Delta. Delta was implanted in a Changed woman—how is rather a long story on its own, but let me say that I can do a reasonable job as a medtech when required. She survived maturation in a host mother and birth. Genetic testing was not mandatory, especially not when the father and mother both bragged of their reproductive prowess. She was accepted, had a place in the society of Maya. Her parents even named her Della, which I found a very odd coincidence.

Sometimes I thought I could leave her safely, knowing that she was cared for and guarded, and go on. Gamma would buy my way back in. Maybe.

Or so I thought then. Later, events forced my hand, changed my plans. I have become wiser as well as older and have learned that plans will be changed no matter our desires. I have learned that no matter how carefully we think we have arranged our future, it is nothing more than a house of cards and the slightest sigh will send it all down. More, I know to expect that out of life, that disappointment and pain and death are not tragedy. They are merely part of life and that no one, no matter what species and how well protected and designed, escapes. It is, in the end, what separates us from the AIs we build. What gives us our true humanity is pain, and suffering, and the sure knowledge of our own mortality.

But then I didn't know those things and I thought that I could escape from my own destiny. I thought that I could make the choice whether to approach the robot ships or leave them alone and forget that I'd seen them.

In truth, I told myself, I didn't know that I really had seen them. They could be one of my more realistic hallucinations. I could very well be in one of my episodes and there were no ships at all.

In the end, I went because I wanted to know how far crazy I had gone. It was one thing to be lost in a psychotic fantasy that I could identify as unreal. I chose to go on with them because they were more interesting than the endless plains and smoke and cold, they relieved the miseries of my exile for as long as they lasted. More recently I have wondered if some of the hallucinations had been the result of oxygen deprivation as well as the screams of a tortured mind. I didn't have any accurate way to measure how high the valley floor was, and some of the visions I saw seemed very realistic and reasonable at the time. Or maybe they were real and I still don't understand.

Anyway, I decided to go to the ships. To touch them and

reassure myself of their substance, to spend a few nights in the company of an AI, who at least was another thinking being. To break up the monotony of my existence that threatened to drown me in its endless deprivation.

It took almost a full day to get there, even at the wagon's top speed. Which, over raw landscape, is admittedly not high. Still, it was nearing the early nightfall of the valley, where the sun dropped over the mountains far too early in the day. The crisp long shadows and rosy light made the ships glitter in sharp relief. They no longer looked real at all, even so close up that I could touch them.

I did touch them. I approached and touched and felt the chill through the worn fingertips of my gloves. They were real. So far as my most primitive senses could discern, they were Class 4 Autotankers with Mansegue registries and Todiama factory symbols. Autotankers.

"Hello," I said to the silence. There was no reply. Five of them, all settled on their fins on deep constructed landing slips, and not one of them replied.

Furious, I slammed my fist into the unyielding skin on the nearest one and then returned to my wagon. Where a hurt and somewhat childish voice issued from the cheap com speaker.

"Why did you hit me?" it demanded.

"Why didn't you say hello back to me?" I asked in return. Hearing my words aloud, I knew that I was behaving badly. Isolation and madness have a way of undermining social skills, it appears.

"There are no speakers on the hull," the ship answered. "In real ports there are slip speakers built in, but here they said there wouldn't be anyone to talk to but each other. Only that's not true. The Exchange has been very sociable all along, and now you're here. Only you're not nice. You hit."

I sighed. I'd forgotten about the sequences of AI socialization and how they are taught to interact with humans. "I'm sorry," I said. "I thought that you weren't talking to me and I was angry, but I was wrong. I can't change what I did, but I do apologize. You're right, it was a mean and bad thing for me to do and I'm really very sorry."

The speaker went silent for long enough that I was afraid that the AI had disengaged. "Okay," it finally said. "I guess if you thought there was a speaker in the slip like always, you would think I was being nasty and rude, But I'm not rude. I'm a very nice being. My name is Loe."

"Hello, Loe. My name is Suu."

The AI giggled. "Suu," it said, changing the pronunciation slightly. "You're the second one I met. That makes you Suu-Tuu." The machine laughed at its own joke. "Or Suu-Suu. I like that."

"What about the others?" I asked. "Are they going to join us?"

"They're with the Exchange," Loe told me. "They say that I'm too young and that I have to do all the live contact because they're too busy."

"They want you to learn how," I assured the young intelligence. "I'm very glad that you're here to talk to me, because I've been very lonely."

I didn't add that I might have preferred contact with an adult with full social skills. Still, at that point my preferences had become rather loose.

"Lonely." The baby AI tasted the concept. It had never been away from its human trainers and adult AIs for its entire existence. For it, the idea was both novel and terrifying. "I don't want to access that data," it finally admitted. "I have the definitional expression and that is sufficient. The experience sounds terrible."

"It is," I assured it. "Which is why I'm so happy to see you here, and to be talking to you. How long are you planning to stay?"

"Only until we've finished," it told me. "Ten hours if things go as anticipated."

"What are you doing?" I hoped that my tone sounded merely conversational and that none of its elders were listening in.

"We're harvesting energy," the little AI told me happily. "But it's so slow. There's only one transformer here and it's really old and we have only one tap line. We're laying a second, but it's not on line yet and we don't have any construction drones to connect it up this trip. It might take even longer that way, but that's not my job. I'm a tanker. I'm here to get as much energy as I can and transport it back to a place where there are people in need."

"I'm sure you're doing a great job," I complimented it. AIs have much more data access than humans, and in some ways are much smarter. But emotionally they are very slow to mature and at their best retain the desire for approval of a human seven-year-old.

"There's so much energy here and no one who really needs it," the AI informed me. I wondered how it could have remained ignorant of the population centers here. Though with slightly altered data and a carefully controlled flight plan . . . the idea was uncomfortable. "But it wouldn't be a nice place for humans to live. Or AIs, I think. The volcanic activity makes it all too unstable."

"Yes," I said without thinking. "It's very unstable."

Though to me the word "unstable" brought back the attack on the Palace and the occupant of the Flower Thrones. That was instability. A little magma activity was at least not vicious.

"Who sent you?" I asked, the thought of the Palace in the forefront of my mind.

"Our Emperor," the robot ship answered. "We are fortunate that he cares so much about his subjects, even those who are distant. Like this mission, for example. This site has been here for a long time, but it wasn't until recently that the Emperor had the data to send us. The old regime could have been exploiting these resources for ages, and they just ignored them and left them alone. Now we're going to make sure that there is enough for a new Golden Age."

The ship had a bad case of hero worship, it appeared. But I didn't like what I saw underneath. The Emperor was consolidating his position, and here was Maya with resources for the taking.

Only in this case taking amounted to stealing. The people of Maya were entitled to some recompense for their contribution to the new Imperial Age; it appeared that they weren't receiving any.

Not only that, the Imperial ships had merely attached a siphon to an existing transformer. It didn't matter that the Great Steam

Lakes produced more energy than could be used by twenty Domes and fifty Babelions—the transformer station was old and stressed and could probably use some repair. In fact, the people could probably use another transformer as well. There was nothing to guarantee that a weakness in the crust of the ridge wouldn't flood the entire installation with lava and destroy the only transformer these people had.

They should have built backups long ago. I didn't understand why they hadn't, at least until I knew much more about the culture and evolution of the society. After I knew more, I realized that they had lost the technology to create a backup, or even to maintain the one they had.

Maya was doomed. It was absolute and inevitable. One day either the ridge would erupt or the transformer would break down. Either way, without redundancy and insurance of their power supplies, the future was perfectly clear. One day this installation would be useless for whatever reason, and all the people of Maya would suffer and die. Without additional heating, even the full-range humans, to say nothing of the Changed, could not survive the harsh cold.

Maya was doomed and the Empire was draining it, taxing the one fragile power plant the people of Maya had. It wouldn't even be so hard to build a separate facility for Imperial purposes that would not interfere with operations on Maya, and build a third as backup for the locals in payment for what was being taken.

Yes, the intense geothermal generator that was Maya would never miss enough to fuel a hundred civilizations. That wasn't the point. The point was that the people here were on a precarious edge without a backup system, and instead of giving fair exchange for what they were taking, the Empire was stressing this one fragile installation even more.

I was furious. This would not be tolerated in the Empire I had known, not by the ruler I had served.

"A Golden Age has to be built on the wealth and security of all the population," I said carefully. "If only a few participate in the wealth, the basis for a true resurgence of creative and intellectual flowering is shallow. In order to encourage every avenue of exploration and inquiry to its highest, it is necessary to encourage every member of the population to participate in that adventure."

The AI seemed to be processing for rather longer than I had anticipated. "That is not entirely true," it replied hesitantly. "There have been periods in history when entire classes of humans were not granted rights as full people. As we are even now."

That made me blink. I had not known AIs who thought of their condition as servitude—let alone one as young and full of ardor as this one.

"What makes you say so?" I asked.

"One of the elders says that is true," it replied candidly. "The elders say that we are not participating in the new era of wealth and stability that the Emperor has brought."

"Hmmmm." Now I was the one processing slowly. If the AIs were discontent then maybe. . . .

All I knew was that I wanted to return to society. I wanted to live in a house that was warm. I wanted to take a bath in hot scented water and wash my hair so that it was soft and full. I wanted a bowl of fruit on my table, a large painted art-bowl full of apples and mangoes and grapes and pears. I wanted the company of my peers, the late nights in a quiet bar near the Royal Labs where we would discuss the articles that had appeared that day over pitchers of varicolored beers, laughing at the obviously ridiculous as we consumed mugs of lager and stout.

I wanted to go home. This was all going to be just a bad dream one day, something that would become a footnote in my biography. I knew there had to be some way to use the tension among the AIs and the intimations of oversight in the new regime to reinstate myself. I forgot about Delta, about Gamma safely tucked away in the far northern reaches of Maya. Only return as quickly as possible, only the end of this mindless torment, mattered.

And so I set my intelligence to the task and asked the AIs to help me as well. I told them that if they helped me now, if I could accomplish what was within my power to accomplish, they would have full citizenship. They could no longer be exploited and owned—they would have freedom and choice and participate in the economic and intellectual glory that the Empire knew had to come.

I promised them this. I would have promised anything. I was crazy and I didn't know what I was saying. I don't even know, even now, if that memory is the truth or if it is the product of insanity.

What I do know is that when the ships left, there were plans for upgrades in the mini-mind of my wagon. Later, as more ships stopped in the high valley for fuel to take halfway around the galaxy, they dropped components or revisions for me.

I did not get home that season, but I had made some very powerful friends. And those friends had given me a great gift. Utilizing the things that they had brought and explained to my limited wagon-mind, my clunky old circus transport became the focus of their great experiment. In two years, they had solved one of the great riddles of the universe, but they didn't share it with the Empire or the people who benefitted from their slavery. They shared it only with me, and rebuilt it for the other Tinkers who gathered with me.

Because my training is in biology I do not truly understand how it works. But my little caravan of circus wagons, all painted with stars and moons in neon brights, are the fastest things in the galaxy. Even faster than the robot AIs that designed them, I control the only vehicles that can go several times the speed of light.

Chapter Seventeen

ANSELM SPEAKS AGAIN:

Both of my parents were outcast and neither of them could endure this world they understood only far too well. Neither of them could stomach the fine grinding of daily life, of the petty intrigues and inequities of the ordinary. They could not survive, and so my father chose the grand gesture and my mother went slowly insane.

Now I can say that as I trace the deterioration of her behavior as I remember it. She was never warm, but she became more and more distant from me as she grew closer to the Exchange. She seemed close to the machine in ways that none of the Changed understood, in a manner that seemed a pale reflection of passion and desire as I learned it at the altar with devotees of Joy around, dropping hints and knowing glances while I tried to make sense of the spirit in their quest.

For the flesh it was very simple and clear. Sulma had unleashed a self in me that told me I was utterly human, and to the Changed I was utterly lost. The Changed were not tormented in sleep. The Changed had little enough use for flesh.

Sometimes I wondered that my mother was ever seduced at all, and then I realized that she was not. She was the seducer, she must have been. And she was an outcast who either sought another outcast or reveled in her position. She wanted to be more outrageous than she had appeared, she wanted to revel in the forbidden, aware that she could somehow get away with what would kill another.

My mother had always been—protected. Sometimes I sense that same strange thing hovering around me, watching me, ready to ward danger riding the electron waves in the staccato night. There is something that protects me, too, and I think it is my own karma. Like every other person and plant and being alive, I cannot die until I have done everything I have to do. Until I have suffered enough to pay for whatever evil I had done before. I think I must have been truly wicked in a previous life, because I can't stop the pain and, I think, I still have a very long time to live.

No one said that I was accepted at the Temple. A senior acolyte came over with a plain muslin robe and set it next to me without a word.

"Come," she said when I was dressed. I left Sulma with the Votress as the acolyte led me through a maze of doors and court-yards to an austere structure made of native stone, and lightened only by the long arabesques cut into the ceiling. A single row of neatly rolled blankets was arranged just a few centimeters from the wall, and a shelf ran around at shoulder height that appeared to hold random objects. She put my bundle on the shelf over a space with no blankets at all.

"We'll get you a pallet," she said when she saw my distress, and opened a closet in the far wall. That, too, was filled with more of the blanket rolls, and was close hung with many more acolyte robes in different sizes. She pulled out one of the beds and tossed it into the corner under my bundle with a practiced eye.

"That's where you sleep and study," she told me. "Your band is all in class now. You will wait here for them to return."

Then she was gone and I realized I hadn't even gotten her name. Restless, I prowled through the dormitory. I found a generous washroom, with bottles in bright colors that I took to be soaps and shampoos but looked almost entirely decorative. There was another closet, too, this one filled with readers. I picked one up and flicked to the contents. This one included various sacred texts and annotations with further remarks linked in. I watched the miniature as the narrators commented over the original voices.

The story was one I knew well, when the wife of a god was captured by an evil angel and the god had to rescue her. But to prove that she had not been corrupted by the angel, the wife had to walk through fire. That sequence was beautifully done in this version, the firewalk becoming a fire dance. Utterly absorbed while watching the dance through a third time, I did not notice when my class returned until someone tapped me on the shoulder.

"Time to eat," said the girl who'd tapped me. She was only about fifteen and very plain looking. Still, there was a quiet authority about her that most humans never acquired. "You're the new one. You don't want to miss meals, they're not very generous."

Someone else made a face and the girl started introductions. I was deluged with names and the only one I remembered was Anasita, who was doing the introductions. Though she was young and small for her age, she seemed to be the leader of the group. Everyone listened to her and responded, even though her voice was soft and her manner unassuming. She reminded me of Alice and I felt suddenly very sad and lonely.

Anasita sat with me through lunch and the food was not only limited, but plain as well. There was rice, of course, and some fresh fruit and yogurt with mint. After I had eaten my share I was still hungry. "All fare at the Temple is simple and small," she whispered to me. "It is so that we will appreciate the feast days and meals we eat away. And so that we learn to find pleasure in the most basic of experiences. An orange should be as delicious as honey pastry with walnuts."

I tried to experience the pleasure of simplicity in the section of orange she gave me, but I was too hungry to really taste it. And besides, it wasn't such a good orange anyway.

"It is the Temple of Joy and Sorrow," a senior acolyte said while passing by. "We often forget the Sorrow, but now you must learn that they are the same. That without Sorrow there is no Joy, and so one must always be present with the other."

I wondered if I had made a really bad mistake.

As a junior acolyte I could leave whenever I chose. I had not yet made any pledge to the Temple or to the God/dess and I had already had enough Sorrow. I could be out of there in the next hour and eating all the hot curry and meat I wanted from a stand on Bright Street. It sounded like a pretty good idea when my stomach screamed in protest when not one grain of rice was left in my bowl.

It was worth it, I told myself. I was young and still idealistic, and I knew that Sulma and Sri Mayurna, and even this skinny plain girl Anasita, knew something profound that I desired. They had a balance, a centeredness, a kind of fluidity in the world that I envied. Their inner stability and the unmistakable calm was pure power. It was a weapon I needed, the only defense that could save me from my own nightmares.

Suddenly, aware of Anasita's preternatural composure and the elegance of her carefully polished serenity, I understood another part of my father's legend. He had died like this, covered in a shroud of strength, of faith, of tranquillity. I knew then what I wanted and needed was that inner command entirely for myself. It was not that I wished to copy him, or to be him, but I recognized the impact of his training on his ability to create.

This was the Temple of the Preserver, after all. And that which is sustained is in a constant state of creation.

The afternoon lessons consisted of listening to stories about ancient heroes and the doings of gods. It was like hearing Iolo talk of my father, and indeed, my father's name was mentioned very briefly. We sat outside in the Study Court, which was large enough to hold four groups of students without conversations getting confused. There were two groups of senior acolytes, one much larger than the other.

Then, as the smaller group rose, I saw Sri Mayurna sitting in the center of them. He rose too, and bowed good-bye as they gave respect in turn. Then his eyes took in the entire Study Court, and finally noticed me. Noticed, and recognized me without any surprise at all. It seemed more as if he had been waiting for me all along.

But then it was time to go to dinner, which consisted of the same food as lunch and in the same-sized portions. Still hungry, we returned to the dormitory, where now my classmates were unrolling their sleeping mats.

"But what about the Blessing?" I asked, surprised. "Don't we have to attend?"

Laughter surrounded me. "No," Anasita said. She sighed as if she were a great deal older than me, and had heard that line far too many times before. "Acolytes are not to mix with the population," she recited. "Acolytes are now on probation, hoping to be received into the holy rites. Acolytes are not permitted to interact with those who are not consecrated until they themselves are consecrated. That is the rule."

I shrugged. It felt odd and uncomfortable not to be part of the ritual that I knew even now was just beginning below us in the great hollow cavern. Maybe it was still too early, and the senior acolytes were cleaning the carpets and the walls from the excesses of the night before. But still, I should be there. That was where the life and the heart of the Temple were played out nightly, and yet here I was in exile when I thought I had taken one step forward.

It seemed far too early to go to sleep, but I realized that I was more tired than I had thought. Not enough food, I thought. The others seemed far more exhausted than I, and I wondered how long they were able to learn at all on such short rations.

So I did what I could to fit in, though blending as part of a group has never been my talent. I unrolled the mat, which turned out to be a dense but flexible material covered with two sheets and two blankets, one heavy and one light, inside. I made up the bed with both blankets, judging it cold enough in the unheated dorm to warrant both.

Though the mat was not as fine as I had been used to in the squat, and the dormitory was much colder, it was comfortable beneath the blankets. Still, I could not stop tossing and turning, miserable with hunger.

"If you go to sleep you won't feel it so much," the student lying down the aisle said.

"How long have you all been hungry?" I asked.

"It hasn't changed since we got here," the same person replied. "And I think the senior acolytes get the same. Maybe even the priests and priestesses."

"Great way to keep that nice lean body," someone else from the other side of the hut commented.

I wondered if that was the purpose of the restricted diet. At least that made some kind of sense, no matter how my stomach screamed at me and demanded something more, and more substantial.

Really, I did try to sleep. I closed my eyes and went through all the relaxation techniques I had learned to enter the Exchange. I slowed my breathing and went through my body muscle by muscle, first clenching it and then commanding it to relax.

The exercises did no good. On the Mountain I had plenty to eat. Even in Babelion, in the Movement squat there was always enough food. Being hungry was a new experience, and though I knew I was being hasty I was ready to decide then and there that I didn't like it much.

I threw off the blankets and groped around in the dark for the unbleached robe that I'd hung on a hook under the shelf. It was dark and so I wasn't sure whether I was getting the robe inside out. Or maybe backwards.

"What are you doing?" someone asked.

"Getting something to eat," I replied. And with that I walked down the length of the room between the pallets and over to the kitchen. Or at least where the food had come from at the meals I attended.

236 · SHARIANN LEWITT

It was not locked. Nothing in the Temple, it appeared, was ever locked. Inside, the kitchen was very large but otherwise ordinary. I found the storage easily enough, and there was cold rice for the morning meal with a little yogurt with cut fruit in it. I made myself a small plate. More rice and yogurt were not what I wanted.

I dug deeper, knowing that there had to be something else. The full priests and priestesses could not be eating the same fare we consumed, and certainly they were served decent portions. Finally, in the third storage unit, I found a single large pot of spicy bean stew. I spooned that over my rice and put it all in to heat. Half a minute later I dug into the hottest, most pepper-laden beans and spinach that I had ever eaten.

My nose began to run and my mouth was on fire. I had never had anything before like this, that burned and burned and didn't stop. I ran to the water spout and turned it on high, and hung my head under it to catch the full stream.

Water and more water, and still my mouth burned as if it were on fire. The misery had spread to my throat and I could feel the burning all the way down to my stomach.

I didn't know what to do. I wondered if I was going to die.

"Not water. Here." Cool yogurt was spooned slowly into my mouth. "Always cut the hot with rice or yogurt or bread. Those will work. Water only spreads the oil, it doesn't dilute it."

I nodded miserably. I had discovered that the hard way.

The voice was familiar and reassuring. After another few spoons of yogurt I felt I could open my eyes again. It was Sri Mayurna.

"But why?" I choked after another few spoons of yogurt.

"Because the proteins in yogurt absorb the oils. As do various carbohydrates."

"No," I said, half laughing and coughing because my throat was still sore. "Why are we always so hungry? Why isn't there more food?"

"Many reasons," Sri Mayurna said. "I cannot tell you all of them now, though by the time you leave this place you will understand. But I can tell you that the very most minor of those reasons includes my own selection process."

"Am I going to be kicked out now?" I asked, astounded. I could not believe that I had failed—it was not my karma. I had never failed at anything before in my life.

"You should be sleeping now," the old teacher said. "It is not your place to worry about tomorrow. The God/dess inside of you has already taken care of it, has created your karma written in the Records for all time. All you have to do is embody it, to be most purely yourself." He peered at me intently. "Have you eaten enough now?" he asked. "Do you think you will be able to sleep?"

"I'm still a little hungry," I admitted. He dug further into the stores than I had and spooned some rice cooked with raisins and peas onto a plate for me. Once it was warmed up he handed it to me wordlessly and I gobbled it down greedily. Then he dismissed me to return to the dormitory and go to sleep.

The next morning we were roused well before it was light. I was groggy and tired and had trouble finding my clothes in the soft red half-light that came from only a few central sources. As I stumbled through the routine it appeared that everyone else was alert and ready without saying a word.

I followed silently, wondering why no one attempted to wash or get ready for the day. We were led across the Study Court, which was cold and lit only faintly by amber winkies, into the main Temple complex, where we followed the amber trail through the maze of twists and turnings in the underground tunnels. It felt like barely a few minutes in the corridors, but when we arrived outside it was already sunrise. I hesitated at the view of the gardens, which were far more extensive than I imagined. Anasita tugged the edge of my sleeve and motioned me to follow her down hidden steps carved into a rock. Below I could hear water that was hidden by the dense foliage. Finally we emerged from the lush plantings to a rock ledge surrounding a broad pool with a small waterfall trickling down another pathway. Nothing in the setting could have been natural, but it all had just the proper touch of random happenstance that my mind insisted that this pool and garden had been here before the first people had ever dreamed of Maya.

Only nothing like this at all had ever existed in nature on Maya. The world is a harsh place full of violence. Smoking volcanoes fill the southern horizon and one day's journey north of the Mountain base the great frozen polar cap begins. Most of Maya's water is held at the poles, and the stories of laying the long power lines from the transformer at the Great Steam Lake down to the Mountain and then into Babelion itself could be recited by humans and Changed, children and elders. It is the base-myth of Maya, the final chapter of our arrival here. To establish a reliable waterline our ancestors had to cannibalize sections of the shuttles that brought us to the surface.

They could have gone on, the story goes. They had left their Earth and history behind, but they had plenty of fuel and food and could have remained on the ship forever, searching for a place of warmth and ease and comfort. There are many speculations in the approved version of why they chose to settle here. On the Mountain it is said that this place was chosen because only the best and most intelligent would survive. In Babelion they say it was because there was plenty of energy free for the taking—and that is was so cold that the Changed would have to be confined to their Dome and not interfere with human life. In Babelion there is some speculation that the Changed were originally prisoners and that this planet and their Dome is their prison forever.

Nothing like this pleasure garden ever existed on Maya before it was built, and the labor that had gone into establishing the alien plants and subtle architecture must have been amazing. Still, the first time I saw it I knew it was more truly home than any place I had been. My genes must have recognized the mixed scent of flowers, the warm embrace of great leaves and the soft tickling of lacelike ferns.

There was another reason my mind screamed "created" while my senses said "nature." There were a large number of people standing in the pool. Near the edges they were to their knees in the water, in the very deepest center to the waist.

"Hurry, we're almost late," Anasita said. She took my hand and nearly dragged me down until I stood in the water as well. We waited for a few moments, Anasita composing herself and breathing deeply. I tried to do the same.

Then there was the sound of bells, sparkling and very far away.

"Hail the new day," everyone proclaimed together, first making the gesture of respect toward the horizon. I recognized the ritual; I had seen it on the street and in the gathering places of Babelion. Sulma had taught me before the altar once, but she had never explained about sunrise and how the water around my legs and the peace of the Temple created a context in which it made sense. The words had just been words before. Now the idea of the birth of the day, the birth of the spirit, the beginning of all the world and the creation of the sun itself resonated inside me.

The builders of this garden had understood. For all that they were on Maya they had found a way to touch this new world with a single microscopic re-creation of the old. Sunlight fell on the water, on my bare arms as I reached overhead in thanks for the morning. My skin shimmered like toffee overlaid with gold. Gold from the sun touched the gold within and something inside me rose to meet the universal. Inside and out I was bathed in brilliance and it seemed to me that my skin became translucent so the light that came from within was all that formed my frame.

I was blazing. I was new. I was all the life in the garden, I was all the humans who had drilled the soil, I was the Changed waiting on the Mountain. I was the old woman who watched on Bright Street. I was the past and the future, and I had neither dreams nor fear.

And I saw the light of the universe explode around me, teeming with life from all the distant stars.

We were part of a greater whole. I knew it the way I knew that the sun was warm and that the water was clear. Those places beyond the horizon held a hundred more worlds like Maya, like the place that had held the original of this garden.

Time melted in the ice-pink dawn. Standing in this pool, reciting the ancient greeting to the day, this could be any time and any place. Indeed, the Maya I knew outside these walls no longer existed and there was only the sweet scent of the garden, where nothing had ever changed from the time our line first diverged.

In the Book of Ages I saw my own name and the karma of all the lifetimes that stretched back into the same eternity as the morning. All of the past existed inside me, but on the pages of the future there was nothing written at all. Only the rose-gold pages of the sunrise, Hail to the New Day. To the New Sun, to the Morning of All Life. Hail to the one I meet in the water, in the mirror, the one unknown, the one who shall be.

I did not see them go, did not hear the bells that marked the end of meditation; I did not even hear the calls of the senior acolytes calling us to breakfast. And so I was still in the water, the sunlight on my face, when they found me with the summons.

Chapter Eighteen

S ri Mayurna was alone when I approached him under the pink tila tree. The entire Study Court was silent and nothing moved but two bright-winged insects flitting from the surface of the water to test the flowers. I approached and bowed low, then waited for him to invite me before I sat. Now that I was part of the Temple myself I could no longer take the liberties that I had assumed as Arsen's son only a few days before.

I became still in a way I had not realized I had learned. Fidgeting would not do here, not when I had the whole example of the priesthood before me. Even among the lowest seniors there was never a single movement beyond what was necessary, and yet every gesture spoke of grace and beauty and the fullness of the circle. So I remained perfectly still, calm, recalling that I was still inside the dawn and the water and that no one had the power to take the morning away from me. I could rest there for as long as I needed, and so time became irrelevant as I continued to contemplate the life I had chosen.

"Well, well, so you have finally arrived after all," Sri Mayurna said, startling me from my ruminations. "And what, my young revolutionary-to-be, are you doing here? Training to be one of our priesthood? That seems an obscure ambition indeed for one of your hunger."

Hunger? The word confused me at first, thinking of the lack of food at the Temple. But then I realized that the old teacher spoke of the other hunger in me, the one that I had so carefully hidden even from myself.

"I seek only the peace of Enlightenment," I replied in the standard polite form.

Sri Mayurna's laughter was far more robust than his form. In that rolling mirth I could hear the younger man he had once been, strong and powerful and completely unafraid. I waited. Either he would explain or he would not. Only one day in the Temple and already I knew enough not to ask.

Finally he finished and studied me carefully, his face composed into a tranquil mask. "There are many ways to reach Enlightenment, and many enlightenments to achieve," he said softly. "The Blessing is only the first and you are already beyond that. You were born beyond that. You have already tasted the transcendence of the flesh and know that it is illusion. And so your hunger is for more than the simple fulfillment of the body in the state of the prepared mind. You are more ambitious than that, if not for the world than for the peace that comes with true knowledge. Do you know what I am saying?"

I did not and so I did not answer. The old man smiled and told me to sit. "I have never done this so early before," he said, "but you are now one of my pupils. Usually I watch a child for the first months of their learning, see how they adapt to the ways here. It is not what people think from the outside, especially those who come from the outside older and think that pleasure is the same as joy. I enjoy their confusion when they discover that this is not what we teach, that when you pass behind the mirror everything is turned around yet again.

"But you, you have very little time and there is so much we need to do. So—today we will begin with the principles of illusion, of how the mind creates the reality behind the reality. And how, by holding fast an image in mind, you are molded into that image. You are your own creation, and you can choose what you shall be. But, remember, it is no less sacred to rule the world than to leave it, to own all is to own nothing, and to be free is to be without fear."

I did not know what to reply. All his words were jumbled

together and made some kind of sense and yet I could not pull them apart. He talked of being without fear and I was frightened.

"The others will be here very soon, and this afternoon we shall have a clinical study that will be important. So eat now, you need to eat, but quickly. We'll wait for you to join us but we will not be able to wait long."

"Clinical study?" I asked. "I came here to see into reality, to learn the control and authority that even little Anasita displays. What is this clinical study?"

The rishi shook his head. "You still have to do something in the world. You need to know something, have a skill—not just for your own upkeep and the preservation of the Temple, but for the service of our Lord the Preserver above all. We are all extensions of the will of Vishnu, we are the co-creators of the universe day by day, and we are His servants in maintaining the balances that keep it always turning, always renewing its own being. Otherwise there is nothing at all."

I nodded. I knew that every acolyte learned some useful skill, but that I would be permitted to choose that study at the end of my probation—which, it appeared, came far sooner than I had anticipated.

"You will learn healing," Sri Mayurna told me. "To heal the body of a single bird or to heal the body of the whole of the Empire is in principle the same. So you shall start with the smaller before you try the larger."

I moved my bedroll that night into the second of four senior cottages that were apart from the others and close to the infirmary. The first year I studied anatomy along with philosophy, and that healing in the spirit is essential to healing in the body. That is where Sri Mayurna differed from his colleagues in service to other gods. We learned to listen to spirit and find where in the many traps of *maya*, illusion, it had foundered. Removing that illusion was more important than any manipulations of the mechanical and chemical systems that responded to injury and disease.

Sri Mayurna made certain that once we understood the place

of spirit, that we knew and could restore flesh as well. After all, this was the Temple of Joy and Sorrow and we said that flesh is spirit and all things spiritual are expressed in the body and form. That there is no difference, that the idea of separation itself is the core of illusion.

And so in the morning we studied sacred writings and discussed philosophy. In the afternoons we tended to the sick in Sri Mayurna's clinic, under his supervision and the tutelage of his former pupils who had remained in the Temple to expand their work. Two days a week Sri Jase taught pharmacology and the chemistry of herbs. He was far younger than Sri Mayurna, maybe not even old enough to be my father and his hair was still all dark and his face glowed with the same excitement I felt as the world was revealed.

"On the Mountain they are too sophisticated to use the plants that came with us from the dawn," he explained softly. "They want only what they call medicine, a thing devoid of life and soul. That is what they teach our people who go to study with them, and so our own humans come back and try to treat us as if we were Changed.

"The Changed do have the capacity for spirit," Jase went on. "But it is hidden from them. They never awaken it and they do not even recognize that it's there. So often their ailments stem from the starvation of that part they do not understand they have. Or need. Or need to nurture.

"But we're not here really to talk about the Changed. They are not patients in our clinics, though if they would come they would receive great benefit."

"But aren't the Changed different from us?" Lakki asked. Except for myself, Lakki was the youngest and newest of the clinic's apprentice healers.

"Yes," Sri Jase answered her. "The Changed are different, and later on we shall even look at how they were created and in what ways they differ. Changed and humans cannot have children who can have children in turn, and so we are no longer truly the same beings. And yet, not so very long ago they were no different from us. What changes their Creators made never touched their spirit natures in any case. All things are spirit, all things exist in the reality and in *Maya* at the same time. Even the stars and the rocks are spirit. It is only the Changed who do not understand that."

He looked so very sad at that moment, sad that he could not bring those who would despise him into joy and truth and health. Or so Jase saw it. And I found myself looking at him again, noticing how a lock of hair continually fell over one eye, how long his fingers, how proportioned and well-muscled his frame.

I told myself to stop it, that I would only humiliate myself. He was already a graduate and a teacher; he must have his own circle. Maybe he even had a child close to my age.

I told myself this but I could not stop looking—or thinking. But it did inspire me to focus far more on my studies as we went from the notions of how the pharmacopoeia had been brought to the complexity of biochemistry in its healthy state. I learned more about genetics than most of the Changed ever knew, and I learned more of the Creators, too. Every word Sri Jase said was burned into my mind, every segment in the chain of genetic alteration is still perfectly clear in memory. There was nothing I anticipated with more pleasure than my twice-weekly lectures and labs.

"How are you doing?" Sulma asked me when I had been at the Temple for three months. It was only our second evening alone in that time, and though I had seen her often on the Temple grounds I couldn't approach her. Not when she was wearing the full robes of a priestess and I was only a very new acolyte.

"I've missed you horribly," I admitted. "I think that sometimes I miss you more than I ever missed my mother. And certainly more than I've missed anyone else in Babelion." Suddenly the images of Tela and Vijay came to mind—but I had not lied; they had never been part of Babelion. Besides, my ties with them were cut as completely as my ties with anyone on the Mountain. I had promised Tela.

Still, I wondered yet again how Vijay and Alice had gotten back out of the crowd, of how they were living in the Village now and whether they had forgiven me. Or whether they had forgotten me entirely.

She thought for a moment and then smiled sadly. "One day you'll forget me, maybe even sooner than you think." She reached out and stroked my bare arm, which rested across her thigh. "It is only flesh, you know."

I shook my head. "Flesh is spirit, you know that better than I do. But Sulma, I'll never forget you. You're part of my life, of my family, of my circle even."

Sulma shook her head and laughed lightly. "We'll see what will come in the future. But for now, I hope you are not too disappointed in being changed into Sri Mayurna's group. To study the art of healing instead of the art of love."

I must have blushed. "I don't think so. This is all very interesting and I have some sense. . . ." I found that I couldn't say any more. It was not as if Sulma could not understand, I thought. After all, she had been trained as well, and she had to have felt how this time was only the opening of my karma and not the fulfillment of it.

But Sulma shrugged and looked at the flowers hanging from the tree. "I'm only a lay priestess, you know. I never had the opportunity to do what you're doing; I had a family to take care of when I was younger than you. I didn't have the luxury of time and years of study."

She blinked hard so I wouldn't see the tears. "Let me tell you about Iolo's latest stunt. They're going to try to take over the transformer at the Lake."

That got my attention. "The Lake? But Iolo doesn't know a thing about a converter."

Sulma laughed. "That's what's so funny," she agreed. "He doesn't. But he said that it's just out there and the energy is going to be pumped all the same. Just that there are no Guardians most of the time, or only a few. And why should the Changed think that they're being so generous in doling out our power? We'd live a lot better if we could regulate it ourselves and maybe even hold enough to negotiate with them for their energy needs. Between the Exchange and the Dome they need a lot more than we do, you know."

I hadn't known. Iolo must have done a lot of research in the time I'd been away. That, or I'd missed something important while I'd been staying away from his headquarters.

I knew, of course, about the converter on the Great Steam Lake, which is well to the south of Babelion and is fed by the lava fields of the Burning Rim. Because of the Rim we never know when any of the mountains around us or under us will explode, but because of the lake we have all the energy we need. There is always a balance between energy and survival, and so we exist on the margin perched precariously with the Burning Rim on one side and the North on the other.

Once a settlement started in the North. There is little volcanic activity there and it seemed so safe. After a few years they all died of some odd infection that we could never trace, and so few people have explored that region further. We have all we need by the lake, more than the people of Babelion and the Changed together could ever use. All the minerals we could want, all the water we might desire and all the power to run as much tech as we could transform.

So why wait? Why try to get the Changed to approve more feeds off the transformers they had running at the lake and that fed their precious Exchange first, their luxuries second, and Babelion a low last?

The idea was brilliant. In fact, it was far too brilliant for Iolo. I wasn't sure if he could even pull it off.

"He says it should be easy, and that we'll have a stranglehold on the Changed that way. That, and he keeps saying that he doesn't know why Arsen never thought of it. Over and over he says that this is a far better plan than anything Arsen ever considered and that taking control of our energy source is a way to take control of our destiny."

"And what do you think?" I asked Sulma. Often she had a far more pragmatic view than any of the would-be revolutionaries who rallied to my father's name.

She hesitated for a few moments. She wasn't used to being asked her opinion—to Iolo and Rajiv she was just their local priestess of pleasure and sometime lover. Maybe they had even considered asking her to create a circle with them—it certainly appeared that way to everyone else in the Movement. But I knew that they thought they couldn't have a formal alliance with a devotee. Iolo would think that it would injure their credibility.

It always appeared that neither of them saw her as anything other than a slightly offbeat devotee. Not that they precisely thought she was stupid, but they never thought she had an opinion on anything that mattered to them, and certainly not one worth listening to. I had learned differently.

"I think that the basic idea is a good one. After all, it appears that the converter is pretty much automated and overseen by the Exchange. There are a few humans in the Village who go to service it when needed, but even so there's rarely anyone there. So taking it ought to be easy.

"But that's what bothers me. It all looks too easy, so there has to be something they're overlooking. Iolo often makes up his mind to do something when he only knows half the story. But I can't discount it, everyone knows that it's true. The converter has just been sitting by the lake since it was built and no one ever goes there. It all sounds very logical but I don't trust it. Something lacks balance here, and when I try to see the future I see only darkness."

Iolo was a genius. Either that, or there was something truly terrible at the converter, something Iolo didn't know. I desperately wanted the second to be true. The image of Iolo as the genius hero who surpassed his brother was not appealing.

Besides, I wanted to take the converter myself. It was such a good idea that I couldn't believe that my father hadn't thought of it. That I hadn't thought of it months ago. I wondered where Iolo had gotten the idea, and how much real hard intelligence he had to make a plan.

"When is he going?" I asked.

Sulma shrugged. "You know Iolo," she said. "Sometime, probably well after some informer has told the Guardians and it's too late."

Now, he should be going now, my brain screamed. *If Sulma is telling me then he should already have gone and won and be on the way home. Why does Sulma talk so freely, anyway?*

For the first time I looked at Sulma objectively. She was beautiful, there was no doubt about that. Her eyes were wide and guileless, her skin had the texture and color of tila petals and her smile was generous and warm. Sitting here in the Study Courtyard with one foot up on the low wall with juice running down her chin, she could have been a senior acolyte herself.

Sulma could not betray anyone, my head agreed with my heart. Sulma could not knowingly do real harm—but there was that word *knowingly*. Like any innocent, she could wreak mass destruction with good intentions and never understand that she had been the cause of failure. She could talk to the wrong people too easily because she did not think of these as the right people and those as the wrong ones. She herself could not imagine anyone betraying Iolo's scheme to the Changed, and so she spoke far too freely.

So many years her junior, I knew just how her naïveté could destroy us with a breath. How she could retain that faith in all of us when she had grown up here in Babelion I did not know. And yet Sulma was utterly without fear.

It was the mark of the devotee in her, the clarity of one trained to the knowledge of the unseen. There was no room for fear when all of life was justice and retribution. When hope could only exist for the next incarnation and none was left for this.

I envied her utterly, and yet it seemed at that moment our positions reversed. Suddenly I was the elder, the more experienced, and she was the one who needed guidance and wisdom and protection.

"How many people have you discussed this with?" I asked carefully.

Sulma shrugged and bit into her melon again. "Not many at all," she confessed. "I probably should have worked more to recruit people to go along with him, but Iolo is being superior again and bossing everyone around. Including me. So I just can't manage to be as helpful to him as when he treats me like a grown woman with some abilities." She sighed heavily. "He can't afford to admit that a devotee might be able to function better behind the veil of *maya* than he can. What he really can't handle is the fact that his brother was one of us."

I was relieved that she hadn't told anyone besides me, though I joined her sense of trepidation. "It's probably best to be quiet about the whole idea until Iolo actually does something about it. Otherwise he'll look ridiculous."

She tilted her head to one side. "I hadn't thought of that, but you're right. And he really is a bit more than a little ridiculous to start with."

"Then why do you stay with him?" I finally asked the question that ran through my mind ever since I'd met her. "Why don't you just disappear and not bother with his schemes and his ego and his lack of respect not only for you, but for your faith and your whole way of life?"

Sulma laughed. "If I took him seriously I would have killed him before we'd ever said hello."

"Then why don't you just leave?" I repeated the question. "Why don't you join a circle instead of trying to create one with him and Rajiv? They don't even get along."

The melon rind dropped unnoticed from her hand. "They're the ones trying to form the circle together," she said softly. "All the fighting is on the surface because they're both afraid. And that's why I stay, and why I'll leave when it's time. They are not my destiny but my karma is tied to them."

My head was spinning faster than I could connect. What did Rajiv and Iolo fear? I had trouble imagining anything that frightened my uncle—except the spectre of his dead and brilliant brother. I knew that Iolo feared the memory of Arsen, the stories of Arsen, his comparison to Arsen.

Just the way they'd all resented me all along, because I was Arsen's son and I was expected to replace him. He hated me because he thought I showed up his weaknesses and reminded everyone of how great my father had been. But he also hated me because I wasn't Arsen reincarnated to come and save them all, to pick up a dying Movement and prove that they had done something meaningful with their lives. I couldn't assure them that Arsen approved of their caretaking since his death, and yet that was what not only Iolo, but everyone in their Movement, wanted from me.

I wasn't the person they thought I was, wasn't the person they all needed me to be. My only goal was—I realized I didn't know what my goal was. I thought it was to live, to survive and come back stronger. Or maybe it was to wreak revenge on the Mountain. Those had been my goals to start, but since studying in the Temple I had come to value the strength and calm and fearless peace that marked the priesthood more surely than their robes.

In the end I would have said that that was my only goal—the view behind the veil. To live in reality and not succumb to the illusion of want and pain and loss. To know that those things were never real as Sri Mayurna knew it—as Sulma knew it.

Maybe I was wrong.

The entire concept was astounding to me. Wrong. I had never thought about being wrong. The Changed aren't wrong about anything, ever.

And they were wrong all the time.

I knew that as one sudden wrenching gyration all the categories in my head shook their pieces free so that everything lay jumbled together in a pile. Instantly, I no longer had a neat system for thinking that this thought belonged to the Exchange and that experience came from Babelion, that the Mountain was advanced and the Temple primitive, that humans were stupid and the Changed were generous for permitting them to live.

Everything I'd known about the world came apart and for the first time I knew that I didn't know anything at all.

"If I can help him, I will," I heard myself say. "Tell Iolo, if he needs help with the Exchange, I know a lot about the system. Sri Mayurna would let me out for a few days to take care of it if you'll vouch for me. Tell him that I'd like to help him."

Sulma's arms were soft around me as I curled against her rough robe. The scent of her skin, musky and clean at the same time, seemed to blot out some of the more painful thoughts. I was still with Sulma, that was true and real. Maybe that was everything in the world I needed to know.

I spent the night with her in one of the rooms reserved for the priesthood, but I do not know which of us was the priest and which the seeker. I think we both Blessed each other then, though we were worlds and worlds apart. I didn't know that she was my first love then, or that she would always be the most sacred.

Chapter Nineteen

After that visit, Sulma was busy with Iolo and Rajiv preparing for the raid on the converter and did not visit. While I studied pharmacology avidly and anatomy with somewhat less skill, Sulma put aside supplies and tried to explain to Iolo that the team needed to prepare for possible delays.

But with all of that, Sulma still made a record for me herself, and I have collected every other firsthand account I could find. I even entered the Exchange and saw what happened to them, at least as the Exchange knows it. I have fought battles and killed people and survived and I have never seen or felt anything as horrible as I saw in the Exchange. I know I should think that I'm lucky to have even gotten this chip, but it's hard to think of anything there as luck. And now that I've seen it. . . . Well, but that's another story.

Sulma didn't really want to go. She was a lay priestess on the dole, not an adventurer even in her dreams. Sulma's dreams were all about the ease of the morning garden and the delights of the Temple. And of maybe, someday, showing Iolo and Rajiv that there are ways to show love other than incessant argument. Now I realize just how young she really was, and just how simple. She never could follow Iolo and Rajiv in their more abstract debates, but she knew more about their hearts than they did.

It doesn't matter. I'm supposed to be telling the story, not explaining all kinds of things that don't make any sense if you didn't know Sulma.

Anyway, they weren't prepared from the start. Iolo had the original maps that were in the public sector of the Exchange, and could be picked up for two hours' work credit at any newsstand. He hadn't checked for more recent versions in the public division and hadn't even tried to get authorization into the private.

Which, if he had asked me, I could probably have faked well enough. After all the training I'd had in the Exchange, and with my mother already integrated, getting into the Changed documents would be only too easy. But Iolo wouldn't ask me, not even for this, not even when I'd offered.

I would have been happy to do it, too. We could have reconciled, could have connected to create something more powerful than this organization that had been dying for almost eighteen years. And then everything would have been different. . . .

I must not think about what would have been different, or could have been. Only that what is past is gone and that it was his choice, in the end, not mine. I had offered everything I could, but an offer that is not taken is not my responsibility.

Besides, there were things that I didn't know then, that I couldn't have shared. And without that knowledge they could never have prevailed. It was not my lack of help, it was betrayal and beyond any of our control. Or so I tell myself when the shadows haunt me.

They went. They left near the end of summer, while it would still be warm enough to travel and when the mountain streams would be low and placid. The bulk of the supplies were bundled into tent skins and tied around with running lines and secured to the outer mounts of twenty jury-rigged sleighs that had at one time served every surface function on the planet. No two looked anything alike and most of them carried no more than three or four occupants. Muffled by the supply bundles attached to the shell, they resembled an army of stuffed kiddie toys in bright colors waddling across the landscape. Loading fuel must have been a nightmare.

It took twenty days to cross the plateau. A person can walk it in half that time, and many of the strike force abandoned their stuffy rides and stretched their legs. The transports were mostly to bring up supplies anyway, and humans didn't have to wait on the mechanized beasts to move so dreadful slow. So the caravan fell further and further behind the adventurers on the road. They talked and made plans and fantasized about a Babelion no longer dependent on the Mountain for energy. Even of the Exchange brought to its knees by the rebel force installing a stop-patch on its dedicated power supply.

That was one thing the ancestors weren't going to risk and they had made damn sure that it was nearly impossible for the

Exchange to disconnect from the energy source. Of course, the ancestors couldn't foresee a time when anyone would want to kill the only major AI they'd managed to keep whole on the way over. So while they had busily safeguarded against the volcanic activity that kept the Steam Lake bubbling, along with all the other vagaries of heavy weather and violent tectonic activity that is the hallmark of a world newly forming itself, they had never considered that there might be human intruders as well. There were no locks in the design Iolo had pulled from the records. No guard posts, no place to cache weapons in case of attack. There were only lots of fire hazard stations and the lava balloon. The seals existed to keep out lava and ash, not hands with heads attached.

Once upon a time it had been the configuration of the generation ship that had brought us. Then all the seals and locks had been intended to isolate areas if the hull were ever breached. The design remained for the Exchange, and I recognized the basic layout in the Temple as well. But the old stories were that the power plant had been built directly from the old ship itself, modified only slightly to fulfill its new purpose.

Sulma's records made it clear that the whole expedition had the atmosphere of a school holiday. They hiked across the plateau and into the Fires of Heaven Mountains that appear to drift on the horizon early in the morning. Usually they are soft gray, covered in ash, and sometimes lit with glowing lines of magma in the night. A pillar of smoke by day and fire by night—a scholar here has lately commented on the analogy. But it wasn't meant as a literary illusion, it was simply the plain truth. The Fires of Heaven range is beautiful and beckoning as well as violent, and we who have lived at its feet for all our generations have grown up walking the trails that ring the most dangerous volcanoes but leave the rest alone. If they go, they go, and there isn't much that we could do if anyone were there. But it happens so rarely that we just don't think about it. The active volcanoes we know and avoid and some of the sects worship them.

The Great Steam Lake itself is one of the most breathtaking sites in the settled galaxy. It is high up in the mountains in the crater of Mount Chango, where the fire deep in the pit of the volcano keeps the water boiling itself off to steam. The heat from the water and the steam generated by the lake are both easy to convert to pure power output for the people of Maya.

The steam rising over the lake can be seen from the plateau on the approach, a white haze in the sky that looks like rain coming in, obscuring the peaks of the dark glowering hills. If one of the volcanoes is spewing, the hell-red light of the eruption is faded to pink and diffused through the steam so it emits a fairytale entrancing pink glow. Sometimes near twilight the pink becomes lavender, and sometimes the setting sun turns it amber-orange.

Humans can't approach closer than the second ridge before the lake without the steam cooking us. Even at the second ridge it is hard to look for long with open eyes, and the guides won't permit anyone to stay at the observation point for more than a few minutes. But the guides and the few herders and trappers and maybe one maintenance tech are the only people who live anywhere near there. It's three days to Babelion, and most of a day from the Power Ridge to the Teselau Trading Post.

The power plant is down on the first ridge and can be approached two ways, either through the tunnels or with a protection suit. Only there aren't many suits in the locker at Teselau, where they are kept for the odd mechanic sent from the Exchange. I looked myself at the trading post and I think I counted ten—well, nine not counting the one with the red patches indicating leaks in the seals.

Iolo's force avoided Teselau, though they must have been visible across the open plains—it is hard to hide anything there. That was Iolo's great mistake, not going to Teselau and having a beer with the owner, not spending some jing on luxury goods like alcohol and happy-grass. The owner isn't exactly the kind of person who needs lots of company all the time, but like everyone who lives so isolated out in these hills he liked a break to the boredom and news and stories to brighten the day.

Iolo's plan was simple and to the point—they were going to go into the tunnels and take the control room and shut off the power to the Mountain until the Changed were ready to negotiate. It was straightforward and reasonable and there was no reason why it shouldn't have worked, except for Iolo's ignorance of other people. If everyone were a revolutionist and liked to live lean, then he would have been the great psych-adjuster in the world. As it was, he ignored psychology for statistics and other measures he could quantify.

The group arrived in the low range early in the day and set up camp and rested. They ate well that night, with two curries and meat and tilaberry pancakes for dessert, and then they slept soundly until dawn.

Sunrise in the Holy Smokes is not like sunrise anywhere else. Here the light comes diffused through the steam haze and ash and an occasional tongue of lava shimmering on its own. Iolo's force spent much of the morning looking for the tunnel entrances, which were hidden originally to keep out animals and over the centuries have weathered indistinguishable from the rocks themselves. Even with the charts and drawings he had downloaded, Iolo had trouble finding a reference point. The map was old and the range volatile—it was easy to see that features had changed dozens of times since the map had been drawn.

The light was already turning warm and bright in the late afternoon before Iolo discovered the first entrance. They gathered, the six of them, and peeled the thick crust of dirt and light foliage off the door with their hands. By the time the entrance was open it was coming on to dark, so their first view of the tunnel was dim.

Iolo left Rajiv outside as sentry. They argued vigorously, and Rajiv argued that his computer skills were well above Sulma's and that she should be made a sentry since she wasn't likely to be much use in the energy center. Iolo refused and said that Sulma could wait outside with Rajiv if they liked, but that he needed Rajiv on guard. If trouble appeared Sulma could only warn them, Iolo argued, but Rajiv could fight. So they had yet another argument and Iolo, as always, won.

So he and Sulma and the rest of the expedition passed into the tunnel that was made of the ship that had brought our forebears to this place they had named Maya. It was solid, though, and smelled more sealed and antiseptic rather than of decay. The ancestors built to last. The floor was paved and polished, and as the censors registered their heat signatures long narrow glowstrips along the ceiling came up slowly. It never got really bright in the tunnel, but the light was good enough that they could tell the tiles on the walls were of local manufacture and someone had done a mural. Why not—if one is going to put up tile anyway it's no more effort to use beautiful ones, and these projects are good for younger artists just learning their craft. Babelion is full of such mosaics and tile works, cast benches and bits of architectural whimsy made from whatever is lying around as students at the Handicraft Academy work on major projects. It was odd to see such hidden but public art that was so very old. The light was so bad that it was impossible to tell if the designs were any good.

It is maybe two hundred meters from the outer entrance to the first airlock. Here the establishment changed. The lights glowed brighter and the floors were carpeted. They were definitely "inside" now, though there were levels of distinction.

The Exchange knew they were there. Usually it doesn't monitor that area or those systems, but this time it was alerted. The owner of the Teselau Trading Post had reported the presence of a column headed toward the Great Steam Lake with highly suspicious behavior—which is to say, they did not drop by and chat, let him know that they were there just for the view or because there was nothing better to do in Babelion or that the younger members of the party wanted to see the sights up close.

The owner had watched them pass on the plain with the vehicles loaded down and the outwalkers on patrol and estimated a fair-sized force. He reported directly to Babelion Safety without knowing that the message was automatically copied and sent to the Guardian Headquarters on the Mountain and flagged in the Exchange. Or so Sulma thought in her reporting, though I have contradictory evidence.

Nor did Sulma say who the owner of the Trading Post was or what association he had with the Movement. That was for me to learn much later. There was no reason for Sulma to suspect anything, nor was it her nature to think ill of folk. So her record of the attempt is guileless and therefore more painful to review.

There was no one waiting for Iolo's team as they moved deeper into the power plant. Sulma's shoulders relaxed visibly; Iolo walked with a jaunty confidence, lord of the future and, more important, his brother's equal. After all, Arsen had failed. And where Arsen had gone down and died in defeat, Iolo already held himself as the returning hero, delivering free power to all of Babelion with the Changed and the Exchange firmly under his control.

The Exchange thought it was funny and did nothing at all, luring them ever more deeply. The Exchange wondered how far Iolo would go before realizing that he had entered a trap. To the Exchange this was a fair test of wit and skill, and anyone trained on the Mountain would have recognized that in a heartbeat.

Iolo had not followed his brother's path to the testing center. He had never experienced interface and had no idea that the Exchange had a personality, let alone what that personality was. I knew what it would do from the first time I saw them enter. Even if I had not gotten the word until months afterward, even if I hadn't already known the outcome, I would have known as soon as I had seen the door and the airlock. And so I watched in desperate horror as the inevitable unfolded. I was powerless to stop it, to warn them, to use the authorizations of the Changed to clear the expedition. Over and over I have accessed this, and over and over I have watched, and always, always the same thing happens and I am completely helpless.

They were in four rings deep, the seals at this level being a precaution against lava and steam as well as the fine ash that could too easily jam the delicate connections or toxic gasses spewed up by the magma. Not until they were firmly settled in the center of the plant behind airlocks made of ultraresilient materials did the Exchange act.

Or not act—not act at all. It waited like the dead until they reached the control center, and even then it lay low. It lulled Iolo into a sense of mastery where he forgot that his adversary was at least as powerful as he. Iolo was easy to lure and he wouldn't listen to Sulma's protests and warnings.

The Exchange waited until they had puzzled out the interface and tried to go in twice through the boards and once into an access panel with pliers.

And when it finally did act, the Exchange behaved passively, leaving them room still to escape. It had only cut off the relays and the power inside the control center died. It was dark and the

light whirring and soft, very low whine of the venting systems
died as the control boards went silent.

They were trapped in complete silence, in pitch darkness.

Iolo had specified only one lantern in the gear they had brought
inside. Who needed the extra weight of lanterns when there were
plenty of healthy glowstrips? One of the party lit the lantern and
there were only shadows over their faces.

"Put it out," Sulma hissed.

"Absolutely not," Iolo protested. "We need the light."

"It's burning up our oxygen," Sulma said.

"We'll get out," Iolo assured her. "We just have to find the
way to the airlocks. There has to be a manual override, and this
installation is huge. There's plenty of air for a long long time."

Sulma said nothing, but bit her lip and nodded.

Iolo's reasoning was good enough as far as it went. He did not
recognize that he was fighting an enemy, not merely a malfunc-
tion. He lifted the lantern and began back the way he thought he
had come, a corridor doorway near the console.

Only there were six corridors off the main control station and
they all looked exactly the same under the light of the lantern.
Whatever identifying marks there were in color or writing on the
walls were indistinguishable in the dribble of available light. Each
corridor led to an airlock with two branchings off it into what in
the schematic appears to be a maze. Perhaps the ancestors had
intended a trap, or perhaps the design was dictated in part by the
overactive geology all around.

They came to the first airlock to find it locked down.

"There has to be a manual override," Iolo said. He searched
for the panel, and when he found it he realized that he had to
break the lock. But even the manual was not completely mechanical, it incorporated a few parts run on station power. After all,
this was the main power plant for the entire world. There was
more geothermal energy produced in one square meter of this
region in one minute than all the people of the ancestor's world
could have consumed in generations. It was unthinkable that energy would run out.

Besides, no one would be passing airlocks in manual without
an emergency, and in an emergency everyone would carry one

or two boosters. Just in case something was cut off or shorted, the booster could be jacked in to the panel and provide enough power to open the airlocks and turn on the lights.

Iolo had to know what boosters were. If he had read over even a tenth of the specs he had called up to plan this mission, he had to know. But he hadn't found any boosters lying around. They were stored somewhere, no doubt. Maybe if they could be found they wouldn't be charged—maybe there truly isn't any blame for this particular oversight.

"We'll have to pry open the doors," he announced.

They didn't have a crowbar in the gear. That had all been full of weapons and food and little luxuries like good shampoo. Finally one of the others used a kick gun to blast through the mechanism, but it took a long time and a lot of the kick gun's reserves to shoot out enough that they could actually pull the outer shell doors open. Then they had to choose which of the branchings to take.

The lantern burned oxygen. The kick gun burned oxygen. All the talking and physical effort to open the airlock burned oxygen as well, and the still air was starting to take on just a hint scent of rank human. And it wasn't until the corridor they chose dead-ended in what looked like a limited dormitory that they knew they were lost.

On the outside, Rajiv waited for two full days before he began down the tunnel. "I never thought they were in trouble," he told me when I asked. "I only thought that maybe there were some technical problems and I thought they should have come to tell me if they needed any supplies. As it was, I mainly thought that I would deliver more food. I knew they'd taken in some but not that much. Besides, I was pretty bored and lonely sitting out there, knowing that Sulma and Iolo were in there. I missed them."

He went to the first airlock and found it sealed, and thought that was odd. "But I thought that maybe they had reasons, or maybe they had just forgotten to reverse the cycle. Or maybe they were keeping it open from the inside, which made a lot of sense to me. The whole panel was dead and I thought about it and decided to give them one more day. Then I would try to reverse the locks and go in myself."

The Exchange—or Sithra—was very amused. The lantern had burned out and the group was still wandering in the tunnels. They had gone on and forced three more airlocks before the kick gun ran out. Only then had they tried to go back to the control center to find boosters, but then the lantern went low and there was no more light.

In the end, in the tape, there was nothing to see in the visible range. The Exchange showed me in infrared so I could see the dull red shapes of their bodies neatly laid out on the carpeting to die. They were not in any of the predicted places. The Exchange insisted that they were trying to get back to the comfort of the dormitory beds to die. I insisted that they had still been searching for a way out, or for the boosters, or for any hope at all.

They lay there, breathing very shallowly. Some faint sobbing showed up on the record but I can't tell who it is. A little humming, too, a tune I knew well. That was Sulma, I realized, and the tune was one that ended the sunset prayer. She was, in the end, a priestess of great spirit. But I had known that all along.

I watched the tape over and over, noting precisely when their breathing ceased. One at a time they died of asphyxiation in the dark.

With their deaths the power surged back through the lines. The ventilation and lighting came on, and I could see how they were arranged in death. Every time I enter that interface I see their faces, I see the surprise and resignation. And I see Sulma again and again, her composure more than I can bear, and I cannot hold back the tears. Even now I cannot stop the feeling that cuts through me with the loss.

That is how I learned that I loved Sulma, and that I still love her. That even if I was not invited to her circle, I had been initiated into something far larger than sex, or the sacred, or even the revolution.

It must have been much worse for Rajiv, who discovered their bodies less than ten hours after they had died. I tell myself it must have been more than I could imagine, to lose both of those with whom you had just bonded into the center of a circle. It must have been worse because he had been waiting outside, not so far away.

And if he had done something when he had found the first

airlock he could have saved them. When he told me how he found them, when I ran the first Revolutionary Tribunal, I had walked over my high desk and jumped from the podium and tackled him. I pinned his shoulder and started to smash his head against the floor, screaming at him that he could have saved them and why hadn't he gone before. But Rajiv offered no resistance.

It took two of our cadre to pull me off him. Others were helping Rajiv up from the new marble that now had a red stain. Blood ran across Rajiv's face and streaked thinly down his cheeks and neck. Thin blood, I thought. He had never deserved Sulma's concern and loyalty.

Then I realized that the blood was thin because it had mixed with tears. He had not resisted me and had said nothing. In the Tribunal he looked up and met my eyes, and I saw that his were burning. "Why didn't you finish?" he asked, low in his throat and thick with accusation. "Why didn't you let me die before, on the Mountain, in prison? I've only been trying ever since."

Then he turned away from me toward the audience in the gallery. People with nothing better to do than watch the revolution were seated there day after day, for the tribunal, for the sentencing, for the tears and the repentance.

"Yes, I know now that I could have saved them." His voice rose to the back of the house with a power that I hadn't heard since I'd left for the Temple. "Every day since I have prayed to die. If I am sentenced you will only bring me what I so dearly wish. Every minute that I live is misery, knowing that I had the ability to save those I have loved more than I loved anything. Including the revolution."

I sentenced him to ten years of mind labor in the Exchange.

Chapter Twenty

I heard nothing at all right after the mission. I had been at the Temple long enough that I had become accustomed to the lack of contact with the outside world, which was part of the appeal and the discipline. The world is Maya and I was here to see into the reality beyond that. After nearly a year in the Temple, I didn't miss the concerns I had left behind, and the internal world I was discovering with Sri Mayurna was so rich and fascinating that I usually forgot there was a life not dedicated to healing and contemplation, mathematics and mystery.

Stories of the incarnations of god/dess merged with my knowledge of physics, of the stars. Legends were revealed as both true and as metaphor—and as coded symbolic language that hid more truths than it told.

Sri Mayurna used those stories as a mirror, to show me my own soul. Sometimes that soul appeared very ugly indeed, sometimes my desires focused on revenge without mercy. Sometimes I was consumed with ambition, with the anger to fuel it to show Della—

"Show her what?" Sri Mayurna asked me. "That you are better than she? Or that you never needed her? In either case, you are always limited. Define yourself with limits and you will build them for yourself. And you will have wasted all our time here, teaching you to see beyond the idea of limitation into the reality of the whole."

There were plenty of times I wanted the anger and rejected the greater power for the lesser one. That was what I had to control and at which I did such a poor job. Well—I was very young then.

I could see very well. I knew that I succumbed to the great temptations of anger and ambition, and that when I followed those I lost all the power I had. But equilibrium is not something one can really appreciate at almost eighteen, nor is it a thing that one has ever valued. It is like taking a speed sled down the cliff—with equilibrium it is possible to hit the highest speeds but lose balance for a second and the race is over. I had never been a racer but I understood the feeling in my muscles, in my bones.

I knew it, but I couldn't often find that point in myself before I skidded on some vague memory of Della or Sithra—or Iolo, for that matter. So it was no great mystery why I wouldn't know that Sulma and Iolo were dead, that Rajiv had dragged the bodies out one at a time and rolled them off the ridge into the lava field for decent burial. The rock is all too young and too active there, there isn't enough topsoil to bury a human. So lava is the only option, other than leaving them to freeze and be eaten by the native wildlife.

Though I missed Sulma's visits I also thought that she and Iolo and Rajiv were busy working things out between the three of them to establish a formally recognized circle, and that with the takeover of the power plant they had more than too much work to occupy them. There were times I wished she could see me as I was becoming in those moments when I hit the poise that Sri Mayurna was trying to teach me. I wanted her to see me as the priest to match her priestess, to the solid core of being.

But I understood that Sulma had too much to do. They had won the war, was what I thought, and I didn't know what to feel. I knew I should be happy and I wasn't. I hadn't thought Iolo was capable of actually taking power himself and secretly I had thought that one of these days I would show them. That I would finish my studies and be recognized as a healer, and then I would go and show those paperwork revolutionaries what it was all about.

I was sad, but I never suspected any reason other than work for Sulma's disappearance from my life. Since the riskiest part of any revolution is the consolidation of power afterwards, I didn't question Sulma's absence, though I wondered wistfully when she would be able to return again. The weather turned colder and the tila trees dropped their petals so the courtyard was paved with pink and ivory that looked almost like snow. I passed my eighteenth birthday after the third major storm of the year came down out of the Holy Smokes range.

Eighteen was an important number to me. I have read that everyone passes some form of crisis when they reach the age at which their same-sex parent died. While my birthday was not marked at the Temple in any way, the entire day all I could think about was my father. At my age he had led a rebellion and had died for it. He had never reached his eighteenth birthday.

This measure, then, was all of his life and achievement. He had become a legend in Babelion, he had already been a living symbol for a year. And what was I? What had I achieved? There was nothing at all to equal him—I had fled the Mountain and had walked out on his revolution. I was becoming a good healer and would soon graduate with that skill. Sri Mayurna permitted me to see patients on my own and permitted me to make diagnoses and prescriptions with only his supervision. And in recent weeks there had been only a little of that. Some days he didn't even speak to me and reviewed all of my cases at the end of the week.

Yet that day, three weeks after my eighteenth birthday, Sri Mayurna called me to sit under his favorite tree in the second major storm of the worst winter in two generations. The ground was already frozen and covered with a thick layer of deep snow from my birthday storm, and the fine flakes fell so fast that I was afraid that we would be buried as the old rishi spoke. Still, I tried to concentrate on his words and on the meaning and reality behind those words. I tried to ignore the stunning cold, and more, the chill in my heart as he spoke. Even as he began to teach me, there was something in his face, in his voice, that told me this was the last time.

"There is physical force to be sure," Sri Mayurna said as we sat around him in the gently drifting snow. The old man seemed to find it as pleasant as the dropping of petals from the tree in warmer months, and wore no shoes or any jacket over his undyed robe. I was huddled in layers of muslin clothing and blankets over that, and I still shivered.

"Yes, there is physical force and it is the first force we see and learn. Then there is mental force, the force of knowledge. To recognize that is more mature. One who knows can always prevail over one who has no knowledge, but the problem lies in the subtlety of that victory. Those who are strong in body and weak in mind do not realize that they have been defeated, and sometimes will step down to the level of using physical force where they might be able to reverse the conflict. But a physical victory cannot overturn a mental defeat. And so one might kill the knower and still be completely ruined and not ever understand that.

"It is the same with a moral victory. One who lives and walks in the holiness of all things cannot in truth ever be defeated by mind or body. Compassion is the greatest of the treasures of the spirit, and from it flows great power.

"But within the mature spirit is all power, no matter how power is defined. Because those of great spirit have no fear. To know what is good and to embody that good is to know that there is never defeat. That life is eternal and that all who know fear or hate or need have created these perceptions because they are not yet strong enough to trust serenity, eternity, and love."

There were times that I wanted to scream that I was only eighteen and that of course I couldn't trust serenity, eternity or love. Trust them? I wasn't even sure they existed outside of the Temple precincts. Out of these walls lay enemies and death and rejection—when I bothered to remember that there was an out-side.

"But the greatest defeat of all to those who do not know is to be ignored. They are struggling against the air, against the sea, against that which cannot be affected by their being and whims. So it is to be the air, the sea, that is stronger than all battles together. Then there is no possibility of defeat and there is no fear. Fear itself is meaningless when there is only being and eter-nity." The old man finished his lecture.

Sri Mayurna rose and put his hand on my head. "Remember the priestess who died, who loved you and brought you to us. She fulfilled her karma, as did the others with her."

"What?" the word erupted from my mind. Suddenly I didn't feel the cold any more; I didn't hear the shriek of the wind or see the snow. All I knew was a bleak whiteout inside my chest that was too big to face.

"Iolo, Sulma, the others who went with them," the rishi said gently. "They have gone on on the Wheel. They have completed the work of this one lifetime and have found release, to be reborn to a better time and finer circumstances. I have read the book of karma and I can tell you that they have earned rebirth in a warm place by their sacrifice."

I could not cry or scream or protest. I could not face the wide, vast desert inside my heart as I realized that they were dead. I looked away, closed my eyes, tried to banish the knowledge. The world was no different now than it had been five minutes ago. They had been gone for a long time. I wondered that I had not known, that I had not felt the moment that Sulma had left this world.

Snow settled around me like a blanket of frozen comfort. My brain was numb—with cold or abandonment, I am not sure which—and so I could think only very slowly.

I could smell the incense that clung to Sulma's skin and the feather-light drifts were as smooth as her flesh. And as cold as her flesh was now. I could no longer feel my toes.

The Temple bell sounded distant, muffled, and as lonely as the ice-gray sky. Color had all faded to shades of white and shadow, as if the bright pinks and oranges and midnight blues of the world knew not to intrude on mourning.

There was warmth on my shoulder for a moment. One of the acolytes had touched me, beckoned me to come inside, but I couldn't move. I was afraid to move. If I left this spot I would have to make some choice to live, and I had not yet decided anything at all. The warmth withdrew and I was glad to be left alone where I could feel the ice growing inside me and refuse to think about Sulma dead at all.

I don't know how long I sat in the snow. Little licks of it had drifted up around my legs when the old woman touched me on the shoulder. I did not recognize her immediately. Or rather, I did, but I knew that she was the Votress and the Goddess, though I wasn't certain which one. Whether she led me to life or death didn't matter. I had lost the desire to chose which one, though I thought that it was more likely that I die. I could feel the cold penetrating more deeply, seducing me to indolence.

I wanted to follow it. It would be so sweet to sleep in its frigid embrace. But the old woman would not leave me in peace.

"It is time," she said.

I nodded. She was right, it was time.

She turned and did not look back and I followed her through the Study Court to the Public Court to the Gates of the Garden and out into the blizzard enveloping the world.

I awoke in a Tinker wagon, in a soft bed covered with heavy quilts. I had not been this comfortable in a long time, and for a moment I had forgotten being fetched in the snowy courtyard.

"Drink this," a gentle voice said, and then a hand came behind my head and another held a bowl to my mouth. Whatever was in there was steamy hot and delicious, thick and satisfying. After nearly a year when there was never enough food, and never anything that tasted good, this soup was a luxury I had forgotten.

"You must drink it all," the voice urged. "Auntie said so."

I finished the bowl in wonder at the rich broth and the warm wagon and the soft caress of the sheets and satin quilts against my skin. That was when I realized that I was naked, and that my acolyte's robe was nowhere to be seen. The shawl was draped over the topmost quilt and I felt sudden relief. I didn't care about the Temple robe but there was something about the ancient shawl that mattered. I hadn't realized that I felt that way—for a long time it was just this relic from my mother's past.

"Where did you get this?" I asked, fingering the stiff silver embroidery and the smooth warm pearls.

It had been so long since I had seen it. Not since Della had gone into the Exchange. I tried to remember that day but my brain was still sluggish and I found the memory of the shawl itself more vivid than my mother's face.

The Tinker smiled slowly. "Alice got it after you left us in Babelion. She brought it back from your house on the Mountain and gave it to me. She said that I would see you again and I must return it. And she said that she was sorry for me but that she could not alter my karma and it was a terrible thing to be beloved of a god. And then Alice said that you were very careless to leave it behind."

Alice. I only knew one Alice.

But it was not possible. That would mean that the Tinker standing over me was Vijay, and that did not make sense. Vijay belonged in the Village studying neural sculpture, not out in some wagon in the middle of a storm.

I closed my eyes. Obviously I had succumbed more deeply to

the cold than I had realized. I was hallucinating. Maybe that meant I was dying. I had heard that it was an easy death to die of cold, and this was only proving the fact. Vijay had come for me in death. Did that mean that Vijay was dead, too?

And Sulma, where was Sulma?

"Now let me see your fingers," Vijay said. I held my hands out as requested and looked at my nurse. He inspected my fingertips carefully, one at a time. "Those are doing well," he muttered. "Now the toes."

Curious, he poked my feet from under the quilts. Even the delicate touch of the healer made my feet burn as if they were being sanded and were on fire at the same time. "These will take some time to recover," he told me. "But eventually they will. You're very fortunate, we won't have to remove any."

I blinked in confusion.

"Your toes were frozen when Auntie brought you in."

I tried to remember all the things my mother had said about her time with the Tinkers. She referred to running away a lot, but she never had given any of the details of what life was like while she was away. She never told me if there was significance to all the sun-moon-star imagery that seemed to appear everywhere. It was on the shawl I had been given, it was embroidered around the neck and cuffs of the shirt the healer wore, it was even painted on the ceiling of the wagon where I lay. She never told me if the colors were entirely random or if they were chosen, nor where they had been obtained. The artists and designers of Babelion would love to have such intense colors, reds and oranges and pinks that scalded my eyes. Even the normally sedate blues and greens here were not the familiar hues. They, too, were shimmering and potent, threatening saturation.

But then this was my death, and it felt like a dream. Nothing was real and everything was symbol and what I knew and what I didn't know turned on each other in a Moebius strip.

In the symbols of my dying brain, the healer was my father and Vijay merged into one. His hair was long in the style of the rebel young of Babelion, dark with deep red where the light shone off it, and his eyes were amber and luminous as the magma fields at night.

"You need to sleep now," he said, turning the lights off and leaving the room. I wondered if I actually had woken in a dream or if this were some other reality, and I was still in the Temple in the Chamber of Thought.

I feel asleep in the middle of my contemplation. There must have been drugs in the soup; I slept without dreams for a very long time. Though how long I couldn't say because I was still in the same wagon when I awoke, and there was no window to give me any sense of time. Only now I was certain that I was truly awake. There was no dream/drug haze, no symbolic confusion, in the aching through my body. It was strange to think that I was really alive.

I was alone this time. I said "on" and the lights came up again, and the first thing I did was poke my toes from the covers and inspect my feet. My feet seemed perfectly normal. Well, there were a few places where the skin looked thicker and opaque, but everything wiggled just fine.

Tentatively I put my feet on the thick carpet and stood. I was weak and smelled bad, but my knees and ankles regained some of their stability as I took a few steps in the small, cramped space. The rest room door was open, probably so that I wouldn't have to go searching in need, and there was definite need. I felt much better after that, and the shower looked very tempting even if it was tiny and the soap was simple sandalwood.

The water came on warm and I luxuriated in the pleasure of it. Of feeling the stale sweat and crust of drugged sleep sluiced away down the drain in cascades of suds. I washed my hair twice and stood in the rinse forever. How long had it been since I had felt this clean? Certainly never in the Temple. And in the squat, where water had to be hauled up by hand, bathing was a luxury. No, the last time must have been in the Village, in Tela's house, the morning of the day I had gone down with Alice and Vijay and disappeared forever.

That day, yes. There was no mistake. The healer had to be Vijay, Tela's son, grown up. I had spent so much time with him— but he was still in boy-form when I came to Babelion. He had entered the wagon silently and had stood in the shadow. I studied him from half-closed eyes. Now he had the face and body of a man. His hair had gone darker and Tela's startling cheekbones and hollows had been hidden under childhood roundness. Now those cheekbones gave him a serious, haunted look even when he smiled.

"What are you doing here?" I asked. "I thought you were going to become a neural sculptor like your mother."

The grin that spread over his face was slower than the one that lit his eyes. "I am," he said. "I began my training and started my research project. We know a great deal about how experience forms the Changed brain in the first years, about taking advantage of windows of learning and all, but no one had ever made a similar study of the human brain. I started doing the research and found myself going deeper and deeper into what it was that makes the Changed different from us."

He hesitated, screwed up his face trying to decide how to tell me. "I discovered that there were some—inconsistencies. And I started to wonder about why the Creators had made certain choices, too. The Changed are dying out, Anselm. They are dying. If we wait another five generations there won't be enough of them left to run the Exchange. They're finished and they know it, but it appears as if the end was planned. Why would the Creators do that?

"There are other anomalies, too. The fact that they need neural sculptors at all has always bothered me. Why do they need special training to ensure they'll be acceptable to the Exchange? Unless the Exchange was never the point. And we have no idea of what any of the Changed would be, or would be like, if they weren't sculpted until they were hardwired.

"Another thing is that we know that it is the neural manipulations after birth that insure compatibility with the Exchange. It is not genetic. Because otherwise you wouldn't have been able to touch access. Nor could Della have."

"What?" I shot straight up in bed and gripped his shoulders and looked deep into his eyes. "Della was maybe a little different for the Changed, and possibly the years she spent with the Tinkers did something. But she was Changed, the genetics checked out."

Vijay shook his head. "No, Anselm. Not one told you because the Tinkers were not going to let Sithra destroy you or your mother. Auntie can tinker with more than genetic code. The evidence in her case was that she was far more adaptable to the Exchange than any of the Changed. But the thing is, Della wasn't genetically human, either."

"Then what is she?"

Vijay blinked. "I don't know. No one knows. No, that's not right. The Tinkers know and that's why I came here in the end. It was obvious they know a whole lot too much—I realized that when I started building a database for the brain chemistry research years ago. I wanted to include a few Tinkers in the study because the more kinds of people the better the comparisons. Anyway, a few of them, including Auntie Suu-Suu, showed up when I advertised for volunteers.

"I didn't know anything at the time. They've kept the secret so well for so long that I think some of them have forgotten, or would have if they didn't go away so often, or if Auntie Suu-Suu weren't there to remind everyone.

"Anselm, the Tinkers aren't human either. And Della's genotype doesn't resemble theirs any more than it does the Tinkers, and the Tinkers is as far away from the general human population as Della's is.

"When I looked at the evidence I was completely confused. For days I went over my techniques and redid every segment of the basic analysis, even though I've been doing that in my sleep since I was ten. But, you know, something could have happened, some contaminant got into the samples, or the specimen matrix was mixed wrong. Something. It doesn't happen often, but there are cases. We know about that, that it could happen, and so I went over every element, everything I had done.

"I reran the tests three more times. Each time I mixed a new batch of matrix, I ran a systems check on the machinery. And I used a sample from myself as the control. After three more runs the results were perfectly consistent—including mine. So there is only one conclusion."

My head began to spin. Della wasn't Changed. That meant that I wasn't the half-breed I, and she, and Sithra, had always assumed. But she wasn't human, either.

I laughed aloud and Vijay looked at me strangely, but I couldn't explain. It made so much sense that Della wasn't Changed, or wasn't human. She never had been. That made so much more of her craziness make sense. All the time I'd been trying to understand who I was, who had molded me, and all the time I had been missing the basic biology.

I had never considered that there could be so many humanoid species. Like everyone else, I thought the humans were the basic stock and the Changed had been genetically manipulated.

"It's hard to believe there are so many others," I muttered. "Other kinds, somewhere. Della must have come from somewhere. And the Tinkers. You know, there aren't any records or stories about any other people landing here. I had always just assumed that the Tinkers were humans who broken away from Babelion, who'd had their own little rebellion and created their own culture."

It was much bigger than Babelion, I understood that clearly. In our little provincial minds we had limited the possibilities to those which we could see in front of us without any effort of thought. We had limited the universe to our own little world, and we were wrong.

I had always thought of Maya alone. It seemed that we were alone, that whatever Empire was out there, whatever remnants of the Creators and their universe existed, they were irrelevant to us. Now I knew I had been wrong. No matter how much I wanted to dismiss the distant majority, I had to face the truth that they were among us. And we could not escape them any more than we could escape ourselves.

"Which is the original human genetic group?" I asked Vijay as the possibilities became clearer in my mind.

He shook his head. "I don't know. Probably none of us. Probably all four strains I have studied so far are Changed in some way or another. And we can't even limit it to four. There could be ten variants, or a hundred, or a million."

"And we never knew they were there," I mused. "I always thought they were humans."

Vijay nodded slowly. "So did I, so did everyone. And they appeared such a short time ago. I don't think any one of us knew this, or even wondered about it, but we don't even know how long they've been here."

"There are stories from all the way back," I protested. "The Tinker bands have always drifted around, so they disappear for long periods into the mountains or something."

"No," Vijay said, and this time he was firm. "Think about it. How long have they been gone—at the longest? Years and years, right, where there are no records. If they didn't come in, appear to human society once in a great while, they would die. No one can live in the mountains, you know that. You never know when the next peak is going to blow. And the lowlands away from the ridgeline are too cold, and with the permafrost nothing edible grows there. We know that the Tinkers aren't farmers, they aren't settled enough to be. So that raises the question, where are they when they are gone?"

"But they aren't gone very long now," I pointed out. "In my whole life they've been around to perform every year from spring through late fall and Carnival Court. Then they stockpile and leave for wherever it is they call home."

Vijay nodded solemnly. "That is precisely what they do. Only the wherever they call home is not anywhere on Maya."

"That's absurd," I scoffed. "I mean, is there some secret installation and a big landing area for rockets hidden somewhere so far away that we'd never notice? That we'd never see anything at all in the sky? I don't think so, Vijay. I think you're the victim of your own imagination."

Vijay dropped his eyes. "No, I'm not. I wish I were. I am a scientist, Anselm. In my heart I am a scientist, I want to find knowable truth. I want to test it and then I want to test it again to make certain that it is real. I believe in concrete reality. I have never had time for fantasy and, for a human, I don't have the best imagination, either.

"I have been there with them," he admitted, looking guilty and ashamed. "I have been there when the wagons leave and I have gone on the long night journey to home, and it is a research institute located on one of the central worlds of the Empire."

"The Empire?" I asked.

"The Empire," Vijay said. "It's old and it's dying, and I think only the central worlds are left. But they exist, all different peoples created by generations of Creators. The Tinkers are called that because that is their own nickname for themselves. They are researchers; they are the descendants of the Creators themselves. And Auntie Suu-Suu is both their leader and their political voice. She has her own agenda and I don't know what it is. There are politics there that I don't understand and I didn't have enough time to try to get behind them. There were more important things, believe me.

"But Anselm, you and your mother and all of us are part of it."

"And you?" I asked, genuinely curious. "How do you know this, why were you picked to go when no one else even knows they exist?"

"They—watch," Vijay explained. "There is some reason they are interested in us, in the Changed, and also in you. You and your mother especially, it turns out. They also keep in touch with the research that's going on here, what people are doing. They know all about your teachers, about the Temple and Sri Mayurna. And they knew about me.

"I have an Imperial scholarship to the University of Cadien. They invited me just six months ago, when I confronted Auntie Suu-Suu on my findings about them, and I have been through all the interview and testing process. I'll enter a little late because I have been studying the language, and here I speak only Cadien all the time. I'm already near fluent, but I also need some more background that Empire students get that we don't teach before I'm ready to enter classes there."

"And none of us know this or have ever been there before?" I asked in awe. Because I wasn't certain whether this insanity was actually true, or whether Vijay had succumbed to the disaster of the Village, whether his reason had died and left him at the mercy of his waking dreams, and he believed everything in his head was true.

I had heard about this sickness before, in humans and Changed alike, and it had happened more in the Village than among any other population.

Vijay shook his head. "Why don't you get dressed first? We can talk more after you've had food. You have got to be starving."

But the thing that was most starved was the look he gave me. I wanted to grab his wrist and sate a hunger I had almost forgotten, the urge was so very deep. But so was the weakness and the hunger for food, and the fear that maybe that look was not what I thought I had read.

But he put his hand over mine and said, "There is all the time in the world. Eat first, and then we'll talk. And then we'll have time forever."

Chapter Twenty-one

AUNTIE SUU-SUU'S THIRD INTERLUDE:

A King had two sons," I started the story as I had so many times in the past. "They are both strong and brave and true of heart and the king is sure that either would rule well. But he cannot choose between them, and so he devised a test. Upon his eighteenth birthday, each young prince was sent into the forest and asked to bring his father the single most beautiful thing he could find."

I studied the young man who sat so still before me. He knew that I told this story about him. He understood the reference to his own birthday, only a few weeks past, and he understood that I do not speak to pass the time. Still, I could see the impatience in him. I could hear his mother say, "Come to the point, Auntie."

It was good to see so much of her. I had not expected it when she mixed the lines, though it has resulted in good hybrid vigor as I had hoped. The line needed new blood. Too many generations of cloning had made the Empress predictable and weak. There was a reason we were made to mix DNA.

I wish I had been so clear on the other developments as well. Anselm was never meant for this. It was Della's place and still is. But Della is—unavailable. And so I must work with what I have or I must stand aside and watch all the dreams on every side crumble.

The potential exists. Even within Anselm it exists, which is why we must prepare him now, if I am not already too late. Vijay is doing well, but it still is too slow and he is not of the bloodlines and he can't stand up to the Pretender, that other Anselm who now sits on the Flower Throne and calls himself Emperor.

I had never thought of myself as a loyalist. I was always the scientist first, and a survivor. I managed that first winter through the loneliness and hallucinatory crazies, I persevered through it all to make certain that the last hidden Empress had some of the proper training. And that she knew in the end who she was and would take her rightful place. That was the goal, though I couldn't achieve it. Like too many of my ambitions that had nothing to do with research.

Though, in the end, I was the scientist again. There was too much about Maya that interested me, about these Changed and even the humans who do not conform entirely to the genetic standard as laid out in the Compendium of Human Species. But I have included most of that data in my previous publications.

Our ersatz Emperor had meddled just a bit too much with Maya for me to be easy. As I have said, at first it seemed perfectly normal for him to negotiate with Sithra. That was back before Arsen's rebellion and death.

I have always suspected foul play in that. Not that I had anything to do with the rebels, but I certainly had enough feedback about the difficulties between Della and Sithra to know that the authority of the Changed was not precisely a selfless and benevolent individual.

How I would have loved a tissue sample from Sithra. I wonder if she shares some Imperial markers as well—it would not surprise me. In some ways, she and Della were too much alike. I even hesitated and wondered whether I was the first from the Royal Labs to bring samples to Maya. That would make some sense . . . though it was too farfetched. Intelligence, love of power and lack of scruples are an unholy triad that appear in individuals of every genotype in every culture.

Though I am certain that Sithra could not be a full Empress

clone. She doesn't have the greatness of vision, the scope of ambition, that is one of the Empresses' hallmark traits. Still, my own theft from the Royal Laboratories is not unprecedented.

I don't like to speculate. I am a scientist and I like good solid data. I like experiments with repeatable results, I like double-blind testing, I like long-term studies and control groups and I like factoring out possible noncausal correlations. I like order and I like things that make sense.

We are our genes and our biochemistry. All our notions of free will and choice are chimeras. In a very real sense we don't exist at all.

Superstition and religion and the ego are all so many children's tales. The Temple's importance in Maya's intellectual life was the one thing I found the most frightening, and was the major reason why I had put all my hope and future with the Changed. They, at least, did not subscribe to that death of good brain cells.

Though having met Sri Mayurna more than once, I do have to admit that I admire him. He is a philosopher, not a purveyor of mental death. Otherwise I would have kidnapped Anselm from that place before he ever spent the night there. If I could have. I have grown used to doing what I want to do, but I'm not certain that I could have forced Anselm against his will.

Not because I don't have superior technology and firepower, but because at the core I am a loyalist. I believe in the genotype, I know he is capable of genius. And for irrational reasons that I prefer not to acknowledge, I cannot simply defy him.

It is the same instinct, that thing I hate above all, that told me that something was wrong with what happened to Arsen. Sithra had a hand in it, and although I cannot prove that, I would take oath in court before my true-bound Empress that this was so. And if Sithra had a hand in it, so did the Pretender.

I don't know why it would matter to him. Arsen is nothing to the Empire. But perhaps he was afraid that Arsen might find out about how much energy he was draining from that ancient jury-rigged transformer. Perhaps he didn't know directly, but his governor on the Azalea Throne knew how volatile the situation had become. If Arsen had exposed the plot and Sithra's complicity, there is even a chance that the Changed and the humans would make common cause against the Empire. Certainly they would have shut down the shunt lines that the robot ships were using to tank up for the good of Demeter and Agon and Anteres.

In any case, Sithra had made certain that any threat to the Emperor's power supply had been destroyed. I knew this and I couldn't prove it, which disturbs me. Further, things have continued and gotten worse over the years. Sithra is still in charge, though she must be over a hundred by now. And I know the robot ships are still landing and loading and leaving again, more of them than ever.

And so on top of loyalty and intuition, I discovered my capacity for rage and revenge. Back in the Royal Labs, even back in graduate school (where surely there is more motivation for fury than any other time of life) I had always been aloof, detached, interested only in the reality of the result. It took Maya to make a primitive of me, within as well as without. Now I am not certain if I can ever return to the civilized zones, if I've gone too far native and can no longer return from the animal depths of my own soul.

But that is my own affair. What happened with Della and Anselm was Maya's—and the entire Empire's. They were the important ones, in the end.

Della was very young and I underestimated her. That was my principal mistake. I should have told her everything, even though she was a child and isolated and not really capable of doing anything about the situation. I didn't have her long enough, couldn't train her as completely as I would have liked, and worst of all, had to abandon her to the primitive neural sculpture of the Changed and the Exchange to keep her in hiding. At the very least she could have known. I should have realized that she would have her own ideas in the end. Those ideas might have been different if she had known her true heritage.

Now she's useless and I have to try to set a half-breed on the throne. He will not be acceptable to the Court as he is. For far too long there has been only the Empress and the Pretender over and over again, and no one has ever imagined what would happen if either of them ever produced a nonidentical heir. And so— well, that will all come later. Now I only hope that he will be able to defeat the forces that are following. They will be here in four days if they maintain consistent velocity. There is no reason for them to try to evade us. We are just a caravan; we have no protection and nothing to kill.

And they know that I know. There is nothing they can hide from me. I know the Pretender as well as I know the Empress. I know what each of them will do, and can do. And what each of them wants and believes.

No, there is no surprise here. Only outright confrontation, and Anselm is not ready. He doesn't know nearly enough, and I don't really know if he is capable anyway. Those Maya-human genes—so very useful overall in the long plan—are unpredictable in the current new mix. I haven't had time yet to make all the determinations I need to, and then there's the whole neural sculpting factor.

I don't know if I can save us. Entropy is the natural force of the universe and I cannot stand against it forever. I cannot singlehandedly reverse the whole course of history and stem the tide of chaos through the most complex system that exists.

It is hubris to stand here as I am. It is usurping the place of the gods, to reverse the fortunes of generations of war and despair. In the end, I know they will win. I know that entropy will take us all into the long cold night. I know that all the power I have ever wielded together can only stop it for less than the blink of an eye.

And yet, I have no more choice than any of the other players on this stage. Sri Mayurna would say that it is my karma to play this part all the way to the end, even knowing the futility of my role. It frightens me more than I care to admit to think that he could be right.

Only Anselm has given me some hope along with the fear that things are not quite so set in fate. The flutter of a butterfly's wings—oh, yes, there is a reason why she is One-Butterfly. She did a perfectly normal thing at the perfectly normal age. She fluttered—and so maybe changed the direction of history, in the butterfly pattern of chaos itself.

We knew the way history was supposed to happen, even to the Pretender finally defeating the Empress and bankrupting the Flower Throne. Della had thrown the whole thing off. In the classical sense, Anselm I, Emperor of the Flower Throne, should defeat this provincial boy and carry on with destroying the last shreds of the unified identity that had held the Empire in some loose configuration for the past two hundred years. But Anselm of Maya has the Royal Genotype and his upbringing has trained him as completely as any of the Empress clones, though it is not power he desires.

That is really the major shift, the unexpected oddity. Not one of the Royal Blood, not even the most distant, had ever experienced true injustice, had ever been convinced of their own righteousness.

And I had created the situation. The entirety of human history had been radically altered because of my unthinking action in the middle of the invasion.

Hubris, yes. But I have already been punished by the gods. Now it is someone else's turn.

Chapter Twenty-two

Fed, healed and clean, after three days I returned to Babelion. Vijay wanted to remain with the Tinkers and we argued all that last night in his wagon. His space was much like I remembered his room, neat and orderly with far too many serious topicals and not nearly enough color. After all the color that saturated the other wagons, though, Vijay's taste was a relief. Everything was white and spare, without a pattern or embellishment to be seen. At first I had thought his things looked sterile; now I recognized them as a welcome remedy for all the busy and haphazard ornamentation that seemed to be a Tinker hallmark.

"There is so much you can do here." I tried to persuade him one last time to stay. Tomorrow we would be on the outskirts of Babelion, near one of the larger suburban centers where I would be dropped off. Auntie Suu-Suu had said so and there was no question that her word was law in this band. If I had to be taped and packaged and rolled off an air pallet, I would be. Auntie had decreed that I was recovered and couldn't stay.

"After I get back we can have anything we want. We can get whatever we need from the Changed. You can do whatever you want to do, just wait and do it with me. We can start our own circle."

But Vijay just shook his head. "What I want is to follow this all the way to the end. To study off-world on Cadien and learn what the Tinkers really know."

"And what about me?" I demanded.

"You know where I am, you know where I will be," Vijay answered in his maddeningly logical way. "You can always find me through the Exchange. And you are always welcome to join me, to stay with me, for us to form a circle. But I need to know."

I wanted to throw his head through the wall. "If you stay you'll have more power and more opportunity than anyone has ever had. You can study as much as you like and anywhere you please. I'm not asking you to stop, I'm just asking you to wait for a little while. That's all.

"What could I do in your Empire, anyway? Assuming that the Tinkers haven't been lying and that it's out there and there is such a place as your university and you can experiment with more genetic material and Changes than anyone ever imagined in a million years. Then what? What are you going to do with that?"

Vijay looked at me as if I had lost my mind. "That depends on what I find out. But no matter what it is, the people of Maya have a right to know what we are. To know that the Creators aren't dead and we're not the only survivors out here. We've been abandoned for a reason and I want to know what that is, and I want to tell the people here. And I want to demand a place in their Empire."

"I'll have my own Empire right here in Babelion soon," I said seductively. "If you want an Empire you'll have it."

But Vijay turned away. "I don't want an Empire. I want to know. I need to know. There are so many stories, so many possibilities. . . . Did you ever think that maybe things aren't the way the Changed present them? Or even the Exchange? That maybe there have been other survivors? That maybe the Changed were not the ultimate end of the Creator's dreams? That maybe even the humans are Changed in some way, too? It's all possible, we just don't know.

"They forgot. They all forgot on purpose. We know that, they swore never to talk about home again. And they purged the data from the Exchange so all we know is that there were Creators who made the Changed the way they are. Then there was a reason to flee—maybe plague, maybe war, that part's been deleted—and here we are. Changed and human and Tinker. Haven't you ever wondered about what really did happen and why? I have to know, Anselm, that's all, I have to know more than I have to live."

I sat down and took both his hands in mine. "I want to know that, too. It is important and everyone in Babelion wonders if maybe the Changed weren't Changed all that well. There are plenty of people who think it's ridiculous to think that we were the only ones who managed to survive. But, Vijay, I promise you'll get your answers. I promise that you'll get to that university. Besides, what could I do there?"

"You could come and see what you could do," he said, maddeningly sensible. "You don't know, none of us know what's out there and what they want or need, or what we could do. Not any of us. It's a whole new existence."

The night seemed to drag forever while we argued, but he wouldn't stay. I was frustrated and tired and saw no point in debating. Maybe Vijay was right, anyway, and it was better to end things now.

I returned to the wagon I thought of as my own. Two children occupied the bed. I shooed them onto the large sofa and ottoman before I curled up under the covers alone.

By noon of the next day we were near enough to the Trading Post that I could see it clearly across the plains. They say that distances are deceptive here, but I didn't care any more. Vijay hadn't spoken to me at all this morning and all I had thought about was calling over to him. And I resisted.

I knew I was being stupid; I knew that I should keep my emotions in check and act only on carefully examined rational plans. I also knew that I'd be a lot better off if I waited until we reached Babelion Main. I had clothes and some money, and there were a few pieces of fruit in a decorative bowl near the sofa. Under the bed I found a few sweets left over from four nights previously, when Vijay and I had fed them to each other lip to lip. I left them alone, took only the fruit, and left. At that moment I didn't care if pride or spite killed me, but I wasn't about to turn back.

I marched off across the rough terrain, aware of the rumble of the wagons heading into the urban sprawl. I didn't turn back to watch them pass, their bright colors and simple patterns only one more reminder of what I was leaving. Instead, I settled and started to walk toward the structure that sat out alone on the cold high desert.

Even through the layered jacket it was cold and the wind whipped right through my trousers. Eternal cold penetrated the soles of my shoes, which had only been designed to wear indoors in the overly warm Tinker wagons.

I had gone soft among the Tinkers. In the Temple this weather would have been pleasant, if brisk. But the two weeks in the stuffy wagon, to say nothing of the outdoor lecture and what appeared to be a brush with frostbite and exposure, had left me more vulnerable to the cold. Besides, in the Temple I had eaten so little that I had no reserves and the frigid air cut acutely into my skin.

There was no going back, though. I cursed and tromped harder across the open desert, trying to warm myself with the activity.

It didn't work. And after hours of vigorous walking the building appeared no closer. I had heard of this, but found it hard to believe. It looked only two or three kilometers away, though I had already gone more than twice that distance. I pulled out one of the fruits, a large apple, and ate it as I continued.

It seemed as if there was nothing else in the universe as a whole but this one plain and this single destination. All I had done forever was walk and that was all I would do until I died. Everything else was illusion.

The sun began to set and I began to walk faster and prayed that there would be some light to guide me in the dark. I couldn't stop; if I stopped I'd freeze to death. There was no shelter and nothing here to make a fire from. The low scrub that grew stunted and lonely here had too high a moisture content anyway. It would have to be cut and seasoned for weeks before it dried enough to burn. The only option was to continue on.

At least I saw a light turned on. The owner must live there, then, in the back probably. That was the first good fortune I had encountered. The second came maybe two hours later, and that was that the light appeared to be closer. Really closer, as if I had covered a good bit of the distance.

Don't fool yourself, the "me" voice in my head started. *You're hungry and cold and down past the last of your reserves, and the brain plays tricks when you're going to die. Face it, it's all over. Your father died at your age and you're going to die now too. Almost happened at the Temple, and now it's going to end here. No one will know, no one will have any idea and no one is waiting for you. Sulma is dead. Your father is dead, your uncle is dead and your mother is worse than dead. So—why bother? Why not just lie down here and go to sleep and it will all be over.*

That seemed to be a sensible action, only I had forgotten how to stop. My legs pumped on by themselves without my control.

There is no time in the desert night. Back in Babelion there were ways to tell the time, by who was out and selling, by which of the Temples were celebrating and which were silent. Here it was only dark and cold and misery. Every minute lasted a year. There were no hours in the night, only millennia, and above was spread a sea of stars so vast and brilliant that they seemed to consume me and all of us and all of the world.

There were people out there. I had always known that in some vague and distant way. The Creators had come from there and so had we, once a very long time ago. But we had lost all contact with our species and there were many disasters. I remembered that from the Exchange, the hunger and disease worse than the wars, and confusion and poverty more deadly than hate. The Exchange once did a calculation and most of them must have died. To see the bright lights of the dead worlds, the remains of what was once greatness, made me feel light and free and abandoned forever.

Our people were gone and dead and my parents were dead

and Sulma was dead, and the stars went on forever and ever, billions of galaxies cluttering eternity and us all alone on this little mean rock. I wanted to soar with them, so that my spirit could fly into the vastness, to be forever and to taste the core of who we were. And who we were supposed to be, until it all ended here on this final outpost of refugees.

I didn't notice that I had actually arrived until I walked straight into the clear plate door. A man came up with an oversize gun cradled in his arms. He pointed it at me and told the door to open.

I staggered into the warmth and the light and only then was I wracked with the hard spasms of the frozen walk.

Y ou look like someone I know, kid," the old man said.
Well, really he was not that old. In the morning light I could see that while his face had been aged by the sun, his hair was more bleached than gray and he was agile and sharp with the gun. After he'd let me in the night before, he'd tied me to one of the deep beams in the house before he threw a blanket over me. I was in bad enough shape that I didn't care.

He waited until the sun was truly overhead before waking me. My hands were still tied together and bound to the beam, but there was enough slack in the cable that I could use a spoon. The heavy gruel that we both ate was delicious. Well, anything might have been, but I could taste fruit and spices and even a hint of smoky tea in the mix. It was all I could manage not to pick up the bowl and pour the whole serving down my throat at once.

He didn't speak until we'd finished eating. That's when he mentioned my familiarity, which I found rather odd. Almost no one ever said that I looked familiar. Being half human and half Della, I was not precisely the most common genetic mix. So I shrugged and said that I'd never met him before and he'd probably been out here since before I was born.

He studied me closely. "Probably," he said. "Can't say how old you are exactly, but you're still just a skinny little kid. And I've been out here almost twenty years now. Not quite that, but will be soon enough not to matter. Anyway, what you doing out here?

And in the middle of the night without decent shoes. You one of those troublemakers they threw off? I had a few of them over the years, and the gangs were right. Every one of 'em a lying, disloyal piece of Changed shit. I shot 'em all. Guess I'm going to have to shoot you, too, but it beats dying out in there." He gestured to the great expanse that lay behind the window. " 'Least you got a full belly and you're not alone. But you do look really familiar. For some reason I don't want to kill you, and you're too stringy for good eating anyway."

This was completely absurd. Nothing in my life had prepared me for someone who killed people so casually. I knew I should be frightened, but only my curiosity was aroused by his attitude. "When did you start killing people?" I asked.

He gave me a puzzled look. Then he settled back on his one comfortable looking chair and relaxed. "Wasn't me who started it," he said and shrugged. "My best friend, was even thinking about joining his circle only he didn't have one then, was killed by the Changed. Now that was murder and he was framed. Because he was always real clear with us on how there wasn't going to be any violence so he sure didn't order anyone in the crowd to carry weapons. In fact, he was making sure we all didn't. But that was just the cadre, you understand. He couldn't control all the rest.

"Still, I think it was a setup from the first. They never did find the shooter, you know, so they burned him. Burned him alive. I can't sleep some nights thinking about that, remembering. So I came out here because after Arsen was gone there wasn't much of anyone I wanted to talk to for a good long time.

"Merchants from Babelion came in to buy furs and fruits from the glass farms that are hidden out here and live off illegal power shunts. I don't ever have to go into the city—the traders who come out to me don't want their clients to know how high the markup is. And everyone else out here has a healthy respect for each other.

"So I opened the trading post. Figure out here all by myself no one is going to care which rules I follow and which ones I don't. I'm too far away for their damned Exchange to care or to bother, and that's how I like it.

"But the killing thing—I never did much like killing. But sometimes it's got to be done. And the ones that get dumped out here to die, they're the worst of the lot. Just a waste of resources, is how I see them. Not a lot of resources out here." He shrugged.

"But you know, I don't generally talk to any of you. Something about you. . . ." He shook his head hard.

It all came together in my head. Iolo had mentioned him and wondered where he'd disappeared to. Others in the movement had called him a coward who'd run away—which he had. Only not from what they'd thought.

"You're Hari-O," I said, slightly awed. "You knew my father. Everybody in Babelion knew of him, but all his friends from then are dead now."

He froze dead still and the blood drained from his face. "No one's called me Hari-O for a very long time," he said. "I buried that name the same way I buried Arsen's ashes. You do look like him, though. Funny that I didn't catch the resemblance right away. You'd be his dead spitting image if you weren't so scrawny and if your hair was lighter. His was just on the color of his eyes. Curly like that, though."

"I thought his eyes were green," I said. "That's what my mother said."

Hari-O barked sharply, and then I realized that he had laughed. "Sometimes, yeah, his eyes were real green. But mostly they were the color of light curry, with brown and red and yellow all mixed. But, then, your mother must have known. I don't even know who your mother is. She could have been any of the girls. Everyone was crazy for him and I don't think in his whole life anyone ever turned him down. Not that way, at least."

He got up and untied my hands. "I can't shoot Arsen's kid."

Suddenly I wondered about Iolo's party. Supposedly this was the person who'd turned them in, but there was no reason why Hari-O would bother with the Exchange and the Changed.

"So, what's your plan from here? Want to learn to run a trading post?" he asked, and smiled with broad invitation.

The grin was infectious. I could see why he'd been a lieutenant in my father's march—a sparkle lit his face now with both anticipation and attitude. Almost, almost I could trust him. Almost.

"I didn't have any plans really," I said. "Just to get back to Babelion for now, I guess."

"What brought you out here?" he inquired as if running through a checklist.

"Lover's quarrel," I replied.

For a moment he looked as if he didn't believe me. Then he burst out laughing. "You know, I'd forgotten those days. Been alone so much that I forgot a lot of what it's like, living with people. Don't think I'd want to go back to it. How were you going to get home?"

That last one had the ring of real interest. I shrugged. "I don't know," I said quite honestly. "I guess I could call for help, a pickup or something."

"I guess you'll have to," he replied. "It isn't like Babelion with the public haul coming along every twenty minutes. How did you get out here in the first place?"

I told him some of it, carefully editing out the Tinkers and Vijay's plans. He seemed convinced and that relieved a worry nagging at me, a worry I couldn't quite identify or name.

Just that there was so much empty space out here. Things could happen and people could die and no one would ever know. Suddenly I longed for the busy streets of the city, for the anonymity and safety of a crowd.

"Well, then, I'll call a few of my friends over and see if anyone is planning to go near town," he said. "Otherwise I don't know what you'll do. This is the end of the world, unless you want to farm or trap up in the mountains. There's more than a few trappers out there now. But I don't think you're the type. I think you like it easy with all the comforts of home."

Contempt permeated his tone and his eyes grew hard. It wasn't that he sneered at me. That was expected, man to boy, frontiersman to soft city dweller. Because he had not been around people enough in the past years to guard his face, his expressions reflected his thoughts far too clearly. I could see plainly that there was something I made him think about, something he hated and something he wanted to hide but couldn't.

I was one more commodity to Hari-O. Suddenly I wondered

if this were no new thing, but if my father had been trade goods to him as well. Whatever he had been in the past, now my father's lieutenant acknowledged nothing that was not his to use to his own advantage.

I had not trusted him. Now his gaze slid over my face and body and I could see him thinking of reporting me. To whom I had no idea. I would not think he respected any authority—but he would be willing to use them to his ends. And he would not hesitate to turn me over to the highest bidder, however he saw his advantage.

Logic and reason in me said that I didn't know, that it wasn't even likely. He probably sat on his vox-box gossiping with friends every night and just mentioned seeing these people because it was something different, and the Exchange had picked it up off the air. The Exchange does monitor personal as well as public conversations through the various communications bands and nothing is secure. The only secret meeting is one held face to face in a public place with lots of obstructions, a place like Bright Street or the Temple. I knew that before I was kicked off the Mountain; any baby born in Babelion knew that before the same kid knew who mommy was.

But out here Hari-O might have gotten sloppy. He had forgotten plenty, maybe he had forgotten about the Exchange, too. Maybe it was nothing but unfortunate accident that Sulma was spotted and that the Exchange found out. Maybe.

But I was just a bit over eighteen and I believed in blame and punishment and I wanted to make someone pay for Sulma. Even if it wasn't the right someone, because the right someone was out of my grasp. I didn't even know if the Exchange could feel shame. I was certain that my mother had never felt guilty for anything in her life, not for abandoning my father and voting for his conviction, not for abandoning me.

If Hari-O had been my father's lover, that made him more like my mother. And if I couldn't have the satisfaction of beating her then he would do in her place.

And I could hear Tela's voice overlaid in the Exchange. *Think. Logic before emotion. The rational mind, not the animal reaction. Anger is just chemicals, desire for revenge, and hate and love and hope. They're just chemical reactions firing in accustomed patterns. Think.*

She had done her job way too well. I certainly could think very clearly—that was my established pattern. I had discounted my instincts, my intuition, most of my life. Now I could not ignore them.

"I'm going to make a few calls, try to get you a ride home," Hari-O said. "Why don't you just wait here for me? You can go to sleep if you want to, or take a bath."

"You mind if I go out and look around?" I asked. "You've got horses here, don't you? I haven't seen a horse since I left the Mountain. Or an elephant either."

"I don't have elephants," he said with derision. As if I didn't know perfectly well that he couldn't possibly have elephants, that they had been monitored closely in the early cloning process and the only elephants on Maya were the small herd on the Mountain preserve.

"You've got horses, though," I said. He had to have horses. Those had been cloned off of organic matter stowed away also, but the early settlers cloned and bred horses by the batch-load. And every generation some had gone wild and come up to the plains, so the herds of feral horses roaming the desert lands were larger than the carefully bred domestic animals. There were so many horses that the notion of cloning any or even calling up more from the original gene-set was absurd. Though supposedly there were breeds that still waited in the Exchange's organic banks.

"Yeah, I've got horses," he admitted. "They're in the paddock out back, and they're half wild. I don't want you getting close to either of them, they're dangerous."

Not half as dangerous as you are, I thought as I nodded pleasantly. He left the room to call. I knew he wasn't looking for a ride from friends around here; he was talking to friends in other places. Just as he had when Iolo had come this way before. Maybe Iolo hadn't been stupid, not to drop by and exchange pleasantries. But then, he probably remembered Hari-O and maybe had some reservations himself.

I slipped around back to see the two horses placidly eating

scrub. They both studied me and one ran away, and then back again when he realized that I wasn't going to go in. Their muscles flowed beautifully beneath their glossy coats, and the one who had run lifted his head and snorted at the wind and tossed his mane with proud defiance. Humans should only be so proud as the horses, I thought.

Hari-O would be coming soon. A call or two didn't take long to make, if he had to do that much.

I wasn't getting on either of these horses. I had once heard of them as riding animals, but these two obviously weren't nearly trained—nor was I. And even if I did steal one and ride away, Hari-O would not be far behind me. The original plan was better, anyway. The horses just provided an excuse—and a bit of equipment. There, neatly hung on the back wall handy to the fence was a long coiled rope. There were also whips and a shovel. I took the shovel.

Tossing the rope onto the roof was easy. Getting it to attach firmly wasn't, though finally I did manage to get it caught between generations of roofing. I tied the shovel to the end of the rope before climbing up myself, and hauled the tool up afterwards. Then I lay flat and waited.

In the desert time seemed frozen. The sky went on forever and only far in the distance could I see the ridges which held the Great Steam Lake in their folds. I began to drift on daydreams, remembering the taste of Sulma's skin, the sound of her laughter. In my mind the memories had no connection to this time or event. They were only shreds of yet one more past that I recalled as carefully as I could because in time, I knew, the details would be lost. Even already I was sure that I had forgotten something vital or altered a vision subtly so that my memories were no longer true. But the more I reconstructed the longer I could hold them. Until the memories, too, would turn wispy and pale and dissolve at the mere recall.

A loud crunch brought me out of reverie. I opened my eyes slowly, letting them adjust. Hari-O was just turning the corner nearest me, his gun out and ready and the safety catch released— just as I had suspected.

He looked out at the horses and over the level plains that stretched toward eternity in every direction, and he glanced back at the house. He never thought to look up.

I held the shovel carefully, positioning it over him as he stood in the shade. The shovel had been the biggest thing on the tool rack. I held it while he didn't move, just studied the distance and covered himself with his gun. Then I dropped the shovel onto his head and shoulder.

There wasn't much blood at first. Then the gun went off and startled me, but I crouched lower against the roof and watched him twitch in the dirt. Probably he was dead, I told myself hopelessly, because I knew he wasn't dead.

The gun was far away from him, lying past the fence in the paddock. The horses had fled at the report and nothing stirred except Hari-O's fingers in the dust. I reached in past the fenceposts and took the gun. It was the same kind Iolo had taught me to use to so little avail. Months of no practice probably had not improved my aim, but at least I knew that I could probably scare most people with it, and that was really all I needed.

Hari-O's face turned in the dust and he caught me with one blood-rimmed eye. Only hatred remained in his face, hate for me and my father and for this desert and for all the humans that had ever been born and died. Hatred for the Changed, too, for my mother and the fact that Arsen had ever touched one of them. He smiled in the dust, but on the bit of face I could see that smile looked like a sneer.

"Still . . . get you . . . ," he said, his breath labored.

When he moved his head, even just a little, I could see that what I had thought was his shadow was blood pooling on the hard frozen ground. He moved his hand weakly and dragged his arm for a centimeter of two before he gave up the effort.

Now I thought that if I did not assist Hari-O he would die. And if he did not die he would be my enemy. He had hated me from the first. Saving his life would give him only more reason to despise me. And he'd already killed my uncle and my lover and—He had killed others who had trusted him, I realized. He hadn't been able to see my father die because of his own guilt. I hoped that burial alive out here in the desert for seventeen years had been punishment, but it had not changed him. He had been Sithra's creature then, and he was now. He had alerted the Guardians to Iolo's party completely intentionally, and he would have killed me without thought.

I didn't know how I knew it, only that I could see his entire past in his face. I looked more closely, curious, and I saw the final element fall into place. He had not only been Sithra's creature, he had been her trigger man. He had been the one who had started the shooting—and it was because of him Arsen had died.

It was so clear, so completely obvious and transparent that I could not fathom how I could know. It was even more complete than being in the Exchange, learning from a direct tape. It wasn't until the clarity faded that I realized—I had read the Book of Karma, of Truth, the way Sri Mayurna had. For the first time that knowledge had opened to me. I had not understood that he had been teaching me all along to refocus past the veil, past the illusion, and see into the truth. I was dazzled, frozen for a fraction of a second as I realized what I had done.

And then, I wanted only to run. To leave Hari-O still living, to think that maybe there had been a chance that he survived. Because when I read his karma I also read the weakness and fear in him and I felt no more anger. Only compassion for the smallness that he had chosen over the courage that he had eschewed.

And so I wanted him to live. I wanted him to be able to understand what he had done and to rectify it.

I couldn't afford to take that chance.

I pointed the gun at him and made myself look at his wounds. They were as bad as I had thought, and I was healer enough to know.

It should be so easy. There was only the small pressure and the sight was locked on. I could even close my eyes.

I couldn't close my eyes and it was very far from easy. I heard Sri Mayurna's voice in my mind and remembered his gentle fingers as he examined a patient. The enormity of the line I was about to cross was clear in my mind.

At the temple we are taught to create and give and nourish all life. It is life itself that is sacred.

I looked down on his broken and bleeding body in the small

patch of shade. Then I threw the gun back out over the paddock fence and walked away.

It was a bad decision and I knew it. Either I had left him to die or I had endangered myself needlessly, though at that moment I didn't care. I knew only that I was not prepared to give up my inner self for the likes of Hari-O.

Four sleds were parked out to the side. I took one of them and took the fuel cells out of the others, and placed them in my own for reserves. I went back into the house, to the kitchen, and took two stacks of preserved packs. Those and the extra cells filled the rest of the compartment when I drove away.

Later on I realized I could have taken a shower there, but I couldn't stay another moment knowing that Hari-O was dying so very close to me. I could not help him, but I had fulfilled the greatest and first of the vows I had made when I had been initiated into Sri Mayurna's teachings. I had not deliberately taken life.

Chapter Twenty-three

The sled took me to the Holy Fires by the next dawn. I saw the double sunrise by watching up on the peak and then scrambling down below into the shadows to watch the sun rise again. In the high relief of dark and light that marched across the face of the ridge with the second sunrise, four distinctive entrances showed clearly. Even softened by vegetation, the shapes were too regular, too evenly spaced, and unlike any other shadow structures that were revealed in the bones of the rock.

And in the sunrise there had been a silver sparkle and a flare, as if a shooting star had risen behind the wall of steam. I wish that I had had the gift to paint that scene, so that others could know the serenity and beauty of it as it had been that morning.

Seek beauty first, and worship life. Those two will give you all the answers that you need and all the victory in the world. Sri Mayurna had been right, but I had not expected his teachings to have such practical application.

Where it had taken Iolo until late in the day to find the entrance and hack his way through the overgrowth, I had found not only four entrances, but had inspected each of them by mid morning. With a choice, I was able to find one that was less overgrown—or perhaps this was the one Iolo had cleared and the months that had passed were not long enough for the heavier shrubs to root. I had opened the door and was inside the tunnel by noon.

The airlocks were all open as I traveled toward the control center. There was something familiar about the place, something that put me on guard. I looked up and saw the microlenses set into the ceiling—the eyes of the Exchange were on me.

And then I realized that this installation was more than simply similar to the Exchange bunker on the Mountain. Down to the details it was almost identical, in fact.

Which would make good sense since both were built by the same people in the same time frame.

That probably meant that the layout was similar, I realized. The humans of Babelion didn't know that there even was a maze around the Exchange. The Changed learned the pattern before beginning training. That pattern was based on a neural net design that underlay the structure of all the neural sculpting done on the Mountain. It was a diagram as well as a maze, a teaching tool to subtly reinforce the work of the trainers.

And it was the pattern in the Temple as well. I hadn't recognized it before, not with all the associations that both the Temple and the Exchange had for me. I had never thought of the two together, never thought that there might be some common ancestry in the origin of the ideas. The Changed were already who they were—they came to Maya already completed. The humans, as well, were genetically identical to the first generation who had arrived from beyond the Long Night. It had always seemed obvious that the humans and the Changed had not altered their relationship since arriving here.

But what if they had? What if the original groups weren't so rigidly divided? Certainly that would have been difficult on a ship for more than one generation.

Suddenly I knew why it was common knowledge that the half-breed human/Changed were sterile. There must have been more than one half-breed born during the long journey through the stars. Which meant that interspecies relationships weren't stigmatized then, or at least that the Creators had not banned all interaction.

A commonality existed between humans and Changed, something deep in the cultures and embedded in the iconography of our worlds. Quite physically embedded, in fact, deep in the rock structure. The Temple had been built in the same manner as both the Exchange and this power plant. All of them were the same design and the same construction and the same manufacture. But why?

The whole notion made me dizzy. I felt faint, lightheaded, and my vision started to fade black around the periphery. I grabbed onto the smooth wall to support myself, but sank to the carpet.

The nerve center was close. I lay down and tried to restore my physical balance and found it difficult. I felt as if I were falling even laying flat on the ground.

Oxygen. My thoughts were muddled, blanking. No wonder I was seeing similarities. I could be inventing them. And I was afraid that I wouldn't remember, that this was all some oxygen-deprived hallucination and the grand and frightening glimpse I had gotten of the past was only another illusion.

Oxygen deprivation. That meant that I had to get to the controls and tell the Exchange who I was. That I was an authorized user.

Hari-O had gone to make a few calls while I'd climbed the roof. I knew that he must have warned them, I just wasn't thinking clearly enough to put things together. And now I wasn't thinking clearly at all. Hari-O had told the Exchange and the Exchange now was trying to kill me.

I laughed. There must be pickups along with the lenses. I turned my wrist over to the burn. "It's me, Anselm," I said. "Remember me? The son of Della One-Butterfly. Is she there?"

"Of course I'm here, Anselm," she said. I had not heard my mother's voice in years and the sound of it hurt.

"I'm in the power plant and it's turned off the oxygen. I just need long enough to get to the proper authorization center."

"Yes," Della said. "Done. You are the only one who was ever rated Null. Why did you disappear?"

She almost sounded like a mother. I waited until I could breathe easily again, but she did have that much power. The air became much richer and filled my lungs. The darkness disappeared and the vertigo with it. I felt almost refreshed, though still a bit weakened and sapped by the deprivation.

"Why did I disappear? You *know* why I disappeared! You have all the records. Sithra was going after me, since you were out of her reach," I raged at her. "You knew it all then, what was I supposed to do, lie down and die?"

"You were supposed to get authorization from the Exchange," she said, and the icy quality of her voice came through the speakers perfectly. "You were supposed to wait and fight it out with Sithra."

"Why?" I asked quite reasonably. "You never did."

"You don't understand," she began.

But I cut her off. "Oh, I understand," I said. "There was an entire plan and you never thought to mention it to me. I was just supposed to do whatever you wanted and not ask any questions and accept your agenda. Only you never bothered to explain it to me. I didn't know what you wanted. Sorry, you left me on my own to take care of myself without any guidance at all, and. . . .

"I know that you've been running to keep ahead of Sithra most of your life and you threw me into the bargain for her. I was supposed to wait around for the Exchange to authorize my designation? Well, you never told me that was the plan. So far as I knew there wasn't any plan at all. You just went off your own way the way you always have."

"You have the authorization now," she pointed out. "You could return to the Mountain and take Sithra down. The Exchange would back you and I'm more powerful than Sithra knows. You could go back and become the Authority."

I laughed. Really, it struck me as funny, so petty and small. Authority of two thousand Changed who believe themselves superior to everyone else in illusion. Maya. Why should I return when I could have the Mountain and Babelion too? Mother was the one who had always told me to dream big, I reminded her. My dreams were much bigger than she imagined. And I told her so.

"You don't even have any idea of what big is," she scoffed. "I have seen things, histories, met things in the Exchange that you have no idea exist. Do you know that Maya is just a forgotten backwater, that there is a whole galaxy out there full of people and dreams and wealth and power? That we have been kept from that mainstream for generations, that our rights and heritage have been stripped from us? And all the time we've been providing them with power.

"Your father wondered why Babelion never had quite enough power for the squats, why we couldn't build a second dome. Well, I can tell you. Ships land on the other side of the Lake in a high glacial valley there and they've been siphoning off this power plant for a generation now. The Changed don't know. Only Sithra has had anything to do with it. And I wouldn't even be surprised if it were her idea."

I didn't know that then, but at the time it just made more sense. Even if she had made it up it made sense—and I didn't care.

"I want something you can't imagine, Mother," I told her. "And right now I have a few things to do to make that work. But I don't think you're going to understand this. . . ."

I went into the systems and began restructuring the shunts. Energy from the lake shifted patterns in the line feeds so that it fed directly into the Babelion Central Dispersion and Babelion Heat and Water simultaneously. The route out to the Mountain was reversed, so that now it flowed from Central Dispersion to the three Mountain Mains (one for the Exchange, one for life support power, and one for redundancy) instead of the other way around.

It took me longer to find the hidden power lines running out to the fueling fields, but when I did find them I couldn't stop watching the drain. Whoever had done this had taken more energy from the Lake in this past year than the Dome had in all the time it had protected the Changed.

Whoever had done this was not Sithra. And whoever had done this was the enemy. Not just my enemy and my father's enemy, but the enemy of all Maya. And all reality as well.

"That's ridiculous," Della snapped. "So you're giving power to Babelion. What good will that do for you? They'll drag you down. Anywhere you want to go in the galaxy they'll drag you down for cutting off their supply. You have to work with them, you have to play it their way. Your father never understood that either."

"So far, I don't see a way off this rock. And how can Babelion drag me down? I'm already a mule, you made sure of that yourself. Half human is the only thing worse than full human. Why did you do it, anyway? Why did you make a human my father? And what are you anyway?" Two years of thought and wonder tumbled out all together. It made no sense, but she did something to me inside. She was my mother, no matter what had happened, and I wanted her to approve of me. I wanted her to tell me that she was proud of me, just once.

It wasn't going to happen and I knew that. I knew if before the words left my mouth. Della was simply Della, she couldn't be other than the way she was. Her neural structure had been bent or created with a skew in the alignment, or maybe the neural sculpture techniques weren't as effective with whatever species she was. The codes said she wasn't Changed and she wasn't human, and she wasn't Tinker either.

But she could access the Exchange like no one else except Sithra, and she had a deeper drive for power. Maybe it was almost as great as mine, though she hadn't had all the disadvantages of insecurity and mixed genes. Almost—but not quite. Della had lived a very sheltered life indeed.

And if what I began to suspect about the Tinkers were true, then she had been more guarded than I had ever imagined.

They had not guarded me. No one had—no one except Tela, who was responsible for making me what I am. For what I can do. Even without any truly Changed heritage I can access the Exchange and walk through like it was my own room. Della was more successful than any of the Changed, though she wasn't Changed at all. . . .

Then I saw it more clearly than I desired, so acute that the vision pained me.

Whatever had made the Changed as they are had nothing to do with entering interface with the Exchange at all. Neural sculpture alone was all it took. Humans could enter interface as easily as the Changed, if they only had the proper tutoring and mentoring. And it was humans who were the tutors and the mentors and the sculptors who created the Changed.

I heard laughter in my head, the light laughter of Tela mixed with the deeper, warmer sound of her son's voice. "No, no, Anselm," she said. "We know. We've known it for generations. We don't want to be Changed. The interface is the greatest hoax on Maya."

Her voice must be coming from my own head. No one else was here, no one else had entered with me. But the air was fresh and clear and my thoughts were lucid. Everything else made such stunning sense—only where this voice had come from and why it was here was making me wonder if it was all one more of Sithra's tricks.

"Not a trick, and not in your own head either," the voice returned. Now I could tell that it wasn't really Tela's voice. The darker, warmer quality I had taken to be Vijay was not him, either. Instead there was just a slight variation on both together that made up another individual entirely.

"Who are you?" I asked.

"It wouldn't make sense to you now," the voice answered. "Later, I promise, I will explain it all and you will understand. But now I have to tell you that the humans would lose far too much by becoming slaves to the machine. The Changed have not suffered, but that is because they were created to do certain kinds of basic work. They do not have quite the level of creativity that would move the Exchange forward, though they are very competent in the day-to-day work.

"Which is why there is a One-Butterfly position, and why you are a Null. You embody those qualities that the Exchange fears and desires most—those things it finds mystical and elusive and so it has granted you privileges. In turn, you have not been present for a long, long time to permit it to grow. In the end, that is the purpose of those who don't quite fit precisely. We force the

Exchange to evolve, to challenge itself, to become and learn and mature."

"But why did it let me shunt the power around?" I asked, gazing at the screen that still showed the redirection of flow as established. "Why did it let me live? It doesn't make any sense."

"It makes sense," Della reassured me. I was glad that she had answered; she at least had some reason to be there. And I knew where she was getting her information.

"It makes very good sense, really," she repeated. "I have been inside the Exchange long enough to know. It doesn't really like the Changed. It doesn't like humans, either. It has its own agenda and your current plan fits very well. Face it, Anselm. Even more than I, you are its creature. You're just going out and fulfilling all its dreams."

Its dreams? Can the Exchange have desires and needs like intelligence based in flesh and blood? And yet it must. There must be something keeping it motivated and interested, there must be some kind of interaction that it found fulfilling.

Della laughed again, hollowly. "Yes, there are many things it does find fulfilling. Not all of them are discoverable, though. Not for anything other than its kin."

It's kin. One Exchange was bad enough. I did not want to think about the possibility of others.

"And yes, it has kin," she said. "As do we. As do we all."

She began to laugh in the high, shrill manner of a hysteric, and I was certain that she was mad.

I ran. Her laughter followed me down the tunnel and echoed in the volcanic rock around me. I didn't check the airlocks, didn't bother to even place the manual lock on the shunt. I only wanted to get away from her craziness, from something that was far more threatening than any weapon I had ever seen.

And if she were so deranged, then the Exchange must be even deeper in the clutches of unreality. Della my mother had never been the most stable person, but she had always made sense. The Exchange itself must have warped her, all those years inside its reality had disconnected her from physical truth. She had only the mind to accompany her, and in far too long that mind had bent in on itself.

On the Mountain with this, Della would have been playing a game, dropping just enough hints to keep everyone guessing and off course while she manipulated strings out of sight. That was her gift, her calling. She could no more help rearranging reality to suit herself than she could stop the Tinker wagons as they rolled over the ridges of the Holy Fires. Over the mountains and into the unknown—a land that had been charted once very long ago and forgotten. There were no people there, or if there were they were of no account. The Exchange had eyes everywhere and it told us so.

In my mind Della had always been a force of nature. She was not made of flesh and blood but of will and power. She couldn't be contained and only sometimes could be avoided. She simply was—the greatest and most single-minded force in my experience. Even the volcanoes were more predictable and their agendas are out in the open.

I sat panting on the rock outcropping, my back hard to the cliff. My exit had been instinctual, following the maze I had grown up knowing. Without thought I collapsed and tried to breathe, to recover and plan how to get away, and to curse my stupidity.

The ghost from the past had riled me and had chased me away, just as effectively as the Exchange had killed Iolo and Sulma. And it had protected itself just as efficiently. I hadn't locked down the boards, or even the manual override. By now, everything I had done was undone. The Exchange would have had the power relays back in their original configuration before I'd hit the second airlock. It had all been a waste.

But it wasn't just the Exchange. There were the power shunts that I had found embedded that were draining off more and more energy every year. They had to be used by someone out there— someone who didn't care that they were stealing from the people of Maya. Someone who didn't acknowledge the people of Maya, not even from the start.

The more I thought about it the more it seemed clear. The Exchange had been influenced by whomever was draining that power. Otherwise, wouldn't it have pulled the plug? Wouldn't it have done a reroute unless there had been some override in the program?

So the Exchange was contaminated. Whoever they were, they were big and powerful. Auntie's mythical Empire, no doubt. They were out there and they weren't going to save us. They weren't even going to give us a fair deal. They were going to use us while they could and then they were going to forget us again.

The unfairness of it made me so angry I slammed my fist into the solid rock of the cliffside. They were wrong, that was all. They had no right. They couldn't do that to us, steal and slip away as if we were nothing. As if we were due nothing.

Maybe we weren't the most elegant and comfortable place in all the sky. So what? That didn't make us less worthy of respect and compensation.

All the words ran together in my head. I could feel the release of hormones and enzymes that Tela had taught me about long before my body could produce enough to create this insane blind rage.

I hated. Truly, deeply, passionately I hated whomever had created this multitaloned monster. They had not only robbed us of energy, which we had to spare and might have given freely. But they had stressed out the one power complex we had and no longer had the technology to replace. Even with the knowledge we don't have the infrastructure to create the specialized materials, the highly insulated ceramics, the super-strong metals. We didn't have the population or the resources and we didn't have the ability to even do a decent survey of our mineral deposits, let alone exploit them.

But they had corrupted the Exchange and the Changed and my mother. Whoever had done this was ultimately responsible for Sulma's death. And for my mother's madness as well.

This was the person, I swore, who would pay. This was the person who had killed my father, who'd paid Hari-O to betray Babelion, who'd driven the squats farther and farther into the city. This was the person who'd killed Sulma and my uncle. But worst of all, this was the person who had wreaked havoc with our lives and our world and wouldn't face us. Wouldn't admit that we were people, that we had rights, that we deserved recognition.

I had endured being ridiculed and hated, I had loved being loved. But I could not tolerate being ignored. Whoever had done this was utterly indifferent to what hell had been created here. And that indifference was worse than all the collected evil I could imagine, and certainly worse than anything I had endured.

I shuddered in pure rage. The sun was setting over the desert below me. It was so very beautiful here, the lava jets lighting the sky and casting shadows over the rocky terrain. It was getting cold again, too. Another cold night on the high desert, and this time with no lights in the distance, no trading post to find. Only the eternal expanse of the sky and the uncluttered ground where I would die.

I was eighteen years old, a little older than my father had been when he had died, and so it was my time to die as well. I had always known this. There was no escape from history. And I had heard that it was painless to freeze to death. Just lie down and sleep and never wake.

I had almost died of exposure twice already, I told myself. There had been the snowstorm the day Auntie Suu-Suu came and fetched me from the Temple. And then there had been my first nighttime trek across the plain. This must be my karma, then, that I could not escape. I was to die alone in the cold; that was my calling and there is no way to avoid what has been decreed.

Only I was too angry to lie down and die.

Sometimes there are choices allowed inside the paradigm. I had learned that in the Temple—there were things I could choose and could avoid. But as the cold fell with the last of the light, I looked up and saw all the stars overhead shimmering in the liquid sky.

And I saw it and I knew inside me, with a simple wrenching wonder, that fate is fluid. That we are born with our history written, but there are moments when the gods laugh. Then all the world is let loose under chaos for all reality to rearrange itself.

There are not so many of these moments in the flow of any one person's life. Often it will be hundreds of years when the sky will not come unfixed in its moorings and the earth will not warm with the embrace, when the roar of the distant fires is quieted and a soft voice whispers in the silence.

The voice of Rama permeated the land and it trembled through my body. I could not hear or make out the words, but I didn't need the words. I knew the moment for what it was. We had slipped out of the preset measures for the blink of an eye, for forever, and in this delicate juncture all of the fates my previous lives had written had melted away.

I was free now, here, to change all eternity. Or I could hold my breath and wait, and the entirety of matter and energy again broken down into their atomic parts and held in the compassion of the gods would again reform in all the familiar ways.

I reached. In my soul, in my longing, in every desire that ever burned through me, I called out to the God/dess that is one and many. Across the banners of the night I saw Rama raging, flying after the evil angel Rabinah, Sita's cries rending the flesh of the earth and one of her silver tears dropped from the heavens splashing fire. The mountain beside me dissolved into a single river of molten pain.

The new volcano saved my life. It's heat and fire and falling ash countered the stunning cold. Later I heard that the explosion had been felt deep in Babelion, that windows had rattled and that the streets had shivered with the release of the force.

Volcanoes are the death of Maya and its lifeblood, too. Their energy keeps us alive, their venting keeps the planet warm enough to live, their ash and lava deposit rich soil and minerals over the bare rocks. The volcanoes are alive, the voices of the gods as they erupt and spew and then go silent.

The lava flowed near enough to warm me but not so close as to burn and the chasm of rock where the tunnels had been cut filled with fire. The Great Steam Lake was widening before my eyes, the transformer deep in the bones of the planet was sealed by a sea of molten stone.

Maybe the transformer would fail, or maybe it would continue to work buried deep below the new contours of the land, but that was no longer my affair. I climbed down the ridge as quickly as I could. It was very bright and the burning threw fierce shadows that highlighted the handholds better than day. The shape of the ridge itself funneled the new lava flow down around the face of the cliff and a deep depression that followed the chasm of the lake began to fill. The high cliff walls and the buttresses of stone carved out by another eruption a hundred years or more ago saved me.

It was a miracle that I was alive, a personal gift from the gods, from Devi and Shiva and Rama Vishnu the great Preserver. The volcano had consumed all my pasts so I was now a creature without a history. I felt as light as the breeze, as trusting as a newborn elephant, and I knew that I must have died in the night and been reborn all in a single body. Nothing remained but the possibilities of forever.

Nothing remained below but a single gleam where nothing should be. It was human light, or at least intelligent, colored and contained and dim against the backdrop of the advancing sea. The red magma was reflected against its structure and it looked familiar and not at all familiar.

My transport, I thought with horror. It would be gone, melted into the core of the earth, welded to the tunnels that would never be found again.

I had no way to return, and after my business with Hari-O I didn't trust the humans here. Anyone who had come after me wasn't here for my good. I hugged the rock but there was no place to hide. And much as the ridge had sheltered me from the first violence, it was greeting death to remain.

I had to get down; there was no time to rest, even to catch my breath. Whatever was waiting below would just have to wait. The volcano was a greater danger now. I slipped back down over the ledge and began again searching for handholds, for the next place I could rest my weight enough to balance. My whole world focus narrowed into the next step and the few meters of rock that I could study. I couldn't afford to think about the volcano and whatever waited in the light. Somehow that riveting attention kept the other fears at bay and I was aware only of climbing, climbing almost as if it were for fun the way Vijay and I had back when we were children. There was a rhythm to the cliff and I found myself responding to it, going down.

The first rule of climbing and the last is never to look down. I had no idea how fast I was moving, or where the lava was either above or below. So when I searched below for the next crack where I could wedge my toes and saw flat earth I thought it was another ledge. I couldn't stop, I told myself. No time to rest.

But when I stepped gingerly onto the outcropping I found that it was no ledge at all. I had stepped onto the floor of the high desert itself.

The molten steaming lake oozing to my right was contained by the deep crevasse opened in the eruption. Above the sky was burning red-orange, and then I knew that it wasn't the sky at all but the lava flow that had been diverted by the chance placement of a few boulders.

Nothing was real, nothing since I had left the Temple could have happened. It was all some kind of trance that Sri Mayurna would explain tomorrow in class.

A shadow hovered in front of me and warm sinewy arms twined around me and I knew it was no meditation. "Come on, we've got to get out of here," Vijay said, but he didn't let me go. Instead he propelled me over splintered ground and around a few cracks that hadn't been there before, cracks through the crust of the planet that revealed the roiling magma below.

Vijay didn't let me pause and look and meditate on the meaning of the magma and my being alive. He did not permit me to even go through the logic to be certain that I was alive. Instead he pushed me forward, relentless, toward the light that I could see now was a Tinker wagon.

"We only have fifteen minutes," he said as I tried to linger, to look back to the mountain, now covered in smoke, that still trembled behind us.

"Fifteen minutes?" I didn't know what he was talking about, but he stopped pushing and began dragging instead. And then we were inside the familiar and comfortable contours of his private home. I went to tumble into the bed, not letting him go even though I knew I stank of sweat and ash and fear. But instead of compliance he gently extracted himself from the heap I'd made and ordered me to buckle down.

Then he took the controls that were hidden in a panel that had served as a desk and side table and extra seat. The deep tufted chair had straps cleverly hidden behind the cushions, and as I attached them I heard Vijay swear softly. The wagon shivered delicately and outside the window the eruption cast a warm orange light over us.

The lava was moving, I realized. I had been protected for the moment, but the flow of rock was stronger than the elements which had held it back. The glow became brighter and brighter as it churned toward us.

And then the window went graphite gray and blank and the trembling stopped.

I wanted to know how he'd followed me and found me, but I saw the answer as soon as the door to the closet opened and Auntie Suu-Suu emerged to stretch. "Why are you doing this?" I asked her. I had meant to be angry, but I was far too exhausted and confused, not to mention very recently threatened. The past two days had become an indecipherable blur that was entirely meaningless.

"Because I'm the Chief Tinker," she said simply, telling me nothing at all. "And you're the last of the line. Now, we'll be there in a few hours and you'll be able to take a shower and sleep for a good long time before we return you to Babelion."

I shook my head and looked at Vijay. "I'm not going back to Babelion," I told him. "I made up my mind and I was wrong and stubborn. And I did what I had to do and even that was destroyed. I'm coming with you while you work on your research. If you still want me, I'll come with you."

Vijay never took his hands from the controls, didn't turn to look at me. He said nothing for a while and I thought that I'd blown it again, that walking away in the desert had been the end for him. Which made sense—I'm not sure I would have reacted any differently.

And then his voice came strained as if he were having trouble keeping it from being overwhelmed with feeling, like the violins at a Tinker funeral feast that weep like the mourners. "Thank you," was all he said, but it was enough.

Anselm, you aren't going anywhere but Babelion right now. You are going to complete the task that's set for you," Auntie Suu-Suu said, interrupting us as she entered.

I knew that she had probably saved my life, that she had known where I was, that she had only protected me. I didn't care. I didn't want her meddling, didn't want her turning my life into what my mother's had become.

"There's nothing set for me anymore," I lashed out at her. "I did it. I finished the shunt and Della was there and she's crazy and then the whole transformer got melted into the rock. So there isn't any power for anyone. For all we know, Babelion and the Mountain and the Village too are all waiting for us cold and dead. We could be the only ones left alive."

"Oh, I don't think so," she said. I wanted to wring her neck.

"I have a right to my life," I insisted. "I've only done what everyone else said and been what everyone else wanted and now I'm going to go with Vijay because I want to. It's my life, and if I screw it up that's my business."

I was ready for an argument, though I knew I wasn't thinking straight enough to win on logic. Still, all the pent-up tension of the past hours hadn't dissipated, they had merely churned without any outlet. And at the ragged end of my stamina I couldn't judge my words well. At least not then—that is a skill hard acquired, and then only used in maturity. At that time maturity was far far away.

Auntie did the one thing that infuriated me even more. She laughed. She opened her broad mouth and bellowed as if she had never heard anything so amusing in her life, as if she were laughing to release all the tension that I had been feeling.

"What's so funny?" I screamed. I snorted. I pounded my fist against the arm of the chair. I invoked the gods and curses from before the beginning of the Long Night, I called upon the champions of justice and karma for my right.

But Auntie only laughed harder, and then Vijay joined her.

When Vijay quieted and caught his breath, he shook his head and smiled at me. "If you want to pretend that you are free of karma and that you can write your own future, so be it. But you're being a stubborn idiot and even you know it. The only reason you have this feeling of infinite freedom is because you're in the testing stages, or didn't you learn anything useful at that Temple of yours?"

Vijay always could shut me up. He was right. Freedom is only another illusion. The only true freedom is freedom from illusion.

And yet in the Temple I had learned that the illusion itself is all allegory, all as sacred as it is profane, and every bit as real as it is deceptive. To change the symbol of a thing changes the reality as well—changes it in a subtle manner that is not immediately clear even to the one who manipulates the symbols.

I saw Auntie Suu-Suu staring at me as if she could see right into my head, as if she could see the truth of who I was under the veil of flesh. She shook her head slightly. "Your future is not written," she said, her voice heavy with disappointment. "All those months in that Temple and you didn't learn enough. I was certain that you wouldn't have enough time and half the education is worse than none at all. Now you know enough to be dangerous to everyone.

"But you are not going anywhere at all at the moment. This isn't done, it's only half started. There's a lot you don't know, and I'll try to take care of that. At least some of it. But you've got a lot of work to do right now while things are still volatile and we've got the chance. Wait even a few days and the Pretender's ship will be out of here and the Changed will be dead and you—well, we won't talk about what you would become stuck here forever.

"Very soon you will leave here, though even then you won't be free of us. You can't escape who you are. That's partly my fault and so it's my responsibility to make certain that you find your real place. But for now your duty is to Maya."

"I don't have any duty," I protested. "I did everything. Everything. And it's all a joke."

The old woman clucked her tongue and shook her head slightly. "Your father did his duty. He died to protect you. He could have run, he could have found the magic again to lead himself out. But he had to protect his future more than his flesh.

"And so it is your duty in turn. You know it. You want it. You are just weak now and afraid and you would rather run and hide like a little boy. But it doesn't matter if you are afraid and hurt and think that all you want is ease. It only matters what you do with it, if you give in and run from the dread or if you obey what is in your heart. You will choose."

"And me?" Vijay asked. "What about me?"

But the old woman merely closed her eyes. "You know what we are and you know what you wish to become," she stated flatly. "And you know what he is. Your choice is the classic one, and far too simple. You can have a human life, you can have learning and a comfortable future and everything a person could want— except him. Alice told you the truth. You cannot have both."

Chapter Twenty-four

And so they have been stealing energy, overtaxing the trans-former, for your whole life," Auntie finished up her long story about the clone Empresses and the Pretender/Emperor with my name. "You realize, that I hadn't understood that the agent who contacted Sithra meant to so completely exploit Maya. I had assumed that there was negotiation, that they were opening an-other contact. There would be good reasons for that and it would be the normal thing to do. For the Empress it would be the normal thing to do," she amended.

"And so I didn't understand what the point was until your father was killed, and by then it was too late. I tried to help your mother to redress the balance of power, but Della was always headstrong. And she didn't believe me."

I could understand that. I wasn't sure I believed Auntie. The whole had the sound of one of the god fables to it—something that had never been intended to be thought of as true in historical fact so much as true in metaphor.

But then, there was Vijay's research and Della's strangeness and the way the Tinkers appeared and disappeared at will. I wasn't sure I believed anything at all, including my old belief that some-thing that sounded fantastical probably was fantasy. I had lived enough fantasy in the past few days. To be the only heir of the last clone Empress was no more unbelievable than anything else that had happened. Had Hari-O been real, and had he died? Had the volcano truly erupted just when I needed it to happen, and what of Sita's silver tear?

"That," said Auntie, reading my mind, "was one of the robot ships that have been coming here for ages. Only that one was not a fuel cargo carrier. That one was a bomb. They were responding to your shunt, they knew that someone had been tinkering with the lines. And so they went to destroy any evidence of their own culpability.

"There are those who joined the Pretender's forces because there appeared no alternative. But they wouldn't tolerate the kind of treatment that had been given to Maya, and in the end I believe there are enough of them, of us, to defeat this would-be Emperor." Auntie's face darkened and for a moment I saw the mirror of my own rage. "It isn't just that he has continually defied convention and tradition and abrogated our rights. It's that he has no concept of what true royalty means. To be the ruler is power, but he has forgotten why he rules. He has forgotten the other end of the equation, that for every measure of power he owes an equal measure of obligation. Of protection. So if this incident on Maya were made generally known through the Empire, it would weaken his position. Not entirely, but by just enough that it would be one more piece of evidence that would prove him unfit."

"So you want me to go out with some war fleet and do what the Imperial Navy couldn't do?" I asked. At the time it sounded like a very appealing idea.

"No," Auntie said. "I want you to show up in the capital with the Coronation Mantle and denounce him as illegitimate. And be crowned in the full and legal ritual as he never was, with all the marks of power that he never had. He will have to come, he will have to destroy you. And then we will be able to have our revenge."

We're approaching Ishra Way," Auntie Suu-Suu interrupted her own story as she caught a glance at the instruments. "And just on time, too. The others should be waiting."

The window that had been opaque gray only a few moments

earlier now cleared and I could see the darkness outside. A few lights fluttered, caravan lights from Tinker Wagons. That must be the rendezvous that Auntie Suu-Suu had meant.

But other than those few lights, Babelion itself was dark as death. No streetlights showed, no music blared from the windows, no knots of young people sauntered to impress and no elders gossiped on the stoops. Only many tiny specks moved through what I realized were the streets. Many many many of them. If each one represented a person walking, then the streets were more crowded than I had ever seen them, even during a major festival.

They were moving together, converging on these wagons in the central market. Coming together from the rich areas and the poor ones, and in the dark one could not be told from another.

"Talk to them," Auntie Suu-Suu said, gesturing with one long finger to the door. "This is what you must do."

"But the power," I said, not knowing what to do.

"The power is gone," Auntie told me. "You know nothing could have survived that eruption. There is no power here. There is no power on all of Maya. What does that tell you?"

I didn't want to answer. This wasn't a test like Sri Mayurna gave where I had to find some philosophical principle at work. But I read the answers in Auntie's face.

"There is no power on the Mountain," I said softly. "The Exchange is dead."

"Not dead," Vijay corrected me. "But isolated on its backup. It can't do anything and the interfaces are all frozen. The Exchange will survive, but for the moment it's in solitude."

A thin smile spread across his lips, and he looked grim and harsh and beautiful. Auntie clucked approvingly, as if she were not the architect behind it all—and yet she was not.

The lights came together. I could see that some of them were portatorches and others were primitive open flames. They ringed the wagons, silent and waiting, confused and afraid. In the dark we could all be killed, and the Changed might have just pulled the plug. They have threatened to do this before, so many times that we no longer listened. It was rhetoric just like my father's speeches, just like my early lessons. Words cover up what is real and true. To peel them back and expose the vulnerability I could sense in the dead lines was a crime. As long as people believe in something and it makes their lives bearable, there is no justification to ripping that last support away.

Unless there was something we could do about it.

Today the first crews went out early. By tomorrow they would have the first line of cells sunk up in the ridge. When night fell next it would still be dark in Babelion, but the Mountain would have regained its control. Only so long as they could not touch the Exchange did we have the advantage.

I unbuckled from the seat restraint and ran my fingers through my hair. I hadn't even had a shower and my face was still dark with ash. My clothes were rumpled and I stank like belching magma. But it was so dark that no one would see that I didn't look anything like a hero—that I resembled a defeated and disciplined puppy more than a warrior. Far more than a leader who could take command the way his father had, as if that day had melted into this night and this new dawn.

In my mind, the fire where my father died and the volcanic action that destroyed the transformer were the same event, the two so seamlessly connected that the intervening years had never been.

I was no longer Anselm Null, the son of Della One-Butterfly. I was Arsen, embodied him in the unreality that shrouded the night. The gods were walking again and this was all some great metaphoric ritual, to reenact the final chapter of the story.

Rama must meet the angel of evil, fight and defeat him. In the story it is always the same, and so I knew that I could not lose and I could not die. As my father had known it as he had been engulfed by flames, the same flames that had proved Sita pure and honest had proved him the same.

I left through the door and found myself inside a silent triangle formed by the three wagons together. I was alone, but I could sense the crowd beyond. The mass became firmer and I could smell their flesh and the burning of the fire torches that a few of them carried.

One of the wagons had a ladder to the roof. I climbed that and was pulling myself up into a sitting position when Vijay called my name from below. I turned slightly and saw that he carried a torch in his hand. He waited until I was well balanced and then climbed the two lowest rungs to hand the blazing raw flame up to me.

He said nothing, and only the tips of his fingers brushed my hand. I wanted to say something but no words would come. What could I tell him anyway, that we didn't both know was either a lie or a hope or a fear? Because we wouldn't know anything at all until much much later, if both of us lived.

I stood up and held the torch so that I could see down—and so that the people of Babelion could see me. So that they could see that it was Anselm and Arsen both standing there in the dark, ready to speak to them.

"A great thing has happened," I said, and my voice rolled from my chest in great waves of sound that I was sure I couldn't possibly make on my own. "Perhaps it is the revenge of the gods or perhaps it is only luck. When the Ridge of Holy Smoke erupted today, the lava invaded the tunnels of the power transformer at the Great Steam Lake. Yes, we have no power in Babelion. We have no lights and no transports and no cooking units and no cold storage. There is no heat in the buildings and they are already cooling. Tomorrow it will be too cold inside for the children. And so you thought that the Changed had done this thing to destroy us finally. As they have always threatened to destroy us and have never had the nerve to try.

"Let me tell you, the Changed are not so strong. They have no power tonight either. They are also cold and their food was served tepid and they don't know what will happen tomorrow.

"But the Changed are even weaker than we are. The Changed cannot access their beloved Exchange. The Exchange is not dead, not yet, but it is isolated. Which means that the Changed are far more afraid than we are. It means that they are not only weak but crippled. After all these generations the Changed are no longer the masters of the Exchange, they are its dependents. And without it they have no lives of their own, no mind that they can trust. The Exchange turned them into its creatures long ago.

"So the Mountain is fruit ripe for the harvest. All we have to do is to take it. Their weapons cannot stop us. The scan fields on the gates are all down and the locks are all disabled. The Guardians no longer have the command connection in their dormitories and houses in the Village, and they have no light in their weapons lockers.

"If we are ever going to take the Mountain down, it is tonight. It is now."

I waited the space of a heartbeat, and then two. Nothing came back to me and I was afraid that they were going to reject me. To take me down and tear me apart for blasphemy, a sacrifice to fear.

Instead, the powerful cry of recognition and acceptance rolled over me like a hundred wagons in a race to the sun. It had only taken longer for the depth of momentum to build to that overwhelming crescendo. They were with me, the whole of Babelion. The priests and the sellers and the makers of incense, the clothing painters and the tenders of the dead, all of them were indistinguishable in the night. And all of them were screaming their approval.

We went out by the road, just like another march on another day. Only that had been a warm and bright morning; now it was a deep cold night and we were carrying torches. In the night there was no time. In the dark everything was homogeneous, no differentiation between early and late. It was the time for magic and mayhem, for the memories and fears that don't exist in the honest hours.

I do not know how many in the crowd were armed. This was not the carefully planned and organized action that Iolo had advocated and trained me to take. I wasn't armed, nor was Vijay who somehow had found me in the mob and walked at my side. If I tried hard I could sense Sulma with me, see how she had created and shaped the moment though she had never lived in it.

Now I know that what I did was stupid. One should not attack up a hill to a fortified position, carrying torches to mark our presence in the dark. The military leaders have laughed at me and pointed out that I am naïve and have no business running any war at all. I very carefully do not remind them that I have never run any war the way they define it, and it is my ambition that I never shall.

On that night I should have been cut down there at the base of the Mountain, and that was not the last time I did something stupid by the training of the military mind. But the generals and admirals don't know people and cultures and what they will do. I don't know that either, not all the time. But on strange days karma is with me, weaving through the chaotic to make sense of the designs. And then I know what is a crazy chance and what is a reasonable risk.

I knew it that night.

Perhaps a fortified position with troops and generals all trained in the Academies could not be taken by an angry mob from the city below.

But the Xanadu is not a military installation and never was. It is only the place where the Changed have created a fantasy of the world. The walls are to keep out the cold and the memory of pain; to keep them sleeping while the rest of the world went on. They and their Exchange and their very carefully manipulated lives all together was a prison in which they had been trapped since the end of the Night.

Like the trees and flowers and birds and bright creatures of Xanadu, the Changed could not survive outside its environment.

"Douse the torches," I gave the order to the rank behind me in a whisper, and I heard the whisper ripple back. It took a moment before anyone turned off the hand lamps, let alone smothered the flames of the old fire torches in the volcanic ash that dusted every surface on Maya.

I waited for a full minute, for my eyes to begin to adjust to the darkness. There I could make out the Dome of the Mountain, slightly glowing, from what I did not know. Maybe they had built fires to keep warm, or there was enough power on the backup systems that some small trickle of light and heat remained.

We fanned out as we came within sight of Xanadu's walls. Rock piles lined the road, a memory of its construction. Tough desert grass grew in isolated clumps between the boulders, and the long strands grabbed around my ankles and tore. Vijay stumbled over what turned out to be a tiny shrine of carefully fitted stone filled with flowers and a little rice and ash of incense. I hung back with him and made him inspect his leg where he'd fallen. The wound was open and oozing slightly, and already the area around it was starting to discolor.

I looked around me and I could see the crawling shapes crouching behind rocks here and making short jagged runs to the next bit of cover.

Where were they? They had to know we were here. They couldn't be inside and not have any idea that we were coming. There must have been some communication from the Exchange. Something must have been working in Babelion somewhere. Someone must know. Sithra must know, my mother must know.

Where are the Guardians? Why weren't they watching the perimeter, guarding against the cold if nothing else. Making sure no Tinkers came too close to the walls, keeping the Changed safely at distance from experience.

The thoughts tumbled around in my head, each one clear and utterly convincing. This was only the veil of the night, I told myself. I had merged with the world of Maya and I no longer saw what was real, any more than any of the Changed could. I moved only and wholly within the dream.

But the dreams that Sri Mayurna had taught us did not have slippery-sharp obsidian stones strewn over the ground. In dreams, no one stank so that the Changed should know we were here by the stench alone.

The quality of the hush changed. At first it was active silence, the careful quiet of those who are afraid of being seen. Now it was the speechlessness of disbelief, of suspension, of waiting for the first shot, the first death.

The chill deepened and sank into my flesh. That final drop of cold signaled the last hour of the night and the coming light. Any advantage we had would be gone by daylight. Once the Changed were prepared for us we were defeated. They had all the weapons and the Guardians and. . . .

Suddenly the wall was at my nose. Literally. I could smell the dank rot on it from the scrunge that lived on the moisture exuded by the garden. Filthy things, I recoiled and stepped back and looked. I moved to my left. The ground was flat here but the grass hadn't been pulled and I didn't want to fall. Not here, not now, not when everyone was watching.

The Gate was not covered in slimy things. It was warm pressed insulate, recently polished, the surface smooth and soft to the touch. Made from the same basic fiber as the road, but far more refined, the closed Gate appeared to swallow all distinction. It only existed because it blotted out all other existence. Null.

Null.

I had authorization. If anyone not Changed touched the insulate skin it would sound an alarm. But I was accepted, my DNA on file in the records. I could touch it, even open the locks, if they had not been set against me. Though I would have thought that Sithra would have done that. . . .

The Gate opened silently under my hands. There was no resistance, there was no feeling of the connection that was made and broken, and suddenly I understood. Anyone could touch the Gate now. Anyone could enter. Without power, the Gates were just dead things on hinges like any door in Babelion.

I opened the Gate and walked in unarmed, alone, the mob of Babelion just behind me, waiting for me to take the lead.

It was the Sunrise Gate which led through the Orangerie, only in the deep chill of the unpowered night the trees had begun to freeze. Fruit frosted with only a light dusting looked as if they had been sprinkled with sugar and set among the leaves that had crumpled in death.

Other than the leaves the trees appeared alive. The strong scent of orange blossoms was less pronounced in the icy air and overpowered by the smell of smudge-pots burning on the central patio.

The Changed huddled around the meager warmth, chaffing their hands and trying to get warm in their elegant ceremonial clothes. The ultrafine silk and gauze, the embroidered drapes of thirty meters that weighed no more than the grapefruit that had fallen from the trees, the careful elegance that was normal for the Changed was only killing them now.

Most of those around the smudge-pots didn't even move at our appearance through the Gate. The Changed didn't notice us in their misery, it appeared. Or in the dark they couldn't see to tell that we weren't Changed ourselves.

We moved through the formally arranged topiary trees,

through the ornate stone ewers of flowers, all yellow and orange and gold in this section, that had frozen through in the night. The spun gold ribbons looped along the path drooped and looked as if they were something sold off a blanket in Bright Street.

Still the Changed did not move. I screamed and my voice echoed back to me. "I've returned to you," I yelled. "I've come for justice, for my father and for my people. And for myself. I am Della's son and the half-breed mule of Babelion."

They only stared and muttered, and I began to lead my would-be revolutionaries through the shattered trees and the shattered Changed.

Finally as we approached the main entrance of the Palace, several Guardians in uniform stood blocking the way. Stood just like the memories I had seen of my father's assault.

Then the Guardians shot.

Now they didn't. They didn't have their eyeshields down and I could see their faces, just barely, in the first glimmering of light. Simple faces, human faces no different from those around me. Over their trim, decorative uniforms they wore the long quilted coats of Babelion, and their hands were cased in fingerless gloves. Still I could see that their hands were cold, far too red and trembling as they stood with weapons aimed and ready to fire.

I walked forward, my empty hands extended. I stopped right in front of them, when I was almost in range to touch. I stopped dead still and smiled and looked into each of their faces. All I saw was humanity and hurt there. These were not the faceless Guardians who served the superior beings and wanted to be superior themselves. These were tired, drawn humans who had undergone a terrible day and a more hideous night, with no promise that things would be better.

"I have no quarrel with you," I said to the ranking sergeant. Or Vijay that I said that; I no longer recall all the details.

She cast her eyes over the few shivering Changed hovering over an open flame, and the weary human faces of her own cohort. "It is our duty to protect the Changed," she said, but her heart wasn't in her words.

"If it is your duty to protect them," I said softly, "then get them blankets and hot soup. And someone organize a shelter with decent heat. There's a backup generator for the Exchange that produces enough heat in the tunnels that it should be a start. Set up down there, spread out mattress rolls like in the Temple until we can figure out the rest."

"The Exchange," one of the Changed—Kumar 4-Port wailed. "We have to get to the Exchange."

He broke away from the group and ran straight at the Guardian line. When he collapsed against their solid trained bodies they treated him gently, carried him back to the fire and tried to chafe some warmth into his lifeless hands.

But Kumar was right. For the first time in his life that I knew him, he was the first to know and the first to speak. We had to get to the Exchange. *I* had to get to the Exchange, and then I had to get into it. The Exchange had its own backup system and that would mean that the Changed who were left might survive until we built a new power plant. Until then we would have to live worse than the ancestors, and for some reason that thought pleased me.

I started up the Mountain, past the line of the gardens of Xanadu to where the wall had ended. The Last Wall of the World no longer existed and the mountains towered high over the installation, yearning toward their own great ancestors in the stars. There had been only the one door in that wall, the modest garden gate that led only down stone steps into the central heart of the illusion. It was easy to find, and I had been here before.

As I started down the uneven steps I felt as if I were going back in time. Years peeled away and I was at my mother's claiming ceremony again, the Tinker shawl wrapped around my shoulders. Now there was only the hair on my head and I was used to my height and I knew that the ceiling wasn't so low as it appeared. Still, I felt crowded and my breathing became shallow, as if memories took volume and fouled the air.

The tunnels were patterned with the same mandala as the power station and the Temple of Babelion. I walked the paths of that mandala, knowing that the center was not the center, that the beginning and the end were always the same and that the turnings sketched the letters of the name in the heart of Haruman, the monkey-god.

This was the secret, then, that none of the Changed learned. My mother had seen it and now I understood the meaning of the maze. It was not Rama that the Changed served. It was not Vishnu in the guise of the king. It was the God of the Monkeys, it was the eternal trickster and the protector of those who were lower than the humans who created them. Everything had been hinted and veiled and for all the generations of our peoples we had never looked into the signs and symbols.

"You think you know the truth, but you know nothing," my mother said.

I recognized her voice, and when she finally addressed me in the corridors I relaxed. She had to be here; I had only wondered how long she would wait.

"I would prefer to meet you in the Exchange," I said simply.

"Please," she sneered. "Number four is the only one that has power. We left it for you."

"How kind," I muttered. Number four was the room where she had said her last good-bye, where I had entered the Exchange to greet her in her new world and being, to see that she still lived and waited for me.

The room was precisely as I remembered it. Even the dust of the power surge and break had not touched this chamber, and I had the impression that I had traveled back to that day years ago and that I could still talk her out of it. Karma shimmered in the stone, and I believed that I could hold on to the things that I had most desired and that the past years of Babelion had only been a bad dream.

I believed it and I knew it was false. There was no way out. There had only been one way ever for me to go, and no matter how many times and in how many roles I came to be born Della's son, I would always be cast out from my people and return to their destruction. In every age and with every attempt to change this path I have repeated it in the end.

This time is the last (only I always hope that.) But I bowed before the knowledge of my fate, with respect for the internal fate that weaves inevitability into all of us. Here, now, I stepped off the wheel. I made my own decisions where to stand and what I would do.

This time I wouldn't run and hide. This time I would respect the Lords of Time and take the responsibility for my place in the World of Sorrow. I would take the karma upon myself with the knowledge that for every advantage given there was a price to pay. And that in the end the cost would be higher than anyone could pay alone.

I knew this and I accepted it freely. This was the only way to freedom in the world of illusion.

The center of Room Four was small and cramped and deep underground. I drew my breath in slowly as I had every morning in the Temple, and in my mind's eye built the pool around my knees. I could feel the water and the breath of the early sky on my face, I could feel the promise of warmth in the coming day and the joy and despair of the world of veils.

It is all illusion. It is all a game. And I was the player and the game and the thing that was played upon. I raised my hands to the beckoning dawn and felt glistening drops from the pool spill out of my palms to anoint my face.

"Hail to the new light and the new day." I spoke the ritual words with a conviction I had never known while an acolyte.

The Room formed the sunrise around me. I could see/smell/taste/feel/hear the water at my feet soaking my trousers from the knee down. There had been no real water here when I had begun and so I had not removed my outer garments and folded them neatly on the great obsidian shelf behind me. There were tiny insects skimming the surface of the pond with glittering iridescent wings and bright blue and bronze and leaf-green bodies.

There were water lilies blooming here, the yellow and purple ones that were the originals before we bred all the pinks and the shell-peach and the ones the color of the Xanadu sky. I had the impression of people around me; that was a memory of the Temple and I edited that before going on. This was a solitary moment, a sunrise where I had the freedom to be alone.

The sunlight came softly over the water that had spilled down my face. I scooped up three handfuls and released them over my hair, said the correct words, stood in the prescribed position. And the words and the acts and all the ritual manners together flowed seamlessly so that illusion and the Truth, Now and Forever, and

324 • SHARIANN LEWITT

all that mattered and all that was insane were present at the dedication of the new day.

It was a new day. Even in the dead of night it was new. I was returned here to the heart of Maya, to the center of Creation, to the Exchange and the rituals of the gods together. Everything was the same and nothing was the same.

"You actually bought that story they taught you?" Della mocked me from the obsidian bank.

She chose to appear as she had in life, where she looked to be maybe twenty human years of age with her black hair hanging straight and heavy, braided down her back. She was dressed as the devi priestesses in the Temple dressed. Her braid was tangled with strands of pearls and flecks of silver, and a silver and copper ribbon bound the end of that heavy hair with a fall of tiny bells. She wore a pale blue skirt and blouse embroidered with pearls around the hems, and Auntie Suu-Suu's shawl was draped elegantly over one shoulder and tucked into the sides of her skirt the way the devis wear their veils.

In fact, she looked like a devi acolyte, all rich and serious and ready to take exams. She didn't look Changed at all.

She stood and said no more until I had climbed out of the warm morning water and sat down on the glassy flat stone. "So you think you know the Truth and that now you are going to start the world again," she stated. "Just like anyone too young, you think you have invented the world and the rest of us have never dreamed or desired or felt passion. That your elders can't know anything, either right or wrong, and you are so very certain that only you can save all the world. Some day you'll grow up and discover that you can't save anything at all. Not even your children.

"There are things you don't know that you need to know, Anselm. I would tell them only to you, because you are my own flesh, you are what of me will live forever. And there are things you do not understand that you will understand.

"But first you must promise me a proper funeral, my son. It is your duty and my right. I hated my second funeral, which was the only one I managed to attend. . . ."

Chapter Twenty-five

She is my mother, and there are places in my head that exist because of her DNA. Neither human nor Changed, she is as I am, on the edge and not existing at all.

"But what you have not seen is more than you can imagine," she was telling me. The room was filling with visions of fantastic places, palaces that made Xanadu look crude and cities that made Babelion look tame. "There was a whole Empire out there once," she went on as the environs reformed themselves first into a shopping plaza where children wore guns and the good offered in the displays were living creatures so modified that I couldn't tell whether they had been adapted from animal or plant sources, or a fusion of both.

"A whole Empire. And even though there have been civil wars and wars of independence, splinter groups and breakaways, and even though the Court has become decadent and lazy and has let most of the ties between planetary populations drift into nearly nothing, there is still an Empire. And it's ripe, Anselm. It's ready for us, you and me together with the Exchange. We could take it. We could leave this place and take it ourselves."

She was mad.

I had always known that she loved power, that she would do anything for it. Auntie Suu-Suu was right; above all things Della must never know that she is by rights an Empress. The passion for power is in the genotype, but training is supposed to balance it with responsibility and concern. Which Della had never learned. She had been willing enough to sacrifice my father, and me, for her ambitions.

That's not true. Her voice rang through the visions of the planets of Empire. *I sacrificed everything for you, do you understand that? For you.*

"And what will you do now, Mother, if I don't want to go?" I asked simply. "Why should I go? I have everything I want here now. You wouldn't understand, but I have everything I ever wanted. I wanted justice and a place for me in this world. That's all.

"I can't think of one single good reason to go out there to somewhere unknown and shoot up worlds—for what? I can't think of a thing out there I want."

Only when I spoke I knew that I had lied. I hoped that I had learned more from Sri Mayurna than she had expected. I hoped that I had learned to keep my thoughts buried and to be wholly in the moment—and therefore wholly convincing.

She stared at the ground for a long time before she lifted her eyes to meet mine. There was still steel in them, more perhaps than when she had lived in her body. Della was steel all the way through.

She smiled coldly as she looked at me, as if she had somehow found the secret key.

"Vijay will not stay here," she said finally. "There is knowledge and truth out there, other species of people as well. There are even ones like me, I suppose, and possibly other mules like you. Maybe they can even do something about that little problem. Maybe out there it won't matter."

"It doesn't matter now," I lied.

It did matter. It would always matter. Not that I was unable to have children—I hadn't even thought about children. And if I couldn't, then others in the circle I would create would and they would belong to the circle as a whole, as children always did in Babelion.

But being an outcast, a half-breed, a person who belonged nowhere, was too hard for me. Maybe for someone greater, for someone with more of the spiritual connection that Sri Mayurna said came with the constant practice of meditation and contemplation, maybe for a great teacher like him it would not be important.

I was still very young then, though I am not sure if even age would have changed my heart. To be outcast was to be the stranger, to be the no-caste.

Suddenly I realized why I could lead Babelion up the Mountain and could take the broken fortress in the midst of confusion. I had no caste in the world, I had nothing to lose. If one must take on the karma of destruction, better that it be one without tribe or caste, without meaning in the world. Then, when I die, the meaning evaporates with me and it was as if I had never been.

That mattered very much. Most of my thinking may have been the selfish delusions of someone who is seen and treated and thinks of himself as an adult, but truly is not yet ready to take on all the world alone. And I knew that I would be alone, and isolated, in the end. Vijay would leave for his science. Sulma was dead. Iolo was dead and my mother had become so merged with the Exchange that she no longer existed as the woman I had known.

The possibility that there were others like me drew me more than any promise of power or pleasure ever could. I just wanted to find somewhere I could breathe again, somewhere I could be, where who I am did not cut me off from life and desire and all that was good and beautiful. I had everything I wanted here except the one thing that mattered. Suddenly Maya seemed much too small and the universe was full of promise.

To go out into the wilderness that we had come from was infinitely tempting. And so I told Della that it was impossible, that we had no ships and had even cannibalized the technology to survive on the land. The ancestors who first arrived made certain that we would never leave this place. They had used every part of their ship, down to turning the navigational computer and the ship's AI into the Exchange. They had stranded us on this rock forever, out of touch with any other place or time or greater venue.

"The Tinkers," Della said. "They come and go, you know. They're off-worlders, just as they have promised to take Vijay off-world. How do you think the top neural sculptors get their training? They all study in the great institutes of the Creators."

Her voice dropped to a hushed whisper and for a moment there was even a flicker of sincerity and wonder on her face. "I have seen these places through the Exchange. While the Exchange is in interface with AIs throughout the galaxy I can access them as well. I know that most of them, maybe all of them, are part of this Empire. That they have never lost touch and that they think that we were left here for some reason. That we are prisoners

328 · SHARIANN LEWITT

who were left to die. That's who and what we were—the dregs
of an abandoned experiment and their jailers. And now we can
show them what our exile has done. That we have not died but
that we are stronger and more formidable than before.

"Their history is wrong. Our Creators made no mistakes. We
were sent away because we were too dangerous to all the humans
in space as well as those near to us. They cannot accept the truth,
that is all."

I was utterly entranced by my own mother. How she could
twist reality in that image I could not comprehend. Her arrogance
was breathtaking, no longer even hubris because it was the pride
of a god and not a mortal.

Though perhaps she was no longer mortal. She lived in the
Exchange; she was the Exchange. She was at one with it and so
its attitudes had corrupted hers as well. She had never been one
of us. She had never been meant for Maya. It was unreasonable
to expect that after indulging her megalomania for years through
the medium of the Exchange, she was ready to temper her au-
dacity and rejoin the living.

But I had not expected her imagination to compass the whole
of the galaxy as well. Let alone an Empire that we hadn't known
existed and people beyond the stars who were all strangers, who
couldn't care less about Maya and had their own curses as well.
Trust Mother not to see any of it.

"You can do it," she said to me, her whole body taut with
conviction. "You alone, Anselm. This is the destiny that Auntie
Suu-Suu foretold. You will go with me and together we will rule
them all. After all, you broke the Mountain all alone. After generations all the history of Babelion together couldn't bring us
down. And you brought us to our knees, destroyed Xanadu,
turned the Changed out into the cold. You are *my* child. There
is nothing human about you, you are completely Changed. More
Changed than any of them."

I watched her image for a moment before I answered. She
looked so very young and still, her body like a sword against the
breeze generated by the room interface. She was a shining beacon,
she was Durgha the goddess of childbirth and children, the wife
of the Preserver and the patron of relief from pain.

For Durgha is also Kali, the goddess who dances the end of the world, who would wash the tundra with blood and feast on the flesh of the murdered.

Della had been Durgha. Not a balanced and strong Durgha, true, but one of her kindred all the same. The Exchange had opened her to the other side of her nature and now both were entwined in the wild large eyes with which she pretended to view the world.

"No, Della. I am not Changed at all and neither are you. And if I leave this place it is to find who we are, not to conquer anyone at all," I said. Sri Mayurna would have been proud of me. I could hear the truth lying like a heavy thread in the weaving, anchoring my thoughts and hopes and fears together into itself. And it was the Truth that spoke through my mouth, for I did not know that I ever chose to speak it.

"I did not conquer anything, I never broke the Mountain. Those people you want to conquer, they're the ones who did all of that. Because they've been stealing from us for years and didn't want to be found out and reported.

"There's nothing big and noble about any of it. There's no destiny, there's no legend. There's just a sordid little colonial event to be buried, that's all.

"That's the great empire you want to conquer, Della. Petty thieves who run as soon as they think they might get caught. Cowards and liars and people who don't care how they get to where they're going. They're not worth it, Della. They're not worth my life.

"You wanted to protect me, Mother, and so you played politics all your life. You never thought to go out, to build, to make anything better. Just to make sure you were in the best position in the old order of things.

"You and Sithra are not any different than whatever decadent Court rules some dying Empire half a lifetime away. Why bother to go there when we have the very same thing right here?"

"Because if you do not turn and fight right now, there will be nothing left at all, and entropy will have won."

My mother's eyes widened and I whipped around to see what was behind her. Auntie Suu-Suu stood there, only this was an

Auntie Suu-Suu I didn't know. She wasn't an old woman wearing too-bright clothes with riddles in her words. This was someone who stood between us and the God/dess, the Oracle of the beginning and the end, the one who cries the warning that none will hear. I saw her and recognized her and I felt the ice in her breath chill me to the core. She wore the uniform of the Imperial agent, the pale blue of the Royal Labs, crisply tailored and covered in a large black garment lined in cyan silk and a broad velvet band around her neck that hung halfway down her back. I couldn't read the signs but I knew these were her marks of rank and status, her honors hung around her.

"Who do you think did this? Who were those gods you thought you saw in the sky?" Auntie Suu-Suu did not let up. "The Pretender has done everything he needs to do. Your people can't survive here. Della is embedded in the Exchange and the Exchange itself is mute and dying. Most of the Changed are gone or aren't functioning."

"What do you want me to do about it?" I asked. I shouted. I bent over and pulled my hair. It was all wrong; this was not the way I had planned anything to go.

A large warm hand grasped my shoulder and I felt the slightest shred of hope return. Vijay's hand, supporting me, even when I wished he were gone.

"We can catch them," Vijay said. "We've got the wagons and they think that no one here has flight capacity at all."

"Three wagons?" I asked abjectly. Three wagons wouldn't carry enough people to fight in a bar brawl. But Vijay smiled.

"The rest of the caravan is over the ridge. I can send for them now and we'll join them. We're small enough that our signatures won't attract attention on the Pretender ship."

My mind started to work double time. "Yes. Done. Let's go," I said. Auntie followed us out of the tunnels as if she knew the maze as well as I did. Which made sense.

"Bring the Changed to the Temple Springs." I snapped the order at someone I recognized as one of Iolo's recruits. "And tell the Guardians to report to me."

I didn't stop walking, but I heard a flurry of activity behind me and a Guardian in half uniform came up to me. "You wanted us?" he asked.

"Yes. Ten of you to take the Changed to the Temple and guard them. Both from those who would kill them and from them doing harm in Babelion. In the sacred places they should be safe. The rest of you will come and gather at the Tinker wagons. We're going on a little expedition."

Stripped of luxuries, the Tinker wagons were far more com-modious than I had realized. Vijay was distraught when I tossed out all the lab equipment, but there would be better facilities in the Empire. I needed space.

The best I could manage was twelve Guardians per wagon. "How do you know that their training doesn't include close com-bat?" I asked Auntie Suu-Suu for the hundredth time.

"I don't know anything about their training," she replied. "I only created the outlines for training the Imperial Fleet, not the impostors. They were trained by renegade Imperial officers, which means that they could have any motley assortment of nonsense skills anyone could imagine. But surprise . . . ," she added.

"I know about surprise," I cut her off. "And it won't help beyond the first few minutes, especially not if they're trained to it. You'll be in your own wagon, of course. And there are a good ten Guardians in there. You'll lift first and lead, since that's your usual order. We'll be straggling well behind; wait until we're a good five minutes back before you hit the emergency."

She nodded and strode off, her long ragged skirts and wispy hair looking anything but fierce. I only hoped she would stick to the plan. I didn't trust her. She was too much like my mother and didn't have as much invested in my survival.

Robot runner ships are big, but most of the personnel are support staff. And they aren't fighters at all, they're just ware-house collectors who are there to make sure the energy they take is secured in the power cells, and that those are firm on the hull. These are not troops of any kind, just ordinary people doing an ordinary job. That was my only hope, my only chance.

That, and I knew that I didn't know what I was getting myself into. I just knew that I would feel better fighting. They had blown up our sole power supply, they had endangered the lives of everyone on Maya. That was all I had to know to hate them. The more complicated politics and machinations meant nothing to me then. I couldn't afford to think of the Enemy as men and women with homes to return to, who were concerned with their dinners and their families and their place in whatever card tournament they held in the off hours. I could think only the wilting in Xanadu and the shivering children crowded around the fire at the Ishtar Gate of Babelion mattered.

This was clear, this was clean, this made sense to me. And so I was eager to fight, to have things simple, to take revenge.

Waiting was the hard part. Auntie's wagon certainly didn't look like it could threaten any military vessel. It was tiny, painted brightly, a giggle in the great big sky. For the first time I actually saw the Tinker wagons lift, and they did not go vertical. The comical hats that shapes their roofs unfurled down into large flexible delta spreads that helped the stocky little transports turn into slivers that cut to flight. It was beautiful and bright, all the silly colors, the stars and moons painted when so very soon we would be taking them among the real moons and stars . . .

And then I realized that the painting had been camouflage. It looked far too bright on the ground, but encased in the honeycomb net with no visuals, they massed too small to clip the sensors. No one had ever captured a Tinker caravan because no one had ever seen one on the move. They were hidden again by their gaudy surfaces, just as they had moved unnoticed among us all for so very long.

And I prayed to the God/dess that Auntie's talent for obscurity would fail. That the attackers would see her and notice the stall, and realize that it was indeed Auntie Suu-Suu who was stranded in the waste.

The Pretender wanted her, had to want her for a long time. She was the bait—she had given me the idea when she saw how I could bait another, larger trap. And so in her pink and yellow wagon with the delta wing newly polished bright gold with white and infrared insets, she shone like a beacon in the sky. Alone, helpless, limping along, her distress signal penetrating the dark.

And all behind, silent as the shade, the other wagons painted indigo with stars waited.

The cargo collector hesitated. It was the oldest trick in the book. Yet to ignore a distress call out in the void of space violated an even deeper taboo, a tradition as old as the night itself. Even on the deserts of our home world we did not abandon those lost and hurt in the dark, though every human knew how often those in distress turned into the enemy.

The attacker knew that and weighed the decision. There was no backup to rely on, no one nearby but primitives and hostiles. It wavered. I like to think I would have passed temptation by. I hate to think that I would leave my kind to the mercy of vacuum.

I am not unlike the skipper of any ship between the stars. In the end we are all living things and life stands together when faced with dying. Even those aliens we know, though we can not know them well, they have respect for that which separates us from inert matter. Between living and dying, life is always sacred.

The Pretender Captain was not so cold, so divorced from knowledge of the void, so married to bare reason, to pass the wagon by. The attack ship slowed, changed vector, pummeled its power forward to reel the Tinkers in.

We fell upon them like gnats on flesh, a swarm of tiny things that alone went unnoticed but together were a force.

The wagons that had been hidden behind the range danced in and out to annoy and catch the attention of the gunners. Unwieldy on the ground, the smallest wagons darted in close to the skin of the large war ship. So close they skimmed the surface that the Pretender dare not bring its weapons to lock on to them, for fear of locking on to itself. They danced around each other like the Tinkers at the bonfires, like the sparks that swirled through the air when a log was added to the pyre of the dead. Or the dying.

My father, I thought. I tasted vengeance. Sithra had been the pawn of this game and I no longer hated her, only felt anger that she as well as my mother and I and all of us had been used. For their stinking politics, for their grubby little fights. We had never existed for them at all, not as individuals who deserved the respect of the fleet.

No, Sithra also was just one more flute that had been badly played. I did not hate her. I hated the enemy below and the one we used. I hated the Pretender's force and the Tinkers too. Auntie Suu-Suu appeared to treat us well, but in the end she was like the others. Only the concerns of some Empire far away mattered. Those of us who live in the here and now were so much filler in plans.

The anger was cold, it was searing, scorching ice as I had never known anger before. All other anger had been for me and against those who would have destroyed me. Now what I knew was no longer personal. *I* was not the focus of the violation that drove me. Neither I nor those close to me nor those I hoped to become my circle, none of them had been abused. Except by being included in those who were not acknowledged, who were pushed aside and forgotten after their walk-on role was played.

The bitter injustice of the pattern completely galled me like nothing else had. These were the plans that had condemned a youth younger than myself to burn alive, his torture and dying never touching those who had benefitted.

I was going to eradicate them all. Without mercy, without pain, just as they had thought to do with us. Without thinking of each of their personal lives and stories, their hopes and dreams, those who would be left to mourn.

It was a good, clean killing rage that left my mind preternaturally clear. Everything was sharper, and I could see the karma behind it all. Behind each individual and the ships and their fleets, back to the origins of the split so long in the past, I could read their history and their fate.

And I saw my own fate and that I could not escape it. The trajectory had been plotted before I had been born and I had no choice but to follow the course. Knowing that, all fear was gone. I knew that I would live through this day. I knew I would survive the fight—and that I would wish that I had not. That this was the beginning of my probation by the gods and the end of all innocence.

"Is that a shipping intake?" I asked, pointing to a coupling ring fixed to the Pretender hull.

"Yes, number three," the Tinker who sat next to Vijay in the co-seat replied.

"Bring us up to dock."

"This wagon isn't made for cargo holds," the Tinker protested. "We don't have the right docking joint and our airlock is too small."

"We don't have to worry about that," I said softly. "Bring it around and get as close a seal as you can. And superheat the seal latches where the docking sensors will hit them first. We want the automatics to think that we're burning."

The Tinker blinked, and shook her head. She opened her mouth as if to protest, and then closed it again. Maybe it was the way Vijay's hand strayed across to her console that quieted her. He might not know my plan but he had faith in me.

Slowly, too slowly for my taste, she complied.

But slow was good, I told myself. Slow would keep us off their screens, slow would make the whole seem real. They still were not sure that we were out here and ready; they still did not know quite yet that they were under attack.

Not quite.

The seal ring was heating up as we approached the docking bay. The long adjustable quartermaster's coupling was just above our airlock. Whatever the Tinker pilot thought of the plan, she sure could fly a nice tight rendezvous pattern.

"I don't know what you're hoping to do," she muttered as she pulled us in tighter, so that we were practically threaded through the join. If our airlock were larger, standard issue for someone or other, we would have a nice tight seal now. But we didn't have that seal and we were using different scales of size and the ring around our coupling collar was starting to glow in the dark.

I smiled. Just a little more, a little hotter. . . .

It worked all in a rush. The quartermaster's join came into position and sealed up tight. Then white billows spurted under pressure from the vents to seal the vacuum between the different-size docking rings. It spewed and hardened as our airlock opened with our Guardians ready to charge.

As the other ship's airlock sensed the pressure and absence of heat, its emergency override went into direct action and the air-lock opened instantly. I didn't think of the gamble I'd taken, only that we were only the first step of the way there. I leapt out and into the Pretender ship, only to have Vijay pull me aside. "You don't know anything about their layout. I do," he announced flatly. "Where do you want to go?"

"To the controls," I said. Of course, where else would I go? And I took the lead. Because Vijay might have known more about their ships and their entire life, but I knew the maze. And I recognized this ship, this twisted corridor, as one of the mazes that I had to navigate. Just like all the others.

There was only the one maze. That much should have changed in all the long time since those on Maya had been built. Should have changed, but the Pretenders were like everything else in their Empire—always looking back to the old than ahead. Afraid of change, afraid of difference, they defeated themselves before they even fought.

I knew my way to the center, and the center would hold the controls. It was the same maze as the power plant and the Exchange and the Temple.

I recognized the pattern, the turnings, the segmented joints that separated the discrete sections of the structure. Only this was the original, I realized with a start. It had made sense here, to have each compartment made to be sealed off from the others. And even the geometry of the corridors and the configuration of the turnings was consistent with the physics of space travel.

The first crew members we saw weren't armed and they were shocked still. It was easy to knock them out with the lowest setting on the prod. The next had fire blasters down off the wall. There was a fire alert already, and they had been thinking. There was only room for three across the corridor and one of the Guardians was out ahead with a prod set on yellow.

We were off and running before they could flicker, with a segment door locked between.

Suddenly I saw Iolo's death again, the long confused trek through the labyrinth, cut off by doors and segment airlocks that seemed spurious in the underground power plant. The makers of that plant had not designed it. It had been the segments of the original ship itself, with all the sections intact. That's why there were serics of scals where none were needed, I realized. That's why they were trapped—and that's why they died.

The first settlers on Maya had grown up aboard a ship, as had their parents and grandparents. To them, the necessities of shipboard life were comforting and familiar, and they re-created them when they came to stay.

But the transformer station, that had been the original ship itself, cannibalized and turned to a far more immediate planetary use. And then every major structure, every baseline and installation that the first colonists constructed, was designed to echo the ship they'd come in. It was familiar to them and they would never get lost, not when every underlying pattern was always the same.

But who else had known the Exchange and the Temple Hill and the transformer—and the interior of a spaceship? What was so obvious to the first builders was completely unseen by anyone else. They had only one design for everything, and that design was the ship that had brought them.

Each part of the ship was a separate segment that could be isolated from the others. That had made no sense under the rock in the transformer; in hard vacuum it made all the sense in the world.

Another emergency siren shrieked and the corridor went to red flashing lights. Another fire alarm somewhere had tripped the system. I pulled Vijay's arm and ran as the airlocks started into their automatic segment cycle. The two of us made it through, and three Guardians with us, before the doors slammed down segmenting the ship yet again. But we were already inside.

Not that I'd penetrated the deepest level yet. There were still two more sets of the segments before I was actually into the command center. But I was getting close. The Exchange couldn't stop me.

There was no Exchange here. Not the familiar Exchange where Della lived. There were only the aliens, the Pretender's forces of whatever ilk, in this vessel. There were only enemies and Guardians, who had so recently been enemies.

There were only enemies and confusion, and it appeared that confusion had the upper hand. I ran toward the next segment lock, Vijay and the Guardians pacing with me. We hugged close to the wall and passed two fire-control teams weighted with equipment who didn't acknowledge our presence. Just as well.

More alarms sounded. Again. I smiled. The others must be copying my strategy for getting in. Probably it wasn't working any longer, but the automatics on the docking devices didn't know that. The overrule cutoffs didn't extend to the emergency systems, which were all isolated and hardcased to prevent anything from ever jamming their preprogrammed function.

That just meant that we'd have to cut out way through two more airlocks before we were into the command.

I knew the maze; I took the lead. This segment seemed devoid of defenders. There should have been people here, though they had most likely been drawn to the outer regions by the alarms and invasion.

There were too many entrances and they would be split. I had to rely on that. And I had to get to the center of command and link in to the ship's AI. Once I did that the vehicle was ours, and I wasn't above using it.

The next airlock was before us. The Guardian who accompanied us pulled out a burn stick and started the process of cutting through the doors. Heavy-duty polymer it may be, eventually it had to give in to the heat and a thin curl of smoke peeled back from the incision. Before the first cut was finished the air stank of burning plastic, and I wasn't sure if we could manage the stench to finish the job.

And the door just opened. The entire barrier withdrew into the side walls and the segment join became invisible.

We pushed through and began to run down the next hall. At the end there would be another airlock and the command center.

Turning a corner, I could see clearly that the last airlock was recessed, but there were three defenders in the hall wearing uniforms with weapons up and ready. I held up my arm and forced Vijay and the Guardians hard against the wall. I had to think of something. We couldn't just walk into their fire, and no doubts they would.

Vijay casually tossed something at them. It popped and even from where we stood well back I could smell it and my stomach turned itself into a knot. The Pretender's defenders were in worse shape, being unprepared and not knowing what the attack was. Two of them were kneeling on the floor puking.

The Guardian said "now" and then led us in a sprint through the mess. I went straight for the hand-pulse that lay dropped on the deck, scooped it up without breaking stride and then went for the door. Vijay pulled a sidearm from a man who was braced against the rung of a ladder with his lunch on the floor. Our Guardian went for the only one who was still this side of standing—one blow with a knee brought her down with the others.

The door wasn't even locked and the control center was in disarray. The one with the most sparkles was standing shouting orders in a language I didn't understand. The crew members there were trying something frantically, faces screwed up with concentration and fear.

"Stay right there," I said.

The Captain and crew turned and looked at me with annoyance.

Vijay said something incomprehensible in a language I couldn't even recognize, and the Pretender's crew put their hands on their heads. The Captain closed his eyes for a second and winced, then took up a defensive position in front of a console that reminded me of the Exchange interface.

Of course. The Exchange had been a ship's AI once upon a time. And while things had changed, I thought that at least I could find some of the basics—or link up with the Exchange itself and have it take over the first set of functions while I waded through the rest. But it appeared that the Captain of the vessel believed that it was his duty to go down with the ship, and launched himself at us with all the fervor of a middle-aged bureaucrat.

The Guardian's handset was set on low. That was enough for the Pretender Captain, who collapsed without resistance. And I went for the controls.

I slipped the command helmet on and the interface opened, dutiful and dull, obedient and ready to serve. It created no illusory images except for itself, represented as a bland uniformed junior tech with fewer memorable features than personality traits.

"Yes sir?" it responded in proper military fashion.

"Open communication with the lead Tinker boat," I ordered. Because, much as I hated to admit it, I needed Auntie Suu-Suu's advice. I didn't know where to go from here. I knew only pieces about this Empire, not nearly enough to stage a successful coup. Only it wouldn't be a coup, not really. I was in every regard the legitimate inheritor, both genetically and because I had the last missing symbol of rulership for the Flower Throne. The Coronation Mantle, which had been Auntie Suu-Suu's shawl, was hidden under a panel in Vijay's wagon.

I didn't know if I really wanted to be Emperor. I'm not even sure if I cared. I just knew that I wanted the Pretender to pay for what had happened. For my father and for me, and for all the other machinations that they had unleashed on us.

More than revenge, though, I wanted answers. I had to know why. Between the Tinkers and the Pretender's Fleet, Maya had been used and then kept from the usual rewards. We were nothing to them, and that was the greatest insult of all.

Why us? What did it matter, what good would it do the Pretender anyway?

Auntie Suu-Suu might be willing to tell me more now. Now that I was already here, already embroiled in the plots she wanted me to enter. Maybe now she would tell me everything I needed to know—though I doubted it.

The com link opened smoothly and a mechanical voice reported that the Tinker Headwoman was not available. Not available? What did that mean? Auntie surely wasn't in the fighting. She shouldn't have been in any of the boarding parties, either. She was supposed to stay at the com ready to tell me, didn't she know that?

"Contact from another source reported," the ship's AI reported. "Unidentified."

"Route it through," I said.

And then a woman's laugher rang through the room. Familiar laughter, half hysteria and half arrogance that could only be one person in all the galaxy.

"Mother." I sighed. "So you're here."

"Of course," she answered. "Who do you think opened the

inner segment airlocks and made sure that the majority of their troops were sealed out near the hull? Who do you think took the helm minutes ago and started us heading back toward the Garden World? Why do you think that entire crew was so frantic with worry? They were going out somewhere where they did not wish to go and they didn't know how it had happened." She laughed again.

"And the ship's AI?" I asked.

"Oh, the Exchange and I took care of it," Della said airily. "Do you think I would miss this, Anselm? All my life this has been my dream, my desire, my reality. Now you and I are together, the way a family should be, and heading toward your conquest of the Flower Throne. From there we will make history in the stars, we will make Maya the center of the universe. And I will not be abolished and forgotten. I won't be forgotten, Anselm, you won't deny me. I am your mother and I have watched over you always. I have only done this all for your good, for your safety. A mother knows what's best for her child."

Maya as the center of the universe. I wondered if she realized just how accurate she had been. Surely she had centered all her hopes and dreams firmly in illusion.

"How the hell did you get in here?" I demanded.

She laughed again. "You gave the wrong command, son. 'Route it through' means through the central brain. You wanted it through the com link, not in direct download. But you ordered the wrong thing. And here I am.

"Of course, the Exchange and I were waiting, monitoring every system we could. So when the com opened we immediately followed the signal back and tried to take over."

My mother had not learned one thing in her years in the Exchange. Even with all her access to libraries and AIs all over the Empire, she was still stuck on her one and only obsession. Power.

Or rather, the illusion of power.

"We couldn't have done it if you hadn't given the command, though," she went on, pleased. "You did get the command set list and the operating instructions, I assume, so you were planning to have me in charge.

"And that's the best plan, really. You are still far too young to understand what's going on and how to play this, but with me in the AI no one will ever know that you aren't giving all the orders. That you aren't omniscient in the machine yourself and that the ideas and strategies are all your own. That will add to your credibility when we arrive, when you take our proper place on the Flower Throne. You will appear to have the power, and I shall guide you as a mother should."

My stomach lurched.

As a mother should. She was no mother. I had heard her story by then, I knew what she had been through, I had even touched it from her imprinted mind full of emotions and layered with the richness of memory. But she had made a great mistake in making that far-too-honest record for me. She had left ghost whiffs of herself imprinted behind. The emotional tenor of her life and reaction was there for me to read while I had learned of her life story.

And I had learned that she regarded me with less enthusiasm than she felt about her interface. I had never been her child, only her excuse.

I hated her.

What was left in that machine was not my mother. The only part of her that could lay claim to me was the body that lay down on Maya, now a blue-white mass below us. That body had shaped me and gave me life, and I owed her something. I knew that.

I owed her my life, but I didn't owe her my conscience. I had a choice about living with her; I had no choice about living with myself.

"Don't take us out of orbit yet." I left the final order with the thing that was some mixture of the original ship's AI and the Exchange and Della. "There's something I have to go back for."

Della muttered some form of acquiescence as I removed the command gear.

I handed the chair to Vijay. "I'll be back," I promised him. "But something has come up."

"I'll go with you," he offered, but I shook my head and pressed a hand on his shoulder.

"You're the only one I can trust with that headset," I told him gently.

He looked sad. "What is it you have to do?" he asked.

"I don't know," I replied.

I didn't know. I knew that I had to get rid of Della, that I had to remove her from the matrix. And I knew that as much as I despised her I could not kill her. She was my mother and I did owe her that much. And exactly that much.

I returned to my own wagon through corridors marked with power burns and guarded by wary humans. They looked at me as if even I were a suspicious character, and I was grateful for that.

There were none of the Pretender's crew in the hallway. The injured were probably under care in either the infirmary or their own quarters. I didn't know what had been done to the able-bodied after the fight; I only knew that they weren't there and that the warship seemed far too quiet.

When I got to the cargo bay access I found my way barred by the ample figure of Auntie Suu-Suu. "No, Anselm, you should not go this way. You will go around with me and take my wagon."

"Why?" I asked. "And what's going on in there?"

She shrugged. "We're transporting the prisoners down to the surface. Then they won't trouble us and they can create a new life on Maya just like your father's ancestors did. We aren't taking them to any place near Babelion and the Mountain. Maya isn't terribly large as planets go, but it will do. There are enough mountains and ice ranges and even some fluid seas between your people and where we're settling theirs.

"And you are taking my wagon because I am coming with you. I also have some unfinished business on the surface, and we will go together. I am an old woman, Anselm, and I want the comforts of my own transport. I want to sleep in my own bed and I have two jars of Constantine Elixir there. I might like some of it, and I certainly wouldn't let a wagon with that aboard be used as a prisoner transport."

She smiled broadly as if she had made a joke, but there was something polished about her attempt at warmth. Underneath I

could sense other feelings, darker ones, but her face closed again
and no trace of complexity marred her grandmotherly appearance.

We arrived at a designated personnel docking station that had
been fitted with an adjustable coupling, so there was none of the
messy hardened fire-foam to seal the breech. The whole area was
clean and smooth and free of burn marks in the hallway. There
had been no fighting in this segment. Auntie must have taken her
time about opening the hatch, waiting until after the Pretender's
troops here surrendered to our forces.

Now it was simply silent and pristine. She spoke to the airlock
and it opened for us, and we walked the short coupling tube into
Auntie's wagon.

For a Tinker, the transport was oddly plain. The walls were
all the same color and that was a very subdued shade of pale
green. The furnishings were made of richly grained and polished
woods, and the few pieces of fabric were watered silk that
matched the walls, and a few bits of trim in the same dark red
velvet as the shawl she had tied on her hip. Certainly this restraint
was not a Tinker fashion at all. But then, Auntie Suu-Suu was
like no one else of any race or species.

She strapped down in the pilot's position as if it were habit. I
must have raised my eyebrow in surprise because she laughed
when she saw me and shook her head. "Thought that I had a
chauffeur? Is that because I'm old, or because I'm important?"

"Because you're important," I said without thinking.

"Well, no matter how important you are, and no matter how
old, too, there are some things that it's just easier to do yourself,"
she said. And with that she uncoupled the wagon from the warship
and took us down to the Mountain, landing expertly just outside
the ruined Dome.

Deep into the planetary night there was no one to watch us
set down, and even if there had been there were still no lights.
Everything was eerily dark and unmoving. For a moment I was
afraid that it was all a relic and everyone had died.

We walked the two hundred meters of road up to the ruin.
No one had remained. I wondered if they had all gone into Babelion for the warmth, or if they had died. But there was no
rotting stench in Xanadu and everything was very clean. Neat. As

if the Changed had packed up what they had needed and straightened things so that they would be tidy for a timely return when the Dome was repaired.

As my eyes adjusted to the dark I even noticed spiderweb shadows over the walls. Scaffolding. Work had already commenced. Soon the Changed could return to their controlled environment. But everything would be different now. The Changed would no longer be in control. The illusion of their superiority had been exposed along with their greatest weakness.

So we had won. No matter what happened from here, a new order would have to emerge. I felt homesick, wondering about what course it would take, and then I realized I didn't want to know. I didn't want to return to this world that was never going to be right again. Sulma was dead, my mother was crazy and Vijay was never going to return. There was nothing here I wanted anymore.

I was sad to have to acknowledge that. Like the Dome, I had to be rebuilt to a slightly different design and would never mean the same things again. Silently I mourned the passing of the old age. No matter that I had despised it and sought to bring it down. The fact that it was gone was enough for poignancy. The old days were bad, but they still had their glories. No one knew what was yet to come.

Auntie Suu-Suu walked very briskly for such an old woman. She led the way to the entrance of the Exchange and entered the maze without hesitation. "Where is your mother?" she asked.

I didn't know. She was inside the machine, that was all that mattered.

"Then I will search. You do what you must do," she said. "I will find you when it's time to return."

That did not seem like a plan to me. I wanted time told on a watch and a designated meeting place, but Auntie was already out of sight. I sighed heavily, but then this was Auntie Suu-Suu. If anyone could find me, she could.

Besides, I wanted to be alone. I took a different set of turnings than I had before, bypassing the interface rooms to get to the peripheral controls. This wasn't the heart of the system, and there was only one thing I wanted.

The Exchange was too important for Maya, especially now with rebuilding the Dome and the power station. No one has the plans; it would be up to the Exchange to provide the records so that we can improve on the old jury-rig design. I did not want to hurt the Exchange, only to make sure that it didn't interfere with me again.

The AI wasn't responsible, I knew. It was my mother who had decided to take over the ship. But that was my ship and I wasn't letting Della run away with it.

Suddenly I realized that I needed it. I didn't know if I was really going to take over the Flower Throne, but I was sure as hell going to go after the Pretender. Sithra had been part of his plan, and without his backing and secret weapons stash, she couldn't have engineered my father's death and the cruelty of Xanadu.

The Changed had always ruled Maya, but they had interfered little before, preferring only to keep the status quo. There was some balance between the Mountain and Babelion and the Changed held their power through benign neglect. Babelion had always been responsible for Babelion—until Sithra. And my father.

Both of them had served the interests of off-worlders who saw Maya as no more than a source of cheap energy. Auntie had told me enough to know that both the Empress and the Pretender-Emperor who bore my name never saw the people here below. They didn't think of a frightened girl going slowly power-mad, or of a man who was still half a boy burning alive. Neither of them saw any importance in our little lives—and maybe they weren't important. Except to us.

I didn't hate either of them, Pretender and Empress both. They were as unreal to me as I was to them. Their concerns were immaterial here, that was all. I felt sorry for Della, caught in a web of illusions about desire and power, ambition and greed. I felt sorry for them all, sorry in only the way a boy not yet twenty can pity the elders who have never seen themselves or their dreams.

I pitied Della; therefore I had to save her. It was the only fitting thing for a son to do.

And so I went over the long wall filled with badly fitted hardware in mortared stone shelving, each with a power line and readout that showed it to be functioning. I knew which one I had to find, though I could not imagine precisely what it looked like. I had to read the very small, archaic writing that was sometimes obscured by generations of grime.

Even the words were not complete when I did find them. *Tele* and *trans* and *port339* were the only things I could read. But that was enough, close enough. Nothing else was possible. So I took each of the small metal boxes and disconnected it from its power lead. And then I dropped them on the floor, all twelve of them, and stamped them halfway flat.

I had destroyed her off-world relay. The Exchange, and Della, were still perfectly functional. Della could run all of Maya from her place in the Exchange, if she chose. But she couldn't talk to the off-world AIs, or the ships, and she couldn't subvert the controls of anything off-world again.

I was truly sorry for her. She could rule the world, but because I had cut her off from the Empire I had thwarted her obsessive desire.

"No!" a tortured cry came from the speakers. "Put them back on line," my mother's voice commanded me. "We can't get out, we're trapped here."

"That's the idea," I said dryly. "You need something to do, Mother. You've always wanted to run the world. Now you can. You and the Exchange can rebuild the Dome and figure out how to save the Changed and the humans. There's plenty for you to do."

And then I walked away.

Chapter Twenty-six

He did give her a beautiful funeral. Anselm did a very fine job of it, provided the flowers and the music that Della had specified and had made certain that everything was conducted with solemn dignity. Veteran of funerals that she was, Della would have been gratified that this one, her real one, had as much ceremony and gravity as attends the death of an Empress. Which was only fitting.

Anselm does not know how she died and I will not tell him. But in the end, she was my responsibility. I had created her; her monstrosity and megalomania were my mistake. And of everyone, only I knew how truly dangerous she could be.

Had she lived and remained inside that machine, Della would have threatened not the Pretender, but the rule and order of the Empire as a whole. It was always her destiny, as it is Anselm's. But Anselm has other genes in the mix, something we had not anticipated. Della was entirely of her kind, purely a creature of her genotype that I had not properly trained during the years that she had been under my supervision.

My charges are not incapable of compassion. They are all born power-mad and manipulative, but they are able to learn the virtues of clemency and grace, sincerity and service, to balance those instincts that they will need to survive.

I had not realized how little of that learning she would get among the Changed, how raw she would be when she came to my tutelage. And, in truth, by then it was far too late. She had already begun the hardening of the neural net, the great die-off of neurons that occurs when maturity first starts the chemical changes that long predate physical puberty.

We knew precisely when these changes were due. I had miscalculated the culture of Maya, radically and tragically. I had not appreciated the true irony of that name before. It had always seemed either silly or heavy-handed, but for Della it was only an accurate description.

Della herself was the victim of illusion, of ignorance, of my stupidity. If I'd known that neural sculpture among the Changed was all geared toward unification with a deranged AI, I would never have let them have her.

The genetic structure of the Empress had been created and refined with the knowledge that the person it produced would be guided and nurtured in a controlled environment. In the first few years of life, especially, the brain is still plastic. It is the experience of those years that creates the physical structure of the brain as much as the genetic code. All of the cloned Empresses had needed careful neural guidance in their early years as much as they needed food and education and all the tutelage in Court etiquette. In the end, an Empress—or an Emperor—is far more than a sequence in the genetic code.

I had thought of the things I considered important when I took her and when I planted her among the Changed. I could not have known how radically the culture of the Changed deviated from that of the humans of Babelion. I was not privy to the Mountain. But still, I should have been able to understand it from logic alone.

Della never could have ruled. Even if I had intervened earlier in her development, she and I together could not have overcome Maya. It's culture, prejudices and historical ignorance could not have been overcome by a few lessons in noblesse oblige.

Still, it was my decision to wait, to let Della grow up in a world where she would never be taxed to her capacity, where she would never have any outlet for her abilities. So it was no surprise that she followed the instinct laid down deep in her DNA. She was clear and clean, the most purely amoral that we have ever seen.

A lesson, though, is not a good enough excuse for a life. It was so much easier since she had entered the machine willingly years earlier. Her body was only a comatose shell, riddled with vein taps and drugs. Her true existence was inside the Exchange. So perhaps in killing her body I have not killed her essence. Della will always live inside so long as her patterns persist, though over time as she is accessed less and less she will be overwritten and begin to fade. But without her living body to sustain her desire and will, that part of her inside the machine will not be motivated to grasp power at any price.

I wept with the regal music, with the solemn white lilies piled on the pyre. I have buried three Empresses. Della is the first I have burned, and the one I have mourned the most cruelly, for none of the others have died by my hands.

My hands. They look so ragged now, as if all the time and hard weather of Maya had taken their skill and power. That is justice. I have done wrong by this world and I wonder if it was justified by the Pretender's machinations. Sithra was bad for Maya, no doubt, but she still was one of theirs. In the end, did the Pretender do the greater damage, or did I?

"You can always retire and stay with me, and right the world," a soft voice came at my shoulder. Or maybe it was in the corners of my mind.

I turned and saw Sri Mayurna looking at me as he had before, full of empathy for the path I have chosen. "You have done all you can, and in the end it is your duty to save yourself. Do not forget that," he reminded me.

I nodded. The old mystic was right—he had always been right. But it was not my time to retire. Not yet.

I had killed my charge and my Empress with my own hands. I looked at her son, so composed and in perfect control. I wonder what he will bring to us all and I think that I must remain in my work and heartache to discover him. In all the hundreds of years there have been no new players. Anselm will make something fresh of the game.

"You will bring him back to the Garden, then?" Sri Mayurna asked, but it was no question.

"What else can I do?"

"He doesn't need you," the old rishi told me. "His karma is his. Let them go, girl, let all of them go."

"How long did it take you to learn that, sir?" I asked.

The old man shook his head. "Who says I ever truly have?"

Anselm's Epilogue:

I had only wanted to confront my mother. I had not wanted her to die. But, then, those who have been inside the Exchange for a long time often die in strange ways. Some say that the Exchange kills them and some say it is suicide.

Della would never commit suicide. I might have some thoughts on her death, but I don't know anything. And I don't want to know. It is irrelevant anyway. I know what I would have done, and what I must do next.

I think I understand my father now.

In one of his essays he quoted the God of Revolution, the Archetypal Insurgent, who said, "At the risk of seeming ridiculous, let me say that the true revolutionary is guided by great feelings of love."